Louise Penny is the Number One *New York Times* bestselling author of the Inspector Gamache series, including *Still Life*, which won the CWA John Creasey Dagger in 2006. Recipient of virtually every existing award for crime fiction, Louise was also granted the Order of Canada in 2014 and received an honorary doctorate of literature from Carleton University ⬛⬛⬛⬛⬛⬛⬛⬛ uébec in 2017. She lives ⬛⬛⬛⬛⬛⬛⬛⬛ real.

Praise for L⬛⬛⬛⬛⬛⬛⬛⬛

'Louise Penny is one of the greatest crime writers of our times' Denise Mina

'She makes most of her competitors seem like wannabes' *The Times*

'A cracking storyteller, who can create fascinating characters, a twisty plot and wonderful surprise endings' Ann Cleeves

'Outstanding . . . a constantly surprising series that deepens and darkens as it evolves' *The New York Times*

'No one does atmospheric quite like Louise Penny . . . a fantastic series' Elly Griffiths

'Louise Penny's writing is intricate, beautiful and compelling. She is an original voice, a distillation of both PD James and Barbara Vine at their peaks and a worthy successor to both' Peter James

'[An] atmospheric, distinctive series' Kate Mosse

'Penny is an absolute joy' *Irish Times*

'The series is deep and grand and altogether extraordinary . . . Miraculous' *Washington Post*

The Gamache series

LOUISE PENNY

A Fatal Grace

HODDER

First published in Great Britain in 2006 by Headline Book Publishing
Published in 2011 by Sphere
This edition published in 2021 by Hodder & Stoughton
An Hachette UK company
Previously published as *Dead Cold* in the UK

1

Map by Rhys Davies

Excerpts from 'Anthem' by Leonard Cohen used with permission of Leonard Cohen.
Excerpts from 'A Sad Child', 'Waiting', 'Up' and 'Half-Hanged Mary' from *Morning
in the Burned House* by Margaret Atwood © 1995.
Used with permission of McClelland & Stewart Ltd, the Houghton Mifflin Company
and Curtis Brown Ltd, London.
Excerpts from *Vapour Trails* by Marylyn Plessner © 2000 by Marylyn Plessner. Used
with permission of Stephen Jarislowsky.
Excerpt from 'A Cradle Song' by W.B. Yeats used with permission of A.P. Watt Ltd
on behalf of Michael B. Yeats.

A CIP catalogue record for this title is available from the British Library

B format ISBN 978 1 529 38818 3
eBook ISBN 978 1 529 38821 3

Typeset in Janson by Palimpsest Book Production Limited, Falkirk, Stirlingshire

Printed and bound in Great Britain by Clays Ltd, Elcograf S.p.A.

Hodder & Stoughton policy is to use papers that are natural, renewable
and recyclable products and made from wood grown in sustainable forests.
The logging and manufacturing processes are expected to conform to the
environmental regulations of the country of origin.

Hodder & Stoughton Ltd
Carmelite House
50 Victoria Embankment
London EC4Y 0DZ

www.hodder.co.uk

A LETTER FROM LOUISE

When I was thirty-five, I thought the best was behind me.

I was lonely, and tired, and empty. Plodding through life.

At thirty-five.

By the time I was forty-five, I was married to the love of my life, and my first book was about to be published.

And now I'm sixty. Living in a beautiful Quebec village, surrounded by friends, with thirteen books to my name. And counting.

This milestone birthday gives me a chance to look back in wonderment. And gratitude. And amazement. That I should be here, happy, joyous, and free.

No one quite appreciates, and recognises, the light like those who've lived in darkness. That awareness is what I try to bring to the books. The duality of our lives. The power of perception. The staggering weight of despair, and the amazement when it is lifted.

The gap between how we appear and how we really feel.

Those are foundations of the Gamache books.

Initially they were called the Three Pines books, which, of course, they are. Three Pines is the tiny hidden village in Québec. Not on any map, it is only ever found by those who are lost.

But, once found, never forgotten.

At their core, though, these books are about the profound decency of Armand Gamache, and the struggles he has to remain a good person. When 'good' is subjective, and 'decent' is a matter of judgement.

These books might appear, superficially, as traditional crime novels. But they are, I believe, more about life than death. About choices. About the price of freedom. About the struggle for peace.

Armand Gamache, of the Sûreté du Quebec, is inspired by my husband, Michael Whitehead. A doctor who treated children with cancer. Who spent his life searching for cures. Who saved countless young lives, boys and girls who now have children of their own.

Despite the dreadful deaths and broken hearts all around him, Michael was the happiest man alive. Because he understood the great gift that life is.

Michael gave that perception to Armand.

Michael died of dementia. And it broke my heart. But I still have Armand. And Clara, and Jean-Guy. Myrna and Gabri and Olivier. And crazy old Ruth.

At thirty-five, I thought the best was behind me.

As I celebrate my sixtieth birthday, I can hardly wait to see what happens next.

Ring the bells that still can ring
Forget your perfect offering
There's a crack in everything.
That's how the light gets in.

Welcome to the very cracked world of Armand Gamache and Three Pines. I am overjoyed to be able to share it with you.

Meet you in the bistro . . .

Louise Penny
March 2018

For my brother Doug and his family,
Mary, Brian, Roslyn and Charles, who showed me
what courage really is. Namaste.

Du Moulin

ONE

—

Had CC de Poitiers known she was going to be murdered she might have bought her husband, Richard, a Christmas gift. She might even have gone to her daughter's end of term pageant at Miss Edward's School for Girls, or 'girths' as CC liked to tease her expansive daughter. Had CC de Poitiers known the end was near she might have been at work instead of in the cheapest room the Ritz in Montreal had to offer. But the only end she knew was near belonged to a man named Saul.

'So, what do you think? Do you like it?' She balanced her book on her pallid stomach.

Saul looked at it, not for the first time. She'd dragged it out of her huge purse every five minutes for the past few days. In business meetings, dinners, taxi rides through the snowy streets of Montreal, CC'd suddenly bend down and emerge triumphant, holding her creation as though another virgin birth.

'I like the picture,' he said, knowing the insult. He'd taken the picture. He knew she was asking, pleading, for more and he knew he no longer cared to give it. And he wondered how much longer he could be around CC de Poitiers before he became her. Not physically, of course. At forty-eight she was a few years younger than him. She was slim and ropy and toned, her teeth impossibly white and her hair impossibly blonde. Touching her was like caressing a veneer of ice. There was a beauty to it, and a frailty he found attractive. But there was also danger. If she ever broke, if she shattered, she'd tear him to pieces.

But her exterior wasn't the issue. Watching her caress her book with more tenderness than she'd ever shown when caressing him, he wondered whether her ice water insides had somehow seeped into him, perhaps during sex, and were slowly freezing him. Already he couldn't feel his core.

At fifty-two Saul Petrov was just beginning to notice his friends weren't quite as brilliant, not quite as clever, not quite as slim as they once were. In fact, most had begun to bore him. And he'd noticed a telltale yawn or two from them as well. They were growing thick and bald and dull, and he suspected he was too. It wasn't so bad that women rarely looked at him any more or that he'd begun to consider trading his downhill skis for cross country, or that his GP had scheduled his first prostate test. He could accept all that. What woke Saul Petrov at two in the morning, and whispered in his ears in the voice that had warned him as a child that lions lived under his bed, was the certainty that people now found him boring. He'd take deep dark breaths of the night air, trying to reassure himself that the stifled yawn of his dinner companion was because of the wine or the *magret de canard* or the warmth in the Montreal restaurant, wrapped as they were in their sensible winter sweaters.

But still the night voice growled and warned of dangers ahead. Of impending disaster. Of telling tales too long, of an attention span too short, of seeing the whites of too many eyes. Of glances, fast and discreet, at watches. When can they reasonably leave him? Of eyes scanning the room, desperate for more stimulating company.

And so he'd allowed himself to be seduced by CC. Seduced and devoured so that the lion under the bed had become the lion in the bed. He'd begun to suspect this self-absorbed woman had finally finished absorbing herself, her husband and even that disaster of a daughter and was now busy absorbing him.

He'd already become cruel in her company. And he'd begun despising himself. But not quite as much as he despised her.

'It's a brilliant book,' she said, ignoring him. 'I mean, really. Who wouldn't want this?' She waved it in his face. 'People'll eat it up. There're so many troubled people out there.' She turned now and actually looked out their hotel room window at the building opposite, as though surveying her 'people'. 'I did this for them.' Now she turned back to him, her eyes wide and sincere.

Does she believe it? he wondered.

He'd read the book, of course. *Be Calm* she'd called it, after the company she'd founded a few years ago, which was a laugh given the bundle of nerves she actually was. The anxious, nervous hands, constantly smoothing and straightening. The snippy responses, the impatience that spilled over into anger.

Calm was not a word anyone would apply to CC de Poitiers, despite her placid, frozen exterior.

She'd shopped the book around to all the publishers, beginning with the top publishing houses in New York and ending with Publications Réjean et Maison des cartes in St Polycarpe, a one-*vache* village along the highway between Montreal and Toronto.

They'd all said no, immediately recognizing the manuscript as a flaccid mishmash of ridiculous self-help philosophies, wrapped in half-baked Buddhist and Hindu teachings, spewed forth by a woman whose cover photo looked as though she'd eat her young.

'No goddamned enlightenment,' she'd said to Saul in her Montreal office the day a batch of rejection letters arrived, ripping them into pieces and dropping them on the floor for the hired help to clean up. 'This world is messed up, I tell you. People are cruel and insensitive, they're out to screw each other. There's no love or compassion. This', she sliced her book violently in the air like an ancient mythical hammer, heading for an unforgiving anvil, 'will teach people how to find happiness.'

Her voice was low, the words staggering under the weight of venom. She'd gone on to self-publish her book, making sure it was out in time for Christmas. And while the book talked a lot about light Saul found it interesting and ironic that it had actually been released on the winter solstice. The darkest day of the year.

'Who published it again?' He couldn't seem to help himself. She was silent. 'Oh, I remember now,' he said. 'No one wanted it. That must have been horrible.' He paused for a moment, wondering whether to twist the knife. Oh, what the hell. Might as well. 'How'd that make you feel?' Did he imagine the wince?

But her silence remained, eloquent, her face impassive. Anything CC didn't like didn't exist. That included her husband and her daughter. It included any unpleasantness, any criticism, any harsh words not her own, any emotions. CC lived, Saul knew, in her own world, where she was perfect, where she could hide her feelings and hide her failings.

He wondered how long before that world would explode. He hoped he'd be around to see it. But not too close.

People are cruel and insensitive, she'd said. Cruel and insensitive. It wasn't all that long ago, before he'd taken the contract to freelance as CC's photographer and lover, that he'd actually thought the world a beautiful place. Each morning he'd wake early and go into the young day, when the world was new and anything was possible, and he'd see how lovely Montreal was. He'd see people smiling at each other as they got their cappuccinos at the café, or their fresh flowers or their baguettes. He'd see the children in autumn gathering the fallen chestnuts to play conkers. He'd see the elderly women walking arm in arm down the Main.

He wasn't foolish or blind enough not to also see the homeless men and women, or the bruised and battered faces that spoke of a long and empty night and a longer day ahead.

But at his core he believed the world a lovely place. And his photographs reflected that, catching the light, the brilliance, the hope. And the shadows that naturally challenged the light.

Ironically it was this very quality that had caught CC's eye and led her to offer him the contract. An article in a Montreal style magazine had described him as a 'hot' photographer, and CC always went for the best. Which was why they always took a room at the Ritz. A cramped, dreary room on a low floor without view or charm, but the Ritz. CC would collect the shampoos and stationery to prove her worth, just as she'd collected him. And she'd use them to make some obscure point to people who didn't care, just as she'd use him. And then, eventually, everything would be discarded. As her husband had been tossed aside, as her daughter was ignored and ridiculed.

The world was a cruel and insensitive place.

And he now believed it.

He hated CC de Poitiers.

He got out of bed, leaving CC to stare at her book, her real lover. He looked at her and she seemed to go in and out of focus. He cocked his head to one side and wondered whether he'd had too much to drink again. But still she seemed to grow fuzzy, then sharp, as though he was looking through a prism at two different women, one beautiful, glamorous, vivacious, and the other a pathetic, dyed-blonde rope, all corded and wound and knotted and rough. And dangerous.

'What's this?' He reached into the garbage and withdrew a portfolio. He recognized it immediately as an artist's dossier of work. It was beautifully and painstakingly bound and printed on archival Arche paper. He flipped it open and caught his breath.

A series of works, luminous and light, seemed to glow off the fine paper. He felt a stirring in his chest. They showed a world both lovely and hurt. But mostly, it was a world where hope and comfort still existed. It was clearly the world the artist saw each day, the world the artist lived in. As he himself once lived in a world of light and hope.

The works appeared simple but were in reality very complex. Images and colors were layered one on top of the other. Hours and hours, days and days must have been spent on each one to get the desired effect.

He stared down at the one before him now. A majestic tree soared into the sky, as though keening for the sun. The artist had photographed it and had somehow captured a sense of movement without making it disorienting. Instead it was graceful and calming and, above all, powerful. The tips of the branches seemed to melt or become fuzzy as though even in its confidence and yearning there was a tiny doubt. It was brilliant.

All thoughts of CC were forgotten. He'd climbed into the tree, almost feeling tickled by its rough bark, as if he had been sitting on his grandfather's lap and snuggling into his unshaven face. How had the artist managed that?

He couldn't make out the signature. He flipped through the other pages and slowly felt a smile come to his frozen face and move to his hardened heart.

Maybe, one day, if he ever got clear of CC he could go back to his work and do pieces like this.

He exhaled all the darkness he'd stored up.

'So, do you like it?' CC held her book up and waved it at him.

TWO

～

Crie carefully got into her costume, trying not to rip the white chiffon. The Christmas pageant had already started. She could hear the lower forms singing 'Away in a manger', though it sounded suspiciously like 'A whale in a manger'. She wondered, briefly, whether that was a comment on her. Were they all laughing at her? She swallowed that thought and continued dressing, humming a bit as she went.

'Who's doing that?' The voice of Madame Latour, the music teacher, could be heard in the crowded, excited room. 'Who's humming?'

Madame's face, birdlike and bright, peeked round the corner where Crie had crept to change alone. Instinctively Crie grabbed her costume and tried to cover her near-naked fourteen-year-old body. It was impossible, of course. Too much body and too little chiffon.

'Was it you?'

Crie stared, too frightened to speak. Her mother had warned her about this. Had warned her never to sing in public.

But now, betrayed by a buoyant heart, she'd actually let some humming escape.

Madame Latour stared at the huge girl and felt a bit of her lunch in her throat. Those rolls of fat, those dreadful dimples, the underwear disappearing into the flesh. The face so frozen and staring. The science teacher, Monsieur Drapeau, had commented that Crie was top in his class, though another teacher had pointed out that one topic that semester had been vitamins and minerals and Crie had probably eaten the textbook.

Still, here she was at the pageant so maybe she was coming out of herself, though that would take a lot of doing.

'Better hurry. You're on soon.' She left without waiting for a reply.

This was the first Christmas pageant Crie had been in in the five years she'd been at Miss Edward's School for Girls. Every other year while the students made their costumes she'd made mumbled excuses. No one had ever tried to dissuade her. Instead she'd been given the job of running the lights for the show, having a head, as Madame Latour put it, for technical things. Things not alive, she'd meant. So each year Crie would watch the Christmas pageant alone in the dark at the back, as the beautiful, glowing, gifted girls had danced and sung the story of the Christmas miracle, basking in the light Crie provided.

But not this year.

She got into her costume and looked at herself in the mirror. A huge chiffon snowflake looked back. Really, she had to admit, more of a snowdrift than a single flake, but still, it was a costume and it was quite splendid. The other girls' mothers had helped them, but Crie had done her own.

To surprise Mommy, she'd told herself, trying to drown out the other voice.

If she looked closely she could see the tiny droplets of blood where her pudgy, indelicate fingers had fumbled the needle and speared herself. But she'd persevered until she finally had this costume. And then she'd had her brainwave. Really, the most brilliant thought in her entire fourteen years.

Her mother, she knew, revered light. It was, she'd been told all her life, what we all strive for. That's why it's called enlightenment. Why smart people are described as bright. Why thin people succeed. Because they're lighter than others.

It was all so obvious.

And now Crie would actually be playing a snowflake. The whitest, lightest of elements. And her own bit of brilliance? She'd gone to the dollar store and with her allowance bought a bottle of glitter. She'd even managed to walk straight past the chocolate bars, stale and staring. Crie had been on a diet for a month now and soon she was sure her mother would notice.

She'd applied glue and glitter and now she looked at the results.

For the first time in her life Crie knew she was beautiful. And she knew, in just a few short minutes, her mother would think so too.

Clara Morrow stared through the frosted mullions of her living-room window at the tiny village of Three Pines. She leaned forward and shaved some frost from the window. Now that we have some money, she thought, we should replace the old windows. But while Clara knew that was the sensible thing to do, most of her decisions weren't really sensible. But they suited her life. And now, watching the snow globe that was Three Pines, she knew she liked looking at it through the beautiful designs the frost made on the old glass.

Sipping a hot chocolate she watched as brightly swaddled villagers strolled through the softly falling snow, waving mittened hands in greeting and occasionally stopping to chat to each other, their words coming in puffs, like cartoon characters. Some headed into Olivier's Bistro for a *café au lait*, others needed fresh bread or a *pâtisserie* from Sarah's Boulangerie. Myrna's New and Used Books, next to the bistro, was closed for the day. Monsieur Béliveau shoveled the front walk of his general store and waved to Gabri, huge and dramatic, rushing across the green from his bed and breakfast on the corner. To a stranger the villagers would be anonymous, even asexual. In a Quebec winter everyone looked alike. Great waddling, swaddling, muffled masses of goose down and Thinsulate so that even the slim looked plump and the plump looked globular. Each looked the same. Except for the tuques on their heads. Clara could see Ruth's bright green pompom hat nodding to Wayne's multi-colored cap, knitted by Pat on long autumn nights. The Lévesque kids all wore shades of blue as they skated up and down the frozen pond after the hockey puck, little Rose trembling so hard in the net even Clara could see her aqua bonnet quiver. But her brothers loved her and each time they raced toward the net they pretended to trip and instead of letting go a blistering slap shot they gently slipped toward her until they all ended up in a confused and happy heap on the verge of the goal. It looked to Clara like one of those Currier and Ives prints she'd stared at for hours as a child and yearned to step into.

Three Pines was robed in white. A foot of snow had fallen

in the last few weeks and every old home round the village green had its own tuque of purest white. Smoke wafted out of the chimneys as though the homes had their own voice and breath, and Christmas wreaths decorated the doors and gates. At night the quiet little Eastern Townships village glowed with light from the Christmas decorations. There was a tender hum about the place as adults and children alike prepared for the big day.

'Maybe her car won't start.' Clara's husband Peter walked into the room. He was tall and slim and looked like a Fortune 500 executive, like his father. Instead he spent his days hunched over his easel, getting oil paints into his curly gray hair as he slowly created his excruciatingly detailed works of abstract art. They went for thousands of dollars to collectors internationally, though because he painted so slowly and produced only one or two a year, they lived in constant poverty. Until recently, that is. Clara's paintings of warrior uteruses and melting trees had yet to find a market.

'She'll be here,' said Clara. Peter looked at his wife, her eyes blue and warm, her once dark hair streaked with gray, though she was only in her late forties. Her figure was beginning to thicken round the stomach and thighs and she'd recently begun talking about rejoining Madeleine's exercise class. He knew enough not to answer when asked if that sounded like a good idea.

'Are you sure I can't come?' he asked, more out of politeness than a real desire to squeeze himself into Myrna's death trap of a car and bounce all the way into the city.

'Of course not. I'm buying your Christmas gift. Besides, there won't be room in the car for Myrna, me, you and the presents. We'd have to leave you in Montreal.'

A tiny car pulled up to their open gate and an enormous black woman got out. This was probably Clara's favorite part of trips with Myrna. Watching her get in and out of the minuscule car. Clara was pretty sure Myrna was actually larger than the car. In summer it was a riot watching her wriggle in as her dress rode up to her waist. But Myrna just laughed. In winter it was even more fun since Myrna wore an ebullient pink parka, almost doubling her size.

'I'm from the islands, child. I feel the cold.'

'You're from the island of Montreal,' Clara had pointed out.

'True,' admitted Myrna with a laugh. 'Though the south end. I love winter. It's the only time I get pink skin. What do you think? Could I pass?'

'For what?'

'For white.'

'Would you want to?'

Myrna had turned suddenly serious eyes on her best friend and smiled. 'No. No, not any more. Hmm.'

She'd seemed pleased and even a little surprised by her answer.

And now the faux-white woman in her puffy pink skin, layers of brightly colored scarves and purple tuque with orange pompom was clumping up their freshly shoveled path.

Soon they'd be in Montreal. It was a short drive, less than an hour and a half, even in snow. Clara was looking forward to an afternoon of Christmas shopping but the highlight of her trip, of every trip into Montreal at Christmas, was a secret. Her private delight.

Clara Morrow was dying to see Ogilvy's Christmas window. The hallowed department store in downtown Montreal had the most magical Christmas window in the world. In mid-November the huge panes would go black and blank, covered by paper. Then the excitement would start. When would the holiday wonderment be unveiled? It was more exciting to Clara as a child than the Santa Claus parade. When word spread that Ogilvy's had finally taken off the paper Clara would rush downtown and straight to the magical window.

And there it would be. Clara would rush up to the window but stop just short, just out of eyeshot. She'd close her eyes and gather herself, then she'd step forward and open her eyes. And there it was. Clara's village. The place she'd go when disappointments and dawning cruelty would overwhelm the sensitive little girl. Summer or winter, all she had to do was close her eyes and she was there. With the dancing bears and skating ducks and frogs in Victorian costume fishing from the bridge. At night, when the ghoul huffed and snorted and clawed beneath her bedroom floor, she would squeeze her tiny blue eyes shut and will herself into the magical window and the village the ghoul could never find because kindness guarded the entry.

Later in her life the most wonderful thing happened. She fell in love with Peter Morrow and agreed to put off taking New York by storm. Instead she agreed to move to the tiny village he loved south of Montreal. It was a region Clara was unfamiliar with, being a city girl, but such was her love for Peter that she didn't even hesitate.

And so it was, twenty-six years ago as a clever and cynical art college grad Clara stepped out of their rattle-trap Volkswagen, and started to weep.

Peter had brought her to the enchanted village of her

childhood. The village she had forgotten in the attitude and importance of adulthood. Ogilvy's Christmas window had been real after all and was called Three Pines. They'd bought a little home by the village green and settled into a life more magical then even Clara had dared dream.

A few minutes later Clara unzipped her parka in the warm car and watched the snowy countryside drift by. This was a special Christmas, for reasons both devastating and wonderful. Her dear friend and neighbor Jane Neal had been murdered slightly over a year before, leaving all her money to Clara. The previous Christmas she'd felt too guilty to spend any. Felt she was profiting by Jane's death.

Myrna glanced over at her friend, her thoughts traveling along the same lines, remembering dear, dead Jane Neal and the advice she'd given Clara after Jane's murder. Myrna was used to giving advice. She'd been a psychologist in Montreal, until she'd realized most of her clients didn't really want to get better. They wanted a pill and reassurance that whatever was wrong wasn't their fault.

So Myrna had chucked it all. She'd loaded her little red car with books and clothes and headed over the bridge, off the island of Montreal, south toward the US border. She'd sit on a beach in Florida and figure it out.

But fate, and a hunger pang, had intervened. In no hurry and taking the picturesque back roads Myrna had been on her journey for only an hour or so when she suddenly felt peckish. Cresting a hill along a bumpy dirt road she'd come across a village hidden among the hills and forests. It came as a complete surprise to Myrna, who was so taken by the sight she stopped and got out. It was late spring and the sun was just gathering strength. A stream tumbled from an old stone mill past a white clapboard chapel and meandered around one side of the village. The village was shaped like a circle with dirt roads running off it in four directions. In the middle was a village green and ringing it were old homes, some in the Québecois style with steeply sloping metal roofs and narrow dormers, some clapboard with wide open verandas. And at least one was fieldstone, built by hand from stones heaved from the fields by a pioneer frantic to beat the oncoming murderous winter.

She could see a pond on the green and three majestic pine trees rising at one end.

Myrna brought out her map of Quebec. After a couple of minutes she carefully folded it up and leaned against the car in amazement. The village wasn't on the map. It showed places that hadn't existed in decades. It showed minuscule fishing villages and any community with two houses and a church.

But not this one.

She looked down at villagers gardening and walking dogs and sitting on a bench by the pond reading. Perhaps this was like Brigadoon. Perhaps it only appeared every number of years, and only to people who needed to see it. But still, Myrna hesitated. Surely it wouldn't have what she craved. Almost turning round and heading for Williamsburg, which was on the map, Myrna decided to risk it.

Three Pines had what she craved.

It had croissants and *café au lait*. It had steak frites and the *New York Times*. It had a bakery, a bistro, a B&B, a general store. It had peace and stillness and laughter. It had great joy and great sadness and the ability to accept both and be content. It had companionship and kindness.

And it had an empty store with a loft above. Waiting. For her.

Myrna never left.

In just over an hour Myrna had gone from a world of complaint to a world of contentment. That had been six years ago. Now she dispensed new and used books and well-worn advice to her friends.

'For Christ's sake, shit or get off the pot,' had been her advice to Clara. 'It's been months since Jane died. You helped solve her murder. You know for sure Jane would be annoyed she gave you all her money and you're not even enjoying it. Should have given it to me.' Myrna had shaken her head in mock bewilderment. 'I'd have known what to do with it. Boom, down to Jamaica, a nice Rasta man, a good book—'

'Wait a minute. You have a Rasta man and you're reading a book?'

'Oh, yes. Each has a purpose. For instance, a Rasta man is great when he's hard, but not a book.'

Clara had laughed. They shared a disdain for hard books. Not the content, but the cover. Hardcovers were simply too hard to hold, especially in bed.

'Unlike a Rasta man,' said Myrna.

So Myrna had convinced her friend to accept Jane's death and spend the money. Which Clara planned to do this day. Finally the back seat of the car would be filled with heavy paper bags in rich colors, with rope handles and embossed names, like Holt Renfrew and Ogilvy. Not a single blinding yellow plastic bag from the Dollar-rama. Though Clara secretly adored the dollar store.

*

Back home Peter stared out the window, willing himself to get up and do something constructive. Go into the studio, work on his painting. Just then he noticed the frost had been shaved off one of the panes. In the shape of a heart. He smiled and put his eye to it, seeing Three Pines going about its gentle business. Then he looked up, to the rambling old house on the hill. The old Hadley house. And even as he looked the frost began to grow, filling in the heart with ice.

THREE

~

'Who did these?' Saul asked CC, holding up the artist's portfolio.

'What?'

'This here.' He stood naked in their hotel room. 'I found it in the garbage. Whose is it?'

'Mine.'

'You did these?' He was staggered. For an instant he wondered whether he'd misjudged her. These were clearly the works of a gifted artist.

'Of course not. Some pathetic little person from the village gave them to me to show around to my gallery friends. Trying to suck up, it was the funniest thing. "Oh please CC, I know how well connected you are." "Oh CC would you mind very much showing my work to some of your contacts?" Very annoying. Imagine asking me for a favor? Even had the gall to ask me to show it to Denis Fortin specifically.'

'What did you say?' His heart sank. He knew the answer, of course.

'Said I'd be delighted. You can put them back where you found them.'

Saul hesitated, then closed the portfolio and put it back in the garbage, hating himself for helping to destroy such a luminous portfolio, and hating himself even more for wanting to destroy it.

'Don't you have something on this afternoon?' he asked.

She straightened the glass and the lamp on the bedside table, moving each a millimeter until they were where they should be.

'Nothing important,' she said, wiping some great carbuncle of dust off the table. Really, at the Ritz. She'd have to speak to the manager. She looked at Saul, standing by the window.

'God, you've let yourself go.'

He'd obviously had a good body once, she thought. But now everything was flaccid. CC had been with fat men. She'd been with buff men. And in her opinion either extreme was all right. It was the transition that was disgusting.

Saul revolted her and she couldn't quite remember why she'd thought this was a good idea. Then she looked down at the glossy, white cover of her book, and remembered.

The picture. Saul was a wonderful photographer. There, above the title, *Be Calm*, was her face. Her hair so blonde it was nearly white, her lips red and full, her eyes a startling, intelligent blue. And her face so white it almost disappeared into the background, leaving the impression of eyes and mouth and ears floating on the cover.

CC adored it.

After this Christmas she'd get rid of Saul. Once he'd finished the last assignment. She noticed he must have bumped into the chair at the desk when he was looking at the portfolio. The chair was now out of alignment. She could feel a tension blossom in her chest. Damn him for deliberately annoying her like that, and damn that portfolio. CC leaped out of bed and straightened the screaming chair, taking the opportunity to also move the telephone parallel to the edge of the desk.

Then she leaped back into bed, smoothing the sheets on her lap. Maybe she should take a taxi back to her office. But then she remembered she did have someplace to go. Someplace important.

There was a sale on at Ogilvy's and a pair of boots she wanted to buy at the Inuit arts store along rue de la Montagne.

It wouldn't be long before she had her own line of clothing and furniture in stores across Quebec. Around the world. Soon all the arrogant chichi designers who'd mocked her would be sorry. Soon everyone would know about Li Bien, her own philosophy of design and living. Feng shui was passé. People were crying for a change, and she'd provide it. Li Bien would be on every tongue and in every home.

'Have you rented a chalet for the holidays yet?' she asked.

'No, I'm going down tomorrow. Why'd you buy a home in the middle of nowhere anyway?'

'I had my reasons.' She felt a flash of anger at him for questioning her judgment.

She'd waited five years to buy a place in Three Pines. CC de Poitiers could be patient if she had to, and if she had a good enough reason.

She'd visited the crummy little village many times, networking with local real estate agents and even talking to shop clerks in nearby St-Rémy and Williamsburg. It had taken years. Apparently homes didn't often come up in Three Pines.

Then a little over a year ago she'd had a call from a real estate agent named Yolande Fontaine. There was a home. A great Victorian Grande Dame on the hill overlooking the village. The mill owner's home. The boss's home.

'How much?' CC had asked, knowing it was almost certainly beyond her. She'd have to borrow against the company, mortgage everything she owned, get her husband to cash in his insurance policy and his RRSP.

But the real estate agent's answer had surprised her. It was well below market value.

'There is one little thing,' Yolande had explained in a cloying voice.

'Go on.'

'There was a murder there. And an attempted murder.'

'Is that all?'

'Well, I guess, technically, there was also a kidnapping. Anyway, that's why the house is so cheap. Still, it's a great buy. Terrific pipes, mostly copper. The roof is only twenty years old. The—'

'I'll take it.'

'Don't you want to see it?' As soon as the question was out Yolande could have kicked herself. If this moron wanted to buy the old Hadley house sight unseen, without inspection or exorcism, then let her.

'Just draw up the papers. I'll be down this afternoon with a cheque.'

And so she had. She'd told her husband a week or so later, when she'd needed his signature to cash in the RRSP. He'd protested, but so feebly it would have been impossible for a casual observer to even recognize it as a protest.

The old Hadley house, the monstrosity on the hill, was hers. She couldn't have been happier. It was perfect. Three Pines was perfect. Or at least it would be, by the time she was finished with it.

Saul snorted and turned away. He could see the writing on the wall. He'd be dumped by CC as soon as the next photo assignment of her in that dreadful hick village was complete. It was for her first catalogue and he'd been told to get pictures of her frolicking among the natives at Christmas. If possible he had to get shots of the locals looking at CC with wonder and affection. He'd need cash for that.

Everything CC did had a purpose. And that purpose came down to two things, he figured: it fed her wallet or her ego.

So why had she bought a house in a village no one had ever heard of? It wasn't prestige. So it must be the other.

Money.

CC knew something no one else did about the village, and it meant money.

His interest in Three Pines perked up.

'Crie! Move, for Christ's sake.'

It was almost literally true. The fine-boned and swaddled issue of a trust fund and a beauty pageant was struggling to be seen behind the drift that was Crie. She'd made it out on stage, dancing and twirling with the rest of the angel snowflakes, and then she'd suddenly stopped. It didn't seem to matter to anyone that snow in Jerusalem made no sense. The teacher, quite rightly, figured if anyone believed in a virgin birth they'd believe there was a snowfall that miraculous night. What did seem to matter, though, was that one of the flakes, a kind of microclimate unto herself, had stalled in the center of the stage. In front of the baby Jesus.

'Move, lardass.'

The insult slid off Crie, as they all did. They were the white noise of her life. She barely heard them any more. Now she stood on stage staring straight into the audience as though frozen.

'Brie has stage fright,' the drama teacher, Madame Bruneau, whispered to the music teacher, Madame Latour, as though expecting her to do something about it. Behind her back even the teachers called Crie Brie. At least, they thought it was behind her back. They'd long since stopped worrying whether the strange and silent girl heard anything.

'I can see that,' Madame Latour snapped. The immense stress of putting on the Miss Edward's Christmas pageant every year was finally getting to her.

But it wasn't the stage that petrified Crie, nor was it the audience. It was what wasn't there that had stopped her dead in her tracks.

Crie knew from long experience it was always the things you didn't see that were the scariest.

And what Crie didn't see broke her heart.

'I remember my first guru, Ramen Das, saying to me,' CC was now walking around the hotel room in her white robe, picking up stationery and soaps and recounting her favorite story, 'CC Das, he said. Ramen Das called me that,' CC said to the stationery. 'It was rare for a woman to have such honor, especially in India at the time.'

Saul thought maybe Ramen Das didn't realize CC was a woman.

'This was twenty years ago. I was just a kid, innocent, but even then I was a seeker of the truth. I came upon Ramen Das in the mountains and we had an immediate spiritual connection.'

She put her hands together and Saul hoped she wasn't about to say—

'Namaste,' said CC, bowing. 'He taught me that. Very spiritual.'

She said 'spiritual' so often it had become meaningless to Saul.

'He said, CC Das, you have a great spiritual gift. You must leave this place and share it with the world. You must tell people to be calm.'

As she spoke Saul mouthed the words, lip-synching to the familiar tune.

'CC Das, he said, you above all others know that when the chakras are in alignment all is white. And when all is white, all is right.'

Saul wondered whether she was confusing an Indian mystic with a KKK member. Ironic, really, if she was.

'You must go back into the world, he said. It would be wrong to keep you here any longer. You must start a company and call it Be Calm. So I did. And that's also why I wrote the book. To spread the spiritual word. People need to know. They've got it all wrong with all those flaky sects just out to take advantage of them. I needed to tell them about Li Bien.'

'Now, I get confused,' Saul said, enjoying the flush of anger this always produced. CC was predictable in the extreme.

She hated anyone suggesting her ideas were in any way muddled. 'Was it Ramen Das who told you about Li Bien?'

'No, you idiot. Ramen Das was in India. Li Bien is an ancient oriental philosophy, passed down through my family.'

'Of ancient Chinese philosophers?' If he wasn't long for this relationship he might as well get his licks in. Besides, it would make a funny story to tell later. Ward off the insipient dullness of his conversation. He'd make CC a laughing stock.

She clicked her tongue and huffed. 'You know my family's from France. France has a long and noble history of colonialism in the East.'

'Oh, yes. Vietnam.'

'Exactly. Being diplomats my family brought back some of the ancient spiritual teachings, including Li Bien. I've told you all this. Weren't you listening? Besides, it's in the book. Haven't you read it?'

She threw it at him and he ducked but not before he felt a sting on his arm as it bit him on the way by.

'Of course I've read your fucking book. I've read it and read it.' He used all his effort not to call it the load of crap he knew it to be. 'I know this story. Your mother painted a Li Bien ball and now it's the only thing you have left from her.'

'Not just from her, you asshole. From my whole family.' Now she was hissing. He'd wanted to anger her but he'd had no idea what he'd unleashed. He suddenly felt two feet tall, an infant cowering as she rose and blocked the sun, blocked all the light from him. He shrank and withered and hunched. Inside. On the outside the grown man stood stock-still, staring. And wondered what had produced such a monster.

CC wanted to rip his arms out. Wanted to pluck his bulging eyes from their sockets, wanted to tear the flesh from his bones. She felt a power growing and aching in her chest and radiating out like a sun gone nova. Her hands strained to feel his heart throbbing in the veins of his neck as she throttled him. And she could. Even though he was bigger and heavier, she could do it. When she felt like this she knew nothing could stop her.

After a lunch of poached salmon and *gigot d'agneau* Clara and Myrna had split up to do their Christmas shopping. But first Clara was heading off in search of Siegfried Sassoon.

'You're going to a bookstore?' asked Myrna.

'Of course not. I'm going to have my hair done.' Really, Myrna had grown quite out of touch.

'By Siegfried Sassoon?'

'Not him personally, but someone in his salon.'

'Or his unit. I understand it's the hell where youth and laughter go.'

Clara had seen pictures of the Sassoon salons and thought that while Myrna's description was a little dramatic it wasn't that far off, judging by the pouting, unhappy women in the photos.

A few hours later, struggling along rue Ste-Catherine, mittened hands grasping the ropes of bags overflowing with gifts, Clara was exhausted and pleased. Her buying spree had gone brilliantly. She'd bought Peter the perfect gift, and smaller items for family and friends. Myrna was right. Jane would be having fun watching her spend the money. And Myrna had also been right, though cryptic, about the Sassoon thing.

'Nylons? Hershey bar?' The lyrical, warm voice came up behind her.

'I was just thinking of you, you traitor. You sent me out into the mean streets of Montreal to ask strangers where I could find Siegfried Sassoon.'

Myrna was leaning against an old bank building, shaking with laughter.

'I don't know whether to be upset or relieved that no one knew I wanted a dead poet from the Great War to do my hair. Why didn't you tell me it was Vidal not Siegfried?' Now Clara was laughing too, and dropped her bags onto the snowy sidewalk.

'It looks great,' said Myrna, stepping back to survey Clara, her laughter finally subsiding.

'I'm wearing a tuque, you moron,' said Clara and both women laughed again as Clara pulled the knitted pompom hat down over her ears.

It was hard not to feel light-hearted in that atmosphere. It was close to four o'clock on 22 December and the sun had set. Now the streets of Montreal, always full of charm, were also full of Christmas lights. Up and down rue Ste-Catherine decorations glowed, the light bouncing off the snowdrifts. Cars crawled by, caught in the rush-hour snag, and pedestrians hurried along the snowy sidewalks, occasionally stopping to look in a bright shop window.

Just ahead was their destination. Ogilvy's. And the window. Even from half a block away Clara could see the glow, and the magic reflected on the faces of the children staring up at it. Now the cold vanished, the crowds, elbowing and nudging moments before, disappeared; even Myrna receded as Clara approached the window. There it was. The Mill in the Forest.

'I'll meet you in there,' Myrna whispered, but her friend had gone. Into the window Clara had climbed. Past the enraptured children in front, over the pile of clothing on the snowy sidewalk and right into the idyllic Christmas scene. She was walking over the wooden bridge now, toward the grandma bear in the wooden mill house.

'Spare some change? *L'argent, s'il vous plaît?'*

A spewing sound cut into Clara's world.

'Oh, gross. Mommy,' a child cried as Clara tore her eyes from the window and looked down. The pile of clothing had thrown up, the vomit gently steaming on the crusted blanket wrapped round him. Or her. Clara didn't know, and didn't care. She was annoyed that she'd waited all year, all week, all day for this moment and some bum on the street had vomited all over it. And now the kids were all crying and the magic had gone.

Clara backed away from the window, and looked around for Myrna. She must have gone inside, Clara realized, and already be at the big event. It wasn't just the window that had brought them to Ogilvy's this day. A fellow villager and good friend, Ruth Zardo, was launching her latest book in the basement bookstore.

Normally Ruth's slim volumes of poetry were slipped to an oblivious public following a launch at the bistro in Three Pines. But something astounding had happened. This elderly, wizened, bitter poet from Three Pines had won the Governor-General's Award. Surprised the hell out of everyone. Not because she didn't deserve it. Clara knew her poems were stunning.

> *Who hurt you once so far beyond repair*
> *that you would greet each overture with curling lip?*
> *It was not always so.*

No, Ruth Zardo deserved the prize. It was just shocking that anyone else knew it.

Will that happen with my art? Clara wondered as she swooshed through the revolving doors into the perfumed and muted atmosphere of Ogilvy's. Am I about to be plucked out of obscurity? She'd finally found the courage to give her work to their new neighbor, CC de Poitiers, after she'd overheard her talking in the bistro about her close personal friend, Denis Fortin.

To have a show at the Galerie Fortin in the Outremont quartier of Montreal was to have arrived. He chose only the very best, the most cutting edge, the most profound and daring of artists. And he was connected worldwide. Even . . . dare she think it? The Museum of Modern Art in New York. The MOMA. MOMA mia.

Clara imagined herself at the *vernissage* at Galerie Fortin. She'd be sparkling and witty, the center of awed attention, lesser artists and major critics hanging on her every insightful word. Peter would be standing slightly outside the circle of admirers, watching with a small smile. He'd be proud of her and finally see her as a fellow artist.

Crie sat on the snowy steps of Miss Edward's School. It was dark now. Inside and out. She stared ahead, unseeing, the snow accumulating on her hat and shoulders. At her side was a bag containing her snowflake costume. Stuffed into it was her report card.

Straight As.

Her teachers had tsked and shaken their heads and bemoaned the fact that such brains had been wasted on someone so damaged. A crying shame, one of them had said and all had laughed at the witticism. Except Crie, who happened to be walking by.

The teachers all agreed they'd have to have a stern talk to whoever it was who'd hurt her so badly she could barely talk or meet an eye.

Eventually Crie got up and began cautiously walking toward downtown Montreal, her balance thrown off by the slippery, steep sidewalks and near unbearable weight of the chiffon snowflake.

FOUR

⁓

As Clara walked through Ogilvy's she wasn't sure what was worse, the stink of the wretched bum or the cloying smell of the perfumeries in the department store. After about the fifth time some slim young thing had sprayed her Clara had her answer. She was offending even herself.

'It's about fuckin' time.' Ruth Zardo limped over to Clara. 'You look like a bag lady.' She gave and received a kiss on each cheek. 'And you stink.'

'It's not me, it's Myrna,' Clara whispered and nodded to her friend nearby, waving her hand under her nose. It was actually a warmer reception than she generally got from the poet.

'Here, buy that.' Ruth handed her a copy of her new book, *I'm FINE*. 'I'll even sign it for you. But you have to buy it first.'

Tall and dignified, leaning on her cane for support, Ruth Zardo limped back to her small desk in a corner of the huge store to wait for someone to ask her to sign her book.

Clara went off and paid for the book then had it signed.

She recognized everyone in the room. There were Gabri Dubeau and his partner Olivier Brulé. Gabri large and soft and clearly going to pot and loving every mouthful of it. He was in his mid-thirties and had decided he'd had enough of being young and buff and gay. Well, not really enough of being gay. Beside him stood Olivier, handsome and slim and elegant. Blond to his partner's dark, he was picking a distressing strand of hair from his silk turtleneck, clearly wishing he could stick it back in.

Ruth needn't have bothered coming all the way to Montreal for the launch. The only people who showed up were from Three Pines.

'This's a waste of time,' she said, her short-cropped white head bending over Clara's book. 'No one from Montreal came, not a goddamned person. Just you lot. What a bore.'

'Well, thank you very much, you old hack,' said Gabri, holding a couple of books in his large hands.

'Great.' Ruth looked up. 'This is a bookstore,' she said, very slowly and loudly. 'It's for people who can read. It's not a public bath.'

'Too bad, really.' Gabri looked at Clara.

'It's Myrna,' she said, but since Myrna was across the way chatting with Émilie Longpré her credibility was lost.

'At least you drown out the stink of Ruth's poetry,' said Gabri, holding *I'm FINE* away from him.

'Fag,' snapped Ruth.

'Hag,' snapped Gabri, winking at Clara. '*Salut, ma chère.*'

'*Salut, mon amour.* What's that other book you have?' Clara asked.

'CC de Poitiers's. Did you know our new neighbor's written a book?'

'God, that means she's written more books than she's read,' said Ruth.

'I got it over there.' He pointed to a pile of white books in the remainder bin. Ruth snorted then stopped herself, realizing it was probably just a matter of days before her small collection of exquisitely crafted poems joined CC's shit in that literary coffin.

A few people were standing there including the Three Graces from Three Pines: Émilie Longpré, tiny and elegant in a slim skirt, shirt and silk scarf; Kaye Thompson, at over ninety years of age the oldest of the three friends, wizened and shriveled, smelling of Vapo-rub and looking like a potato; and Beatrice Mayer, her hair red and wild, her body soft and plump, and ill-concealed beneath a voluminous amber caftan with chunky jewelry about the neck. Mother Bea, as she was known, held a copy of CC's book. She turned and glanced in Clara's direction, only for a moment. But it was enough.

Mother Bea looked overtaken by some emotion Clara couldn't quite identify. Fury? Fear? Extreme concern of some sort, that much Clara was sure of. And then it was gone, replaced by Mother's peaceful, cheery face, all pink and wrinkled and open.

'Come on, let's go over.' Ruth struggled to her feet and took Gabri's offered arm. 'There's nothing much happening here. When the inevitable hordes arrive, desperate for great poetry, I'll race back to the table.'

'*Bonjour*, dear.' Tiny Émilie Longpré kissed Clara on both cheeks. In winter, when most Québecois looked like cartoon characters, wrapped in wool and parkas, Em managed to look both elegant and gracious. Her hair was dyed a tasteful light brown and was beautifully coiffed. Her clothes and make-up were subtle and appropriate. At eighty-two she was one of the matriarchs of the village.

'Have you seen this?' Olivier handed Clara a book. CC stared back, cruel and cold.

Be Calm.

Clara looked over at Mother. Now she understood why Mother Bea was in such a state.

'Listen to this.' Gabri started reading the back. 'Ms de Poitiers has officially declared feng shui a thing of the past.'

'Of course it is, it's ancient Chinese teaching,' said Kaye.

'In its stead,' Gabri persevered, 'this new doyenne of design has brought us a much richer, much more meaningful philosophy which will inform and indeed color not just our homes but our very souls, our every moment, our every decision, our every breath. Make way for Li Bien, the way of light.'

'What is Li Bien?' Olivier asked no one in particular. Clara thought she saw Mother open her mouth, then shut it again.

'Mother?' she asked.

'Me? No, dear, I don't know. Why do you ask?'

'I thought since you have a yoga and meditation center you might be familiar with Li Bien.' Clara tried to put it gently.

'I'm familiar with all spiritual paths,' she said, exaggerating slightly, Clara thought. 'But not this one.' The implication was clear.

'But still,' said Gabri, 'it's a strange coincidence, don't you think?'

'What is?' Mother asked, her voice and face serene, but her shoulders up round her ears.

'Well, that CC should call her book *Be Calm*. That's the name of your meditation center.'

There was silence.

'What?' said Gabri, knowing he'd somehow put his foot into it.

'It must be a coincidence,' said Émilie, evenly. 'And it's probably a tribute to you, *ma belle*.' She turned to Mother, laying a thin hand on her friend's plump arm. 'She's been in the old Hadley place for about a year now; she's no doubt been inspired by the work you do. It's a homage to your spirit.'

'And her pile of crap is probably higher than yours,' Kaye re-assured her. 'That must be a comfort. I didn't think it was possible,' she said to Ruth, who looked at her hero with delight.

'Nice hair.' Olivier turned to Clara, hoping to break the tension.

'Thank you.' Clara ran her hands through it, making it stand on end as though she'd just had a scare.

'You're right.' Olivier turned to Myrna. 'She looks like a frightened doughboy from the trenches of Vimy. Not many people could carry off that look. Very bold, very new millennium. I salute you.'

Clara narrowed her eyes and glared at Myrna whose smile went from ear to ear.

'Fuck the Pope,' said Kaye.

CC straightened the chair again. She stood dressed and alone in the hotel room. Saul had left without a goodbye kiss offered or expected.

She was relieved to see him go. Now, finally, she could do it.

CC held a copy of *Be Calm* and stood at the window.

Slowly she brought the book up to her chest and pressed it there as though it was the piece that had been missing all her life.

She tilted her head back and waited. Would this be the year they eluded her? But no. Her lower lip trembled slightly. Then her eyes fluttered and a small lump fizzed in her throat. And then they came, racing cold down her cheeks and into her now open, cavernous, silent mouth. And she tumbled down that dark chasm after them and found herself in a familiar room, at Christmas.

Her mother stood beside a long dead and undecorated pine tree propped in the corner of the stark, dark room, a sprinkling of sharp needles on the floor. A single ball hung on the tree and now her mother, hysterical and howling, yanked it off. CC could still hear the storm of needles hitting the floor and see the ball racing toward her. She hadn't meant to catch it. Had only put her hands up to protect her face, but the ball had landed right in her palms, and stuck there, as though finding a home. Her mother was on the floor now, rocking and crying, and CC was desperate for her to stop. Desperate to shut her up, silence her, calm her before the neighbors called the police again and again her mother was taken away. And CC was left alone, in the company of strangers.

For an instant, though, CC hesitated and looked at the ball in her hands. It glowed and was warm to the touch. On it was painted a simple image. Three tall pine trees grouped together like a family, snow nestled on the bowing branches. Below it was written, in her mother's hand, *Noël*.

CC leaned into the ball, losing herself in its peace and calm and light. But she must have looked too long. A banging on the door tore her away from the three pines and back to the horror in front of her.

'What's going on in there? Let us in,' the man's voice demanded from the other side of the door.

And CC had, though it was the last time she ever let anyone in, anywhere.

Crie walked by the Ritz, stopping to stare into the plush hotel. A doorman ignored her, not offering to let her in. She moved on slowly, her boots sodden with slush, her woolen mittens hanging off her hands, the caked snow dragging them to the ground.

She didn't care. She trudged along the dark, snowy, congested streets, pedestrians bumping into her and giving her disgusted looks, as though fat children had spread their feelings like icing on slabs of cake, and swallowed them.

Still she walked, her feet freezing now. She'd left the house without proper winter boots, and when her father had vaguely suggested maybe she wanted something warmer she'd ignored him.

Like her mother ignored him. Like the world ignored him.

She ground to a stop in front of *Monde de la musique*. There was a poster of Britney Spears, dancing on a hot, steamy beach, her happy backup singers grinning and gyrating.

Crie stood before the window a long time, no longer feeling her feet or her hands. No longer feeling anything.

'I beg your pardon?' Clara asked.

'Fuck the Pope,' Kaye repeated, as clear as day. Mother Bea pretended she hadn't heard and Émilie stepped slightly closer to her friend, as though positioning herself in case Kaye collapsed.

'I'm ninety-two and I know everything,' Kaye said. 'Except one thing,' she conceded.

There was another long silence. But curiosity had replaced embarrassment. Kaye, normally so taciturn and abrupt, was about to speak. The friends gathered closer.

'My father was with the Expeditionary Force in the Great War.' Of all the things they thought she might say, this wasn't one of them. She was speaking softly now, her face relaxing and her eyes drifting off to stare at the books on the shelves. Kaye was time-traveling, something Mother Bea claimed to do while yogic flying, but had never achieved to this degree.

'They'd formed a division especially for Catholics, mostly Irish like Daddy and Québecois, of course. He'd never talk about the war. They never did. And I never asked. Imagine that? Did he want me to, do you think?' Kaye looked at Em, who was silent. 'He told us only one thing about the war.' Now she stopped. She looked around and her eyes fell on her fluffy knitted hat. She reached out and put it on, then looked at Em, expectantly. No one was breathing. They stared back, waiting to hear more.

'For Christ's sake, woman, tell us,' Ruth rasped.

'Oh, yes.' Kaye seemed to notice them for the first time. 'Daddy. At the Somme. Led by Rawlinson, you know. Fool of a man. I looked that much up. My father was up to his chest in muck and shit, horse and human. Food was infested with maggots. His skin was rotting, sores all over. His hair and teeth were falling out. They'd long since stopped fighting for king and country, and were now just fighting for each other. He loved his friends.'

Kaye looked at Em then over to Mother.

'The boys were lining up, and told to fix bayonets.'

Everyone leaned forward slightly.

'The last wave of boys had gone over a minute or so earlier and were mowed down. They could hear the screams and see the twitching body parts that had flown back into the trench. It was their turn, my father and his friends. They waited for the word. He knew he was going to die. He knew he had moments to live. He knew he could say one last thing. And do you know what those boys screamed as they went over the top?'

The world had stopped turning and had come down to this.

'They crossed themselves and screamed, "Fuck the Pope."'

As one the friends recoiled, as though wounded by the words, by the image. Kaye turned to Clara, her rheumy blue eyes searching.

'Why?'

Clara wondered why Kaye thought she'd know. She didn't. And she was wise enough to say nothing. Kaye dropped her head as though it suddenly weighed too much, the back of her thin neck forming a deep trench into her skull.

'Time to go, dear. You must be tired.' Em put a delicate hand on Kaye's arm and Mother Bea took the other and the three elderly women walked slowly out of the bookstore. Heading home to Three Pines.

'And time for us to go as well. Need a lift?' Myrna asked Ruth.

'No, I'm here to the bitter end. All you rats, don't feel bad. Just leave me here.'

'Saint Ruth Among the Heathens,' said Gabri.

'Our Lady of Perpetual Poetry,' said Olivier. 'We'll stay with you.'

'There once was a woman named Ruth,' said Gabri.

'Who was getting quite long in the tooth,' said Olivier.

'Come on, let's go.' Myrna dragged Clara away, though Clara was quite curious to see what they'd come up with to rhyme with 'tooth'. Mooth? Gooth? No, probably better if it's an actual word. Being a poet was harder than it looked.

'There's one quick thing I need to do,' said Clara. 'It'll just take a minute.'

'I'll get the car and meet you outside.' Myrna rushed off. Clara found the small brasserie in Ogilvy's and bought a panini and some Christmas cookies. She also bought a large coffee, then headed for the escalator.

She was feeling badly about the homeless person she'd stepped over to get into Ogilvy's. She had a sneaking, and secret, suspicion that if God ever came to earth He'd be a beggar. Suppose this was Him? Or Her? Whatever. If it was God Clara had a deep, almost spiritual feeling that she was screwed. Getting on the crowded escalator up to the main floor Clara saw a familiar figure descending. CC de Poitiers. And CC had seen her, she was sure of it.

CC de Poitiers gripped the rubber handrail of the escalator and stared at the woman getting on at the bottom. Clara Morrow. That smug, smiling, self-righteous villager. That woman always surrounded by friends, always with that handsome husband, showing him off as though it was more than some freak of nature that she'd landed one of the Montreal Morrows. CC could feel a rage building inside her as Clara approached, looking so wide-eyed and happy.

CC gripped harder, willing herself not to launch herself over the sleek metal divider and onto Clara. She balled up all her rage and made a missile of it and, like Ahab, had her chest been a cannon she'd have fired her heart upon Clara.

Instead, she did the next best thing.

Turning to the man next to her she said, 'I'm so sorry, Denis, that you think Clara's art is amateur and banal. So she's just wasting her time?'

As Clara passed CC had the satisfaction of seeing her smug, arrogant, ugly little face crumple. A direct hit. CC turned to the baffled stranger beside her and smiled, not really caring whether he thought she was nuts.

Clara got off the escalator in a dream. The floor seemed a very long way off and the walls receded. Breathe. Breathe, she ordered herself, a little frightened that she might actually die. Murdered by words. Murdered by CC. So casual and so cruel. She hadn't recognized the man next to CC as Fortin, but then she'd only seen pictures of him.

Amateur and banal.

And then the pain started and the tears, and she stood in Ogilvy's, the place she'd been yearning to enter all her life, and wept. She sobbed, and lowered her precious presents to the marble floor, and placed the sandwich there and the cookies and the coffee, carefully, as a child places food for Santa. Then she knelt there herself, the final offering, a tiny ball of pain.

Amateur and banal. All her suspicions, all her fears had been true. The voice that whispered to her in the dark while Peter slept hadn't lied after all.

Her art was crap.

Shoppers swirled around her, no one offering to help.

Just as, Clara realized, she hadn't helped the vagrant outside. Slowly Clara gathered herself and her packages up, and shuffled through the revolving door.

It was dark and cold, the wind and snow now picking up and surprising her warm skin. Clara stopped to allow her eyes to adjust to the darkness.

There, under the window, still slumped on the ground, was the bum.

She approached the beggar, noticing the vomit had stopped steaming and was frozen in place. As she got closer Clara became convinced the beggar was an old woman. She could see a scraggle of iron-gray hair and thin arms hugging the crusty blanket to her knees. Clara bent down and caught a whiff. It was enough to make her gag. Instinctively she pulled back, then moved closer again. Putting her weight of bags on the ground she laid the food next to the woman.

'I brought you some food,' she said first in English, then in French. She inched the bag with the sandwich closer and held the coffee up, hoping the bag lady might see it.

There was no movement. Clara grew concerned. Was she even alive? Clara reached out and gently lifted the grime-caked chin.

'Are you all right?'

A mitten shot out, black with muck, and cupped itself round Clara's wrist. The head lifted. Weary, runny eyes met Clara's and held them for a long moment.

'I have always loved your art, Clara.'

FIVE

⌐⌐

'**B**ut that's incredible.' Myrna didn't want to sound as though she doubted her friend, but really, 'incredible' was charitable. It was unbelievable. And yet despite the cup of tea and fire in the grate her forearms broke out in goose bumps.

They'd driven home from Montreal in silence, listening to the Christmas Concert on CBC Radio. The next morning Clara was at her bookshop bright and early and eager to talk.

'It is,' Clara agreed, sipping tea and taking another star-shaped shortbread cookie, wondering when she could in all conscience start eating from the bowls of licorice goodies and candied ginger Myrna had scattered around.

'She really said, "I've always loved your art, Clara"?'

Clara nodded.

'And this was right after CC said your work was, well, whatever.'

'Not just CC but Fortin as well. Amateurish and banal, he'd called it. Doesn't matter. God likes my work.'

'And by God you mean the shit-covered bag lady?'

'Exactly.'

Myrna leaned her bulk forward in her rocking chair. Around her were the usual stacks of books waiting to be inspected and priced. Clara had the impression they sprang legs and followed Myrna about the village. Wherever she was there were books, like very unwieldy calling cards.

Myrna thought back. She'd noticed the vagrant, but then Myrna noticed most vagrants. She wondered what would happen if she ever recognized one. For years she'd seen patients at the mental hospital in Montreal, then one day, not so out of the blue as she liked to pretend, a memo appeared. Most of the clients – the patients overnight had become clients – were to be released. She'd protested, of course, but had eventually given in. And so she'd found herself looking across her battered desk at a succession of 'clients', and into their eyes, and giving them a piece of paper that lied, that said they were ready to live on their own, with a prescription and a prayer.

Most quickly lost their prescription and never really had a prayer.

Except, perhaps, Clara's woman.

Was it possible – Myrna watched her friend over the rim of her mug – that Clara had met God on the streets? Myrna believed in God and prayed God wasn't one of the men or women she'd betrayed by signing their release. Myrna's weight wasn't all carried around her middle.

Clara was looking past the wooden shelves full of books and out the window. Myrna knew exactly what Clara was seeing. She'd sat in that very chair countless times staring out that window, dreaming. Her dreams were simple. Like Leigh Hunt's Abou Ben Adhem, all she'd ever had was a deep dream of peace. And she'd found it here, in this simple, forgotten village in the Eastern Townships. After decades of treating people who never got better, after years of looking out windows at lost souls wandering toward a street that would become their new home, Myrna longed for another view.

She knew what Clara was seeing. She was seeing the village green, now covered in a foot of snow, and an irregular skating rink, and a couple of snowmen and three enormous pine trees at the far end that were lit at night with cheery Christmas lights of red and green and blue. And on the top of the tallest a brilliant white star shone visible for miles around.

Clara was seeing peace.

Myrna got up and went to the wood stove in the center of her shop, and taking an old coffee pot from the top she poured herself another cup. She wondered whether she should get out the small pan and warm up some milk for hot chocolate, but decided it was a little too early.

On either side of the stove she'd placed a rocking chair, and facing it a sofa Peter had found while dumpster diving in Williamsburg. A Christmas tree she and Billy Williams had dragged from the woods stood in a corner and filled the shop with its sweet scent. Now it was decorated and under it were brightly wrapped gifts. A tray of cookies sat beside it for anyone who dropped by and bowls of candy were placed within easy reach around the store.

'So how'd she know your art?' Myrna had to ask.

'How d'you think?' Clara was genuinely curious to hear Myrna's thoughts. They both knew what Clara believed.

Myrna thought for a moment, holding a book in her hand. She always thought better when holding a book. Still, no answer came.

'I don't know.'

'Are you sure?' asked Clara with a grin.

'You don't know either,' said Myrna. 'You want to believe it was God. I have to tell you, people are locked up for less.'

'But not for long.' Clara caught Myrna's eye. 'Now, in my place what would you believe? That CC was right and the work is crap or that a vagrant was God and the work is brilliant?'

'Or you could stop listening to the outside world and decide for yourself.'

'I've tried that.' Clara laughed. 'At two in the afternoon my art is brilliant, at two in the morning it's crap.' She leaned forward until her hands were almost touching Myrna's. She looked into her friend's warm eyes and said very quietly, 'I believe I met God.'

Myrna smiled, not in a patronizing way. If Myrna knew one thing it was how little she really knew.

'Is that Ruth's book?' Clara picked up *I'm FINE*. 'May I buy it?'

'But you bought one yesterday. We both did. Even had her sign it. You know, I think I saw her signing some books by Auden too.'

'I lost mine somewhere. I'll get this and if she signs an Anthony Hecht I'll buy that too.'

Clara opened the book and read, at random.

> *'Well, all children are sad*
> *but some get over it.*
> *Count your blessings. Better than that,*
> *buy a hat. Buy a coat or pet.*
> *Take up dancing to forget.*

'How does Ruth do it? I swear she's just an old drunk.'
'You thought that about God, too,' said Myrna.
'Listen,

> *Forget what?*
> *Your sadness, your shadow,*
> *whatever it was that was done to you*
> *the day of the lawn party*
> *when you came inside flushed with the sun,*
> *your mouth sulky with sugar,*
> *in your new dress with the ribbon*
> *and the ice-cream smear,*
> *and said to yourself in the bathroom,*
> *I am not the favorite child.'*

Myrna looked out the window and wondered whether their peace, so fragile and precious, was about to be shattered. Since CC de Poitiers had arrived there'd been a gathering gloom over their little community. She'd brought something unsavory to Three Pines, in time for Christmas.

SIX

The days leading up to Christmas were active and full. Clara loved the season. Loved everything about it, from the sappy commercials to the tacky parade for Père Noël through St-Rémy sponsored by Canadian Tire, to the caroling organized by Gabri. The singers moved from house to house through the snowy village, filling the night air with old hymns and laughter and puffs of breath plump with song and snowflakes. Villagers invited them into their living rooms and they carried on around pianos and Christmas trees, singing and drinking brandy eggnogs and eating shortbread and smoked salmon and sweet twisty breads and all the delicacies baked in the festive ovens. The carolers sang at every home in the village over the course of a few evenings, except one. By unspoken consent, they stayed away from the dark house on the hill. The old Hadley place.

Gabri, in his Victorian cape and top hat, led the carolers. He had a beautiful voice but longed for what he couldn't have. Each year Ruth Zardo visited the bistro as Father Christmas, chosen, Gabri said, because she didn't have to grow a special beard. Each year Gabri would climb onto her lap and ask for the voice of a boy soprano and each year Father Christmas offered to kick him in the Christmas balls.

Every Christmas Monsieur and Madame Vachon placed the old *crèche* on their front lawn, complete with the baby Jesus in a clawfoot bathtub surrounded by three wise men and plastic farm animals who slowly became buried under snow and emerged unchanged in spring, another miracle, though one not shared by every villager.

Billy Williams hitched his percherons to his bright red sleigh and took boys and girls round the village and into the snow-covered hills. The children crawled under the ratty bearskin rug and cradled hot chocolate while the dignified gray giants pulled them along in a manner so calm and measured it was as though they knew their cargo to be precious. Inside the bistro parents were granted the window seats where they could sip hot cider and watch their children disappear over rue du Moulin, then they'd turn back to the warm interior with its faded fabrics, mismatched furniture and open hearths.

Clara and Peter finished their decorations, putting up splays of pine branches in their kitchen to complement the huge Scotch pine in the living room. Their home, like everyone else's, smelled of the forest.

All the presents were wrapped and placed under the tree. Clara walked by them every morning thrilled that finally, thanks to Jane's will, none of their gifts came from the Williamsburg dump. Finally they'd exchange gifts that didn't need disinfecting.

Peter hung their stockings on the mantelpiece. The short-bread cookies were baked into stars and trees and snowmen and decorated with silver balls that could have been buckshot.

In the living room each evening before caroling Peter would tend the fire and read his books while Clara noodled on the piano, singing carols off key. Many nights Myrna or Ruth, Gabri or Olivier would drop by for drinks or an easy dinner.

Then, before they knew it, it was Christmas Eve and they were all off to Émilie's for her *réveillon* party. But first, midnight service at St Thomas's church.

'Silent night, holy night,' the congregation sang, with more gusto than talent. It actually sounded slightly like the old sea shanty, 'What shall we do with the drunken Sailor'. Gabri's beautiful tenor naturally led them, or at least made it clear they were wandering in a musical wilderness, or lost at sea. Except one. From the back of the wooden chapel came a voice of such exquisite clarity it staggered even Gabri. The child's voice swooped out of the pew and mingled with the meandering voices of the congregation and hovered around the holly and pine boughs the Anglican Church Women had placed all over so that the worshippers had the impression they were not in a church at all, but a forest. Bare maple limbs had been attached to the rafters by Billy Williams, and the ACW, led by Mother, had asked him to twine small white lights loosely about the branches. The effect was of the heavens sparkling above the small gathering of faithful. The church was filled with greenery and light.

'Green is the heart chakra,' Mother had explained.

'I'm sure the Bishop will be pleased,' Kaye said.

On Christmas Eve St Thomas's was also filled with families, children excited and exhausted, elderly men and women who'd come to this place all their lives and sat in the same pew and worshipped the same God and baptized and married and buried those they loved. Some they never got to bury, but instead immortalized in the small stained glass window placed to get the morning, the youngest, light. They marched now in warm yellows and blues and greens, for ever perfect and petrified in the Great War. Etched below the brilliant boys were their names and the words 'They Were Our Children'.

This night the church was full of Anglicans and Catholics and Jews and non-believers and people who believed in something undefined and unrestricted to a church. They came because St Thomas's on Christmas Eve was full of greenery and light.

But, unexpectedly, this Christmas it was also full of the most beautiful singing.

'All is calm,' the voice sang, rescuing the sinking congregation. Clara turned, trying to find the child. Many were also craning to see who was leading them. Even Gabri was forced to relinquish his place in the unexpected and not totally welcome presence of the divine. It was as though an angel, as Yeats would have it, became weary of the whimpering dead and chose this lively company.

Clara suddenly had a perfect view.

There at the back stood CC de Poitiers wearing a fluffy white sweater made of either cashmere or kittens. Beside her was her husband, florid and mute. And beside him an enormous child was wearing a sleeveless sundress of the brightest pink. Her underarms bulged and flopped and the rolls of her waist made the skin-tight dress look like a melting strawberry ice cream. It was grotesque.

But her face was beautiful. Clara had seen this child before, but only from a distance and only with a sullen unhappy face.

But now that face was tilted toward the glowing rafters and held a look Clara knew to be bliss.

'All is bright.' Crie's exquisite voice played in the rafters with the lights then slipped under the door of the old chapel and danced with the gently falling snowflakes and parked cars and bare maples. The words of the old carol glided across the frozen pond and nested in the Christmas trees and seeped into every happy home in Three Pines.

After the service the minister hurried out, late for Christmas Eve celebrations in nearby Cleghorn Halt.

'*Joyeux Noël*,' said Peter to Gabri as they gathered on the steps outside the church for the short stroll across the village to Émilie's house. 'What a beautiful night.'

'And what a beautiful service,' said Clara, coming up beside Peter. 'Can you believe that child's voice?'

'Not bad,' admitted Gabri.

'Not bad?' Mother Bea oscillated up to them, Kaye on her arm like a muff and Émilie on her other side. 'She was unbelievable. I've never heard such a voice, have you?'

'I need a drink,' said Kaye. 'When're we leaving?'

'Right now,' Em assured her.

'Olivier's getting the food from the bistro,' said Gabri. 'We made a poached salmon.'

'Will you marry me?' asked Myrna.

'I bet you ask all the girls,' said Gabri.

'You're the first,' admitted Myrna and laughed. But her laughter was cut short.

'You're a stupid, stupid girl,' a voice hissed from the other side of the church. Everyone froze, surprised to stillness by the words that cut through the crisp night air. 'Everyone was staring at you. You humiliated me.'

It was CC's voice. There was a side door to the church and a path that was a short cut to de Moulin and the old Hadley house. CC must be there, they realized, standing in the shadow of the church.

'They were laughing at you, you know. Deep and crisp and even,' CC sang in a mocking voice, off key and childish. 'And your clothes. Are you sick? I think you're mentally unstable.'

'Now CC,' came a man's voice so meek and weak it barely penetrated the flurries.

'She's your daughter. Look at her. Fat and ugly and lazy. Like you. Are you crazy, Crie? Is that it? Is it? Is it?'

The crowd was frozen in place as though hiding from a monster, silently pleading, please, please, someone stop her. Someone else.

'And you've opened your Christmas gift, you selfish child.'

'But you told me I—' came the tiny response.

'Me, me, me. That's all I hear from you. And have you even thanked me?'

'Thank you for the chocolates, Mommy.' The voice and the girl were so diminished as to be almost non-existent.

'Too late. It doesn't count if I have to beg.' The end of the sentence was barely audible as CC clicked down the path as though walking on claws.

The congregation stood speechless. Beside Clara Gabri started humming, low and slow, then, barely audible, came the words to the old carol: 'Sorr'wing, sighing, bleeding, dying. Sealed in the stone-cold tomb.'

They'd evaded the monster. Instead, it had devoured a frightened child.

SEVEN

'*Joyeux Noël, tout le monde*,' Em beamed, opening the door to greet her guests a few minutes later. Her year-old shepherd Henri raced out the door and leaped on everyone before being bribed back with a piece of Christmas cake. The chaos and happy turmoil helped banish the unease after CC's outburst. It seemed the entire village arrived at once, bounding up the steps of Em's wide veranda, shaking snow from their hats and coats.

Émilie's home was a sprawling old clapboard cottage across the green from the Morrow place. Olivier paused just outside the circle of light from her porch, balancing his poached salmon on its platter.

Approaching Em's cottage, especially at night, always enchanted him. It was like walking into those fairy tales he'd read by flashlight under his bedcovers, full of rose-covered cottages and small stone bridges, glowing hearths and content couples hand in hand. His relieved father had thought he was reading *Playboy* but instead he was doing something infinitely more pleasurable and dangerous. He was dreaming of the day he'd create this fairy-tale world for himself, and he'd succeeded, at least in part. He had himself become a fairy. And as he looked at Em's cottage, its buttery light beaconing, he knew he'd walked right into the book he'd used to comfort himself when the world seemed cold and hard and unfair. Now he smiled and walked toward the house, carrying his Christmas Eve offering. He walked carefully so as not to slip on the ice that might be waiting under the thin covering of snow. A layer of pure white was both beautiful and dangerous. You never really knew what lurked beneath. A Quebec winter could both enchant and kill.

As people arrived food was taken to the familiar kitchen and too many casseroles and pies were stuffed into the oven. Bowls overflowing with candied ginger and chocolate-covered cherries and sugar-encrusted fruit sat on the sideboard beside puddings and cakes and cookies. Little Rose Lévesque stared up at the *bûche de Noël*, the traditional Christmas log, made of rich cake and coated with the thickest of icing, her tiny, chubby fingers curling over the tablecloth embroidered with Santa Claus and reindeer and Christmas trees. In the living room Ruth and Peter made drinks, Ruth pouring her Scotch into what Peter knew to be a vase.

The lights on the tree glowed and the Vachon children sat beside it reading the tags on the mountain of brightly wrapped presents, looking for theirs. The fire was lit, as were a few of the guests. In the dining room the gate-legged table was open full and groaning with casseroles and *tortières*, home-made molasses-baked beans and maple-cured ham. A turkey sat at the head of the table like a Victorian gentleman. The center of the table was saved every year for one of Myrna's rich and vibrant flower arrangements. This year splays of

Scotch pine surrounded a magnificent red amaryllis. Nestled into the pine forest was a music box softly playing the Huron Christmas Carol and resting on a bed of mandarin oranges, cranberries and chocolates.

Olivier carried the whole poached salmon to the table. A punch was made for the children, who, unsupervised, stuffed themselves with candy.

Thus did Émilie Longpré hold her *réveillon*, the party that spanned Christmas Eve and Christmas Day, an old Québecois tradition, just as her mother and *grandmère* had done in this very same home on this very same night. Spotting Em turning in circles Clara wound her arm round the tiny waist.

'Can I help?'

'No, dear. I'm just making sure everyone's happy.'

'We're always happy here,' said Clara, truthfully, giving Em a small kiss on each cheek and tasting salt. She'd been crying this night and Clara knew why. At Christmas homes were full of the people there and the people not there.

'So when do you plan to take off your Santa beard?' Gabri asked, sitting next to Ruth on the worn sofa by the fire.

'Bitch,' muttered Ruth.

'Slut,' said Gabri.

'Look at that.' Myrna sat on the other side of Ruth, her bulk almost catapulting the other two off the sofa. Myrna motioned her plate in the direction of a group of young women standing by the Christmas tree critiquing each other's hair. 'Those girls think they're having a bad hair day. Just wait for it.'

'It's true,' Clara said, looking around for a chair. The room was full, people yakking away in French and English. She eventually sat on the floor, putting her overflowing plate on the coffee table. Peter joined her.

'What're you talking about?'

'Hair,' said Myrna.

'Save yourself,' said Olivier, reaching out to Peter. 'It's too late for us, but you can get away. I understand there's a conversation on prostates at the other sofa.'

'Sit down.' Clara pulled Peter down by his belt. 'Those girls over there all think they have it bad.'

'But wait 'til menopause,' confirmed Myrna.

'Prostates?' Peter asked Olivier.

'And hockey,' he sighed.

'Are you guys listening?'

'It's so hard being a woman,' said Gabri. 'There's our periods, then losing our virginity to you beasts, then the kids leave and we no longer know who we are—'

'Having given the best years of our lives to thankless bastards and selfish kids,' nodded Olivier.

'Then, just when we've signed up for pottery and Thai cooking courses, bang—'

'Or not,' said Peter, smiling at Clara.

'Watch it, boy.' She poked him with her fork.

'Menopause,' said Olivier in a sonorous CBC announcer voice.

'I've never told a man to pause,' said Gabri.

'The first gray hair. Now there's a bad hair day,' said Myrna, ignoring the guys.

'How about when the first one appears on your chin,' said Ruth. 'That's a bad hair day.'

'God, it's true.' Mother laughed, joining them. 'The long wiry ones.'

'Don't forget the moustache,' said Kaye, creaking down where Myrna offered her seat. Gabri got up so that Mother could sit. 'We have a solemn pact.' Kaye nodded to Mother and looked over at Em talking to some neighbors. 'If one of us is unconscious in the hospital, the others will make sure it's pulled.'

'The plug?' Ruth asked.

'The chin hair,' said Kaye, eyeing Ruth with some alarm. 'You're off the visitors list. Mother, make a note.'

'Oh, I made that note years ago.'

Clara took her empty plate back to the buffet and returned a few minutes later with trifle and brownies and Licorice Allsorts.

'I stole them from the kids,' she said to Myrna. 'Better hurry up if you want some. They're getting wise.'

'I'll just eat yours,' and Myrna actually attempted to take one before a fork menaced her hand.

'Addicts, you're pathetic.' Myrna looked over at Ruth's vase of Scotch, half gone.

'You're wrong there,' said Ruth, following Myrna's gaze. 'This used to be my drug of choice. In my teens my drug of choice was acceptance, in my twenties it was approval, in my thirties it was love, in my forties it was Scotch. That lasted a while,' she admitted. 'Now all I really crave is a good bowel movement.'

'I'm addicted to meditation,' said Mother, eating her third helping of trifle.

'There's an idea.' Kaye turned to Ruth. 'You could visit Mother at the center. She can meditate the crap out of anyone.'

Silence met this statement. Clara scrambled for something to replace the repulsive image that had sprung to her mind and was grateful when Gabri picked up a book from the stack under the coffee table and waved it around.

'Speaking of crap, isn't this CC's book? Em must have bought it at your launch, Ruth.'

'She probably sold as many as I did. You're all traitors,' said Ruth.

'Listen to this.' Gabri opened *Be Calm*. Clara noticed that Mother shifted in her seat as though to get up but Kaye laid a claw on her arm, stopping her there.

'Therefore', Gabri was reading, 'it stands to reason that colors, like emotions, are harmful. It's not a coincidence that negative emotions are given colors, red for rage, green for envy, blue for depression. But, if you put all the colors together, what do you get? White. White is the color of divinity, of balance. The goal is balance. And the only way to achieve it is to keep the emotions inside, preferably beneath a layer of white. This is Li Bien, an ancient and venerable teaching. In this book you'll learn how to hide your true feelings, to keep them safe from an unkind and judgmental world. Li Bien is the ancient Chinese art of painting from the inside. Keeping the colors, the emotions, in. That is the only way to achieve peace, harmony, and calm. If we all kept our emotions to ourselves there would be no strife, no harm, no violence, no war. In this book I am offering you, and this world, peace.' Gabri snapped the book shut. 'She didn't exactly have Li Bien coming out the yin-yang tonight.'

Peter laughed with the others but was careful not to catch anyone's eye. Privately, beneath his layer of white skin, Peter agreed with CC. Emotions were dangerous. Emotions were best hidden away beneath a calm and peaceful veneer.

'But this doesn't make sense,' Clara said, flipping through the book and puzzling over a particular passage.

'And that other stuff did?' asked Myrna.

'Well, no, but here she says she got her philosophy of life in India. But didn't she just say Li Bien was Chinese?'

'You're actually looking for sense in there?' Myrna asked. Clara had buried her face back in the book and slowly her shoulders started heaving, then her back, and finally she raised her face to the circle of concerned friends.

'What is it?' Myrna reached out to Clara, who was crying.

'The names of her gurus,' said Clara between sobs. Myrna was no longer sure whether she was crying or laughing.

'Krishnamurti Das, Ravi Shankar Das, Gandhi Das. Ramen Das. Khalil Das. Gibran Das. They even call her CC Das.' By now Clara was roaring with laughter as were most of the others.

Most. But not all.

'I see nothing wrong with that,' said Olivier, wiping his eyes. 'Gabri and I follow the way of Häagen Das. It's occasionally a rocky road.'

'And one of your favorite movies is Das Boot,' Clara said to Peter, 'so you must be enlightened.'

'True, though that's Das backward.'

Clara fell laughing against Peter and Henri came over to leap on them both. When she'd regained herself and calmed Henri Clara was surprised to see that Mother had left.

'Is she all right?' she asked Kaye, who was watching her friend walk toward the dining room and Em. 'Did we say something wrong?'

'No.'

'We didn't mean to insult her,' said Clara, taking Mother's place beside Kaye.

'But you didn't. You weren't even talking about her.'

'We were laughing at things Mother takes seriously.'

'You were laughing at CC, not Mother. She knows the difference.'

But Clara wondered. CC and Mother had both named their businesses Be Calm. They both now lived in Three Pines, and they both followed a similar spiritual path. Clara wondered whether the women were hiding more than their emotions.

Calls of 'Merry Christmas' and '*Joyeux Noël*' faded into the cheerful night as the *réveillon* broke up. Émilie waved to the last of her guests and closed the door.

It was two thirty on Christmas morning and she was exhausted. Putting a hand against a table to steady herself she walked slowly into the living room. Clara, Myrna and the others had cleaned up, quietly doing the dishes while she'd sat with a small glass of Scotch and spoken to Ruth on the sofa.

She'd always liked Ruth. Everyone had seemed stunned more than a decade ago by her first book of poetry, stunned that such an apparently brittle and bitter woman could contain such beauty. But Em knew. Had always known. That was one of the things she shared with Clara, and one of the many reasons Em had taken to Clara, from the first day she'd arrived, young and arrogant and full of piss and talent. Clara saw what others couldn't. Like that little boy in *The Sixth Sense*, but instead of seeing ghosts, Clara saw good. Which was itself pretty scary. So much more comforting to see bad in others; gives us all sorts of excuses for our own bad behavior. But good? No, only really remarkable people see the good in others.

Though, as Em well knew, not everyone had good to see. She walked to the stereo, opened a drawer and delicately lifted out a single woolen mitten. Beneath it she found a record. She put the record on, reaching out to touch the play button, her finger crooked and trembling like a feeble version of Michelangelo's *Creation*. Then she walked back to the sofa, delicately holding the mitten as though it still contained a hand.

In the back bedrooms Mother and Kaye slept. For years now the three friends had stayed together on Christmas Eve and celebrated the day in their own quiet way. Em suspected this was her last Christmas. She suspected this was Kaye's last too, and perhaps Mother's. Two thirty.

The music began and Émilie Longpré closed her eyes.

In the back bedroom Mother could hear the opening notes of Tchaikovsky's violin concerto in D Major. Christmas Eve was the only time Mother ever heard it, though it had once been her favorite piece. It had once been special to them all. Em most of all, but that was natural. Now she only played it once a year, in the small hours between Christmas Eve and Christmas Day. It broke Mother's heart to hear it and to think of her friend alone in the living room. But she respected and loved Em too much to deny her this time alone with her grief and her son.

And this night Mother had her own grief to keep her company. She repeated over and over, be calm, be calm. But the mantra which had comforted her for so many years was suddenly empty, its power to heal stolen by that horrible, twisted grotesque of a woman. Damn that CC de Poitiers.

Kaye creaked over in her bed. Even the act of rolling onto her side was unbearable. Her body was giving up. Giving up the ghost, it was called. But it was really the opposite. She was actually becoming a ghost. She opened her eyes and allowed them to adjust to the darkness. Way far away she heard Tchaikovsky. It was as though it entered her body not through her failing ears, but through her chest and straight into her heart, where the notes lodged. It was almost too much to bear. Kaye took a deep, rattling breath, and nearly cried out for Émilie to stop. Stop that divine music. But she didn't. She loved her friend too much to deny her this time with David.

The music made her think of another child. Crie. Who called their child Crie? Cry? Names mattered, Kaye knew. Words mattered. That child had sung like an angel tonight and she'd made them all divine, more than human, for a brief time. But with a few well chosen words her mother had made ugly what minutes before had been exquisite. CC was like an alchemist, with the unlikely gift of turning gold into lead.

What had Crie's mother heard that could have provoked such a reaction? Surely she hadn't heard the same voice. Or maybe she had and that was the problem. And maybe she heard other voices as well.

She wouldn't be the first.

Kaye tried to shove that thought away, but it kept intruding. And another thought, another voice, appeared, lyrical and Irish and masculine and kind.

'You should have helped that child. Why didn't you do something?'

It was always the same question and always the same answer. She was afraid. Had been afraid all her life.

Here it is then, the dark thing,
the dark thing you have waited for so long.
And after all, it is nothing new.

The lines of Ruth Zardo's poem floated into her mind. Tonight the dark thing had a name and a face and a pink dress.

The dark thing wasn't CC, it was the accusation that was Crie.

Kaye shifted her gaze, her fists balled in the flannel sheet under her chin, trying to keep warm. She hadn't really been warm in years. Her eyes caught the red numbers on her digital clock. Three o'clock. And here she was in her trench. Cold and trembling. She'd had a chance this night to redeem herself for all those moments of cowardice in her life. All she had to do was defend the child.

Kaye knew the signal would soon be given. And soon she'd have to crawl out of her trench and face what was coming. But she wasn't ready yet. Not yet. Please.

Damn, damn that woman.

Em listened as the notes of the violin visited familiar places. They played around the tree and searched for gifts and laughed at the frosted window looking onto the brightly lit pine trees on the familiar green. The concerto filled the room and for a blessed moment, her eyes closed, Em could pretend it wasn't Yehudi playing, but someone else.

Each Christmas Eve was the same. But this was worse than most. She'd heard too much. Seen too much.

She knew then what she must do.

*

Christmas dawned bright and clear, the dusting of snow from the day before balanced finely on the branches of the trees outlining the world in sparkles. Clara opened the mudroom door to let her golden retriever Lucy out and took a deep breath of frigid air.

The day moved along at a leisurely pace. Peter and Clara opened their stockings full of puzzles and magazines and candy and oranges. Cashews spilled out of Peter's stocking and Gummy Bears didn't last long from Clara's. Over coffee and pancakes they opened their larger gifts. Peter loved his Armani watch, putting it on immediately and shoving the sleeve of his terrycloth robe up over his elbow so it would be visible.

He rummaged beneath the tree with great drama, pretending to have misplaced her gift, and finally emerged, face flushed from bending over.

He handed her an orb wrapped in reindeer paper.

'Before you open it I want to say something.' He flushed some more. 'I know how hurt you were by that whole Fortin thing and CC.' He held up his hand to stop her protests. 'I know about God too.' He felt unbelievably stupid saying that. 'What I mean is, you told me about meeting God on the street even though you knew I wouldn't believe it. I just want you to know that I appreciate that you told me and trusted I wouldn't laugh at you.'

'But you did.'

'Well, but not much. Anyway, I wanted to say I've been thinking about it and you're right, I don't believe God's a vagrant—'

'What do you believe God is?'

He was just trying to give her a gift and here she was asking him about God.

'You know what I believe, Clara. I believe in people.'

She was silent. She knew he didn't believe in God and that was all right. He certainly didn't have to. But she also knew he didn't really believe in people. At least, he didn't think they were good and kind and brilliant. Perhaps once he might have, but not after what happened to Jane.

Jane had been killed, but something inside Peter had died as well.

No, much as she adored her husband she had to admit the only thing he believed in was himself.

'You're wrong, you know,' he said, sitting down beside her on the sofa. 'I can see what you're thinking. I believe in you.'

Clara looked at his serious, lovely, Morrow face and kissed it.

'CC and Fortin are idiots. You know I don't understand your work, probably never will, but I do know you're a great artist. I know it here.'

He touched his own breast, and Clara believed him. Maybe she was getting through to him. Or maybe he was getting better at telling her what she wanted to hear. She'd take either.

'Open your gift.'

Clara ripped away at the paper, making Peter wince. As tiny pieces flew off the orb he picked them up and smoothed them out.

Inside was a ball. No surprise there. What was surprising was that it was beautiful. It seemed to shine in her hands. On it was painted a very simple image. Three pine trees, covered in snow. Below was the single word, *Noël*. While the image was simple it wasn't primitive or naive. It had a style like nothing Clara had ever seen. An easy elegance. A confident beauty.

Clara held it up to the light. How could a painted ball be so luminous? But then she looked closer. And smiled. She looked up at Peter, his anxious face leaning in to hers. 'There's no paint on the outside. It's all glass. The paint is on the inside. Imagine that.'

'Do you like it?' he asked softly.

'I love it. And I love you. Thank you, Peter.' She hugged him, still holding the sphere. 'It must be a Christmas decoration. Do you think it's a picture of Three Pines? I mean, of course it's three pine trees but they actually look like our pines on the village green. But I guess any three evergreens together are going to look alike. I adore it, Peter. It's the best gift ever. And I won't even ask where you found it.'

He was very grateful for that.

By mid-morning the chestnut stuffing was in the turkey and the turkey was in the oven, filling the house with more wonderful Christmas smells. Peter and Clara decided to wander over to the bistro, passing villagers as they went. Most took a moment to recognize since they'd almost all received brand new tuques in their Christmas stockings, the old ones being both familiar and well eaten by dogs and kittens. All winter long the family pet would worry the pompoms until most of the villagers ended up looking like candles, with wicks on the tops of their heads instead of the woolly balls.

At the bistro Clara found Myrna by the fire sipping mulled wine. They struggled out of their coats, which didn't seem to want to let them go, and put their tuques and mitts on the radiator to keep warm. Cherry-faced villagers and children kept arriving, in from cross-country skiing or snowshoeing, tobogganing down the hill above the mill or skating on the pond. Some were just heading off for half a day's downhill skiing at Mont St-Rémy.

'Who's that?' Myrna pointed to a man sitting by himself.

'Monsieur Molson Canadian. Always orders the same beer. Good tipper,' said Olivier, placing two Irish coffees on the table for Peter and Clara along with a couple of licorice pipes. 'Merry Christmas.' He kissed them both then nodded to the stranger. 'He showed up a couple of days ago.'

'Probably a renter,' said Myrna. It was unusual to find strangers in Three Pines, only because it was hard to find and people rarely stumbled on it by accident.

Saul Petrov sipped his beer and took a bite of his roast beef sandwich on a baguette with melting Stilton cheese and arugula. Beside it on his plate was a diminishing pile of shoestring fries, lightly seasoned.

It was perfect.

For the first time in years Saul felt human. He wasn't quite up to approaching these friendly people but he knew when he did they'd ask him to join them. They just seemed that sort. Already a few had smiled in his direction and lifted their drinks, mouthing '*Santé*' and '*Joyeux Noël*'.

They seemed kind.

No wonder CC loathed them.

Saul dipped a fry into his small saucer of mayonnaise and wondered which of the people here was the artist. The one who'd done that amazing melting tree. He didn't even know if it was a man or a woman.

He wondered if he should ask someone. Three Pines was so small he was sure someone would be able to tell him. He'd like to congratulate the artist, buy him or her a beer, talk about their shared art and craft. Talk about things creative instead of the dark places he went with CC. First, though, he had business in Three Pines. But once that was done he'd find the artist.

'Excuse me.' He looked up and a huge black woman was smiling down at him. 'I'm Myrna. I own the bookstore next door. I just wanted to tell you there's a community breakfast and curling match tomorrow in Williamsburg. We all go. It's a fundraiser for the local hospital. You may not know about it, but you're welcome to attend.'

'Really?' He hoped he didn't sound as thick as he felt. Why was he suddenly afraid? Not of this woman, surely. Was he afraid, perhaps, of her kindness? Afraid she'd mistaken him for someone else? Someone interesting and talented and kind.

'The breakfast's at the legion at eight and the curling starts at ten on Lac Brume. Hope you can make it.'

'*Merci.*'

'*De rien. Joyeux Noël,*' she said in accented but beautiful French. He paid for his lunch, leaving an even larger tip than usual, and left, getting in his car for the short drive up the hill to the old Hadley house.

He'd tell CC about the event. It was perfect. Just what he was looking for.

And when the event was over he'd have finished what he'd come to do, and then, perhaps, he could sit at the same table as these people.

EIGHT

⌒

'Did you find something?'

Chief Inspector Armand Gamache poured his wife a glass of Perrier and kissed the top of her head as he leaned over to peer at the document in her hand. It was Boxing Day and they were in his office at Sûreté headquarters in Montreal. He was in gray flannels, a shirt and a tie, which he always wore to the office, and an elegant cashmere cardigan, an acknowledgment that he was on holiday, after all. Though he was only in his early fifties there was an old world charm about Gamache, a courtesy and manner that spoke of a time past. He smiled down at his wife, his deep brown eyes taking in the soft wave of her graying hair. From where he stood he could just faintly pick up the subtle fragrance of Joy by Jean Patou, the eau de toilette he gave his wife each Christmas. Then he moved round in front of her and eased himself into the leather chair opposite, finding the familiar curves worn into the seat. His body spoke of meals enjoyed and a life of long walks rather than contact sports.

His wife, Reine-Marie, was sitting in another leather chair, a huge red and white check napkin on her lap, a dossier in one hand and a turkey sandwich in the other. She took a bite then dropped her reading glasses from her face, to dangle on their strings.

'Thought I'd found something, but no. I thought there was a question the investigating officer hadn't asked, but I see here he did a little later.'

'Who was it?'

'The Labarré case. Man pushed in front of the metro car.'

'I remember.' Gamache poured himself some water. Around them on the floor were neat stacks of file folders. 'I didn't realize it wasn't solved. You didn't find anything?'

'Sorry, my love. I'm not doing so well this year.'

'Sometimes there's just nothing to find.'

The two of them picked up fresh folders and resumed reading in companionable silence. It had become their Boxing Day tradition. They'd take a picnic lunch of turkey sandwiches, fruit and cheese to Gamache's office in the homicide division and spend the day reading about murder.

She looked across at her husband, head buried in a file, trying to tease from it the truth, trying to find in the dry words, in the facts and figures, a human form. For in each of these manila folders there lived a murderer.

These were the unsolved murders. A few years earlier Chief Inspector Gamache had approached his opposite number in the Montreal Metropolitan Police and over cognac at the Club Saint-Denis had made his proposal.

'An exchange, Armand?' Marc Brault had asked. 'How would that work?'

'I suggest Boxing Day. It's quiet at Sûreté headquarters and probably in your office as well.'

Brault had nodded, watching Gamache with interest. He, like most of his colleagues, had immense respect for the quiet man. Only fools underestimated him, but Brault knew the service was full of fools. Fools with power, fools with guns.

The Arnot case had proved that beyond doubt. And had almost destroyed the large, thoughtful man in front of him. Brault wondered whether Gamache knew the whole story. Probably not.

Armand Gamache was speaking, his voice deep and pleasant. Brault noted the graying of the dark hair at the temples and the obvious balding head, without attempt to comb it over. His dark moustache was thick, well trimmed and also graying. His face was lined with care, but also laughter, and his deep brown eyes, looking at Brault over his half-moon glasses, were thoughtful.

How does he survive? Brault wondered. Brutal as the world inside the Montreal police could be, he knew the Sûreté du Québec could be even worse. Because the stakes were higher. And yet Gamache had risen to run the largest and most distinguished department in the Sûreté.

He'd go no further, of course. Even Gamache knew that. But unlike Marc Brault, who was ambition itself, Armand Gamache seemed content, even happy with his life. There had been a time, before the Arnot case, when Brault had suspected Gamache was a bit simple, a bit beyond his depth. But he didn't think that any more. He knew now what was behind the kind eyes and calm face.

He had the strangest feeling just then that Gamache understood everything that was going on, in Brault's head and in the labyrinthine minds at the Sûreté.

'I suggest we give each other our unsolved cases and

spend a few days reading over them. See if we can find something.'

Brault took a sip of his cognac and leaned back in his chair, thinking. It was a good idea. It was also unconventional and would probably cause a stink if anyone found out. He smiled at Gamache and leaned forward again.

'Why? Don't you have enough work through the year? Or maybe you're desperate to get away from your family at Christmas.'

'Well, you know if I could I'd move into my office and live off vending machine coffee. I have no life and my family despises me.'

'I've heard that about you, Armand. In fact, I despise you.'

'And I you.'

The two men smiled. 'I would want someone to do this for me, Marc. It's pretty simple and pretty selfish. If I was murdered I'd like to think the case wouldn't just sit unsolved. Someone would make an extra effort. How could I deny someone else that?'

It was simple. And it was right.

Marc Brault reached out and shook Gamache's large hand. 'Done, Armand, done.'

'Done, Marc. And if anything happened to you, it wouldn't remain unsolved.' It was said with great simplicity and it surprised Brault how much it meant.

And so for the past few years the two men had met in the parking lot at Sûreté headquarters to exchange boxes, ironically, on Boxing Day. And each Boxing Day Armand and Reine-Marie opened the boxes and looked for murderers inside.

'Now this is odd.' Reine-Marie lowered her dossier and

caught him staring at her. She smiled and continued. 'Here's a case from just a few days ago. I wonder how it made it into the pile.'

'Christmas rush. Someone must have made a mistake. Here, give it to me and I'll put it in the out tray.' He held out his hand, but her eyes had dropped once again to the file and she was reading. After a moment he lowered his hand.

'I'm sorry, Armand. It's just that I knew this woman.'

'No.' Gamache set his own dossier aside and came beside Reine-Marie. 'How? What's the case?'

'She wasn't a friend or anything. You probably knew her too. That bag lady down by the Berri bus station. You know, the one with all the layers in all weather. She'd been there for years.'

Gamache nodded. 'Still, it can't be considered an unsolved case yet. You say she's only been dead a few days?'

'She was killed on the twenty-second. And this is strange. She wasn't at the Berri bus station. She was over on de la Montagne, by Ogilvy's. That's a good, what? Ten, fifteen blocks away.'

Gamache resumed his seat and waited, watching Reine-Marie as she read, a few strands of her graying hair falling across her forehead. She was in her early fifties and lovelier than when they'd married. She wore little make-up, comfortable with the face she'd been given.

Gamache could sit all day watching her. He sometimes picked her up at her job at the Bibliothèque nationale, intentionally arriving early so he could watch her going over historic documents, taking notes, head down and eyes serious.

And then she'd look up and see him watching her and her face would break into a smile.

'She was strangled.' Reine-Marie lowered the file. 'Says here her name was Elle. No last name. I can't believe it. It's an insult. They can't even be bothered to find her real name so they call her She.'

'These things are difficult,' he said.

'Which is probably why kindergarten children aren't homicide detectives.'

He had to laugh as she said it.

'They didn't even try, Armand. Look at this.' She held the dossier up. 'It's the thinnest file there. She was just a vagrant to them.'

'Would you like me to try?'

'Could you? Even if it's just to find her name.'

He found the box for Elle's case, stacked with the others from Brault against one wall of his office. Gamache put on gloves and removed the contents, spreading them on the floor of his office. Before long it was full of rancid, putrid clothing, and a smell that put their blue cheese to shame.

Old newspapers, curling and filthy, sat next to the clothing. Used for insulation, Gamache suspected, against the brutal Montreal winter. Words could do many things, he knew, but they couldn't halt the weather. Reine-Marie joined him and together they sifted through the box.

'She seems to have literally surrounded herself with words,' said Reine-Marie, picking up a book. 'Those papers for insulation and even a book.'

Opening it she started to read at random.

'Long dead, and buried in another town,
my mother hasn't finished with me yet.'

'May I see that?' Gamache took the book and looked at the cover. 'I know this poet. I've met her. It's Ruth Zardo.' He looked at the cover. *I'm FINE*.

'The one from that small village you liked so much? She's one of your favorite poets, isn't she?'

Gamache nodded and flipped to the beginning of the book. 'It's one I don't have. Must be new. I don't think Elle even read it.' He looked up the publication date and noticed the inscription: 'You stink, love Ruth.'

Gamache went to the phone and made a call.

'Is this the Ogilvy bookstore? I'm calling to find out about – yes, I'll hold.' He cocked his head at Reine-Marie and smiled. She was putting on evidence gloves and reaching for a small wooden box that had also come out of the evidence box. It was simple and worn. Reine-Marie turned it over and found four letters stuck to the bottom.

'What do you make of that?' she asked, showing it to Armand.

B KLM

'Does it open?'

She gently pried the top off and looked inside, and her face grew even more puzzled.

It was full of letters of the alphabet.

'Why don't you – yes, hello?' He raised his eyebrows in apology. 'I'm calling about Ruth Zardo's latest book. That's right. Many people? I understand. Well, *merci*.' He hung up. Reine-Marie had turned the contents of the box onto his desk and was organizing the letters into neat piles.

Five of them. Bs, Cs, Ms, Ls and Ks.

'The same as the bottom, except the Cs,' she said. 'Why these letters and why capitals?'

'Do you think it's significant they're all capital letters?' Gamache asked.

'I don't know, but I know from the documents I handle at work when a series of capital letters is used it's because each letter represents a word.'

'Like RCMP or DOA.'

'Always a cop, but that's the idea. For instance, *I'm FINE*,' she pointed to Ruth's book now on Gamache's desk. 'I bet that stands for something else. What did the bookstore say?'

'Ruth Zardo launched this book a few days ago, at the Ogilvy store. December twenty-second.'

'The day Elle died,' said Reine-Marie.

Gamache nodded. Why would Ruth give a copy to a vagrant and sign it 'love Ruth'? He knew the old woman well enough to know she didn't toss around the word 'love'. He reached for the phone again, but it rang just as he touched it.

'*Oui, allô?* Gamache here.'

There was silence for a moment on the other end.

'*Oui, bonjour?*' He tried again.

'Chief Inspector Gamache?' A voice came down the line. 'I didn't think you'd answer your own phone.'

'I'm a man of many parts.' He laughed disarmingly. 'How may I help you?'

'My name is Robert Lemieux. I'm the duty officer at the Cowansville police station in the Eastern Townships.'

'I remember. We met during the Jane Neal investigation.'

'Yes sir.'

'What can I do for you, son?'

'There's been a murder.'

After getting the information Gamache hung up and looked at his wife. She sat in the chair composed and calm.

'Do you have your long underwear?' she asked.

'I do, madame.' He slid open his top desk drawer to reveal a lump of deep blue silk.

'Don't most officers keep guns there?' she asked.

'I find long underwear protection enough.'

'I'm glad.' She gave him a hug. 'I'll leave you, my dear. You have work to do.'

At the door she watched as he made his calls, his back to her, staring out the window at the Montreal skyline. She watched him move in ways she knew, and she noticed how his hair curled slightly at his neck and she watched his strong hand as it held the phone at his ear.

Within twenty minutes Armand Gamache was on his way to the scene, his second in command Inspector Jean Guy Beauvoir at the wheel as they drove over the Champlain bridge and onto the autoroute for the hour and a half trip into the heart of the Eastern Townships.

Gamache stared out the window for a few minutes then opened the book once again, finishing the poem Reine-Marie had begun reading to him.

When my death us do part
Then shall forgiven and forgiving meet again,
Or will it be, as always was, too late?

NINE

~

'Her name was Cecilia de Poitiers,' said Agent Robert Lemieux in answer to Gamache's first question. 'But everyone called her CC. This is where it happened, sir.' Lemieux was trying not to sound too eager. But best not to sound blasé either. He stood up straighter and tried to look like he knew what he was doing.

'Here?' Gamache was bending over the snow.

'Yes sir.'

'How do you know?' Jean Guy Beauvoir asked. 'It all looks the same to me.'

And it did. Snowy footprints everywhere. The Santa Claus parade might as well have marched through his murder scene. Beauvoir shoved his black ski hat further down his head and tugged the ear flaps into place. It was the closest thing he could find to an attractive hat that was also almost warm. Jean Guy Beauvoir was constantly at war with himself, at odds over his need to wear clothes that showed off his slender, athletic build, and his need not to freeze his tight ass off. It was nearly impossible to be both attractive and warm in a

Quebec winter. And Jean Guy Beauvoir sure didn't want to look like a dork in a parka and stupid hat. He looked at Gamache, so composed, and wondered whether he was as cold as Beauvoir, but just didn't show it. The chief was wearing a gray tuque, a yellow cashmere scarf and a long Arctic-weight parka in soft British khaki. He looked warm. And Beauvoir was struck by how attractive warm looked at minus ten, parka, funny hat, bulbous gloves and all. He began to suspect maybe he was the one who looked funny. But he pushed that unlikely thought away as a gust of wind tore through his attractive bomber jacket and lodged deep in his bones. He shivered and stomped his feet. They were standing on a frozen lake, bleak and cold. The shore was a hundred yards behind them and the far shore just a dark strip in the distance. Beauvoir knew that round the rugged point of land off to their left was the town of Williamsburg, but standing there now he had the impression they were very far from civilization. They were certainly standing at a spot where something very uncivilized had take place.

Someone had been murdered right there.

It was a shame no one had realized it at the time.

'Tell me what you know,' said Gamache to Lemieux.

This was one of Beauvoir's favorite moments. The beginning of another mystery. But Gamache knew this mystery, like all murders, had begun long ago. This was neither the beginning nor the end.

Gamache walked a few paces further onto the frozen lake, his boots breaking through the thin crust of snow to the softer layer beneath. Gamache felt the telltale trickle down his ankles and knew snow had found its way into his boots.

'According to witnesses the victim simply collapsed,' said

Lemieux, watching the chief, trying to read whether he was satisfied with his answers. He looked uncomfortable and Lemieux privately cringed. Had he done something wrong already? 'They tried to revive her, thinking it was a heart attack, then they got her into a truck and took her to the hospital.'

'So they trampled all over the murder scene,' said Beauvoir, as though it had been Lemieux's fault.

'Yes sir. They were doing their best, I think.'

Lemieux waited for another rebuke, but none came. Instead Beauvoir huffed and Gamache said, 'Go on.'

'The emergency room physician, Dr Lambert, called the police about half an hour later. At around eleven thirty this morning. He said he had a suspicious death. Said he'd called in the coroner and it looked as though the victim had been electrocuted. As I said, officially he called it a suspicious death, he has to until it's ruled a homicide, but when we arrived he made it clear he had no doubts. She was murdered.'

'Please use her name, agent,' said Gamache, without reproach. 'We need to see Madame de Poitiers as a person.'

'Yes sir. She, Madame de Poitiers, was electrocuted right here.'

It was what Lemieux had said on the phone, and hearing it in his office had sounded strange enough to Gamache, but standing at the scene it was even more bizarre.

How does someone get electrocuted in the middle of a frozen lake? You used to be able to electrocute someone in a bathtub but that was before most appliances had automatic shut-offs. Toss a toaster into your spouse's bath these days and all you'll get is a blown fuse, a ruined appliance and a very pissed-off sweetheart.

No. It was almost impossible to electrocute someone these days, unless you were the governor of Texas. To do it on a frozen lake, in front of dozens of witnesses, was lunacy.

Someone had been insane enough to try.

Someone had been brilliant enough to succeed.

How? Gamache turned slowly, but nothing new presented itself. Certainly there were no vintage televisions or toasters smoldering on the ice. But there were three aluminum lawn chairs sitting on the snow, one toppled over. Towering behind the chairs was what looked like a huge chrome mushroom, fifteen feet high. About twenty feet off to the left was a set of bleachers.

Everything was facing onto the lake toward a clearing on the ice twenty feet or so in front of the bleachers. Gamache walked toward it, trying to avoid more deep snow, and saw it was a rectangle, long and narrow, with large round stones scattered about.

Curling.

Gamache had never played the sport, but he'd watched the Briar on television and knew enough to recognize a curling stone when he saw one. The rink had an eerie feel to it now, as all abandoned sites did. Gamache could almost hear the rocks roll down the ice, the voices of the team members, calling to each other. Just hours ago this place had been full of happy people. Except one. One had been so unhappy, so wretched and diseased, he'd had to take a life. Gamache tried to imagine what that person had done. Where had he sat? With the others in the bleachers, or had he distanced himself from the rest, knowing he was about to commit an act that would mark him for ever as different? Was he excited or scared to death? Had he planned the murder to the last detail or suddenly been overtaken with a rage so profound he'd had to act? Gamache stood very still and listened carefully now to see whether he could hear the voice of the murderer, whether it distinguished itself from the ghostly laughter of the children and the collegial calls of the team-mates.

But he couldn't. Yet.

And maybe there were no voices, just the wind as it skittered across the surface of the lake whisking up snow and creating small, frozen waves.

Technicians were putting out the yellow crime scene tape, photographing every inch of the terrain, picking up anything that looked like evidence. Measuring and bagging and finger-printing, not an easy task at minus ten Celsius. They were racing time, Gamache knew. It was almost two thirty, three hours since the murder, and the elements were closing in. Any murder scene outside was difficult but a lake in the middle of winter was particularly hard.

'How can someone be electrocuted here?' Beauvoir asked petulantly. 'What do the witnesses say?'

'The curling started at about ten,' said Lemieux, consulting his notebook. 'Maybe ten thirty by the time everyone was here. Almost everyone was in the stands over there but the victim and another woman were sitting in those chairs.'

'The victim in the one that was overturned?' Beauvoir asked.

'I don't know.' It killed Lemieux to admit it. Strangely enough it was the first time Gamache looked at him with more than polite interest. 'The first anyone knew there was a problem was when the other woman sitting there called out. At first no one heard because of all the noise at the rink.'

'There was a curling riot?' asked Beauvoir, incredulous. The only riot he could imagine was a stampede to leave.

'I guess someone made a good shot,' said Lemieux.

'Best not to guess,' said Gamache quietly.

'Yes sir.' Lemieux lowered his head and tried not to look too upset by the simple criticism. He didn't want to appear like an eager schoolboy. This was a delicate time. It was important to give just the right impression.

'Once people realized what had happened they tried to revive Madame de Poitiers. There were members of the volunteer fire department here.'

'Including Ruth Zardo?' asked Gamache.

'How'd you know?'

'I met her at the last investigation. She still the head of the volunteer fire department in Three Pines?'

'Yes sir. She was here along with a few others. Olivier Brulé, Gabri Dubeau, Peter and Clara Morrow – '

Gamache smiled at the names.

' – they did CPR then got the victim onto a nearby truck and took her to Cowansville where she was declared dead.'

'How'd the doctor know she'd been electrocuted?' asked Beauvoir.

'Burning. Her hands and feet were scorched.'

'And no one noticed this while they were giving her CPR?' Beauvoir asked.

Lemieux knew enough now to be silent. After a moment he continued.

'Madame de Poitiers had a husband and a daughter. They were here and went with her to the hospital. I have their names and address.'

'How many people saw this happen?' asked Gamache.

'About thirty, maybe more. It was the annual funspiel. There was a community breakfast at the legion beforehand.'

All around them now the Crime Scene Investigators were working, every now and then stopping to approach Gamache with a question or an observation. Beauvoir went off to oversee the gathering of evidence and Gamache paused on the ice to watch his team at work, then slowly began to circle the scene, his pace measured, his gloved hands behind his back. Agent Lemieux watched as the Chief Inspector seemed to walk into his own world.

'Come with me, please.' The Chief Inspector had stopped and turned so suddenly that Lemieux was caught staring into Gamache's lively brown eyes. Galumphing through the snow Lemieux caught up with the chief and walked beside him, wondering what was expected of him. After a minute or two he realized maybe all he had to do was keep the man company. So Lemieux, too, put his hands behind his back and walked slowly round and round the periphery of the crime scene until their boots had worn a snowy path and in the center of their circle, like a bull's-eye, a smaller circle marked the spot where CC de Poitiers had died.

'What's that?' Gamache finally spoke, pointing to the huge mushroom that towered over the scene like a very small and frozen A-bomb.

'It's a heating element, sir. Like a lamp post, except it throws heat.'

'I've seen them on the *terrasses* in Quebec City,' said Gamache, remembering the glasses of white wine on the old stone *terrasses* in Vieux Québec, and the heating elements that allowed people to enjoy outdoor dining into the early autumn. 'But they were much smaller.'

'Most are. These are industrial. Used for outdoor construction sites in the winter and some sporting events. I imagine that one was borrowed from the Bantam hockey league in Williamsburg. They play most of their games outside and a few years ago they had a big fundraiser to build bleachers and get something to keep spectators warm.'

'Are you from round here?'

'Yes sir. I was raised in St-Rémy. My family's moved but I wanted to come back here after police college.'

'Why?'

Why? The question surprised Lemieux. No one had asked him that. Was this a test, a trick on the part of Gamache? He looked at the large man in front of him and decided probably not. He didn't seem the sort who needed tricks. Still, it was best to give a diplomatic answer.

'I wanted to work with the Sûreté and I figured I'd have an advantage working here since I know so many people.'

Gamache watched him for a moment. An uncomfortable moment, then he turned back to look at the heat standard. Lemieux relaxed a little.

'That must be electric. The electricity that killed Madame de Poitiers probably came from that. And yet she was so far from it when she collapsed. Could the heater have had a bad connection, and somehow Madame de Poitiers came in contact with it and managed to stagger a few paces before collapsing, I wonder? What do you think?'

'Am I allowed to guess?'

Gamache laughed. 'Yes, but don't tell Inspector Beauvoir.'

'People use generators all the time round here to make electricity. Everyone has one. I think it's possible someone attached her to one.'

'You mean used a jumper cable and clipped the two prongs onto her?' He tried not to sound incredulous, but it was difficult. 'Do you think she might have noticed?'

'Not if she was watching the curling.'

It seemed young Agent Lemieux and Chief Inspector Gamache had different experiences with curling. Gamache liked it enough to watch the national finals on television. It was almost a Canadian requirement. But riveting it never was. And he'd certainly know if Reine-Marie suddenly started up a generator and attached a couple of huge alligator clips to his ears.

'Any other ideas?'

Lemieux shook his head and tried to give the impression of massive thought.

Jean Guy Beauvoir had broken away from the CSI and joined Gamache, now standing near the heat lamp.

'How was this powered, Jean Guy?'

'Not a clue. We've dusted and photographed it so you can touch it if you like.'

The two men circled the lamp, alternately bowing and looking heavenward, like two monks on a very short pilgrimage.

'Here's the on switch.' Gamache flipped it and, not surprisingly, nothing happened.

'One more mystery.' Beauvoir smiled.

'Will it never end?'

Gamache looked toward Agent Lemieux sitting on the bleachers, blowing on his frozen hands, and writing in his notebook. The chief had asked him to put his notes in order.

'What do you think of him?'

'Lemieux?' Beauvoir asked, his heart sinking. 'He's all right.'

'But . . .'

How'd he know there was a but? Not for the first time Beauvoir hoped Gamache couldn't actually read his mind. There was a lot of junk up there. As his grandfather used to say, 'You don't want to go into your head alone, *mon petit*. It's a very scary place.'

The lesson had stuck. Beauvoir spent very little time looking around his own head, and even less looking into others'. He preferred facts, evidence, things he could see and touch and hold. He left the mind to braver men, like Gamache. But now he wondered whether the chief hadn't discovered a way into his own mind. He'd find a lot of embarrassing stuff up there. More than a little pornography. A fantasy or two about Agent Isabelle Lacoste. Even a fantasy about Agent Yvette Nichol, the disastrous trainee from a year or so ago. That fantasy involved dismemberment. But if Gamache was ferreting around in Beauvoir's mind, he'd only find respect for himself. And if he dug deep enough Gamache might eventually find the room Beauvoir tried to keep hidden even from himself. In that room waited Beauvoir's fears, fetid and hungry. And slouching there, hidden below the fear of rejection and intimacy, sat the fear that someday Beauvoir would lose Gamache. And beside that fear, in that hidden room, sat something else. It was where Beauvoir's love hid, curled into a tiny protective ball and rolled into the furthest corner of his mind.

'I think he's trying too hard. There's something wrong. I don't trust him.'

'Is that because he defended the villagers who were trying to help Madame de Poitiers?'

'Of course not,' Beauvoir lied. He hated to be contradicted, especially by a kid. 'He just seemed beyond his depth, and he shouldn't be. Not for a Sûreté officer.'

'But he's not trained in homicide. He's like a GP who suddenly has to operate on someone. Theoretically he should be able to do it, and he's probably better trained than a bus conductor, but it's not what he does. I'm not sure how well I'd do if I was suddenly transferred to narcotics or internal affairs. I suspect I'd make a few mistakes. No, I think Agent Lemieux hasn't done badly.'

Here we go, thought Beauvoir. 'Not doing badly isn't good enough,' he said. 'That's a pretty low bar you're setting, sir. This is homicide. The elite division in the Sûreté.' He could see Gamache bristle as he always did when that was said. For some reason unfathomable to Beauvoir, Gamache resisted this statement of the obvious. Even the top bosses admitted as much. The best of the best made it into homicide. The smartest, the bravest, the people who got up each morning from the comfort of their homes, kissed their children and went into the world to deliberately hunt people who deliberately killed. There was no place for the weak. And trainees, by their very nature, were weak. And weakness led to mistakes and mistakes led to something going horribly wrong. The murderer could escape to kill again, maybe even a Sûreté agent. Maybe even you, maybe – the door crept open slightly and a ghoul escaped the well hidden room – maybe Armand Gamache. One day his need to help young agents will kill him. Beauvoir slammed the door shut, but not before feeling a bristling of rage against the man standing before him.

'We've been through this before, sir,' his voice now hard and angry. 'This is a team. Your team, and we'll always do as you ask. But please, please stop asking this of us.'

'I can't, Jean Guy. I found you at the Trois-Rivières detachment, remember?'

Beauvoir rolled his eyes.

'You were sitting among the reeds in a basket.'

'Weed, sir. How many times must I tell you, it was weed. Dope. I was sitting with stacks of dope we'd confiscated. And it wasn't a basket, it was a bucket. From Kentucky Fried Chicken. And I wasn't in it.'

'Now I feel badly. I told Superintendent Brébeuf I found you in a basket. Oh dear. You do remember, though? There you were buried alive under stacks of evidence, and why? Because you'd so annoyed everyone they'd assigned you permanently to the evidence room.'

Beauvoir remembered that day every day. He'd never forget being saved. By this large man in front of him, with the trim graying hair, the impeccable clothes and the eyes of deepest brown.

'You were bored and angry. I took you on when no one else wanted you.' Gamache was speaking so softly no one else could hear. And he was speaking with open affection. Beauvoir suddenly remembered the lesson he always hurried to forget. Gamache was the best of them, the smartest and bravest and strongest because he was willing to go into his own head alone, and open all the doors there, and enter all the dark rooms. And make friends with what he found there. And he went into the dark, hidden rooms in the minds of others. The minds of killers. And he faced down whatever monsters came at him. He went to places Beauvoir had never even dreamed existed.

That was why Armand Gamache was their chief. His chief. And that was why he loved him. And that was why Jean Guy

Beauvoir struggled every day trying to protect this man who made it clear he neither wanted nor needed protection. Indeed, every day he tried to convince Beauvoir the protection was a travesty, a ruse. All it did was block his view of whatever horrible thing was heading his way. Best to see it, and meet it. And not try to hide behind armor that won't protect anyway. Not against what they hunted.

'But I'll tell you what, Jean Guy,' now Gamache smiled brilliantly and completely, 'if you don't want Agent Lemieux I'll take him. I won't impose him on you.'

'Fine, take him, but don't come crying to me when you find out he's the murderer.'

Gamache laughed. 'I have to admit, I've made a lot of bad choices, especially recently,' he meant, but would never say, Agent Yvette Nichol, 'but that would be the winner. Still, better to risk than live in fear.'

Gamache patted him on the arm with such easy affection it almost took Beauvoir's breath away. And then he was gone, walking purposefully across the ice, nodding to the other investigators, as he made his way to Agent Robert Lemieux, to make the young man's day. His week. His career.

Beauvoir watched as Gamache quietly spoke with Lemieux. He saw the young man's face open in a look of such astonishment Beauvoir felt maybe the angels had appeared. It was a look Beauvoir had often seen from people speaking to Gamache. And had never, ever seen from anyone looking at him.

Beauvoir shook his head in wonderment and returned to the task at hand.

TEN

‘Look who’s here,’ Peter called from the kitchen into the living room. Clara closed her book and joined her husband at the sink. Holding the curtains back she could see a familiar, well-liked figure coming up their path and beside him came someone else. A stranger.

Clara hurried into the mudroom to open the door, stepping over Lucy, who showed no interest in protecting the home. The only person she barked at was Ruth and that was only because Ruth barked back.

‘Cold enough for you?’ Clara called.

‘Snow’s coming, I hear,’ said Gamache.

Clara smiled as he spoke. She hadn’t seen him for more than a year, since Jane’s murder. She’d sometimes wondered whether, upon seeing Gamache again, some of the old hurt would also come back. Would she for ever associate him with that horrible time? Not just the loss of Jane, but those terrifying minutes trapped in the basement of the old Hadley house? But now, seeing him arrive, all she felt was gladness. And comfort. And she’d forgotten the delight of hearing perfect English, with a slight British accent, coming from a senior Sûreté officer. She'd meant to ask him where he'd learned it, but kept forgetting.

Gamache gave Clara a kiss on both cheeks and shook Peter's hand with affection. 'May I present Agent Robert Lemieux. He's been seconded to us from the Cowansville Sûreté.'

'*Enchanté*,' said Lemieux.

'*Un plaisir*,' replied Clara.

'So it was murder,' said Peter, taking their coats. He'd gone to the hospital with CC and had known long before they'd arrived that she was dead. He'd been on the curling rink watching Mother's magnificent last shot when he'd looked over to the bleachers and seen the crowd that should have been watching the curlers rising from their seats and watching something else entirely. He'd dropped his broom and raced over.

And there she was, CC de Poitiers, unconscious on the snow. All her muscles taut as though straining against some force.

They'd tried to revive her, had called an ambulance, and had finally concluded it was fastest to take her to the hospital themselves. So they'd piled her into the open back of Billy Williams's pickup and bumped and jostled along at break-neck speed on the snow-covered back roads, making for Cowansville. He and Olivier and Ruth in the open truck while Billy Williams drove like a maniac. Beside Billy in the cab sat CC's lump of a husband and their daughter. Staring straight ahead. Silent and unmoving, like snowmen. Peter knew he was being uncharitable, but he couldn't help being annoyed at the man who did nothing to save his wife while perfect strangers did everything.

Olivier was leaning rhythmically on and off CC's chest, massaging her heart. Ruth was counting the beats. And Peter drew the short straw. He'd had to breathe into her dead lungs. And they were dead. They all knew it, but still they kept it up as Billy hit every pothole and ice patch between Williamsburg and Cowansville. Kneeling on the frozen metal floor Peter could feel himself lift with each bump and crash down on his knees, bruising them more and more each time. But still he persevered. Not for CC. But because beside him Olivier was suffering the same fate. And holding CC's head tenderly and firmly was Ruth, also kneeling, her bad hip and old knees slamming into the floor, her voice never wavering as she counted the beats. He'd continued CPR, pressing his warm lips to CC's increasingly cold and rigid ones, until finally it felt as it had when he was a child and had kissed his ski poles. Just to see. They were so cold it burned, and his lips had refused to come away. He'd finally peeled them off, leaving a thin layer of himself on the poles. His lips bleeding, he'd quickly looked around to make sure no one had seen.

Giving CPR to CC had felt like that. He'd had the impression that if he kept it up eventually his moist lips would solder to hers and he'd be stuck there until he finally ripped them away, leaving part of him for ever on her, a bloody kiss of life.

It was the most repulsive thing he'd ever had to do, all the more so since he'd found her pretty repulsive in life. Death hadn't improved her.

'It was murder. Madame de Poitiers was deliberately electrocuted,' said Gamache.

Clara turned to her husband. 'You knew the doctors suspected murder.'

'I heard Dr Lambert talking to a police officer. Wait a minute. Was that you?' Peter asked Lemieux.

'*Oui, monsieur.* I recognize you as well. In fact, I believe we've met at a few community events.'

'It's certainly possible. Electrocution,' said Peter thoughtfully. 'Well, there was a smell. Barbecue.'

'Do you know, now that you mention it, I remember that as well,' said Clara with disgust. 'There was such a commotion it's hard to remember back.'

'That's what I'm going to ask you to do,' said Gamache, motioning to Lemieux to take notes. Peter led them into the cozy living room and threw a birch log on the fire, the flames grabbing and crackling and leaping as the bark burst into flames. Gamache noticed again the honey pine wide-plank flooring, the mullioned windows looking out onto the village green, the piano and the bookcase, crammed with books and covering one wall. A sofa faced the open hearth and two easy chairs bracketed it. The hassocks in front of the seats were covered with old newspapers and magazines and books, splayed open. The only thing different about the familiar room for Gamache was the huge and exuberantly decorated Christmas tree, giving off a sweet aroma. Clara followed with a tray of tea and biscuits and all four sat round the warm hearth. Outside the sun was setting, and clouds were gathering on the dim horizon.

'Where would you like to start?'

'This morning, please. I understand there was a community breakfast?'

'In the Royal Canadian Legion, on rue Larry in Williamsburg. Peter and I got there early to help set up. It's a fundraiser for the hospital.'

'We got there at about seven this morning,' Peter picked up the story, 'and were joined by a few other volunteers. Myrna Landers, Émilie Longpré, Bea Mayer and Kaye Thompson. We have it down pat by now. Put out the tables and chairs, Clara and I do that, while the others get the coffee going and organize the food.'

'The truth is, by Boxing Day morning most people aren't actually all that hungry. They pay ten dollars and get an all-you-can-eat breakfast,' said Clara. 'Peter and I do the cooking while Em and Kaye serve up. Kaye's about two hundred years old and still manages to help but now she finds something she can do sitting down.'

'Like bossing everyone around,' said Peter.

'She never bosses you. That's my job,' said Clara. 'It's voluntary.'

'Very civic minded.' Peter smiled with a long-suffering look.

'What did the others do?' Gamache asked. Lemieux was surprised by the question. He'd run out of notebook soon if they kept going into such detail over something that was hours away from the murder. He tried to write smaller.

'Who's left?' Peter turned to Clara. 'Myrna Landers and Bea Mayer.'

'Bee?' Lemieux asked.

'Her name's Beatrice, but everyone calls her Bea.' Peter spelled Beatrice for Lemieux.

'Actually, everyone calls her Mother,' said Clara.

'Why?' asked Gamache.

'See if you can figure it out,' said Clara. Lemieux looked at the chief to see if he was annoyed by her flippant and familiar tone, but he was smiling.

'What did Myrna and Bea do at the breakfast?' Gamache asked.

'They cleaned up between sittings and served coffee and tea,' said Peter.

'Oh, yeah,' said Clara, 'Mother's tea. It's some herbal brew. Disgusting. I don't mind tea,' Clara raised her mug to them, 'even tisane, but I hate to think what goes into the one Mother offers each year. She's kind of amazing. No one ever takes it and yet she keeps on trying.'

There's a fine line between noble perseverance and insanity, reflected Gamache. 'Were Madame de Poitiers and her family there?'

'I don't really know,' said Clara after a moment's thought. 'We were cooking the whole time so we didn't get a chance to look out.'

'Did anything unusual happen at the breakfast?' Gamache asked.

Peter and Clara thought about it then shook their heads.

'Peter was curling on Em's team this year, for the first time, so he left early.'

'By the time I got outside Em and Mother were already at the lake. It's just down the road then off to the right. It's about a five-minute walk from the Legion.'

'And your team didn't wait for you?'

'Well, Georges did. He was the other man on our team. This was his first year curling as well.'

'Georges who?'

'Simenon,' said Peter and smiled at Gamache's raised brow. 'I know. His mother was cursed with the pleasure of reading.'

'And cursed her son,' said Gamache.

'Georges and I walked over to Lac Brume and found Em

and Mother there. Billy Williams had already cleared the ice surface so we could curl and he'd put up the bleachers a few days before Christmas.'

'The ice was frozen enough?'

'Oh, long ago. Besides, it's close to shore and I think Billy uses his auger to check the ice thickness. He's a very prudent man is our Billy.'

'What else did you notice at the lake?'

Peter cast his mind back. He remembered standing at the side of the road looking over the small incline down to the snow-covered lake. Mother and Bea were over by their chairs.

'Chairs,' said Peter. 'Mother, Em and Kaye always bring chairs to sit close to the heat lamp.'

'How many chairs were there this morning?' Gamache asked.

'Three. Two were close to the heat lamp, the other was a little way ahead.'

'So what happened?' Gamache leaned forward, cradling the warm mug in his large hands, his eyes lively and alert.

'Everyone seemed to arrive at once,' said Peter. 'Em and Mother had been sitting on their chairs when Georges and I joined them. We talked strategy for a while then the other team arrived and soon it seemed the bleachers were full.'

'I got there just as the curling started,' said Clara.

'Where did you sit?'

'In the stands, between Myrna and Olivier.'

'And where was CC?'

'In one of the chairs by the lamp.' Clara smiled very slightly.

'What is it?' Gamache asked.

Clara blushed a little at being caught in a private moment. 'I was remembering CC. It was like her to take the best seat.

In fact, the one she chose was closest to the lamp. It's the one Kaye should have had.'

'You didn't like her, did you?' he asked.

'No. I thought she was cruel and selfish,' said Clara. 'Still, she didn't deserve to be killed.'

'What did she deserve?' he asked.

The question staggered Clara. What did CC deserve? She gave it some thought, staring into the fire, watching the flames leap and pop and play. Lemieux shifted his position and almost said something, but Gamache caught his eye and he shut his mouth.

'She deserved to be left alone. That should have been her punishment for treating people with such disdain, for causing such hurt.' Clara was trying to keep her voice firm and calm, but she could feel it wavering and quivering and hoped she wasn't about to cry. 'CC couldn't be trusted in the company of others.'

Gamache was silent, wondering what CC could have done to have hurt this fine woman so much she'd visit such a horror on her. Because Gamache knew, as did Clara, that isolation was far worse than death.

He knew then that this case wouldn't be solved easily. Anyone so damaged as to cause this much harm led a life full of secrets and full of enemies. Gamache moved a little closer to the fire. Outside the sun had set and night had fallen on Three Pines.

ELEVEN

'She wasn't so bad,' said Ruth Zardo, slapping the cork back into a bottle of wine. She'd poured herself another while offering her guests none.

Gamache and Lemieux were sitting in the white resin pre-formed garden chairs Ruth called her dining set in her near freezing kitchen. Ruth wore a couple of moth-eaten sweaters, while the men had kept their parkas on.

Agent Lemieux rubbed his hands together in a ball-and-socket motion and tried to resist the urge to blow on them. He and Gamache had crossed the village green after interviewing the Morrows and made for the smallest house Agent Lemieux had ever seen. It looked little more than a shack, with two windows on the main floor and a single window up top. The white paint was chipping and one of the porch lights was out.

The door was opened by a ramrod. Straight and scraggly, everything about her was thin. Her body, her arms, her lips and her humor. As they made their way down the dim corridor lit with low voltage bulbs, he tripped a few times over stacks of books.

'I see the Sûreté is now hiring the handicapped,' said Ruth, waving her cane at him. 'Still, he's got to be better than the last one you brought round. What was her name? Doesn't matter. Complete disaster. Very rude. Sit if you must but don't get too comfortable.'

Lemieux rubbed his hands again, then took up his pen and began writing.

'I've heard CC de Poitiers described as cruel and selfish,' said Gamache, surprised he couldn't see his breath.

'So?'

'Well, that doesn't sound very good.'

'Oh, she wasn't very good, but she wasn't so bad either. I mean, really,' the old poet took a gulp of her wine, then put the glass back on the round plastic table, 'who isn't cruel and selfish?'

Gamache had forgotten the complete joy that was Ruth Zardo. He laughed out loud and caught her eye. She started laughing too.

Robert Lemieux didn't get it.

'What did you think of Madame de Poitiers?'

'I think she was bitter and petty and yes, very cruel. But I suspect there was a reason for it. We just didn't know her well enough, yet, to figure it out.'

'How long have you known her?'

'Just over a year. She bought Timmer Hadley's old place.' Ruth watched Gamache closely as she said this for a reaction, but she was to be disappointed. His reaction had come half an hour earlier at Clara and Peter's home. Clara had told him about CC buying the old Hadley place. They'd all sat silently then, and again Agent Lemieux was left to wonder what he was missing.

The last time Armand Gamache had been in the Hadley place it had almost killed him along with Peter, Clara and Beauvoir. If there was ever a house that wept it was that one.

Gamache would never forget that basement and the darkness. Even now in front of the cheery fire, with a warm mug in his hands and friends and colleagues around him, Gamache felt a tremor of fear.

He didn't want to go back into that dark place, but he knew now he'd have to.

CC de Poitiers had bought it. And that spoke more eloquently about the woman than any number of adjectives.

'She used it only on weekends,' Ruth continued when her bombshell proved a dud. 'Came down with her husband and daughter. Now, there were a couple of losers. At least CC had some spark to her. Some life. Those two looked like great lumpen masses of indulgence. Fat and lazy. And dull. Very dull.'

For Ruth Zardo, dull was one of the greatest insults. It ranked right up there with kind and nice.

'What happened at the curling?' Gamache asked.

Talking about CC's family seemed to have angered Ruth. She became even more curt and abrupt.

'She died.'

'We're going to need more than two words,' Gamache said.

'Em's team was losing, as usual. Then CC died.' Ruth sat back in her chair and glared at Gamache.

'Don't play games with me, Madame Zardo,' he said pleasantly, contemplating her with interest. 'Do we really have to do this again? Don't you ever tire of it?'

103

'Of anger? It's as good as this.' She raised her glass to him in a mock salute.

'But why are you angry?'

'Doesn't murder anger you?'

'But you're not angry at that,' he said thoughtfully, almost kindly. 'Or at least, not exclusively. There's something else.'

'Clever boy. I bet you heard a lot of that at school. What time is it?'

Gamache seemed unfazed by the abrupt change of topic. He looked at his watch.

'Quarter to five.'

'I have to go in a few minutes. Appointment.'

'What happened at the curling?' Gamache tried again. Lemieux held his breath. He didn't know why, but this seemed an important moment. The old poet stared at Gamache, her face and figure full of loathing. Gamache simply stared back, his face open and thoughtful and strong.

Ruth Zardo blinked. Literally. It seemed to Lemieux she'd closed her eyes in rage then opened them to a new world. Or at least a new attitude. She took a deep breath and nodded her gray hair. She smiled slightly.

'You bring out the worst in me, Chief Inspector.'

'You mean you're about to be decent?'

'I'm afraid so.'

'My apologies, madame.' Gamache rose momentarily from his plastic chair and bowed. She inclined her head toward him.

Lemieux wasn't at all sure what had just happened. He thought perhaps it was some weird Anglo code, a dance of aggression and submission. This rarely happened in francophone encounters, in his limited experience. The French, he felt, were far more open about their feelings. The English? Well, they were devious. Never really knew what they were thinking, never mind feeling.

'I was in the stands, next to Gabri. The curling had been going on for a while. Em was losing, as I said before. Poor Em always loses. It got so bad she once called her team Be Calm. At some point Gabri poked me in the side. Someone shouted that there'd been an accident.'

Ruth described the scene for them, replaying it in her head. Swaying back and forth, trying to get a clear view of what was causing the commotion. All the bulky parkas and tuques and scarves blocking her view, then the stands clearing as people began shuffling, then walking and finally running toward the crowd gathering near the overturned chair.

Ruth had made her way through, expecting to see Kaye collapsed there, shouting, 'Fire chief coming through, clear the way.'

Of course, there wasn't a fire, nor did Ruth expect to find one. Still, she'd learned that most people, while claiming to hate authority, actually yearned for someone to take charge. To tell them what to do.

CC was flat on her back. Dead. Ruth knew that immediately. But she still had to try.

'Olivier, you do the massage. Peter? Where's Peter Morrow?'

'Here, here.' He was making his way through the crowd, having had to sprint across the lake from the curling rink. 'What's happened?'

'You give her mouth-to-mouth.' To his credit Peter didn't

hesitate. He fell to his knees beside Olivier, ready to go, both men staring up at Ruth. But there was one more order she had to give.

'Gabri, find her husband. Clara?'

'Here.'

'Find the daughter.'

Then she turned her back on them, certain her orders would be followed, and started counting.

'Did you have any idea what had happened to her?' Gamache asked, bringing her back to this world.

'None.'

Was it his imagination or had her hard eyes wavered? He kept silent for a moment but nothing else came.

'What happened then?'

'Billy Williams said he had his truck ready to go and we should put her in. Someone had already called the hospital but it would take twenty minutes for the ambulance to arrive and twenty minutes to get back. This was faster.'

She described the horrific journey to Cowansville and it pretty much tallied with what he'd heard earlier from Peter Morrow.

'What time is it?' she demanded.

'Five to five.'

'Time to go.' She got up and led the way down the hall, without looking at them, as though her salvation lay beyond her front door. Agent Lemieux heard clinking and rattling in the closets as their heavy feet passed by. Skeletons, he thought. Or bottles. Or both.

He didn't like Ruth Zardo and he wondered why the chief seemed to.

'Out.' Ruth held open the door and they'd barely gotten

their boots on before she was shoving them out with an arm far stronger than he'd have thought.

Gamache reached into his parka pocket and produced not the tuque or mitts Lemieux expected to see, but a book. The chief walked over to the single porch light that split the darkness and placed the book under it for Ruth to see.

'I found this in Montreal.'

'You are brilliant. Let me guess. You found it in a bookstore?'

'Actually, no.' He decided not to tell her yet.

'And I suppose you've chosen this moment to ask me to sign it?'

'You've already done that. Could you come and look, please?'

Agent Lemieux braced for the acerbic response but none came. She limped over and Gamache opened the slim volume.

'You stink, love Ruth,' Ruth read out loud.

'Who did you give this to?'

'You expect me to remember what I say in every book I sign?'

'You stink, love Ruth,' Gamache repeated. 'It's an unusual inscription, even for you. Please think, Madame Zardo.'

'I've no idea, and I'm late.'

She stepped off her porch and walked across the village green toward the lights of the village shops. But she stopped halfway, and sat down.

In the dark. In the cold. On a frozen bench in the middle of the green.

Lemieux was both impressed and amazed by the woman's gall. She'd kicked them out claiming an appointment then brazenly sat on a bench to do absolutely nothing. It was clearly an insult. Lemieux turned to ask Gamache about it but the chief seemed lost in thought himself. Ruth Zardo was staring at the magnificent lighted trees and the one shining star, and Armand Gamache was staring at her.

TWELVE

⁓

Lemieux had decided to jog ahead to their car, parked outside the Morrow home, and turn it on. They weren't heading back yet, but night had fallen and the car would take a few minutes to warm up. If he started it now, by the time they got back in it would be toasty warm and the frosted windows would be clear, both advantages on a chilling December night.

'I don't get it, sir,' he said as he returned to Gamache.

'There's a lot not to get,' said Gamache with a smile. 'What in particular is troubling you?'

'This is my first murder case, as you know.'

'I do.'

'But it seems to me if you wanted to kill someone there are a whole lot of better ways.'

'Like?'

'Well, *franchement*, just about anything other than electrocuting a woman in the middle of a crowd on a frozen lake. It's nuts.'

And that's what worried Gamache. It was nuts.

'I mean, why not shoot her, or strangle her? It's Quebec in the middle of winter, why not take her for a drive and shove her out the car? We'd be using her as an ice sculpture in the Cowansville Fête des Neiges. It makes no sense.'

'And that's lesson number one.' They were walking toward Olivier's Bistro. Lemieux struggled to stay beside the large man as he strode with measured but long strides toward the brightly lit restaurant. 'It makes sense.'

Gamache suddenly stopped and Lemieux had to twist out of the way to avoid ramming into him. The chief looked at the young agent seriously.

'You need to know this. Everything makes sense. Everything. We just don't know how yet. You have to see through the murderer's eyes. That's the trick, Agent Lemieux, and that's why not everyone's cut out for homicide. You need to know that it seemed like a good idea, a reasonable action, to the person who did it. Believe me, not a single murderer ever thought, "Wow, this is stupid, but I'm going to do it anyway." No, Agent Lemieux, our job is to find the sense.'

'How?'

'We collect evidence, of course. That's a big part of it.'

'But there's more, isn't there?' Lemieux knew that Gamache had a near perfect record. Somehow, while others were left baffled, he managed to figure out who would kill. Now Lemieux stood very still himself. The big man was about to tell him how he did it.

'We listen.'

'That's it?'

'We listen really hard. Does that help?' Gamache grinned. 'We listen 'til it hurts. No, agent, the truth is, we just listen.'

Gamache opened the door to the bistro and stepped in.

'*Patron.*' Olivier came over and gave Gamache a kiss on both cheeks. 'Snow's coming, I hear.'

'Couple inches tomorrow.' Gamache nodded sagely. 'Maybe more.'

'That Météo Média or the Burlington forecast?'

'Radio Canada.'

'Oh, *patron*, they thought the Separatists would win the last referendum. You can't trust a Radio Canada prediction.'

'You might have a point, Olivier.' Gamache laughed, and introduced Lemieux. The bistro was packed, full of people enjoying a drink before dinner. He nodded to a few. 'Good crowd.'

'Always is over Christmas. Lots of families visiting, and what with the events of the day, well, everyone comes to Rick's.'

Rick's? Rick's what? Lemieux was already lost. This might be a record. So far in this case it had taken him a few minutes in each interview to become disoriented, and generally with the English. Now the chief was speaking French to another Québecois and Lemieux was already lost. This didn't bode well.

'People don't seem too upset,' said Gamache.

'*C'est vrai,*' Olivier agreed.

'The monster's dead and the villagers are celebrating,' said Gabri, appearing at Gamache's elbow.

'Gabri,' Olivier admonished. 'That's terrible. Haven't you heard you must only say good things of the dead?'

'Sorry, you're right. CC's dead.' Gabri turned to Gamache. 'Good.'

'Oh, dear Lord,' said Olivier. 'Stand back. He's channeling Bette Davis.'

'It's going to be a bumpy night,' Gabri agreed. '*Salut, mon amour.*' Gabri and Gamache exchanged a hug. 'Have you left your wife yet?' Gabri asked.

'Have you?'

Gabri moved to stand beside Olivier. 'There's an idea, now that it's legal. The Chief Inspector could be our best man.'

'I thought Ruth was going to be our best man.'

'True. Sorry, chief.'

'Perhaps I could be your matron of honour. Let me know. I hear you had a tough time of it today trying to save Madame de Poitiers.'

'No more than Peter, and I suspect considerably less than Ruth.' Olivier jerked his head toward the window and the invisible woman sitting alone in the cold. 'She'll be in soon for her Scotch.'

Her important appointment, thought Lemieux.

Gamache said to Gabri. 'I'd like to book into your B&B. Two rooms.'

'Not for that horrible trainee you had last time, I hope.'

'No, just Inspector Beauvoir and me.'

'*Merveilleux.* We'll book you in.'

'*Merci, patron.* We'll see you tomorrow.'

Walking to the door he whispered to Lemieux, 'Rick's is from the film *Casablanca*. Here's lesson number two. If you don't know something, ask. You have to be able to admit you don't know something, otherwise you'll just get more and more confused, or worse, you'll jump to a false conclusion. All the mistakes I've made have been because I've assumed something and then acted as though it was fact. Very dangerous, Agent Lemieux. Believe me. I wonder if you haven't already leaped to a false conclusion?'

This cut Lemieux deeply. He was desperate to impress Gamache. He needed to impress him if he was to get the job done. But now, for some reason, the chief felt he might be on the wrong track. As far as Lemieux knew he wasn't on any track, nor had he come to any conclusions about the case. Who could, so early?

'You need to tread very carefully, Agent Lemieux. I often think we should have tattooed to the back of whatever hand we use to shoot or write, "I might be wrong."'

Standing outside the bistro Chief Inspector Gamache's face was in darkness, but Lemieux assumed he was smiling. It must be a joke. The head of homicide for the Sûreté du Québec couldn't possibly be advocating such self-doubt.

Still, he knew his job was to learn from Gamache. And he knew if he watched the chief, and listened, not only would the mystery be revealed, but so would Gamache.

And Robert Lemieux was eager for that to happen.

He took out his notebook and in the biting cold he wrote down the two lessons. Then he waited in case there was more, but Armand Gamache seemed frozen in place, his tuque on, his mitts on, everything ready. Except the man.

He was staring at something in the distance. Something beyond the charming village, something beyond Ruth Zardo and her lit Christmas trees. He was staring at something in the darkness.

As he looked more closely, and let his eyes adjust to the night, Agent Robert Lemieux became aware of the outline of something even darker than the night. A house on the hill overlooking the village. As he stared the darkness seemed to take shape and an image of turrets appeared against the dark sky and darker pine forest. From one of the chimneys he saw just a hint of smoke before it was dragged away like a wraith into the woods.

Gamache took a breath, exhaling puffy white air, and turning to the young man beside him he smiled.

'Ready?'

'Yes sir.'

Lemieux didn't know why but he was suddenly a little afraid and suddenly very glad to be in the company of Armand Gamache.

At the top of the hill Agent Lemieux glided the car to a stop beside a snow bank, hoping he'd left enough room for the chief to squeeze out.

He had, and Gamache stood for the briefest moment surveying the large, dark house before beginning to walk decisively down the long path to the unlit front door. As the old Hadley house got closer Gamache tried to banish the impression it was watching him, its blinds half drawn like hooded serpent eyes.

It was fanciful, but that was a side to himself he'd come to accept and even encourage. It helped sometimes. But sometimes it hurt. Gamache wasn't sure which this was.

From inside the house Richard Lyon watched the two men approach. One was clearly in charge. Not only was he walking first down their path, but he seemed in command. It was a quality Lyon noticed in others, mostly as a counterpoint to his complete lack of it. The other figure was smaller and slimmer and walked with a bit of a bounce, like a younger man.

Deep breath. Suck it up. Be a man. Be a man. They were

almost at the door now. Should he go and open it before they arrived? Should he wait for them to ring? Would making them wait be rude? Would opening the door show anxiety?

Richard Lyon's mind was racing, but his body was frozen. It was his natural state. He had a very slim brain and a very generous body.

Be a man. Firm handshake. Look him in the eye. Lower your voice. Lyon hummed a little, trying to get his voice below the soprano register. Behind him in the gloomy living room his daughter Crie stared into space.

Now what? Normally at a time like this CC would have told him exactly what to do. Be a man. Suck it up. He wasn't totally surprised to hear her voice in his head still. It was almost comforting.

God, you're such a loser.

Almost comforting. It would be helpful if she'd say something constructive, like 'Go open the door, you idiot' or 'Sit down and make them wait. Jesus, do I have to do everything?'

The doorbell peeled and Richard Lyon jumped out of his skin.

What an idiot. You knew they were there. You should have gone to the door to let them in as they approached. Now they'll think you're rude. God, what a loser.

Armand Gamache stood at the door, Lemieux behind him, trying not to remember the last time he was there. Trying to see the old Hadley house as just a building. And buildings, he told himself, were just everyday materials. The same materials went into this house as his own in Outremont.

There was nothing special about this place. But still the house seemed to moan and shiver.

Armand Gamache braced himself, putting his shoulders back a little and lifting his head more. He was damned if he was going to let a house get the better of him. Still, part of him felt like a six-year-old who'd approached the haunted house on a dare and now wanted to run home as fast as his desperate legs would take him.

Wouldn't that be a sight, he thought, imagining Lemieux watching as Chief Inspector Gamache ran shrieking past him and down into the village below. Best not to do that. Not just yet.

'Maybe they're not home.' Lemieux was looking around hopefully.

'They're here.'

'Hello.' The door suddenly yanked open, startling Lemieux, and a short, squat man stood there speaking in a very low voice. He sounded to Gamache like a person just recovering from laryngitis. The man cleared his throat and tried again.

'Hello.' It came out in a more healthy register.

'Mr Lyon? My name is Armand Gamache. I'm the head of homicide for the Sûreté du Québec. I'm sorry to intrude.'

'I understand,' said Lyon, pleased with his tone and his words. They didn't sound rehearsed. 'A terrible, terrible day. We're devastated, of course. Come in.'

To Gamache's ear the man sounded rehearsed. But not, perhaps, quite enough. He had the words right but the tone wrong, like a poor actor speaking from his head and not his heart.

Gamache took a deep breath and crossed the threshold. He was almost surprised to find that ghosts and demons weren't swirling around his head, that something cataclysmic and catastrophic didn't happen.

Instead, he found himself in a dreary front hall. He almost laughed.

The house hadn't changed all that much. Its dark wood paneling still greeted guests in the unwelcoming entrance hall. The cold marble floors were spotless. As they followed Lyon through the hall into the living room Gamache noticed there didn't seem to be any Christmas decorations up. Nor were many lights on. A few pools of light here and there, but not nearly enough to take the gloom from the room.

'I wonder if we might turn on more lights?' Gamache nodded to Lemieux who went quickly round the room, switching on lamps until the place was bright, if not cheerful. The walls were bare, except for the rectangles where old Timmer Hadley had had pictures. Neither CC nor her husband had bothered to repaint. In fact, they didn't seem to have bothered to do anything. The furniture looked as though it probably came with the house. It was heavy and ornate, and, as he was about to discover, extremely uncomfortable.

'My daughter Crie.' Lyon waddled ahead of them and pointed to a huge girl wearing a yellow sundress and sitting on the sofa. 'Crie, these men are with the police. Please say hello.'

She didn't.

Gamache sat down beside her and looked at her staring straight ahead. He wondered whether she was autistic. She was certainly withdrawn, but then she'd just witnessed her mother's murder. It would be unusual for a child not to be.

'Crie, my name is Armand Gamache. I'm with the Sûreté. I'm so sorry about what happened to your mother.'

'She's always like this,' explained Lyon. 'Though she's good at school apparently. I guess it's natural for a young girl. Moody.' This is going all right, he said to himself. You have him fooled. Just don't screw up. Be sad about your wife but supportive of your daughter. Be a man.

'How old is Crie?'

Lemieux sat at a small chair in a corner and took out his notebook.

'Thirteen. No, wait. She's twelve. Let me see. She was . . .'

Oh oh.

'That's all right, Mr Lyon, we can look it up. I'm thinking perhaps we should talk in private.'

'Oh, Crie won't mind, will you?'

There was silence.

'But I will,' said Gamache.

Listening to this and taking notes Lemieux tried to heed Gamache's advice and not jump to conclusions about this weak, jabbering, mincing, stupid little man.

'Crie, would you go up and watch television for a while?'

Crie continued to stare.

Lyon reddened a little. 'Crie, I'm speaking to you. Please leave . . .'

'Perhaps we should go to another room.'

'It's not necessary.'

'Yes it is,' Gamache said gently and got up. He held out his arm, guiding Lyon before him. The little man waddled ahead and across the entrance hall into the room beyond. At the door Gamache looked back at Crie, plump and plucked, as though bred for the pot.

This was still a tragic house.

THIRTEEN

'Yes, we were at the community breakfast this morning,' said Lyon.

'All three of you?'

'Yes.' Lyon hesitated.

Gamache waited. They were in the dining room now.

'We arrived in separate cars, CC and I. She was visiting a colleague.'

'Before breakfast?'

'It's a very stressful time for her. A very important time. Big things happening.'

'What did your wife do?'

'You don't know?' Lyon seemed genuinely surprised.

Gamache raised his eyebrows and shook his head.

Lyon got up and ran out of the room returning a moment later with a book. 'This is CC.'

Gamache took it and stared at the cover. It was all white with arched black eyebrows, two piercing blue eyes, nostrils, and a red slash of lips hovering in the middle. It was artful and bizarre. The effect was repellent. The photographer, Gamache thought, must have despised her.

The book was called *Be Calm*.

Gamache tried to recall why that sounded familiar. It would come to him, he knew. Below the title was a black symbol.

'What's this?' Gamache asked.

'Oh, yes. That didn't turn out so well. It's supposed to be the logo for CC's company. An eagle.'

Gamache looked at the black blotch. Now that Lyon had told him he could see the eagle. Hooked beak, head in profile, mouth open in a scream. He hadn't taken any marketing courses but he supposed most companies chose logos that spoke of strength or creativity or trust, some positive quality. This one evoked rage. It looked like one pissed-off bird.

'You can keep that. We have more.'

'Thank you. But I still don't know what your wife did.'

'She was Be Calm.' Richard Lyon didn't seem to be able to grasp that not everyone rotated in CC de Poitiers's orbit. 'The design firm? Li Bien? Soft palettes?'

'She designed dentures?' Gamache made a guess.

'Dentures? No. Houses, rooms, furniture, clothes. Everything. Life. CC created it all.' He opened his arms wide like an Old Testament prophet. 'She was brilliant. That book is all about her life and her philosophy.'

'Which was?'

'Well, it's like an egg. Or really more like paint on a wall. Though not on the wall, of course, but Li Bien. Beneath the wall. Painting inside. Kinda.'

Lemieux's pen hovered over his notebook. Should he write this down?

Dear God, thought Lyon. Shut up. Please, shut up. You're a fat, ugly, stupid, stupid loser.

'When did she leave this morning?' Gamache decided to try another tack.

'She was gone when I got up. I snore I'm afraid so we have separate bedrooms. But I could smell coffee so she must have just left.'

'And what time was that?'

'About seven thirty. When I got to the Legion about an hour later CC was already there.'

'With the colleague?'

Did he hesitate again?

'Yes. A man named Saul something. He's rented a place down here for the Christmas holidays.'

'And what does he do for your wife?' Gamache hoped Lemieux had managed to keep a straight face.

'He's a photographer. He takes pictures. He took that picture. Good, isn't it?' Lyon pointed to the book in Gamache's hand.

'Was he taking pictures of the breakfast?'

Lyon nodded, his eyes round and puffy and somehow imploring. But imploring him to do what, Gamache wondered.

To not pursue this line of questioning, he suddenly knew.

'Was the photographer there during the curling match?' he pursued.

Lyon nodded unhappily.

'You know what this means, don't you?'

'That's just rumor. Vile, baseless lies.'

'It means he might have taken a picture of the person who killed your wife.'

'Oh,' was Lyon's startled reply. But try as he might Gamache couldn't figure out whether Lyon was surprised-happy or surprised-terrified.

'Who do you think did it?' Clara asked, passing a glass of red wine to Peter before sitting back in the easy chair and sipping from her own.

'Ruth.'

'Ruth? Really?' Clara sat up and stared at Peter. He was almost never wrong. It was one of his more annoying features. 'You think Ruth killed CC?'

'I think if I keep saying that eventually I'll be right. Ruth's the only one here, as far as I know, who could kill without a second thought.'

'But you don't really think that of her?' Clara was surprised, though she didn't necessarily disagree.

'I do. It's in her nature. If she hasn't murdered someone before now it's only because she's lacked the motive and opportunity. The ability is there.'

'But would she electrocute someone? I always figured if Ruth killed someone it would be with her cane, or a gun, or she'd run them down with her car. She's not a great one for subtlety.'

Peter went to their bookcases and searched the volumes stacked and piled and crammed in together. He scanned the titles, from biographies to novels to literature and history. Lots of murder mysteries. And poetry. Wonderful poetry that sent Clara humming and moaning in the bath, her favorite place to read poetry since most volumes were slender and easy to hold with slippery hands. Peter was jealous of the words that brought such pleasure to his wife. She made sounds as though the words were caressing her and entering her and touching her in a way he wanted to keep just for himself. He wanted all her moans. But she moaned for Hecht and Atwood and Angelou and even Yeats. She groaned and hummed with pleasure over Auden and Plessner. But she reserved her greatest pleasure for Ruth Zardo.

'Remember this?' He brought over a small book and handed it to Clara. She flipped it open and read, at random,

> *'You were a moth*
> *brushing against my cheek*
> *in the dark.*
> *I killed you*
> *not knowing*
> *you were only a moth,*
> *with no sting.'*

She flipped to another poem, again at random, and another and another.

'They're almost all about death, or loss,' she said, lowering the book. 'I hadn't realized that. Most of Ruth's poems are about death.' She closed the book. It was one of Ruth's older volumes.

'Not just about death,' said Peter, throwing a birch log on the fire and watching it spit, before heading to the kitchen to check the casserole warming for dinner. From there he shouted, 'But also very subtle. There's a great deal to Ruth we don't see.'

'You were only a moth, with no sting.' Clara repeated the words. Was CC only a moth? No. CC de Poitiers had a sting. To come anywhere near the woman was to feel it. Clara wasn't sure she agreed with Peter about Ruth. Ruth got all her bitterness out in her poetry. She held nothing in, and Clara knew the kind of anger that led to murder needed to ferment for a long time, often sealed beneath a layer of smiles and sweet reason.

The phone rang and after a few short words Peter hung up.

'Drink up,' he called from the doorway. 'That was Myrna inviting us for a quick one at the bistro.'

'I have to gulp one drink to get another?'

'Like old times, isn't it?'

Armand Gamache stood outside the old Hadley house. The door had closed and he felt he could exhale. He also felt foolish. He'd toured the gloomy old pile with Lyon and nothing he'd seen had made him like the place more, but neither did it hide any ghouls. It was just tired and sad and it longed for laughter. Like its inhabitants.

Before he left he'd gone back into the living room where Crie was still sitting in her sundress and flip-flops. He'd put a blanket round her and sat across from her, watching her impassive young face for a moment then closing his eyes.

He tried to let her know it would be all right. Eventually. Life wouldn't always be this painful. The world wouldn't always be this brutal. Give it time, little one. Give it another chance. Come back.

He repeated that a few times, then opening his eyes he saw Lemieux at the door watching.

Now, outside, Gamache shrugged deeper into his coat and walked down the path toward the car. The flurries were just beginning, fluffy and light and lovely. He looked down at the village below, all sparkling in the light from the decorations and the flurries. Then something Gabri'd said floated like a flurry into his head. 'The monster is dead and the villagers are celebrating.' An allusion to Frankenstein. But in that story the villagers weren't just celebrating the death of the monster, they'd killed him themselves.

Was it possible this sleepy, lovely, peaceful place had banded together and killed CC de Poitiers?

Gamache almost dismissed it. It was a crazy idea. But then he remembered. It was a crazy death.

'Do you have a question for me?' Gamache asked, not turning back to the young man behind him.

'No sir.'

'Lesson number three, son. Never lie to me.' He turned round now and looked at Agent Lemieux in a way the young man would never forget. There was caring there, but there was also a warning.

'What were you doing in the living room with the daughter?'

'Crie is her name. What did it look like?'

'You were sitting too far away to be talking to her. And, well . . .'

'Go on.'

'Your eyes were closed.'

'You're right.'

'Were you praying?' Lemieux was embarrassed to ask. Prayer, in his generation, was worse than rape, worse than sodomy, worse than failure. He felt he'd just deeply insulted the chief. Still, the man had asked.

'Yes, I was praying, though not, I suppose, in a conventional way. I was thinking about Crie and trying to send her the message that the world could be a good place, and to give it another chance.'

This was more information that Agent Robert Lemieux wanted. Way more. He began to wonder how difficult this assignment was going to be. But as he watched the chief walk slowly, thoughtfully, back to the car Lemieux had to admit Gamache's answer had somehow comforted him. Maybe this wasn't going to be so hard. He brought out his notebook and while the two of them sat in the now warm vehicle Gamache smiled to see young Agent Lemieux write down what he'd said.

Shaking snow off their coats Peter and Clara hung them on the rack by the door and looked around. The bistro was full, the conversation robust. Servers wound expertly between the little round wooden tables, balancing trays with drinks and food.

'Over here.' Myrna stood by the sofa in front of the fireplace. Ruth was with her and a couple was just getting up to leave.

'You can take our seats,' said Hanna Parra, their local elected representative, as she and her husband Roar wrapped scarves round their necks. 'Snow begun?'

'A bit,' said Peter, 'but the roads should be fine.'

'We're just off home. An easy drive.' Roar shook their hands while Hanna kissed them on both cheeks. Departing was not an insignificant event in Quebec.

But then neither was arriving.

After making the rounds and kissing everyone on both cheeks Clara and Peter subsided into the soft wing chairs. Peter caught Gabri's eye and soon the big man had arrived with two glasses of red wine and two bowls of cashews.

'Can you believe what happened?' Gabri took a sip of Clara's wine and a handful of nuts.

'Are they sure it was murder?' Myrna asked.

Peter and Clara nodded.

'That great oaf Gamache is in charge again,' said Ruth, reaching for Peter's wine, 'and you know what happened last time.' She took a swig.

'Didn't he solve the case?' said Myrna, moving her Scotch to the other side of the table.

'Did he?' Ruth gave her an arch look. 'Luck. I mean, look at it. This woman collapses on the ice and he thinks she was electrocuted? By what? The hand of God?'

'But she was electrocuted,' said Peter, just as Olivier arrived.

'You're talking about CC,' he said, looking longingly at the empty chairs by the fire. But he had a restaurant full of patrons and to sit down now was to be lost.

'Peter thinks you did it, Ruth,' said Clara.

'And maybe I did. And maybe you're next.' She smiled maniacally at Peter who wished Clara had kept her mouth shut.

Ruth reached for the nearest drink on the table.

'What did you tell the police?' Olivier asked Peter.

'I just described what happened.'

'The Chief Inspector booked into the B&B.' Olivier picked up Peter's empty wine glass and tilted it toward him in a silent question. Peter, surprised it was empty, shook his head. Two was his limit.

'You don't think she was electrocuted?' Clara asked Ruth.

'Oh, I know she was. Knew it right away. I was just surprised that nincompoop Gamache glommed onto it so quickly.'

127

'How could you know right away?' asked a skeptical Myrna. Ruth said,

'A smell of burning filled the startled air.
CC de Poitiers was no longer there.'

Myrna, despite herself, started to laugh. It was a particularly appropriate quote, or misquote. A smell of burning had indeed filled the startled air.

'Actually,' said Clara, 'another poem came to my mind.

This world he cumbered long enough
He burned his candle to the snuff
And that's the reason some folks think,
He left behind so great a stink.'

Clara's poem fell into the silence round the fire. Behind them conversations ebbed and flowed, bursts of laughter were heard, glasses clinked together. No one was mourning the death of CC de Poitiers. Three Pines was not diminished by her passing. She'd left behind a stink but even that was lifting. Three Pines felt lighter and brighter and fresher for its loss.

Gamache could smell the stew before he made it through the door. *Boeuf bourguignon*, with its aroma of sirloin and mushrooms, of tiny pearl onions and Burgundy wine. He'd called Reine-Marie from the office to let her know he was back, and on her request had picked up a fresh baguette from the local bakery round the corner from their house. Now he struggled through the door carrying the evidence box, his satchel and the precious baguette. He didn't want to break bread before he'd even made it through the door, though it wouldn't be the first time.

'Is that the pool boy?'

'*Non, Madame Gamache, désolé*. It's just the baker.'

'With a baguette, I hope.' She came out of the kitchen wiping her hands on a towel. When she saw him her face broke into a warm smile. She couldn't help it. There he was standing in the hall, both hands holding the box, his leather satchel falling off his shoulder and trying to drag his giant caramel coat with it, and the baguette under his arm rubbing crust into his face.

'It's not, I'm afraid, as robust as it once was.' He gave her a wry smile.

'It's just perfect for me, monsieur.' She carefully tugged it out from under his arm, freeing him to bend down and drop the box to the floor.

'*Voilà*. It's good to be home.' He took her in his arms and kissed her, feeling her soft body beneath his coat. They'd both swelled since they'd first met. There was no way either would get into their wedding clothes. But they'd grown in other ways as well, and Gamache figured it was a good deal. If life meant growth in all directions, it was fine with him.

Reine-Marie hugged him back, feeling his coat wet from the falling snow making her own sweater damp. But she figured it was a good deal. In exchange for a little discomfort, she got immense comfort.

After he'd showered and changed into a clean turtleneck and tweed jacket he joined her for a glass of wine in front of their fireplace. It was the first quiet night for weeks, what with family and the crush of Christmas parties.

'Should we eat here?' he asked.

'What a wonderful idea.'

He put out folding tables in front of their chairs while she served the *boeuf bourguignon* on egg noodles, with a basket of sliced baguette.

'What a strange couple,' said Reine-Marie, when he'd finished telling her the events of his day. 'I wonder why CC and Richard stayed together. I wonder why they married at all.'

'I do too. Richard Lyon's so passive, so befuddled, and yet I wondered how much was an act. Either way, he'd be a very annoying person to live with, unless you're also kind of vague, or very patient, and it doesn't sound as though CC de Poitiers was either. Have you heard of her?'

'Never. But she might be known in the English community.'

'I think she was only famous in the mirror. Lyon gave me this.' He reached into the satchel lying beside his easy chair and pulled out *Be Calm*.

'Self-published,' Reine-Marie commented after examining the cover. 'Lyon and his daughter saw the whole thing?'

Gamache nodded, taking a forkful of the tender stew. 'They were in the stands. Lyon didn't know anything was wrong until he noticed everyone looking over to where CC had been sitting. Then people began leaving their seats. Gabri went to him and said there'd been an accident.'

He realized he'd spoken of Gabri as though Reine-Marie had met the man. And she seemed to feel the same way.

'And the daughter? Crie did you say her name was? Why call a child Crie? What a hideous thing to do to a child, poor one.'

'More than you know. She's not well, Reine-Marie. She's

withdrawn, almost catatonic. And she's immense. Must be fifty, sixty pounds overweight and she's only twelve or thirteen. Lyon couldn't remember.'

'Being fat isn't a sign of unhappiness, Armand. At least, I hope it isn't.'

'True. But it's more than that. It's as though she's disconnected. And there's something else. When the murder happened Lyon described seeing CC lying there and the rescuers working on her but he didn't know where Crie was.'

'You mean he didn't look for her?' asked Reine-Marie, her fork stopped partway to her mouth in astonishment.

Gamache shook his head.

'Odious man,' said Reine-Marie.

It was hard not to agree, and Gamache was left to wonder why he was trying so hard not to.

Maybe, came the answer, maybe it's too easy. Maybe you don't want the solution to be anything as pedestrian as the scorned, humiliated, cuckolded husband murdering the selfish wife. Maybe that was too easy for the great Armand Gamache.

'It's just your ego,' said Reine-Marie, reading his mind.

'What is?'

'The reason you're not agreeing with me about Lyon. You know he probably did it. You know they must have had a sick relationship. Why else would she treat him like that and why else would he take it? And why else would their daughter withdraw until she all but disappeared? I mean, by your description, no one even noticed whether she was there or not.'

'She was there. She went with them in the truck. But you're right.'

'About what?'

'I don't want Richard Lyon to be guilty.'

'Why not?' She leaned forward.

'I like him,' said Gamache. 'He reminds me of Sonny.'

'Our dog?'

'Remember how he'd wander from backyard to backyard, looking for picnics?'

'I remember he once got on the 34 bus and ended up in Westmount.'

'Lyon reminds me of Sonny. Eager to please, hungry for company. And I think he's got a good heart.'

'Good hearts get hurt. Good hearts get broken, Armand. And then they lash out. Be careful. I'm sorry, I shouldn't have said any of that. You know your business better than I. Forgive me.'

'It's always good to be reminded, especially about my ego. Who was that character in Julius Caesar who described his job as standing behind the emperor and whispering, "You're only a man."'

'So now you're an emperor? This isn't going in a promising direction.'

'Careful,' he said, wiping the last of the gravy off his plate with a crispy piece of baguette, 'or you'll crush my ego completely. Then I'll disappear.'

'I'm not worried.' She gave him a kiss as she collected their plates and made for the kitchen.

'Why wasn't CC sitting with her family?' she asked a few minutes later as Gamache washed up and she dried. 'Doesn't that strike you as strange?'

'The whole thing strikes me as strange. I'm not sure I've ever had a case where so little made sense from the get-go.' Gamache's sleeves were rolled up and his hands soapy as he vigorously scrubbed the Le Creuset pot.

'Why would a woman leave her family in the cold stands while she took a comfortable chair under the heater?' Reine-Marie seemed genuinely perplexed.

'I guess that answers it.' Gamache laughed, handing her the pot. 'It was comfortable and warm.'

'So she was selfish and he's odious. If I were Crie I'd disappear too.'

Once the dishes were done they took their coffee tray into the living room and Gamache carried over the box with the evidence from Elle's murder. It was time to change gears, at least for a while. Sipping coffee and occasionally lowering a report to stare into the fire, he went through the box more thoroughly than he'd been able to that morning.

He picked up the small engraved wooden box and opened it, staring at the strange assortment of letters. Homeless people weren't famous for their good sense, but even so, why would she have cut out all those letters? C, B, L, K and M. Turning it over he saw again the letters taped to the bottom. B KLM.

Maybe the C fell off. Maybe it sat in that hole between the B and K.

He picked up the autopsy report. Elle had been strangled. Alcohol was found in her bloodstream and there were signs of chronic alcoholism. No drugs. Some bruising round her neck, of course.

Why kill a bag lady?

The murderer was almost certainly another homeless person. Like any sub-culture, this one interacted mostly with itself. A regular pedestrian would probably not care enough about Elle to kill her.

He opened the craft paper envelope which held the crime

scene photographs. Her face was smudged and surprised. Her legs were splayed and wrapped in layers of clothing and newspapers. He lowered the picture and peered into the box. There they were. Some yellowing newspaper, some fresher, curled into the shape of Elle's legs and arms and torso, like a dismembered ghost.

There were pictures of Elle's filthy hands, her nails grotesque. Long and twisted and discolored with God knew what beneath them. Actually, the coroner knew what. Gamache consulted the report. Dirt. Food. Excrement.

One hand had some blood on it, her own blood according to the report, and a few fresh cuts in the center of the palm, like stigmata. Whoever had killed her might have gotten some blood on him. Even if the clothes were washed there would still be some DNA left. Blood was the new albatross.

Gamache made a note of that and turned to the final photograph. It was of Elle naked on the coroner's cold gurney. He stared at it for a moment, wondering when he'd get used to seeing dead bodies. Murder still shocked him.

Then he picked up his magnifying glass and slowly examined her body. He was looking for letters. Had she written or taped K L C B and M onto her body? Perhaps the letters were some obsessive talisman. Some madmen drew crucifixes all over their bodies and all round their homes, to ward off evil. Maybe these letters were Elle's crucifix.

He lowered the magnifying glass. Her body, while free of consonants, was thick with dirt. Years of it. Even the occasional bath or shower at the Old Brewery Mission couldn't lift it off. It was engraved on her body, like a tattoo. And like a tattoo it told a story. It was as eloquent as a Ruth Zardo poem.

I understand. You can't spare
anything, a hand, a piece of bread, a shawl
against the cold,
a good word. Lord
knows there isn't much
to go around. You need it all.

A good word. That reminded him of something else. Crie. Like Elle, she longed for a good word. Begged for it as surely as Elle had begged for food.

The tattoo of filth spoke of Elle's external life, but was mute about what happened inside, beneath the layers of fetid clothing and dirt and alcohol-shriveled skin. Staring at the picture of the body on the gurney Gamache wondered what this woman had thought and felt. Gamache knew those things had probably died with her. Knew he might find her name, might even find her killer, but he would probably never find her. This woman had been lost years ago.

Like Crie, only further down the road?

And then he saw it. A small discoloration different from the rest. It was dark and circular, too even to be random filth. It was on her chest, on her breastbone.

Lifting his magnifying glass again he spent some time looking at it. He wanted to be certain. And when he looked up Armand Gamache was.

He took out the other pictures again and stared at one in particular. Then he rooted through the evidence box, looking for one small thing. Something that would be easy to over-look. But it wasn't there.

He carefully replaced everything in the box and put it by the door. Then he returned to his warm chair by the fire and sat a moment watching Reine-Marie reading, her lips moving ever so slightly now and then and her brows rising and lowering in a way only he, who knew her so well, could see.

Then he picked up *Be Calm* and started reading.

FOURTEEN

⌐

J ean Guy Beauvoir reached for his Tim Horton's Double
   Double coffee, cradling it in his hands to keep them warm.
The huge black wood stove in the center of the room was
trying its best, but so far it hadn't managed to throw much
heat.

It was ten o'clock on a snowy morning, almost exactly
twenty-four hours after the murder, and the Sûreté team had
assembled in their situation room in Three Pines. They
shared it with a large red fire truck. The white walls above
the dark wood wainscoting were plastered with detailed maps
of the area, diagrams of firefighting strategies and a huge
poster commemorating past winners of the Governor-
General's Awards for Literature.

This was the home of the Three Pines Volunteer Fire
Department, under the baton of Ruth Zardo.

'*Tabernacle*. She's a senile old hag. Won't let us move that
out.' Beauvoir shoved his thumb toward the truck taking up
half the room.

'Did Madame Zardo give you a reason?' Gamache asked.

137

'Something about needing to make sure the truck doesn't freeze up in case there's a fire,' said Beauvoir. 'I asked her when the last fire was and she told me it was confidential. Confidential? Since when was there a secret fire?'

'Let's get started. Reports, please.' Gamache sat at the head of the table wearing a shirt and tie and crew neck merino wool sweater beneath his tweed jacket. He held a pen in his hand, but rarely took notes. All around technicians were wiring phones and faxes and computers, setting up desks and blackboards and unloading equipment. But Gamache heard none of that. He concentrated totally on what was being said.

Agent Robert Lemieux had put on his Sunday best and polished his shoes and now was grateful the little voice of instinct had spoken, and even more grateful it had been heard. Beside him a young woman agent sipped her coffee and leaned forward attentively. She'd introduced herself as Agent Isabelle Lacoste. Lemieux wouldn't describe her as attractive, not the kind you'd notice immediately in a bar. But then she didn't seem the sort to hang around bars. More the kind you'd find on Mont St-Rémy. Natural and relaxed, without artifice. Her clothes were simple and well cut to fit her comfortable body, a light sweater, scarf and slacks. Her dark eyes were alert and her light brown hair was held off her face by a wide band. Lemieux noticed a string of earrings piercing one ear. She'd come up immediately and welcomed him. Instinctively he'd checked her left hand, and found, to his surprise, a wedding band.

'Two kids,' she said, with a smile, her eyes not leaving his face and yet she'd followed his quick glance. 'A boy, René, and a girl Marie. *Toi?*'

'Not married. Not even a girlfriend.'

'Just as well. At least while the investigation is on. Pay attention.' She'd leaned in and whispered, 'And be yourself. The chief only chooses people who don't pretend.'

'And who are good at their jobs, presumably,' he said, thinking he was giving her a compliment.

'*Oh, mais, franchement,* you can't be good at this job if you don't know who you are. How can you possibly find the truth about someone else if you won't admit the truth about yourself?'

'*Bon.*' Beauvoir leaned forward. 'The good news is, I know how the electricity got to the curling rink on the lake. Yesterday afternoon I interviewed Billy Williams, the guy who drove the truck with CC to the hospital. He told me he wired up that heat lamp. Here, let me show you. Some of you haven't been to the site yet.'

Beauvoir picked up a chocolate-glazed doughnut in one hand and a magic marker in the other and walked to a large sheet of paper tacked to the wall.

'This is Lac Brume, and this is the town of Williamsburg. Here's the Legion. Right?'

Beauvoir was no Picasso, which was a good thing for a homicide inspector. His drawings were always very clear and straightforward. A large circle was Lac Brume. A smaller circle, like a moon, touched its edge. Williamsburg. And an X marked the Legion Hall, close to the shores of the lake.

'Now, you can't actually see the lake from the Legion. You have to go down this road and round a corner. Still, it's only about a five-minute walk. Everyone was at a community breakfast at the Legion just before the curling. Billy Williams told me he'd gotten to the rink before the breakfast and driven his truck onto the ice.'

'Is that safe?' one of the officers asked.

'The ice is about a foot and a half thick right there,' said Beauvoir. 'He tested it before Christmas when he put up the stands and the lamp. All he had to do the day of the curling, yesterday, was shovel the rink again and wire up the heat lamp. It was a clear morning so he decided to do both before going to the Legion himself for breakfast. Here's where he parked his truck. You can see the tire tracks in the crime scene photos.' He handed out the pictures after marking a small X on his drawing. It was on the ice near the shore.

'Now, this is important. Here's his truck, here's the heat lamp – it's called a radiant heater – here're the stands and out here,' he drew a rectangle on the paper, 'is the curling rink. Billy Williams is the Canadian Automobile Association's mechanic in the area, so he has this monster truck. I saw it. Huge mother. Wheels up to here.' Gamache cleared his throat and Beauvoir remembered where he was. 'Anyway, he has a generator on the flatbed of his truck for boosting cars. But again, not just any generator. This is immense. Says he needs the power to boost frozen semis and construction equipment. So he simply took his booster cables and connected them onto his generator at one end and the heat lamp at the other. *Voilà*. Power and heat.'

Agent Lemieux shifted in his seat then caught the eye of Agent Lacoste. She looked at him and gave a curt nod. Of encouragement? he wondered. She nodded again and widened her eyes.

'Sir,' he said, grateful his voice didn't break. Beauvoir turned surprised eyes on the newcomer who had the audacity to interrupt.

'What is it?'

'Well, those things' – he motioned to the drawing – 'the heating thing? When we saw it yesterday I had a question but I wanted to check it out before I said anything. Those heaters are almost always powered by propane. Not electricity.' He looked round the table. All eyes were on him. 'I called a friend who's an electrician. He also plays hockey in a men's league here.'

To Lemieux's surprise Beauvoir smiled. An easy, open smile that made his face seem quite youthful.

'You're right. This one was propane once too,' he said. 'But it broke and was going to be thrown away when Billy Williams saved it. Knew he could wire it up and it would work well enough for the once-a-year curling extravaganza. That was a couple of years ago. So far it's held up. But he needs a generator to juice it up.'

'Agent Lemieux here suggested a generator to me yesterday.' Gamache nodded to Lemieux who sat up a little taller in his chair. 'I'm afraid I didn't take the suggestion seriously. I'm sorry.'

Lemieux had never had a superior apologize to him. He didn't know what to do, so he did nothing.

'Was Mr Williams's generator powerful enough to kill?' Gamache asked.

'That's the question. The other stop I made yesterday was to the Cowansville hospital to speak to the coroner, Dr Harris. She gave me the autopsy report. She knows Williams and says his generator is powerful enough to do the job. In fact, it doesn't really take much.' Beauvoir returned to his seat and ate the last bite of his doughnut while stirring his coffee with a pen. 'She wants to speak to you, chief. Says she'll be by later this morning with a more detailed report and the clothing the victim was wearing. But she made it clear this was no accident, in case any of you were wondering.'

Beauvoir looked down at his notes. He didn't really know where to start. He certainly didn't want to repeat that this was a bizarre, even possibly insane way to commit a murder. Chief Inspector Gamache already knew that. They all did. But Dr Sharon Harris had said it to him yesterday afternoon several times.

'I don't think you completely appreciate the situation, Inspector. Look at this.' Dr Harris had taken the white sheet off the victim. There on the cold, hard gurney lay a cold, hard woman. She had a snarl on her face and Beauvoir wondered whether her family would recognize the look. Sharon Harris had spent a few minutes circling the woman, pointing out areas of interest like a necropolitan tour guide.

Now, in the morning briefing, he passed out more pictures, these ones taken by Dr Harris at the autopsy. The room grew silent as everyone went through them.

Gamache looked carefully at the images then passed them to Agent Lacoste. He turned slightly in his chair, crossed his legs and stared out the window. Snow was falling and gathering on the cars and houses and piling up on the branches of the trees. It was a peaceful scene, in sharp contrast to the pictures and conversation inside the old railway station. From where he sat he could see the arched stone bridge that connected their side of the Rivière Bella Bella with Three Pines. Every now and then a car would pass slowly and silently, the sound muffled by the snow.

Inside, the room smelled of wood smoke and industrial coffee in wet cardboard with a slight undercurrent of varnish and that musky aroma of old books. Or timetables. This had once been the railway station. Now abandoned like so many small stops along the Canadian National Railway the village of Three Pines had found a good use for the old wood and brick building.

Gamache brought his hand, warmed by his coffee, to his nose. It was cold. And a little wet. Had he been a dog it would have been a better sign. Still, the room was warming up and there was nothing quite like the comfort of being cold, then slowly feeling the heat approaching and arriving and spreading.

That's how Armand Gamache felt now. He felt happy and satisfied. He loved his work, he loved his team. He'd rise no further in the Sûreté, and he'd made his peace with that because Armand Gamache wasn't a competitive man. He was a content man.

And this was one of his favorite parts of the job. Sitting with his team and working out who could have committed the murder.

'You see her hands? And feet?' Beauvoir held up a couple of the autopsy pictures. 'They're charred. Did any of the witnesses report a smell?' he asked Gamache.

'They did, though it was very faint,' Gamache confirmed.

Beauvoir nodded. 'That's what Dr Harris suspected. She thought there'd be a smell. Burning flesh. Most of the electrocution victims she sees these days are more obvious. Some are actually smoking.'

A few of the homicide investigators winced.

'Literally,' said Beauvoir. 'Most people who die this way are killed by the high tension wires. They're hydro workers or maintenance men or people just unlucky enough to come in contact with one of those wires. They blow down in a storm or get cut accidentally and *pouf*. Killed immediately.'

Beauvoir paused. Now Armand Gamache leaned forward. He knew Jean Guy Beauvoir well enough to know he didn't go in for dramatics. Disdained them in fact. But he did enjoy his little pauses. They almost always gave him away. Like a liar who cleared his throat before telling a big one, or a poker player who rubbed his nose, Beauvoir telegraphed some big piece of news with a dramatic pause.

'Dr Harris hasn't seen a death by low voltage in more than ten years. The automatic shut-offs put an end to that. She says it's almost impossible.'

Now he had everyone's attention. Even the technicians, so busy in their work a moment earlier, had slowed down and stopped to listen.

A near impossible murder.

Doughnuts and coffee were arrested on their way to mouths, photographs were laid on the table, breathing seemed to have stopped.

'Almost,' repeated Beauvoir. 'A number of things had to come together for this to work. CC de Poitiers had to have been standing in a puddle. In the middle of a frozen lake at minus ten Celsius she had to be standing in water. She had to have had her bare hands come in contact with something that was electrified. Bare hands.' He brought his hands up, as though perhaps the homicide team needed the reminder of what hands looked like. 'Again, in freezing cold temperatures she had to have taken off her gloves. She then had to touch the one thing in the whole area that was electrified. But even that wasn't enough. The current had to travel through her body and out her feet, into the puddle. Look at your feet.'

Everyone looked at him.

'Your feet, your feet. Look at your feet.'

All faces disappeared below the table, except Beauvoir's. Armand Gamache bent down and looked at his boots. They were nylon on the outside. Inside there were layers of Thinsulate and felt.

'Look at the soles of your feet,' an exasperated Beauvoir said.

Down they went again.

'Well?'

'Rubber,' said Agent Isabelle Lacoste. Beauvoir could tell by her clever face that she understood. 'Pre-formed rubber with ridges for traction, so we don't slip on the ice and snow. I bet we all have rubber soles.'

Everyone agreed.

'That's it,' said Beauvoir, barely able to contain himself. 'We'll have to call round to confirm, but I bet there isn't a boot sold in Quebec that doesn't have rubber soles. That was the final element, and maybe the most unlikely in a series of unlikely events. Had CC de Poitiers been wearing boots with rubber or even leather bottoms she wouldn't have died. She grabbed onto something metal. Metal conducts electricity. The earth conducts electricity. Our bodies conduct electricity. According to Dr Harris, electricity is like a living thing. It's desperate to stay alive. It races from one form to another, through the metal, through the body, and into the earth. And along the way it races through the heart. And the heart has its own electrical current. Amazing, isn't it? Dr Harris explained all this to me. If the electricity goes right through the body it only takes a few seconds to affect the heart. It screws up the normal rhythms and causes it to' – he checked his notes – 'fibrillate.'

'Which is why they use those electrified paddles to start the heart,' said Lacoste.

'And why pacemakers are implanted. Those are really just batteries, giving the heart an electrical impulse,' agreed Beauvoir, excited by the topic. Thrilled to have facts to deal with. 'When CC touched the metal her heart was affected within seconds.'

'But', Armand Gamache spoke and all eyes turned to him, 'Madame de Poitiers had to have been grounded.'

The room sat in silence. By now it had warmed up, but still Gamache felt a chill. He looked at Beauvoir and knew there was more to come.

Beauvoir reached into a bag at his side and plunked a pair of boots onto the table.

Before them sat CC de Poitier's footwear, made of the youngest, whitest, finest baby seal skin. And on the bottom, where everyone else would have rubber, the investigators could see tiny claws.

Beauvoir turned one of the boots on its side so that the sole was visible. Twisted and charred and grotesque, the claws were revealed to be metal teeth, protruding from the leather sole.

Armand Gamache felt his jaw clench. Who would wear such boots? The Inuit, maybe. In the Arctic. But even they wouldn't kill baby seals. The Inuit were respectful and sensible hunters who'd never dream of killing the young. They didn't have to.

No. Only brutes murdered babies. And only brutes supported that trade. Sitting in front of them were the carcasses of two babies. Animals, certainly, but all senseless killing appalled Gamache. What sort of woman wore the bodies of dead babies shaped into boots, with metal claws imbedded in them?

Armand Gamache wondered whether CC de Poitiers was at that very moment trying to explain herself to a perplexed God and a couple of very angry seals.

FIFTEEN

—

Beauvoir stood in front of another sheet of paper tacked to the wall. CC's boots sat in the middle of the table like a sculpture, and a reminder of how strange both murderer and murdered were.

'So, to recap, four things had to come together for the murderer to be successful.' Beauvoir wrote as he spoke. 'A: the victim had to be standing in water. B: she had to have taken off her gloves; C: she had to touch something that was electrified and D: she had to be wearing metal on the bottom of her boots.'

'I have a report from the crime scene,' said Isabelle Lacoste, who'd been in charge of the Crime Scene Unit the day before. 'It's preliminary, of course, but we can answer one question anyway. About the water. If you look at the photographs again you'll see a slight blue tinge to the snow around the overturned chair.'

Gamache looked closely. He'd taken that area for a shadow. On snow, in certain angles and lights, shadows were blue. But not, perhaps, this particular shade. Now that he looked more closely he recognized it and almost groaned. He should have seen it right away. They all should have.

The murderer could only have created a puddle in two ways. Melt the ice and snow that was there, or spill some new liquid. But if he spilled some coffee or tea or a soft drink it would freeze in very little time.

What wouldn't freeze?

Something specially designed not to.

Anti-freeze windshield washer fluid. The ubiquitous light blue liquid everyone in Canada poured by the gallon into their cars. It was designed to be sprayed onto the windshield to wipe away the slush and salt. And not to freeze.

Was it that easy?

'It's windshield washer fluid,' said Lacoste.

Apparently so, thought Gamache. At least something about this case was straightforward.

'How did the murderer spill washer fluid there without being seen?' Lacoste asked.

'Well, we don't know that the murderer wasn't seen,' said Gamache. 'We haven't asked that question. And someone was sitting right beside Madame de Poitiers. That person might have seen.'

'Who?' Beauvoir asked.

'Kaye Thompson.' Now Gamache got up and walked to the drawing Beauvoir had made of the scene of crime. He told them about his interviews of the day before then he drew three Xs clustered round the heat lamp.

'Lawn chairs. They were meant for the three elderly women who brought them, but only one ended up using a chair. Kaye Thompson was sitting in this one.' Gamache pointed to one of the Xs. 'The other two women were curling and CC sat in the chair closest to the lamp. Now this chair,' he circled the chair closest to the curling rink, 'was on its side. It's also the one with the fluid under it, am I right?' he asked Lacoste, who nodded.

'It's in the lab being tested but I suspect we'll find that the chair was the murder weapon,' she said.

'But wasn't it the heat lamp?' one of the agents asked, turning to Beauvoir. 'I thought you said the victim touched the thing that was electrified. That's the heat lamp.'

'*C'est vrai*,' Beauvoir conceded. 'But it appears that wasn't what killed her. The chair did, we think. If you look at the wounds on her hands, they're consistent with the aluminum tubing at the back of the chair.'

'But how?' one of the technicians asked.

'That's what we have to find out,' said Beauvoir, so wrapped up in the mystery he failed to tell the technician to get back to work. She'd asked the right question. How did a charge get from the heat lamp to create an electric chair?

An electric chair.

Jean Guy Beauvoir rolled the concept round in his clear, analytical mind. Was that somehow important? Was there a reason the murderer had chosen to kill CC de Poitiers by electric chair?

Was this retribution? Revenge? Was it punishment for some crime of CC's? If so, it was the first such execution in Canada in fifty years.

'What do you think?' Gamache turned to the technician who'd asked the question, a young woman in overalls and a toolbelt. 'And what's your name?'

'Céline Provost, sir. I'm an electrician with Sûreté technical services. I'm just here to wire up the computers.'

'*Bon, Agent Provost.* What's your theory?'

She stared at the diagram for a full minute, considering. 'What was the voltage of the generator?'

Beauvoir told her. She nodded and thought some more. Then she shook her head.

'I was wondering whether the murderer could have attached some more booster cables from the lamp to the chair, then buried the wires under the snow. That would electrify the chair.'

'But?'

'But it would mean the chair was live with electricity the whole time. As soon as the murderer attached the cables the chair would be electrified. Anyone touching it would get the charge. The murderer couldn't guarantee Madame de Poitiers would be the first to touch it.'

'There'd be no way to turn the current on and off?'

'None, except from the truck generator and they make a lot of noise. Everyone would have noticed it going off. And if the murderer put the cables on at the last minute, that woman you said was sitting right there, well, she would have seen for sure.'

Gamache thought about it. She was right.

'Sorry, sir.'

'Other reports?' Gamache asked as he sat back down.

For the next twenty minutes various agents reported on the crime scene findings, the preliminary analyses, the initial background checks.

'So far,' Agent Lacoste reported, 'we know that Richard Lyon works as a glorified clerk in a clothing factory. He does their paperwork and makes out shift assignments. But in his spare time he's invented this.' She held up a diagram.

'Enough mysteries,' said Beauvoir. 'What is it?'

'Silent Velcro. Apparently the US military has a problem. Now that they're doing more and more close quarters combat silence is crucial. They sneak up on their enemies.' Lacoste crouched down at her desk and mimicked skulking around. 'Then get ready to shoot. But they keep all their equipment attached to their uniforms by Velcro. As soon as the pocket is opened the Velcro rips off and their position is given away. It's become a huge problem. Anyone who can invent silent Velcro will make a fortune.'

Gamache could see the wheels turning in everyone's head.

'And Lyon did?' he asked.

'Well, he invented this. It's a system of keeping pockets shut using magnets.'

'Ingenious,' said Gamache.

'Except that to work through heavy khaki the magnets need to be quite heavy. And you need two per pocket and the average uniform has about forty pockets. The magnets add about fifteen pounds to an already heavy load.'

There were a few snickers.

'He has nine patents, for various things. All failures.'

'A loser,' said Beauvoir.

'Still, he keeps trying,' Lacoste pointed out. 'And if he gets one right, he could be rich beyond his wildest dreams.'

Gamache listened to this and remembered Reine-Marie's question of the night before. Why had Richard Lyon and CC de Poitiers married? And why had they stayed married? One so ambitious and selfish and cruel, the other so weak and bumbling? He'd have expected CC to kill him, not the other way round.

He realized then that he was almost taking it for granted

that Lyon had killed his wife. Very dangerous, he knew, to take anything for granted. Still, was it possible Richard Lyon had finally hit upon an invention that worked? Had he murdered his wife to keep her from sharing in the fortune?

'There's something else strange about this case.' Lacoste smiled her apology to Inspector Beauvoir. The two had worked together on many cases and she knew his mind to be sharp and analytical. This kind of clutter and chaos was torture to him. He braced himself and nodded. 'I also ran CC de Poitiers through the computer and found nothing. Well, a driver's license and health card. But no birth certificate, no passport, nothing from more than twenty years ago. I then tried CC Lyon, Cecilia Lyon, Cecilia de Poitiers.' She lifted her hands in surrender.

'Try Eleanor and Henri de Poitiers,' Gamache suggested, looking down at the book in front of him. 'According to her book, they were her parents. And look up Li Bien.' He spelled it for her.

'What's that?'

'Her philosophy of life. A philosophy she was hoping would replace feng shui.'

Beauvoir tried to look both interested and knowledgable. He was neither.

'A philosophy,' Gamache continued, 'she was hoping would make her very rich indeed.'

'A motive for murder?' Beauvoir perked up.

'Perhaps, had she actually succeeded. But so far it looks as though CC de Poitiers was about as successful as her husband. Is that all before we hand out assignments?' He made to get up.

'Sir, there is one more thing.' Agent Robert Lemieux. 'You

gave me the garbage from the Lyon home. Well, I've sorted through it and I have the inventory list here.'

'That'll wait, agent, thank you,' said Gamache. 'We have a busy day. I'm going to speak to Kaye Thompson, find out what she saw. I want you to find that photographer Richard Lyon talked about,' he said to Beauvoir, who nodded briskly, eager for the hunt to begin. 'At the very least he took pictures at the community breakfast and the curling. He might even have photographed the murder. His name is Saul someone.'

'Saul Petrov.' The big red fire truck spoke, in a female voice.

From behind it a young woman appeared.

'I've found him.'

As she approached she couldn't help but notice the looks of shock and even horror on the faces of the men and women round the table. She wasn't surprised. She was prepared for this.

'Good morning, Agent Nichol,' said Armand Gamache.

SIXTEEN

B eauvoir handed out the assignments while Gamache spoke to Agent Yvette Nichol in private. There was one enclosed room which used to belong to the ticket taker. Latterly it was taken over by Ruth Zardo. It housed a desk, a chair and about three hundred books. It was, in all certainty, a fire hazard.

Chief Inspector Gamache had risen to his feet as soon as Agent Nichol appeared, as a man about to be executed might rise to face what was coming. He'd nodded to Beauvoir and his second in command knew instinctively what was being said. Without a word Gamache walked across the floor to meet Nichol halfway, and guide her into the small room.

Now Beauvoir watched his team work their computers and the phones, but his mind was on the chief. And Nichol. That rancid, wretched, petty little woman who'd almost ruined their last case, and had proved a deeply divisive element in a team that thrived and depended on harmony.

'Explain yourself, please.' Gamache stood in the small room, towering over the petite agent. Her short mousy hair was not only disheveled from taking off her tuque, but seemed to have been cut by a drunken gardener with tree shears. Her clothes were ill fitting and drab and Gamache thought he saw a bit of egg yolk clinging to her prickly wool sweater. Her face was scarred and purple from severe acne as a teen, and where it wasn't purple it was pasty. The only spark her gray eyes held was fear. And something else, Gamache thought. Cunning. She's afraid of someone, he thought, but not me.

'I was assigned to you, sir.' She watched him closely. 'Superintendent Francoeur called this morning and told me I was to report to you. It surprised me as well.' She tried to sound contrite and only succeeded in sounding whiny. 'I read the field notes you and Inspector Beauvoir had written.'

'How?'

'Well, the Superintendent forwarded them to me at home. I noticed your note about the photographer and that you considered that the priority. I agreed—'

'I'm relieved to hear it.'

'I mean, I thought you were right. Well, of course you were.' Now she was getting flustered. 'Here.' She thrust out her hand with a piece of paper. He took it and read.

Saul Petrov, 17 rue Tryhorn.

'I looked it up on the map. See, here.' She pulled a map from her jacket pocket and handed it to him. He didn't take it. He simply stared at her.

'I called about fifteen rental agencies in the area. No one knew him but finally I found a restaurant in St-Rémy, Le Sans Souci. People advertise chalets for rent there. I asked the owner and he remembered getting a similar call from a guy in Montreal a few days ago. Guy rented the place right away. So I called and sure enough, it's this photographer. Saul Petrov.'

'You spoke to him?'

'Yes sir. Had to. To confirm his identity.'

'And suppose he's the murderer? Suppose at this moment he's burning his pictures or loading up his car? How long ago did you call?'

'About two hours.' Yvette Nichol's voice had faded to a whisper.

Gamache took a deep breath and stared at her for a moment, then strode out the door.

'Inspector Beauvoir? Please take an agent and find out if this is the photographer we're looking for. Agent Lemieux, stay here. I need to speak to you.' He turned back to Nichol. 'Sit down and wait for me.'

She plunked down on the chair as though her legs had been cut out from underneath her.

Beauvoir took the piece of paper, consulted the map on the wall and was out the door in a matter of minutes, but not before he'd gotten a look at Agent Nichol sitting in the tiny, cramped room, looking about as miserable as a person still alive could look. He surprised within himself a certain sympathy for her. Chief Inspector Gamache's bad side was legend. Not because it was so bad, but because it was so well hidden. Hardly anyone had ever found it. But those that did never ever forgot.

'I have an assignment for you,' Gamache said to Lemieux. 'I want you to go into Montreal and ask some questions for me. It's about a woman named Elle. That's not her real name. She was indigent and was murdered just before Christmas.'

'Is this about the de Poitiers case?'

'No.'

'Have I done something wrong?' Lemieux looked crest-fallen.

'Not at all. I need some questions asked about that case and it'll be good training for you. You haven't worked in Montreal?'

'Barely visited,' Lemieux admitted.

'Now's your chance.' He could see the anxiety in Agent Lemieux's face. 'You'll be fine. I wouldn't send you if I didn't think two things. First, that you can do it and second, that you need to do it.'

'What do you want me to do?'

Gamache told him, and the two of them went to Gamache's car where the chief took a cardboard evidence box from his trunk and handed it to Lemieux with instructions.

Gamache's eyes followed Lemieux as his car drove slowly over the old stone bridge, onto the Commons and round the village green before mounting rue du Moulin and heading out of Three Pines. The chief stood in the steadily falling snow and his stare fell on the figures on the village green. Some carried bags of shopping from Sarah's Boulangerie or Monsieur Béliveau's general store. Some families were skating. Some walked dogs. One dog, a young shepherd, was rolling and digging and tossing something into the air.

He missed Sonny.

Through the snow everyone looked much the same. All bundled up in fluffy parkas and tuques, making them anonymous. He supposed if he knew the children and the dogs, he'd be able to figure out who the adults were.

And that was one of the problems they were facing. Everyone looked alike in the Quebec winter. Like colorful marshmallows. It was hard to even distinguish men from women. Faces, hair, hands, feet, bodies, all covered against the cold. Even if someone had seen the murderer, could they identify him?

He watched the dogs frolic and recognized with a smile what they were playing with. Sonny's favorite winter treat.

Frozen poop. Poopsicles.

He even missed that.

'You're not welcome on my team, Agent Nichol.' Gamache looked into the scarred, scared face a few minutes later. He was done with her manipulation, her arrogance, her anger. He'd had enough of that during the last case.

'I understand, sir. It wasn't my idea either. I know what a mess I made of the last assignment with you. I'm so sorry. What can I do to prove I've changed?'

'You can leave.'

'I wish I could.' She looked miserable. 'I really do. I knew you'd feel like this and honestly I don't blame you. I don't know what I was thinking last time. Stupid. Arrogant. But I think I've changed. A year in narcotics.' She looked into his face to see whether this was making any impact.

It wasn't.

'Goodbye, Agent Nichol.'

He walked out of the room, put his coat back on and got into his car without looking back.

'I'm sorry, Chief Inspector, but Kaye Thompson isn't here right now. She spent the night at her friend's home. Émilie Longpré.'

The matron of the seniors' home in Williamsburg looked

kindly and efficient. The home itself was in a converted mansion, the rooms large and gracious, though perhaps a little tired and definitely smelling of talcum. Like the residents themselves.

Armand Gamache at least had the sense to laugh at himself. Madame Longpré lived in Three Pines and might even have been one of the anonymous figures he'd watched walking across the village green. He'd been so angry at Agent Nichol he'd stormed out like the petulant child he believed her to be, gotten in his car and zoomed away. So there. And here he was, kilometers away from the witness who had in fact been just meters away in the first place. He smiled and the matron was left to wonder what the large man found so funny.

Instead of going straight back to Three Pines, Gamache parked the car at the Legion and walked in. It wasn't locked. Most places weren't. He wandered around the hall, his boots echoing slightly in the large, empty room. One wall was opened up to form a cafeteria-style pass-through from the kitchen. He imagined the bustle of the Boxing Day breakfast, the shouted greetings, the calls for more tea or coffee. Beatrice Mayer offering her noxious brew.

Now, why was she called Mother? Clara had seemed to think he could figure it out without even meeting her. Beatrice Mayer? Mother Bea? He shook his head, but knew he'd get it, eventually. It was the sort of little puzzle he enjoyed.

He went back to his imagination, joining these people for Boxing Day breakfast. The place warm and cheery and festooned with the tackiest Christmas decorations imaginable. He didn't have to spend energy imagining them. They were still up. The plastic and crepe paper stars and snowflakes.

The fake tree, missing at least half its plastic and wire branches. The paper bells and crayoned green and blue snowmen made by the excited and exhausted, and not overly gifted, daycare children. The upright piano in the corner almost certainly had pounded out carols. The room must have been full of the aroma of pancakes and maple syrup, drawn from trees surrounding the town. Eggs and cured Canadian back bacon.

And CC and her family? Where had they sat? Had anyone joined her for her final meal? Had any of them known it was her final meal?

One of them had. Someone had sat in this very room, eating and drinking and laughing and singing Christmas carols on Boxing Day, and planned a murder.

Outside Gamache paused to get his bearings, then, checking his watch, he set out for Lac Brume. He'd always liked Williamsburg. It was quite different from St-Rémy, which was more French while Williamsburg was traditionally more English, though this was changing as the two languages and cultures mixed. As he walked he noticed the lovely homes and shops, all covered in pure white snow. It was quiet: that peace and calm that came in winter as though the earth was resting. Cars barely made any noise on the cushion of snow. People walked silently along the sidewalks, their steps making not a sound. Everything was muffled and mute. It was very, very peaceful.

Four and a half minutes it had taken him to get from the Legion to the lake. He'd not hurried, but he had long legs and he knew most people would take slightly longer. But it was a pretty good average.

He stood at the side of the road looking down over the

lake, empty and obscured now by the snow. The curling rink was almost invisible and the only real evidence anything had happened here were the stands, empty and lonely as though waiting for company that would never come.

What to do about Yvette Nichol? The peace of the place gave him a moment to mull the problem. And problem she was. He knew that now. He'd been fooled by her once, but Armand Gamache wasn't a man to be fooled twice.

She was there for a reason, and the reason wasn't necessarily CC de Poitier's murder.

Inspector Beauvoir drove out of Three Pines and turned toward St-Rémy. After a few minutes down wooded and snowy back roads he turned into a driveway and up to a rambling wooden house. He'd brought an agent with him, just in case. Now he knocked on the door and stood loose-limbed, trying to give the impression he was relaxed, maybe even distracted. He wasn't. He was ready to give chase at any moment. Actually hoped chase would be necessary. Sitting and talking was Chief Inspector Gamache's territory. Running was his.

'*Oui?*' A disheveled middle-aged man stood on the threshold.

'Monsieur Petrov? Saul Petrov?'

'*Oui, c'est moi.*'

'I'm here about the murder of CC de Poitiers. I understand you knew her?'

'I've been waiting for you. What took so long? I have some pictures that might interest you.'

Gamache shrugged out of his huge coat, readjusting his jacket and sweater which had bunched up underneath. Like everyone else in winter, he looked as though someone had put a mouse down his back. He paused for a moment, gathering his thoughts, then walked into the small private room, picked up the phone, and dialed.

'Oh, it's you, Armand. Did you get my present?'

'If you mean Agent Nichol, I did, Superintendent Francoeur. *Merci.*' Gamache spoke jovially into the phone.

'What can I do for you?' Francoeur's voice was deep and smooth and intelligent. No hint of the cunning, the devious, the cruel man who lived in that head.

'I want to know why you sent her.'

'It seemed to me you were too hasty in your judgment, Chief Inspector. Agent Nichol's worked here in narcotics for a year and we're very pleased with her.'

'Then why send her to me?'

'Are you questioning my judgment?'

'No, sir. You know I have no need to wonder why you do anything.'

Gamache knew he'd made a direct hit. Venom poured down the line and filled the great, bare silence.

'Why have you called, Gamache?' snarled the voice, all pretense dropped.

'I wanted to thank you, sir, for sending Agent Nichol. *Joyeux Noël.*'

He hung up then, but he'd already heard the line go dead in his hand. Gamache had what he needed.

He knew he was being frozen out of decision-making at the highest level of the Sûreté du Québec, a level he had once enjoyed. Officially he was still head of homicide and a senior officer in the force. But privately things had changed. Since the Arnot case.

But it was only recently he'd come to appreciate how much had changed. He had had no more requests for Beauvoir to lead other investigations. Agent Isabelle Lacoste had been reassigned more than once since the Arnot case to minor jobs in minor departments, as had other members of his homicide squad. Gamache hadn't thought anything of it, assuming the temporary transfers had been made because they were necessary. It had never occurred to him his people were being punished for something he himself had done.

Until his own boss and friend, Superintendent Michel Brébeuf, had invited Reine-Marie and him for dinner a few weeks ago and had taken him aside after the meal.

'*Ça va, Armand?*'

'*Oui, merci, Michel.* Kids are a worry. Never listen. Young Daniel has quit his job and wants to travel the world with Roslyn. Annie is working too hard, defending poor besieged Alcoha from all those unfair charges. Imagine believing a corporation would knowingly pollute?' Gamache grinned.

'Shocking.' Brébeuf offered him a cognac and a cigar. Gamache accepted the drink but refused the smoke. They sat in Brébeuf's study in companionable silence, listening to Radio Canada and the murmur of the women laughing and getting caught up.

'What did you want to say to me?' Gamache had turned in his chair and was looking directly at Brébeuf.

'One day you're going to be wrong, Armand,' smiled his friend, often at a loss to know how Gamache could guess what he was thinking. But he couldn't divine everything.

'According to you, Michel, I have been wrong, and spectacularly. That day has been and gone.'

'No. Not gone.'

There it was. And as the silence settled once more over the two friends like a snowfall Gamache could suddenly see the depth of the problem. And that he'd unwittingly taken Beauvoir and the others with him. And now they were being buried beneath layers of lies and loathing.

'The Arnot case isn't over, is it?' Gamache held Brébeuf's unblinking eyes. He knew then the courage his friend had shown in telling him this.

'Be careful, Armand. This is more serious than even you know.'

'I believe you're right,' Gamache admitted.

And now Superintendent Francoeur had sent Agent Nichol back. Of course, it could mean nothing. Probably only meant she'd annoyed them so much Francoeur had decided to get his little revenge by sending Nichol to him. Yes, that was the most likely explanation. A malicious little joke, nothing more.

SEVENTEEN

———

'Success,' Beauvoir said, striding into the warm situation room and shedding his heavy coat. He tossed his tuque onto his desk and his mitts soon followed. 'You were right. The photographer has the pictures.'

'Wonderful,' said Gamache, clapping him. 'Let's see.'

'Well, he doesn't have them on him,' said Beauvoir, as though that was really too much to expect.

'Where are they?' asked Gamache, his voice somewhat less thrilled.

'He mailed the film to the lab he uses in St-Lambert. They went by priority post so they should arrive by tomorrow.'

'At the lab.'

'*Précisément.*' Beauvoir could sense a little less enthusiasm than he would have wanted. 'But he says he took hundreds of pictures at the breakfast and the curling.'

Beauvoir looked around. Isabelle Lacoste was engrossed in her computer and Agent Yvette Nichol sat off at the other end of the table by herself, as though on an island, watching the mainland that was Gamache.

'Did he see anything?' Gamache asked.

'I asked. He claims that as a photographer he's so focused on taking the pictures he's not actually paying attention to what's happening, so he was as surprised as anyone when CC keeled over. But he did say his assignment was to photograph CC, and only her, so his camera was trained on her the whole time.'

'Then he must have seen something,' said Gamache.

'He might have,' conceded Beauvoir, 'but maybe he didn't know what he was seeing. Had she been stabbed or bludgeoned or strangled he probably would have reacted, but this was less obvious. All CC did was get up and touch the chair in front of her. Nothing strange in that, certainly nothing threatening.'

It was true.

'Why did she do it?' Gamache asked. 'It's true what you say, though: it certainly wouldn't attract any attention, but it's still an odd thing to do. And we only have Petrov's word that he was busy photographing his client and not busy electrocuting her.'

'I agree,' said Beauvoir, warming his hands by the woodstove and reaching for the coffee pot. 'He seemed eager enough to help. Maybe too eager.' In Beauvoir's world anyone helpful was immediately suspect.

Émilie Longpré set the table for three, folding and smoothing the cloth napkins more than they needed. There was something comforting in the repetitive gesture. Mother hadn't arrived yet, but she'd be there soon. According to the clock on the kitchen wall Mother's noon meditation class would be over soon.

Kaye was having a nap but Em couldn't rest. Where normally she'd be sitting quietly with a cup of tea reading that day's *La Presse*, instead she found herself wiping the tops of cookbooks and watering plants that were already soaked, anything to distract her racing mind.

She occupied herself with the pea soup, stirring the ham bone in the large pot, making sure the flavors combined. Henri was sitting patiently at her feet, staring up at Em with his intense brown eyes as though willpower alone could force the bone to levitate out of the pot and into his eager mouth. His tail wagged as Em bustled around the kitchen and he made sure he got in her way whenever possible.

The corn bread was ready to be put into the oven and by the time it was baked Mother would be there.

And sure enough, half an hour later Mother's car pulled into Em's drive and Mother waddled out, walking without hesitation on the slippery path. Her center of gravity was so low Kaye often remarked that she couldn't fall down even if she wanted to. Nor, according to Kaye, could Mother drown. Kaye, for some reason Em couldn't figure out, never tired of analyzing the ways Bea might meet her maker. Mother Bea returned the favor by endlessly explaining that she at least would meet Him.

Now the three old friends helped themselves to bowls of soup and slices of fresh, warm bread, the butter melting into it. They sat at the comfortable kitchen table. Henri, ordered out of the room, curled up under the table and prayed for crumbs.

Ten minutes later, when Gamache arrived, the food was still in front of each of them, cold and untouched. Had Gamache thought to sneak up to the side window and look in he would have seen the three friends holding hands, encircling the table in a prayer apparently without end.

'Don't worry about the snow, Chief Inspector,' Em said, after Gamache looked behind him at their snowy boot prints on the stone floor of her mudroom. 'Henri and I track it through the house all the time.' She nodded to a German shepherd puppy about six months old who looked as though he was going to explode with excitement. Instead his tail wagged furiously and his bottom, while still technically on the floor, moved with such ferocity Gamache thought he might be able to create fire with it.

Introductions were made, boots removed, and apologies offered for interrupting their lunch. The kitchen smelled of homemade French Canadian pea soup and fresh-baked bread.

'Namaste,' said Mother, putting her hands together and bowing slightly to the men.

'Oh, Christ,' said Kaye. 'Not that again.'

'Namaste?' Gamache asked. Beauvoir hadn't asked because she was old, she was *anglaise* and she was wearing a purple caftan. People like that said ridiculous things all the time.

The chief bowed back, solemnly. Beauvoir pretended he hadn't seen.

'It's an ancient and venerable greeting,' said Beatrice Mayer, smoothing her wild red hair and shooting a concerned look at Kaye, who simply ignored her.

'May I?' The chief pointed to Henri.

'At your peril, monsieur. He might lick you to death,' warned Em.

'Drown in drool is more like it,' said Kaye, turning to walk back into the body of the house.

Gamache knelt down and rubbed Henri's ears, which stood up from his head like two sails. The dog immediately lay on his back and presented his tummy to be rubbed, which Gamache did.

Em led the way through the kitchen and into the living room. The house was inviting and comfortable and had the feel of Grandma's cottage, as though nothing bad could happen here. Even Beauvoir felt relaxed and at home. Gamache suspected everyone felt at home in this place. And with this woman.

Now Émilie Longpré excused herself and returned a moment later with two bowls of soup.

'You look hungry,' she said simply and disappeared again into the kitchen. Before the men could protest they found themselves sitting before the hearth, two steaming bowls of soup and a basket of corn bread in front of them on tray tables. Gamache knew he was being a bit disingenuous. He certainly could have spoken up sooner to stop the three elderly women from waiting on them, but Émilie Longpré was right. They were hungry.

Now the Sûreté homicide investigators ate and listened while the elderly trio answered their questions.

'Can you tell us what happened yesterday?' Beauvoir asked Kaye. 'I understand there was a curling match.'

'Mother had just cleared the house,' began Kaye and Beauvoir immediately regretted his decision to start with her. Nothing in that sentence made sense.

Mother had just cleared the house. *Rien*, no sense at all. Another wacky Anglo. This one, though, was not a complete surprise. He could see her rolling out of the nuthouse for miles. Now she sat in front of him, nearly submerged under layers of thick sweaters and blankets. She looked like a laundry hamper. With a head. A very small, very worn head. All ten hairs on her tiny wizened scalp were standing straight up from the winter static in the house.

She looked like a Muppet with strings.

'*Désolé, mais qu'est-ce que vous avez dit?*' he tried again, in French.

'Mother. Had. Just. Cleared. The. House.' The old woman spoke very distinctly in a voice surprisingly strong.

Gamache, taking everything in, noticed Émilie and Beatrice exchanging smiles. Not maliciously but as a kind of familiar joke as though they'd lived with this all their lives.

'Are we talking about the same thing, madame? Curling?'

'Oh, I see.' Kaye laughed. It was a nice laugh, Beauvoir realized. It changed her face from suspicious and pinched to very pleasant. 'Yes, believe it or not I'm talking about the match. Mother is her.' She pointed a gnarled finger at her friend in the caftan. For some reason it didn't surprise him. He'd taken an immediate dislike to 'Mother', and this was one more reason. Mother. Who insisted on being called Mother? Unless she was a Mother Superior, and, looking at her, Beauvoir doubted it.

She was trouble, he knew. He could sense it, though he'd never use those words and certainly never in front of Gamache.

'What does that mean, madame?' Beauvoir turned back to Kaye, and took a bite of corn bread, trying not to let the butter dribble down his chin.

'"Clearing the house" is a curling term,' said Kaye. 'Em can explain better. She was the skip. That's the captain of the team.'

Beauvoir turned to Madame Longpré. Her blue eyes were thoughtful and lively and perhaps a little tired. Her hair was dyed to a subtle light brown and styled beautifully to her face. She looked contained and kind and she reminded him of Reine-Marie Gamache. He looked briefly at the chief who was listening with his usual calm concentration. When he looked at Madame Longpré did the chief see his wife in thirty years?

'Have you ever curled, Inspector?' Em asked Beauvoir.

Beauvoir was surprised, even offended, by the question. Curl? He played center on the Sûreté hockey team. At thirty-six he creamed men ten years his junior. Curl? He felt embarrassed even thinking the word.

'I can see you probably don't,' Em continued. 'Shame really. It's a marvelous sport.'

'Sport, madame?'

'*Mais oui*. Very difficult. It requires balance and a keen hand-eye co-ordination. You might want to try.'

'Would you show us?' It was the first time Gamache had spoken since they'd sat down. Now he looked at Em warmly and she smiled back, inclining her head.

'How is tomorrow morning?'

'Perfect,' said Gamache.

'Can you describe what was happening up to and including when you realized something was wrong?' Beauvoir turned back to Émilie. Might as well try the sane one.

'We'd been curling for almost an hour. It was a funspiel, so it was shorter than regular games, and being outside we didn't want everyone to get too cold.'

'Didn't work. It was freezing. Coldest I remember,' said Kaye.

'We were losing, as usual,' Em continued. 'At some point I realized the other team had put a whole lot of rocks in the house.'

Seeing Beauvoir's expression she explained. 'The house is the bull's-eye, those red rings painted on the ice. That's where you want your rocks to end up. The other team had done a good job and the house was full of their stones. So I asked Mother to do what's called "clearing the house".'

'I wind up and toss my stone down the ice.' Mother stood up and moved her right arm out in front of her, then swung it behind her, then in one fast movement brought it down and out in front again, pantomiming a pendulum swinging. 'The stone shoots down the ice and hits as many of the rocks out of the house as possible.'

'It sounds like doing the break in pool,' said Beauvoir and realized by their faces that made about as much sense to them as 'clearing the house' had to him.

'It's a lot of fun,' said Mother.

'In fact,' added Em, 'it's so much fun it's become a tradition at the Boxing Day funspiel. I'm convinced most people go just to see Mother clear the house.'

'It's very dramatic, rocks banging everywhere,' said Mother.

'Noisy,' said Kaye.

'It normally signals the end of the match. After that we give up,' said Em. 'Then we all go back to the Legion for a hot buttered rum.'

'Except yesterday,' said Beauvoir. 'What happened yesterday?'

'I didn't know there was any problem until everyone started running toward where Kaye and CC de Poitiers were,' said Mother.

'Neither did I,' said Em. 'I was watching Mother's stone. Everyone was. Then there was a huge cheer, but that suddenly stopped. I thought—'

'What did you think, madame?' Gamache asked, seeing her stricken face.

'She thought I'd keeled over,' said Kaye. 'Didn't you?' Em nodded.

'No such luck. She'll outlive us all,' said Mother. 'She's a hundred and forty-five years old already.'

'That's my IQ,' said Kaye. 'I'm actually ninety-two. Mother's seventy-eight. You don't meet many people whose age is greater than their IQ.'

'When did you realize something had happened?' Beauvoir asked Kaye, casually, trying not to show that this was the key question. Sitting in front of them was really the only witness to the crime.

Kaye thought about it for a moment, her small, wrinkled face looking like a Mrs Potato Head that had been left too long in the sun.

'That woman who died, CC? She was sitting in Em's chair. We always brought our own lawn chairs and put them under the heat lamp. People were very kind and allowed us the warmest seats. Except that horrible woman—'

'Kaye,' said Émilie, a reproach in her voice.

'She was and we all know it. Always bossing people about, moving things, straightening things. I'd put the salt and pepper on the tables for the Legion breakfast and she went around moving them. And complained about the tea.'

'That was my tea,' said Mother. 'She'd never had natural, organic, herbal tisane even though she pretended to have been in India.'

'Please,' said Émilie. 'The poor woman's dead.'

'CC and I were sitting side by side, about five feet apart. As I said, it was quite cold and I was wearing a lot of clothing. I think I might have dozed off. The next thing I know CC's standing at Mother's chair gripping the back of it as though she's going to pick it up and throw it. But she's kind of trembling. Everyone around is cheering and clapping but then I realized CC wasn't cheering at all, but screaming. Then she lets go of the chair and falls down.'

'What did you do?'

'I got up to see what had happened, of course. She was lying on her back and there was a strange smell. I think I must have called out because the next thing I knew there were all these people around. Then Ruth Zardo took over. Bossy woman. Writes horrible poetry. Nothing rhymes. Give me a good bit of Wordsworth any time.'

'Why did she get out of her chair?' Beauvoir asked hastily before Kaye or Gamache or both started quoting.

'How should I know?'

'Did you see anyone else around the chairs? Anyone bending over them, say? Or maybe spilling a drink?'

'Nobody,' said Kaye, firmly.

'Did Madame de Poitiers speak to you at all?' Gamache asked.

Kaye hesitated. 'She seemed disturbed by Mother's chair. There was something about it that was upsetting her, I think.'

'What?' Mother said. 'You never told me that. What could possibly upset her about my chair, except the fact it was mine? She was out to get me, that woman. And now she died holding my chair.'

Mother's face matched her caftan and her bitter voice

175

filled the calm and tranquil room. She seemed to realize how she sounded and regained herself.

'What do you mean, madame?' asked Gamache.

'About what?'

'You said Madame de Poitiers was out to get you. What did you mean by that?'

Mother looked at Émilie and Kaye, as though suddenly lost and frightened.

'She means,' said Kaye, jumping in to save her friend, 'that CC de Poitiers was a stupid, vapid, vindictive woman. And she got what she deserved.'

Agent Robert Lemieux was deep in the bowels of Sûreté headquarters in Montreal, a building he'd seen in recruitment posters, but never actually visited. In recruitment posters he'd also seen a whole lot of happy Québecois gathered respectfully round a Sûreté officer in uniform. That was something else he'd never seen in real life.

He'd found the door, closed, and the name Chief Inspector Gamache had given him stenciled onto the frosted glass.

He knocked and adjusted the leather of his satchel over his shoulder.

'*Venez*,' the voice barked. A thin, balding man looked up from his slanting desk. A pool of light from a small lamp shining on it was the only light in the room. Lemieux had no idea whether the room was tiny or cavernous, though he could guess. He felt claustrophobic.

'You Lemieux?'

'Yes sir. Chief Inspector Gamache sent me.' He took a step further into the room with its formaldehyde smell and intense occupant.

'I know. Otherwise I wouldn't be seeing you. I'm busy. Give me what you've got.'

Lemieux dug into his satchel and pulled out the photograph of Elle's dirty hand.

'So?'

'Well, here, you see?' Lemieux waved an index finger over the middle of the hand.

'You mean these bloodstains?'

Lemieux nodded, trying to look authoritative and praying to God this curt man didn't ask him why.

'I see what he means. Extraordinary. Right, tell the Chief Inspector he'll get it when he gets it. Now go away.'

Agent Lemieux did.

'Well, that was interesting,' said Beauvoir as the two men walked through the gathering snow back to the Incident Room.

'What struck you as interesting?' Gamache asked, his hands behind his back as he walked.

'Mother. She's hiding something.'

'Perhaps. But could she be the murderer? She was curling the whole time.'

'But she might have wired up the chair before the curling began.'

'True. And she might have spilled windshield washer fluid. But how did she get CC to touch the chair before anyone else? There were children running around. Any of them might have grabbed the chair. Kaye might have.'

'Those two fought the whole time we were there. Maybe Madame Thompson was supposed to get electrocuted. Maybe Mother killed the wrong person.'

'It's possible,' said Gamache. 'But I don't think Madame Mayer would risk other lives.'

'So the curlers are out?' Beauvoir asked, disappointed.

'I think so, but when we meet Madame Longpré tomorrow at the lake we'll have a better idea.'

Beauvoir sighed.

He was frankly astonished the entire community hadn't died of boredom. Just talking about curling was sucking the will to live right out of him. It was like some Anglo joke, an excuse to wear plaid and yell. Most Anglos, he'd noticed, didn't like to raise their voices. Francophones were constantly gesturing and shouting and hugging. Beauvoir wasn't sure why Anglos even had arms, except perhaps to carry all their money. Curling at least gave them an excuse to vent. He'd watched the Briar once on CBC television, for a moment. All he remembered was a bunch of men holding brooms and staring at a rock while one of them screamed.

'How could someone have electrocuted CC de Poitiers and no one notice?' Beauvoir asked as they entered the warm Incident Room, stomping their boots to get the worst of the snow off.

'I don't know,' admitted Gamache, walking right past Agent Nichol, who was trying to catch his eye. She'd been sitting at an empty desk when he'd left and she was still there.

Shaking his coat off Gamache hung it up. Beside him Beauvoir was fastidiously brushing the small drift from the shoulders of his own coat.

'Glad I don't have to shovel this.'

'Let every man shovel out his own snow, and the whole city will be passable,' said Gamache. Seeing Beauvoir's puzzled expression he added, 'Emerson.'

'Lake and Palmer?'

'Ralph and Waldo.'

Gamache walked back to his desk, knowing his mind should be on the case, but finding it lingering on Nichol, wondering whether they were both in too deep.

Emerson, Ralph and Waldo? What was that? thought Beauvoir. Some obscure hippy group from the '60s probably. The lyrics didn't even make sense.

While Beauvoir hummed 'Lucky Man', Gamache downloaded his messages, read for half an hour, listened to reports, then put his coat, tuque and gloves back on and took himself off.

Round and round the village green he walked, through the falling snow. He passed people on snowshoes and others gliding along on cross-country skis. He waved at villagers shoveling their paths and driveways. Billy Williams came by, driving a snowplow, throwing cascades of snow off the road and onto people's lawns. No one seemed to mind. What's another foot?

But mostly Gamache thought.

EIGHTEEN

'S ir.'
   'Sir.'
'Sir.'

As Gamache walked back into the Incident Room he was met with a chorus of people wanting to speak to him.

'Sir, Agent Lemieux's on the line from Montreal.'

'Ask him to hold for a moment. I'll take it in there.' He nodded to the small office.

'Sir,' Agent Isabelle Lacoste called across the room. 'I've got a problem here.'

'Sir.' Beauvoir came up beside him. 'We've called the lab about the photos. They don't have them yet, but will let us know as soon as they arrive.'

'Good. Go see if you can help Agent Lacoste. I'll be there shortly. Agent Nichol?'

All activity in the room stopped. It seemed impossible that the cacophony could cease so quickly, but it did. All eyes turned to Nichol, then swung back to Gamache.

'Come with me.'

All eyes, and Nichol, followed Gamache into the tiny office.

'Please sit.' Gamache nodded to the only chair in the room, then picked up the phone. 'Put Lemieux through, please.' He waited a moment. 'Agent? Where are you?'

'I'm at the Old Brewery Mission. But I just came from headquarters. He'll do what you asked.'

'Any idea when?'

'No sir.'

Gamache smiled. He could imagine Lemieux in that horrible room with that brilliant, gifted, horrible man. Poor Lemieux.

'Good work.'

'Thank you. You were right, though. They knew the vagrant here at the Mission.' He sounded excited, as though he'd just split the atom.

'As Elle?'

'Yes sir. They have no other name. But you were right about the other thing. I have the director of the Mission with me. Should I put him on?'

'What's his name?'

'Terry Moscher.'

'*Oui, s'il vous plaît*. Put Mr Moscher on.'

After a pause a deep, authoritative voice came down the line.

'*Bonjour*, Chief Inspector.'

'Monsieur Moscher, I want to make it clear this is not our jurisdiction. This is a murder in Montreal, but we've been invited to make certain discreet inquiries.'

'I understand, Chief Inspector. In answer to your question, Elle stuck to herself a lot. Most do here, so I didn't know her well; none of the staff did. But I asked around and a few of the kitchen staff remember her having a pendant round her neck, some old silver thing they think.'

Gamache closed his eyes in a small prayer for the answer to the next question.

'Did anyone remember what it looked like?'

'No. I asked and one of the cooks said she'd once commented on it to Elle, by way of making conversation, and Elle immediately covered it up. It seemed important to her, but then the strangest things can seem important to street people. They get fixations, obsessions. This seemed to be one of Elle's.'

'One? Did she have others?'

'Probably, but if she did we don't know about it. We try to respect their privacy.'

'I'll let you go, Monsieur Moscher. You must be busy.'

'Winter's always busy. I hope you find out who killed her. Normally it's the weather that gets them. It'll be a killing cold tonight.'

Both men hung up thinking it would be nice to meet the other.

'Sir.' Beauvoir poked his head in the door. 'Could you come out and see what Agent Lacoste has?'

'I'll be there in a minute.'

Beauvoir closed the door but not before glancing at Agent Nichol sitting like a statue on the chair, her clothes dull and ill fitting, her hairstyle ten years out of date, her eyes and complexion gray. Most women in Quebec, certainly the Québecoises, were stylish and even elegant. The younger ones were often daring in their dress. Even in the Sûreté. Agent Lacoste, for instance, was only slightly older than

Nichol but she seemed a world away. She carried herself with élan. Her hair was always clean and cut in a casually elegant fashion, her clothes were simple with a dash of color and individuality. Of course, Nichol's attire and demeanor were also unique. Their dullness set her apart. Beauvoir wished he could stay and hear the chief give her hell for daring to show up again.

Once the door closed, Gamache turned to consider the young woman sitting in front of him.

She annoyed him. Just looking at her pathetic, 'poor-me' demeanor set his skin on edge. She was manipulative and bitter and arrogant. He knew that.

But he also knew he'd been wrong.

That's what he'd been considering as he'd circled the village green. Round and round he'd gone but always came back to the same place.

He'd been wrong.

'I'm sorry,' he said, looking her directly in the eye. She looked back expectantly, as though bracing herself for more. I'm sorry, but you're fired. I'm sorry, but you're going home. I'm sorry, but you're a pathetic loser and I don't want you anywhere close to this investigation.

And she was right. There was more.

'I ignored you and that was wrong.'

Still she waited, watching his face. Watching those deep brown eyes, so stern and thoughtful. He looked down at her, his hands folded casually in front of him, his hair and moustache well groomed. The small room smelled slightly of sandalwood. It was so subtle she wondered whether she was imagining it, but thought not. All her senses were heightened, waiting for the execution. The next sentence that would send her back to Montreal in disgrace. Back to narcotics. And back to her tiny, immaculate home in east end Montreal, with its front vegetable garden now under snow, and her father, so proud of her successes.

How could she tell him she'd been fired, again? This was her last chance. Too many people were counting on her. Not just her father, but also the Superintendent.

'I'm going to give you another chance, agent. I want you to look into the backgrounds of Richard Lyon and his daughter Crie. School, finances, friends, family. I'd like the information by tomorrow morning.'

Nichol rose as though in a dream. In front of her Chief Inspector Gamache had a small smile on his face and warmth in his eyes for the first time since she'd shown up.

'You said you've changed?'

Nichol nodded. 'I know I was horrible last time. I'm so sorry. I'll do better this time. Really.'

He looked at her closely and nodded. Then extended his hand. 'Good. Then maybe we can begin again. A fresh start.'

She slipped her small hand into his.

The asshole believed her.

Outside in the Incident Room Beauvoir saw the handshake and fervently hoped they were saying goodbye, but he had his doubts. Nichol left the room and he hurried over.

'You didn't.'

'Didn't what, Jean Guy?'

'You know perfectly well. You didn't put her back on the team?'

'I had no choice. Superintendent Francoeur assigned her to me.'

'You could have refused.'

Gamache smiled. 'Choose your battles, Jean Guy. This isn't one I need to fight. Besides, she might have changed.'

'Oh, God. How many times are you going to try to kick that football?'

'You think I'm making the same mistake?'

'Don't you?'

Gamache looked out the window to Nichol already on a computer.

'Well, at least I'll know when to cringe.'

'You're cringing a little now, sir. You don't really believe her, do you?'

Gamache walked out of the tiny room and made for Agent Isabelle Lacoste's station.

'What've you got?'

'I've been at it all morning and I can't find anything on Cecilia de Poitiers or her parents. Nothing. I scanned her book, weird stuff by the way, to see if I could find any clues there. You'd mentioned France, so I'd already put in a request to the Sûreté there. Half an hour ago I got this reply.'

Gamache leaned into the computer and read the email from Paris.

Do not bother us with hoaxes.

'Well, *zut alors*,' said Gamache. 'What did you do?'

'I wrote this.' She showed him another email.

Dear stupid, ridiculous fuckers, You running dog assholes in the almighty Sûreté in Paris have your heads so far up your asses you wouldn't know a legitimate inquiry if one bit you on your scrawny little testicles. We're busy solving crimes here while you're dreaming of the day you have half the intelligence we have, you pig-shit farts.

Sincerely, Agent Isabelle Lacoste, Sûreté du Québec.

'That's certainly one way to handle it.' Gamache smiled.

Beauvoir was impressed and looking forward to another fantasy.

'I didn't send it.' Lacoste looked wistfully at the message. 'Instead I placed a call to the homicide squad in Paris,' she said. 'If I don't hear from them in a few minutes I'll call again. I don't understand their answer. Have you had dealings with them, sir?'

'A few. I've never had a reply like that.' He looked again at the terse message from Paris. It was yet another thing about this case that seemed to make no sense.

Why would they think this was a hoax?

Gamache sat at his desk and began to go through the stack of papers and messages waiting for him. He came across Lemieux's list of the contents of CC de Poitiers's garbage. It was a routine check and rarely helpful since murderers were almost never stupid enough to just throw evidence in their own trash. But Richard Lyon had struck Gamache as, if not stupid, at least close kin to it.

He got himself a coffee, sat down and began reading.

Assorted foods

Milk and pizza cartons

Old, broken bracelet

Two wine bottles, cheap variety

Newspapers

Empty cereal box, fruit loops

A video cassette – *The Lion in Winter*

Plastic juice containers

Candy wrappers – Mars bars

Gift wrapping

Box from Inuit shop in Montreal

These people certainly didn't believe in recycling, thought Gamache. He presumed the video was broken and that the box from the Inuit shop had contained the boots. There was no material for wiring up a heat lamp. There was no empty container of windshield washer fluid.

Too much to ask, really.

Saul Petrov paced the living room of his rented chalet. Outside the snow was beginning to let up. Should he tell the cops about what CC had said? She'd been looking for something in Three Pines, she'd made that clear enough. Money, he was sure. Had she found it?

He'd visited her husband that morning after talking to the Sûreté, just to try to get a feel for the place, and maybe snoop around. Richard Lyon had been cool; unwelcoming even. In fact, his response had surprised Petrov. He hadn't thought the man capable of standing up for himself. Lyon had always seemed so weak, so bumbling. But he'd managed to make it clear that Saul wasn't welcome.

Lyon had reason to dislike him, Saul knew. And soon he'd have even more reason.

Now Petrov paced from one end of the overstuffed living room to the other, kicking the day's newspapers out of his way and toward the fireplace. He was losing patience. What should he tell the cops? What should he keep for himself? Maybe he'd wait until the pictures were developed. He'd told the cops the truth. He had sent them off to his lab. But not all. He'd kept one roll back. One roll that might make him enough money to finally retire and maybe buy this place, and get to know the people of Three Pines. And maybe even find that fantastic artist whose portfolio CC had trashed.

He smiled to himself. CC might not have found her treasure in Three Pines, but he had. He picked up the small roll of film and looked at it, black and hard in his palm. He was an ethical man, though his ethics were situational and this was a very promising situation indeed.

'Vous avez dit "l'Aquitaine"? J'ai besoin de parler à quelqu'un là-bas? Mais pourquoi?' Isabelle Lacoste was struggling to keep the annoyance out of her voice. She knew the person she was most annoyed at was herself. She felt stupid. It was not something she felt often, but here was a quite patient and apparently intelligent agent with the Sûreté in Paris telling her to call the Aquitaine. She didn't even know what the Aquitaine was.

'What is the Aquitaine?' she had to ask. Not to would have been even stupider.

'It's a region in France,' he said, his voice in his nose. Still, it was a nice voice and he wasn't trying to make her feel bad, just trying to give her information.

'Why would I want to call there?' This was turning into a game.

'Because of the names you gave me, of course. Eleanor de Poitiers. Eleanor of Aquitaine. Here's the number of the local gendarmerie there.'

He'd given her the number and the officer there had also laughed and said no, she couldn't speak to Eleanor de Poitiers, 'unless you're planning to die in the next moment'.

'What do you mean?' She was getting tired of hearing laughter, and getting tired of asking the same question. Still, working with Armand Gamache she'd watched his near endless supply of patience and knew that was what was called for here.

'She's dead,' the constable said.

'Dead? Murdered?'

More laughter.

'If you have something to tell me, please do.' She'd practice patience tomorrow.

'Think about it. Eleanor de Poitiers.' He said it very slowly and loudly as though that would help. 'I must go. My shift ends at ten o'clock.'

He hung up. Lacoste automatically checked her watch. Quarter past four. In Quebec. Quarter past ten in France. The man had at least given her extra time.

But to what end?

She looked around. Gamache and Beauvoir had left. So had Agent Nichol.

Turning back to her computer Agent Lacoste went to Google and typed in 'Eleanor of Aquitaine'.

NINETEEN

⁓

The walls of the meditation room were a soothing aqua. The floor was carpeted in a deep, warm green. The ceiling was cathedral and a fan moved lazily around. Some pillows were piled in the corners, awaiting bottoms, Gamache guessed.

He and Beauvoir had driven into St-Rémy to visit Mother Bea at her meditation center. He turned around, taking in the floor to ceiling windows looking into the darkness. All he could see was his own reflection, and Beauvoir behind him standing as though he'd entered the Gates of Hell.

'You expecting some spirit to attack?'

'You never know.'

'I thought you were an atheist.'

'I don't believe in God, but there might be ghosts. Do you smell something?'

'It's incense.'

'I think it's making me sick.'

Gamache turned to the back wall. Written in fine calligraphy across the top was *Be Calm*. The name of Madame

Mayer's center was Be Calm. Coincidentally, it was also what CC had called her business and her book.

Be Calm.

Ironically, neither woman, from what he could tell, was gifted with calm.

Below the words there was more writing on the wall. The sun had set and the room was lit discreetly. He couldn't make out the writing from where he was so he moved closer but as he approached Mother arrived, her purple caftan billowing behind her and her hair sticking out like a firestorm.

'Hello, welcome. Have you come for the five o'clock class?'

'No, madame.' Gamache smiled. 'We came to visit you, to ask for your help.'

Mother stood in front of him, warily. She seemed a woman used to traps, or at least to imagining them.

'It's obvious to me you're a woman of sensitivities. You see and feel things others don't. I hope I'm not being presumptuous.'

'I don't think I'm any more intuitive than anyone else,' she said. 'If anything I've been blessed to have been able to work on myself. Probably because I needed it more than most.' She smiled at Gamache and ignored Beauvoir.

'The enlightened are always the last to say it,' said Gamache. 'We wanted to speak to you in private, madame, to get your help. We need your insights on Madame de Poitiers.'

'I didn't know her well.'

'But you wouldn't have to, would you? You're a teacher; you see so many people from all walks. You probably know them better than they know themselves.'

'I try not to be judgmental, Chief Inspector.'

'Not judgment, madame, discernment.'

'CC de Poitiers was, I believe, in a lot of pain.' Mother led them over to a gathering of pillows and indicated one. Gamache sat, more or less falling the last third of the way down. He only just stopped himself from tumbling over backwards. Beauvoir decided not to risk it. Besides, it was ridiculous and perhaps even insulting to offer a homicide investigator a pillow to sit on.

Mother lowered herself expertly, landing in the center of the crimson pillow like a paratrooper. Granted, she hadn't all that far to fall.

'A lost soul, I believe. Had she not been murdered and had she had the humility to ask I believe I could have helped her.'

Beauvoir thought maybe he was going to throw up.

'She came here once, you know. I was heartened to see her, imagining she'd come to seek guidance. But I was wrong.'

'What did she want?'

'I have no idea.' Now Mother looked genuinely puzzled. It was, Beauvoir thought, the first real thing about her. 'I came in and she was standing over there, straightening the pictures.' Mother indicated some framed photographs on the wall and a couple on what looked like a small shrine. 'She had her fingers on everything in the room. Everything had been moved.'

'How so?'

'Well, kind of lined up. When the classes are over the students just toss the pillows into the corners, as you can see. I like it like that. It's God's will where the pillows land. I don't like imposing myself too much.'

Another wave of nausea washed over Beauvoir.

'But CC didn't seem to be able to enter a room without touching and straightening everything. Very unevolved. No room for the spirit if you need to do that. All the cushions were neatly stacked and lined up with the wall, all the pictures in perfect alignment, everything just so.'

'Why did she come here?' Gamache asked.

'I don't really know. When she saw me she looked surprised, as though I'd caught her doing something wrong. After she left I looked around to see if anything was missing, she'd looked so guilty. She tried to cover it up by being aggressive. Very typical.'

'Of what?' Gamache asked.

The question seemed to stump Mother and Beauvoir wondered whether she wasn't used to being questioned.

'Well, of unhappy people, of course,' she snipped after a moment. 'I had the impression she was looking for something, and I don't mean enlightenment. I think she was so deluded she actually thought she had that. But a less enlightened person would be hard to find.'

'Very discerning of you,' said Gamache. Mother looked closely for signs of sarcasm. 'What makes you think she thought she was enlightened?'

'Have you read her book? It's smug and self-satisfied. She had no center, no real beliefs. She grabbed whatever philosophy floated by. A bit of this, a bit of that. She'd cobbled together a bumpy, pitted, muddy spiritual path. It reminded me of Frankenstein. She'd cannibalized all sorts of faiths and beliefs and came up with that Li Bien.'

The word 'crap' was implied.

'She wasn't balanced.' Mother lifted her arms and spread them out in what looked like an embrace, the folds of her purple caftan dripping down so that she resembled something out of a Renaissance painting, by a not very good artist.

'Tell me about Li Bien,' Gamache said.

'It has something to do with holding emotions inside. She seemed to think emotions were at the root of all our problems, so the trick was to not show them and best of all not feel them.'

'And Li Bien itself, is that an ancient teaching, like Zen?'

'Li Bien? Never heard of it. As far as I know, she made it up.'

Gamache, who'd read CC de Poitiers's book, was interested to see that Mother, while strictly accurate, had left some crucial pieces out. Like the Li Bien ball. The basis of CC de Poitiers's teachings and the one thing passed on to her from a long dead mother. She talked about it in some detail in the book and it had struck Gamache as the only part of her story that was actually meaningful to her. It was as though CC had indeed been given this gift from her mother and knew it to be precious, but didn't know how or why. And so she'd manufactured an entire belief system around it.

She made the Li Bien ball into something holy. And now it was nowhere to be found. He'd had agents search her home in the Notre Dame de Grace *quartier* of Montreal. They'd come up with nothing, except a desire to leave its antiseptic atmosphere. Agents had again searched the old Hadley house, and found nothing.

Of course, it was possible he was wrong and the Li Bien ball never existed. Maybe Mother was right and she'd made that up too.

'Wasn't there something about light too?' he asked, wondering what Mother would say to that.

'Well, yes, but that was even more convoluted. She seemed to think anything light or white was spiritual and colors, like red or blue, were evil. She even went so far as to assign each color an emotion. Red was anger, blue was depression, yellow was cowardice or fear, something like that. I can't remember, except that it was pretty weird. I don't know if she believed it herself, but the message she was peddling was that the lighter and whiter you were the better.'

'Was she a racist?'

Mother hesitated. It seemed to Gamache she was longing to paint CC in as bad a light as possible, and racist was pretty bad. But, to give her credit, she didn't.

'I don't think so. I think she was talking about interior stuff. Emotions and feelings. Her idea was that if all our emotions are kept inside, and if they're in alignment, then we're balanced.'

'What did she mean by alignment?'

'You must remember science class? This is where CC was actually quite clever, and very dangerous in my opinion. She'd take something that had a bit of truth or fact and then stretch it beyond recognition. In science we learn that white is the presence of all colors. If you combine them all you get white, whereas black is the absence of color. So, according to CC, if emotions are colors and you're emotional, angry, sad, jealous, whatever, then one color is dominant and you're out of balance. The idea is to achieve white. All colors, all emotions, in alignment.'

All Beauvoir heard was blah, blah, blah. He'd long since stopped paying attention and was staring at a poster of India on the wall, trying to pretend he was standing on the barren mountain beside the man in the loincloth. Anything was better than this.

'Was she right?'

Mother was taken aback by the simple question.

'No, she wasn't right. Her beliefs were ludicrous and insulting. She advised people to swallow their emotions. Her book, if followed by anyone, would lead to serious mental illness. She was nuts.'

Mother took a deep breath and tried to recover her own balance.

'And yet,' Gamache continued in a pleasant voice, 'isn't that what's often taught in meditation? Not the absence of emotion, or swallowing them, but not allowing them to run the show? And isn't one of the disciplines in meditation the chakras?'

'Yes, that's true, but that's different. I myself teach the chakra method of meditation. I learned it from him.' She pointed to the poster Beauvoir had entered. 'In India. It's a method for achieving balance, inside and out. There are seven centers in the body, from the top of your head to, well, your privates. Each has a color, and when they're in alignment you're balanced. If you're interested, come to one of my classes. In fact, one's about to start.'

She rocked herself out of the cushion and to her feet. Gamache also got up, but slightly less gracefully. She waddled toward the door, hurrying them out. Gamache stopped and looked more closely at the writing on the wall.

Be Calm, and know that I am God.

'That's beautiful,' he said. 'It sounds familiar.'

Did Mother hesitate a moment before answering?

'It's from Isaiah.'

'You called your center Be Calm. Did you get the name from this?' He nodded toward the wall.

'Yes. I'm a little embarrassed about having what's essentially a Christian saying on my walls, but this is an inclusive community. The people who come here to do yoga and meditate believe all sorts of things. Some are Christians, some Jews, some follow the Buddha, some lean more toward the Hindu teachings. We take what's meaningful from each faith. We're not dogmatic here.'

Gamache noticed that when she did it, it was a virtue, whereas when CC did it it was grotesque.

'Though Isaiah is the Old Testament, so you're off the Christian hook.' Gamache smiled. 'Why did you choose that particular saying?'

'It's actually quite close to the Buddhist belief that if we're quiet and calm we'll find God,' Mother explained. 'It's a beautiful thought.'

'It is indeed,' said Gamache, and meant it. 'Quiet and calm.' He turned away from the saying and looked down directly into the eyes of the elderly woman beside him. 'And still.'

Mother barely hesitated. 'And still, Chief Inspector.'

'*Merci, Madame.*' He put a firm hand on Beauvoir's arm and guided him to the door. Beauvoir didn't even bother zipping his coat. He dived out the door and into the frigid evening feeling as though he'd plunged into a cold mountain stream. He coughed and sputtered as the freezing air hit his lungs, but he didn't care. He was finally coming back to his senses.

'Here, give me the keys.' Gamache held out his hand and Beauvoir, without protest, dropped them in. 'You all right?' He got the Inspector into the passenger's seat.

'I'm fine. That woman, that place.' He waved a weary hand

around his head. He still felt nauseous and hoped he'd be able to hold it in until they got back to the B&B. But he couldn't.

Five minutes later Gamache was holding Beauvoir's head at the side of the road as he vomited and coughed and cursed that woman and her cloying claustrophobic calm.

TWENTY

~

'I'll be fine.' Beauvoir looked like death.

'Eventually, yes,' said Gamache as he practically carried the man up the stairs and into Beauvoir's bedroom at the B&B. He helped Beauvoir undress and ran a bath, and eventually, clean and warm, Beauvoir subsided into the large comfortable bed, with its soft flannel sheets and eiderdown duvet. Gamache fluffed up the pillows and brought the duvet up to Beauvoir's chin, all but tucking him in. He placed the tray with tea and crackers within reach.

Beauvoir's feet rested on a hot water bottle, wrapped in a cozy, the warmth spreading slowly from his freezing feet up his shivering body. Beauvoir had never felt so sick or so relieved.

'Feel better?'

Beauvoir nodded, trying not to let his teeth chatter. Gamache put his huge cool hand on the younger man's brow and held it there a moment, looking into Beauvoir's feverish eyes.

'I'll get you another hot water bottle. How does that sound?'

'Yes please.'

Beauvoir felt as if he was about three years old, sick, and looking beseechingly into his father's strong and certain eyes. Gamache returned a few minutes later with the hot water bottle.

'She cursed me,' said Beauvoir, curling himself round the hot water bottle, no longer caring whether he looked like a little girl.

'You have the flu.'

'That Mother woman cursed me with the flu. Oh, God, do you think I've been poisoned?'

'It's the flu.'

'Bird flu?'

'People flu.'

'Or SARS.' Beauvoir struggled up. 'Am I dying of SARS?'

'It's the flu,' Gamache said. 'I need to leave. Here's the cell phone, here's a cup of tea. Here's the wastepaper basket.' He held the tin bucket up for Beauvoir to see, then placed it on the floor by the bed. His own mother had called it a 'burp bowl' when he'd been sick as a child, though they both knew burping wasn't the problem. 'Now rest and sleep.'

'I'll be dead when you get back.'

'I'll miss you.' Gamache straightened the fluffy white duvet, felt the man's forehead again, and tiptoed out. Beauvoir was already asleep.

'How is he?' Gabri asked as Gamache descended the staircase.

'Asleep. Will you be here for a while?'

'I'll make sure I am.'

Gamache put his coat on and stood at the threshold. 'Getting colder.'

'Snow's stopped. I hear tomorrow's supposed to get down to minus twenty.'

Both men looked out the door. The sun had long since set and the trees and pond were lit. A few people were walking their dogs and skating. The bistro was throwing its welcoming light and the door opened and closed as villagers went for their late afternoon toddy.

'Must be five,' said Gabri, nodding toward the village green. 'Ruth. She looks almost lifelike.'

Gamache left the warmth of the B&B and hurried round the Commons. He considered pausing to speak to Ruth but decided against it. Something about the woman warned against casual, or any kind of, conversation. His feet squeaked on the snow, a sure sign that the temperature was plunging. His face felt as though he was walking through a cloud of tiny needles and his eyes watered slightly. With regret he walked past the bistro. It had been his intention to sit in the bistro each afternoon with a quiet drink to review his notes and meet the villagers.

The bistro was his secret weapon in tracking down murderers. Not just in Three Pines, but in every town and village in Quebec. First he found a comfortable café or brasserie, or bistro, then he found the murderer. Because Armand Gamache knew something many of his colleagues never figured out. Murder was deeply human, the murdered and the murderer. To describe the murderer as a monstrosity, a grotesque, was to give him an unfair advantage. No. Murderers were human, and at the root of each murder was an emotion. Warped, no doubt. Twisted and ugly. But an emotion. And one so powerful it had driven a man to make a ghost.

Gamache's job was to collect the evidence, but also to collect the emotions. And the only way he knew to do that was to get to know the people. To watch and listen. To pay attention. And the best way to do that was in a deceptively casual manner in a deceptively casual setting.

Like the bistro.

As he walked by he wondered whether the murderer was in there now, enjoying a Scotch or hot cider on this cold night. Warming himself by the open hearth and by the company of friends. Or was the murderer out here, in the cold and dark? An outsider, bitter and brittle and broken?

He walked over the arched stone bridge, enjoying the silence of the village. Snow did that. It laid down a simple, clean duvet that muffled all sound and kept everything beneath alive. Farmers and gardeners in Quebec wished for two things in winter: lots of snow and continuous cold. An early thaw was a disaster. It tricked the young and vulnerable into exposing themselves, only to be nipped in the root. A killing frost.

'And then he falls, as I do,' quoted Gamache to himself, surprised by the reference. Wolsey's farewell. Shakespeare, of course. But why had he suddenly thought of that quote?

The third day comes a frost, a killing frost;
And, when he thinks, good easy man, full surely
His greatness is a-ripening, nips his root,
And then he falls, as I do.

Was he falling? Was he being lulled into believing he was in control, that everything was going to plan?

The Arnot case isn't over, his friend Michel Brébeuf had warned. Is a killing frost on the way? Gamache clapped his arms round himself a few times for warmth and reassurance. He snorted in amusement and shook his head. It was quite humbling. One moment he was the distinguished Chief Inspector Gamache, head of homicide for the Sûreté du Québec, investigating a murder, the next he was chasing his imagination all over the countryside.

Now he paused and again took in the venerable village, with its ring of old, well-loved homes, inhabited by well-loved people.

Even Ruth Zardo. It was a tribute to this quiet, calm place that its people found space in their hearts for someone as wounded as Ruth.

And CC de Poitiers? Would they have been able to find a place for her? Or her husband and child?

He reluctantly raised his eyes from the glowing circle of light that was Three Pines up to the darkness and the old Hadley house, sitting like the error that proved the point. It stood outside the circle, on the verge of the village. Beyond the pale.

Was the murderer in there, in that foreboding and forbidding place that seemed to breed and radiate resentment?

Gamache stood in the freezing cold and wondered why CC had wanted to breed resentment. Why had she created it at every turn? He had yet to find a soul saddened by her death. Her departure diminished no one, from what he could see. Not even her family. Perhaps especially not her family. He tilted his head slightly to one side as though that might help his thinking. It didn't. Whatever small idea he'd had was lost. Something about breeding resentment.

Now he turned and walked toward the old railway station, lit and almost as welcoming as the bistro.

'Chief,' Lacoste called as soon as he entered, cold air clinging to him. 'Am I glad to see you. Where's the Inspector?'

'Sick. He thinks Beatrice Mayer put a curse on him.'

'Wouldn't be the first woman.'

'True.' Gamache laughed. 'Where's Agent Nichol?'

'Gone. Made a few calls then disappeared a couple of hours ago.' She watched to see if his face reflected how she felt. Nichol had buggered up again. It was as though she had a compulsion to screw up her career and their cases. But Gamache didn't react.

'What've you got?'

'A mountain of messages. The coroner called. She says she'll meet you in Olivier's Bistro at five thirty. She lives around here, doesn't she?'

'In a village called Cleghorn Halt, down the railway line. This is on her way home. Does she have something?'

'The completed autopsy report. Wants to talk to you about it. Also you have a call from Agent Lemieux in Montreal. He says he sent something to you over the internet. It's from headquarters. But he also wants a callback. But, before you do . . .' She walked back to her desk, Gamache following. 'I found Eleanor de Poitiers.'

Lacoste sat and clicked her computer. A picture appeared. It was a black and white drawing of a medieval woman on horseback carrying a flag.

'Go on,' said Gamache.

'That's it. That's her. Eleanor de Poitiers was Eleanor of Aquitaine. Her.' She pointed to the screen. Gamache pulled up a chair and sat beside Lacoste, his brows drawn together and his whole body leaning forward, drawn to the screen. He stared, trying to make sense of it.

'Tell me what you know.'

'What I know or what I think? Either way, it's not much. CC de Poitiers listed her mother and father as Eleanor and Henri de Poitiers, of France. In her book,' Lacoste pointed to the copy on her desk, 'she describes her childhood of privilege in France. Then there was some sort of financial catastrophe and she was sent away to Canada, to live with distant, unnamed relatives, right?'

Gamache nodded.

'Well, Eleanor is her.' Once more Lacoste nodded to the medieval equestrienne, then she clicked again and the screen changed. 'And that's her father.' A picture came up of a stern, strong, blond man wearing a crown. 'Henry Plantagenet. King Henry the Second of England.'

'I don't understand.'

'The only Henry and Eleanor de Poitiers in France are them.' Again Lacoste pointed to the screen, now split and showing both old drawings.

'But it doesn't make any sense,' said Gamache, struggling with the information.

'You've never been a teenage girl.'

'What do you mean?'

'This is the sort of thing that appeals to romantic girls. A strong and tragic queen, a noble king. The Crusades. Eleanor de Poitiers actually went on crusade with her first husband. She created an army of three hundred women and rode bare-breasted part of the way. At least, that's the story. She eventually divorced Louis of France and married Henry.'

'And lived happily ever after?'

'Not exactly. He put her in prison, but not before she'd had four sons. Richard the Lionheart was one. She was amazing.' Lacoste gazed at the woman on horseback and imagined being part of her army. Riding bare-breasted through Palestine in the wake of this remarkable woman. It wasn't just teenagers who were drawn to Eleanor of Aquitaine.

'Richard the Lionheart?' Gamache asked. 'But no daughter named CC?'

'Who was a designer living in Three Pines? No. King Henry died in 1189. Eleanor in 1204. So either CC de Poitiers was long overdue for death herself or, just maybe, she was lying. No wonder the entire Sûreté in Paris was laughing at me. Thank God I told them I was Agent Nichol.'

Gamache shook his head. 'So she made them up. She reached back almost a millennium to create parents. Why? Why would she do it? And why them?'

The two sat in silence for a moment, thinking.

'So who were her real parents?' Lacoste finally asked.

'I think that might be an important question.'

Gamache went to his desk. It was twenty past five. Just time to speak to Lemieux before meeting Dr Harris. He downloaded his messages and dialed the number left by Lemieux.

'Agent Lemieux,' came the shouted answer.

'It's Gamache,' he shouted back down the line, not sure why he was shouting.

'Chief, I'm glad you called. Did you get the drawing from the Sûreté artist? He said he'd email it to you.'

'I'm just opening my messages now. What did he say and why are we yelling?'

'I'm at the bus station. A bus just arrived. The Sûreté artist said it looked as though Elle had been holding something in her hand as she died, and it had cut into it.'

'And that explains the pattern of cuts in her palm?'

'Exactly.' The bus must have left or shut off because the background noise settled down. Lemieux spoke normally. 'I gave him the autopsy picture and he drew a sketch as you asked. It's not very precise, as you'll see.'

As Lemieux spoke Gamache was going through his messages, looking for the one from the eccentric artist in the bowels of Sûreté headquarters. He clicked on it and waited while the excruciatingly slow dial-up connection downloaded the image.

Little by little a picture emerged.

'I've talked to other vagrants here about Elle,' Lemieux continued. 'They're not a very talkative lot but most remember her. There was a scuffle over her spot when she left. Apparently she had the equivalent of a penthouse suite. Right over one of the heating grates. Strange that she'd leave it.'

'Strange indeed,' Gamache mumbled as he watched the image haltingly appear on his screen. It was only half there. 'You've done well, Lemieux. Come home.'

'Yes sir.'

Gamache smiled. He could almost see the grin on Lemieux's face.

For the next five minutes Gamache stared at the screen, watching the image download. A centimeter at a time. And when it was finished Gamache sat back in his chair, hands folded over his stomach, and stared.

He suddenly remembered himself and looked at the clock. Five thirty-five. Time to meet the coroner.

TWENTY-ONE

—

Dr Sharon Harris had just settled into her easy chair and ordered a Dubonnet when Gamache arrived, full of apologies and smiles. He joined her in a Dubonnet and sat down. They had a window seat, looking through the mullions at the frozen pond and Christmas trees. Over her shoulder he could see the fire crackling and playing in the hearth. Dr Harris was absently toying with a discreet white tag hanging from their table. She glanced at it.

'Two hundred and seventy dollars.'

'Not the Dubonnet, I hope.' Gamache stopped his untouched drink partway to his mouth.

'No.' She laughed. 'The table.'

'*Santé.*' He took a sip and smiled. He'd forgotten. Everything in the bistro was an antique, collected by Olivier. And everything was for sale. He could finish his drink and buy the cut crystal glass. It was, actually, a lovely glass. As he held it up and looked through it the crystal picked up and refracted the amber light from the fireplace, splitting it into parts. Like a very warm rainbow. Or the chakras, he thought.

'Are you still looking to move here?' he asked, bringing himself back to the table and catching her wistful gaze out the window.

'If a place comes up I would, though when they do they get bought fast.'

'The old Hadley home came up about a year ago.'

'Except that place, though I have to admit I looked at the listing. Cheap. Almost gave it away.'

'How much were they asking?'

'I can't remember exactly but it was less than a hundred thousand.'

'*C'est incroyable*,' said Gamache, taking a handful of cashews.

Dr Harris looked around the bistro, filling up with patrons. 'No one seems too bothered by the murder. Not a popular woman, our victim?'

'No, it seems not. She was the one who bought the Hadley house.'

'Ahh,' said Dr Harris.

'Ahh?' questioned Gamache.

'Anyone who'd buy that house must have been insensitive in the extreme. I didn't even like looking at its picture on the computer listing.'

'People have different sensibilities.' Gamache smiled.

'True,' she agreed, 'but would you buy it?'

'I don't even like going in it,' he whispered to her conspiratorially. 'Gives me the willies. What've you got for me?'

Dr Harris leaned down and drew a dossier from her briefcase. Placing it on the table she took a handful of nuts, leaned back and looked out the window again, sipping her drink between salty mouthfuls.

Gamache put on his half-moon reading glasses and spent

the next ten minutes going over the report, finally putting it down and taking a contemplative sip of Dubonnet.

'Niacin,' he said.

'Niacin,' she agreed.

'Tell me about it.'

'Besides the niacin she was a healthy, though perhaps underweight, forty-eight-year-old woman. She'd given birth. She was pre-menopausal. All very natural and normal. Her feet were charred from the shock and her hands were blistered, in the same pattern as the tubing of the chair. There was a tiny cut underneath that but it was old and healing. It's all consistent with electrocution except for one thing. The niacin.'

Gamache leaned forward, taking his glasses from his face and tapping them gently on the manila folder. 'What is it?'

'A vitamin. One of the B complex.' She leaned forward so that they were both talking over the table. 'It's prescribed for high cholesterol and some people take it thinking it can increase brain power.'

'Can it?'

'No evidence.'

'Then why do they think that?'

'Well, what it does produce is a facial flush, and I guess someone thought that meant blood was rushing to the brain and you know what that can only mean.'

'More brain power.'

'Isn't it obvious?' She shook her head in disdain. 'Fitting that people with so little brain power would come to that conclusion. A normal dose is five milligrams. It's enough to slightly raise the heart rate and the blood pressure. As I said, it's often prescribed by doctors, but it's also available over the counter. I don't think you can overdose on it. In fact, it's even put into some breakfast cereals. Niacin and thiamin.'

'So if the normal dose is five, what did CC have in her?'

'Twenty.'

'Phew. That's a lot of cereal.'

'Captain Crunch a suspect?'

Gamache laughed, the wrinkles round his eyes falling into familiar folds.

'What would twenty milligrams have done to her?' he asked.

'Produced quite a flush. A classic hot flash. Sweating, discoloration of her face.' Dr Harris thought some more. 'I'm not all that familiar with it so I looked it up in the pharmacopoeia guide. There's nothing dangerous about niacin. Uncomfortable, yes, but not dangerous. If the person was hoping to kill her, he got it wrong.'

'No, I think he got it just right. He did kill her, and niacin was an accomplice. CC de Poitiers was electrocuted, right?'

Dr Harris nodded.

'And you more than anyone knows how hard that is.'

Again she nodded.

'Especially in the middle of winter. She had to not just touch a power source, but she had to be standing in a puddle with metal boots and . . .'

He left it dangling. Dr Harris thought about it for a moment. Tried to see the scene in her mind. The woman standing in a puddle at the chair, reaching out – 'Bare hands. She had to have bare hands. That's how he did it. And I thought you'd asked for the extensive blood work in case of poisoning.'

'The gloves. I kept asking myself, why did she take off her gloves? Why would anyone?'

'Because she was hot,' said Dr Harris. She loved her job but she envied Gamache and Beauvoir the ability to put all the pieces together.

'Someone at the community breakfast slipped her enough niacin to produce a flush. How long would it take?' Gamache asked.

'About twenty minutes.'

'Enough time for her to be at the curling when it came on. At some point she began to get flushed and removed her gloves and probably her hat. We'll see in the pictures tomorrow.'

'What pictures?'

'There was a photographer there. CC hired him to take publicity shots of her mingling with the common folk. His film gets to the lab tomorrow.'

'Now why would she do that?'

'She was a designer, a kind of minor Martha Stewart. Just came out with a book and was considering a magazine. The pictures would have been for that.'

'Never heard of her.'

'Most people hadn't. But she seemed to have this image of herself as a successful and dynamic motivator. Like Martha, her business went beyond what colors the walls should be – white, by the way – into a personal philosophy of life.'

'Sounds odious.'

'I can't get a grasp of it,' admitted Gamache, leaning back comfortably. 'I don't know whether she was completely delusional or whether there was something almost noble about her. She had a dream and she pursued it, and damn the doubters.'

'You agree with her philosophy?'

'No. I spoke to someone today who described it as a kind of Frankenstein. I think that was quite accurate. Actually, that reference keeps popping up in this case. Someone else talked about the villagers celebrating the death of the monster, like in Frankenstein.'

'The monster wasn't Frankenstein,' Dr Harris reminded him. 'Dr Frankenstein created the monster.'

Gamache felt his chest tighten as she spoke. There was something there. Something he'd been approaching and missing throughout this case.

'So what now, *patron*?' she asked.

'You've taken us a huge step forward with the niacin. Thank you. Now we just follow the headlights.'

'Sorry?'

'I always think a case is like driving from here to the Gaspé. A great long distance and I can't see the end. But I don't have to. All I have to do is keep throwing light in front of me, and follow the headlights. Eventually I'll get there.'

'Like Diogenes with his lamp?'

'In reverse. He was looking for one honest man. I'm looking for a murderer.'

'Be careful. The murderer can see the man with the lamp coming.'

'One more question, doctor. How would someone give her niacin?'

'It's water soluble, but quite bitter. Coffee would probably mask it. Orange juice I guess.'

'Tea?'

'Less likely. It's not strong enough.'

She gathered her things and taking her key from her pocket she pointed it out the window and pressed a small button.

Outside a car came to life, headlights on and presumably the heater struggling to warm the inside. Of all the inventions in the last twenty years Gamache knew the two best were car seat warmers and automatic ignition. Too bad for Richard Lyon he'd invented magnetized soldiers instead.

Gamache walked her to the door, but just as she was about to leave something else occurred to him. 'What do you know about Eleanor de Poitiers?'

Dr Harris paused for a moment.

'Nothing. Who is she?'

'How about King Henry the Second?'

'King Henry the Second? You're not seriously asking me about some long dead British royal? My favorite was Ethelred the Unready. Will he do?'

'What a repertoire you have. Ethelred and Captain Crunch.'

'A Catholic education. Sorry I couldn't help.'

'Niacin.' He pointed to the dossier still on their table. 'You saved the day.'

She felt absurdly pleased.

'Actually,' he said as he helped her into her coat, 'there is one more thing. Eleanor of Aquitaine.'

'Oh, that's easy. *The Lion in Winter*.'

'Honey, could you get the door? I'm in my studio,' Clara called. There was no answer. 'Never mind,' she called after the second knock. 'I'll get it. Don't bother yourself. No really. I don't mind.' She yelled the last at the closed door to his studio. She was pretty certain he was in there playing free cell.

It was unusual to hear a knock. Most of the people they

knew walked right in. Most helped themselves to whatever was in the fridge. Peter and Clara sometimes came home to find Ruth asleep on their sofa, a glass of Scotch and the *Times Literary Review* on the hassock in front of her. Once they found Gabri in the bath. Apparently the hot water in the B&B had run out, and so had Gabri.

Clara yanked open the door, prepared for the blast of cold air and not totally surprised to see Chief Inspector Gamache, though a tiny part of her still hoped it might be the chief curator of the MOMA, come to see her works.

'Come on in.' She stepped aside and quickly closed the door after him.

'I won't keep you long.' He gave a tiny bow and she bowed back, thinking maybe she should have given a subtle curtsy. 'Do you have a video player?'

Now there was a question she wasn't expecting.

He unzipped his parka and brought out a video, kept warm against his body.

'*The Lion in Winter*?' She looked at the box.

'*Précisément*. I'd very much like to watch it, as soon as possible.' He was perfectly contained and relaxed, but Clara knew him well enough to know this wasn't a casual request or a nice way to spend a quiet winter evening in the country.

'We do. Ruth and Myrna are coming over for dinner, though.'

'I don't want to be in the way.'

'Never.' She took his arm and led him into the warm and inviting kitchen. 'Always room for more, but I want to make sure you don't mind the company. Peter's made a family specialty from the leftover turkey and vegetables. It looks horrible but tastes like heaven.'

Before long Peter had emerged from his studio and the others had arrived, Myrna enveloping everyone in her generous arms and Ruth making for the bar.

'Thank God,' was Ruth's reaction when told Gamache wanted to watch a video. 'I thought I'd have to make conversation yet another night.'

Clara prepared a basket with dinners for Richard and Crie and Myrna volunteered to deliver it.

'May I drive you up?' Gamache offered.

'It's a short walk. Besides, if I walk that'll give me permission to have seconds.' Myrna smiled as she wrapped a huge colorful scarf round her neck until she looked like an African tribesman in a cold spell.

'Could you check on Crie when you're there?' Gamache lowered his voice. 'I'm worried about her.'

'What're you thinking?' Myrna asked, her normally jovial face searching and serious. 'It's natural for a child who just saw her mother murdered to be abnormal for a while.'

'True, but this seems like more. Could you just see?'

She agreed and was off.

Agent Yvette Nichol edged up to the car in front of her in the fast lane of the autoroute, heading from Montreal back to the Townships. Her bumper was just inches from the car in front. Any minute now the driver would notice.

That was the moment. That exquisite moment. Would he hit the brake? Even a slight tap would send their cars careering together at 140 kilometers an hour and they would be a fireball within seconds. Nichol gripped her steering wheel tighter, her eyes keen with concentration and rage. How dare he slow her up? How dare he use her lane? How dare he not pull over? Slow, stupid man. She'd show him, as she showed anyone who stood in her way. Rage made her invincible. But there was something else too.

Glee.

She was going to scare the shit out of the driver.

'I read your book,' said Gamache to Ruth as the two of them sat in front of the cheery fire while Peter puttered in the kitchen and Clara browsed her bookshelves for something to read.

Ruth looked as though she'd rather be sitting in scalding oil than next to a compliment. She decided to ignore him and took a long gulp of her Scotch.

'But my wife has a question.'

'You have a wife? Someone agreed to marry you?'

'She did and she was only a little drunk. She wants to know what FINE means in your title.'

'I'm not surprised your wife has no idea what fine means. Probably doesn't know what happy or sane means either.'

'She's a librarian and she was saying in her experience when people use capital letters it's because the letters stand for something. Your title is *I'm FINE* with the FINE in capitals.'

'She has brains, your wife. She's the first to notice that, or at least to ask. FINE stands for Fucked up, Insecure, Neurotic and Egotistical. I'm FINE.'

'You certainly are,' agreed Gamache.

Agent Robert Lemieux eased over into the slow lane, allowing the maniac tailgating him on the autoroute at 140 kilometers an hour to pass. If he'd been in the mood he'd have put his flasher on the roof and chased the psycho, but he had other things on his mind.

He was sure he'd done well in Montreal. He'd convinced the police artist to do the drawing. He'd visited the bus station and the Old Brewery Mission. He'd advanced the Elle case, which Gamache seemed to want to keep private.

He'd made a note of that in his book.

Agent Lemieux had achieved what he wanted and needed. He was pretty sure Chief Inspector Gamache trusted him. And that was the key. A lot was riding on gaining Gamache's trust.

'The only person I remember moving around at the curling match was that photographer person,' said Myrna a few minutes later. As soon as she'd returned Peter and Clara had put the dinner out for people to help themselves. Gamache had taken her aside briefly and Myrna had agreed there was something very wrong with Crie. They arranged to get together the next day to talk.

Now their dinner was on tray tables in the living room. Clara had been right. It looked like something found in the bottom of the sink on Christmas Day once the dish water had been drained. But it tasted wonderful. Mashed potatoes, roast turkey, gravy and peas, all mushed together in a steaming casserole. Fresh bread and a green salad sat in bowls on the coffee table, with Lucy drifting around like a hungry shark.

'The photographer popped up everywhere,' agreed Clara, taking a hunk of bread and spreading it with butter. 'But he only took pictures of CC.'

'He was hired to do that. Where were all of you?' asked

Gamache. He took a sip of red wine and listened as the others talked.

'In the stands, next to Olivier,' said Ruth.

'I was sitting between Myrna and Gabri,' said Clara, 'and Peter was curling.'

'Richard Lyon was beside me,' said Myrna.

'Was he there the whole time?' Gamache asked.

'Definitely. I'd have noticed if he left. Body heat. But what about Kaye Thompson?' Myrna looked at the others. 'She was sitting right next to CC. She must have seen something.'

Everyone nodded and looked at Gamache expectantly. He shook his head. 'I spoke to her today. She says she saw nothing. Only knew something was wrong when CC started screaming.'

'I didn't hear that,' said Ruth.

'Nobody did,' said Gamache. 'It was masked by the noise of Mother clearing the house.'

'Oh, right,' said Peter. 'Everyone was cheering.'

'How about Crie?' Gamache asked. 'Did anyone notice her?'

Blank stares.

Gamache was again struck by how sad it must be to be Crie. She'd swallowed all her feelings, all her pain. She carried such an enormous weight, and yet she was invisible. No one ever saw her. It was the worst of all possible states, he knew, to never be noticed.

'Do you have a Bible?' Gamache asked Clara. 'Old Testament, if you have one. In English, please.'

They wandered over to the bookcase and Clara finally found it.

'May I return it tomorrow?'

'You can return it next year if you like. Can't remember the last time I read the Old Testament,' said Clara.

'The last time?' Peter asked.

'Or the first time,' admitted Clara with a laugh.

'Would you like to watch the movie now?' Peter asked.

'Very much,' said Gamache.

Peter reached out to pick up the cassette from the living room table, but Gamache stayed his hand.

'I'll do it, if you don't mind.' Gamache took out a handkerchief and slipped the movie out of its sleeve. Everyone noticed, but no one asked, and Gamache didn't volunteer the information that this particular tape had been found in the garbage of the dead woman.

'What's it about?' asked Myrna.

'Eleanor of Aquitaine and her husband King Henry,' said Ruth. Gamache turned to her, surprised. 'What? It's a great film. Katharine Hepburn and Peter O'Toole. All the action takes place at Christmas, if I remember well. Strange, isn't it. Here we are at Christmas too.'

There were many strange things about this case, thought Gamache.

The opening credits started, the Metro-Goldwyn-Mayer lion roared, the powerful Gothic music filled their quaint little living room and grotesque images of gargoyles leered on the screen. Already the film reeked of power and decay.

And dread.

The Lion in Winter began.

Agent Nichol's car skidded round the snowy corner, barely making the turn off the main road onto the tiny secondary road that led to Three Pines. Gamache hadn't invited her to stay at the B&B with them, but she would anyway, even if she had to pay her own way. While in Montreal, after interviewing the headmistress of Crie's snooty private school, Agent Nichol had driven home to pick up a suitcase, stopping briefly to have a bite with her relatives gathered in the tiny, fastidious house.

Her father always seemed nervous on these occasions and had instructed his daughters never to mention the family history in Czechoslovakia. Growing up in the immaculate little home in east end Montreal Nichol had seen a parade of distant relatives and friends of friends come to live with them, though it was less a parade than a cortege. They trudged through the door, all in black with stone stern faces, speaking words she couldn't understand and sucking all the attention the world had to offer. They demanded and yelled and wailed and complained. They came from Poland and Lithuania and Hungary and young Yvette listened to them and came to believe each person must have their own language. Hovering near the doorway in the tiny, crowded, chaotic living room, a room that had once been so pleasant and calm, young Yvette struggled to understand what was being said. At first the newcomers would speak kindly to her, then when she didn't react they'd speak more loudly, until finally they screamed at her in the universal language that said she was lazy and stupid and disrespectful. Her mother, once so gentle and kindly, had become impatient too, and yelled at her. In a language she did understand. Little Yvette Nikolev had become the foreigner. All her life she'd stand just on the outside. Longing to belong, but knowing she didn't, when even her mother sided with others.

It was then she began to worry. If her home was this

baffling and overwhelming, what was waiting outside? Suppose she couldn't make herself understood? Suppose something happened, but she couldn't follow the instructions? Suppose she needed something? Who would give it to her? And so Yvette Nichol had learned to take.

'So, you're back with Gamache,' her father had said.

'Yes sir.' She smiled at him. He was the only one who had ever stood up for her as a child. The only one who'd protected her against those invaders. He'd catch her eye and wave her over and give her a butterscotch candy wrapped in noisy cellophane. He'd instruct her to hide someplace to open it. Away from prying and greedy eyes. Their secret. Her father had taught her the value and necessity of secrets.

'You must never tell him about Czechoslovakia. Promise me now. He wouldn't understand. They only want pure Quebecers in the Sûreté. If he found out you're Czech you'd be kicked out. Like Uncle Saul.'

The very idea of being compared to stupid Uncle Saul made her nauseous. Stupid Uncle Saul Nikolev who'd washed out of the Czech police and couldn't protect the family. And so they'd all perished. Except her father, Ari Nikolev, and her mother and the discontented and bitter relatives who'd used their home like a latrine, dropping their shit all over the young family.

In the small, neat back bedroom Ari Nikolev watched as his daughter packed her suitcase with the dreariest, drabbest clothes in her closet. At his suggestion.

'I know men,' he'd said, when she'd protested.

'But men won't find me attractive in these.' She'd jabbed her finger at the pile of clothes. 'I thought you said you wanted Gamache to like me.'

'Not to date. Believe me, he'll like you in those.'

As she turned to find her toiletry bag he slipped a couple of butterscotch candies into the suitcase, where she'd find them that night. And think of him. And with any luck never realize he had his own little secret.

There was no Uncle Saul. No slaughter at the hands of the communists. No noble and valiant flight across the frontier. He'd made all that up years ago to shut up his wife's relatives camped in their home. It was his lifeboat, made of words, which had kept him afloat on their sea of misery and suffering. Genuine suffering. Even he could admit that. But he'd needed his own stories of heroics and survival.

And so, after helping to conceive little Angelina and then Yvette, he'd conceived Uncle Saul. Whose job it was to save the family, and who had failed. Saul's spectacular fall from grace had cost Ari his entire fictional family.

He knew he should tell Yvette. Knew that what had started as his own life raft had become an anchor for his little girl. But she worshipped him, and Ari Nikolev craved that look in her gray eyes.

'I'll call you every day,' he said, lifting her light case from the bed. 'We need to stick together.' He smiled and cocked his head toward the cacophony that was the living room as the relatives shouted at each other from entrenched positions. 'I'm proud of you, Yvette, and I know you'll do well. You have to.'

'Yes, sir.'

None of the fucking relatives lifted their heads as she left, her father carrying her case to the car and putting it in the trunk. 'In case there's a crash, it won't hit you on the head.'

He hugged her and whispered in her ear, 'Don't mess up.'

*

And now she approached Three Pines. At the top of du Moulin she slowed, her car skidding slightly to the side on the slippery road. Below her the village glowed, the lights off the tall trees reflected red and green and blue on the snow and the ice, like a giant stained glass window. She could see figures moving back and forth in front of the windows of the shops and homes.

A feeling roiled in her chest. Was it anxiety? Resentment perhaps about leaving her own warm home to come here? No. She sat in the car for a few minutes, her shoulders slowly sagging from up round her ears and her breath coming in long, even puffs. Trying to identify this strange feeling. Then, knitting her brows together and staring out the windshield at the cheery little village, she suddenly knew what she was feeling.

Relief. Was this what it felt like to let the weight down, the guard down?

Her cell phone rang. She hesitated, knowing who it was, and not wanting to leave her last thought.

'Oui, bonjour. Yes sir, I'm in Three Pines. I'll be polite. I'll win him over. I know how important this is. I won't mess up,' she said in response to his warning.

She hung up and took her foot off the brake. Her car glided into the village and came to a stop in front of the B&B.

Eleanor and Henry were going at it hammer and tongs. Their sons were fracturing, turning on each other and their parents. Each character was exploding, sending shards into each other. It was devastating and brilliant. By the end Gamache looked down, surprised to see his plate empty. He didn't remember eating. He didn't remember breathing.

But he did know one thing. Given a choice, Eleanor and Henry would be the last people on earth he'd want as parents. Gamache sat staring at the closing credits, wondering what he'd missed, because he'd surely missed something. There was a reason CC had the tape and a reason she'd taken the name de Poitiers, and presumably a reason she'd thrown out a perfectly good video. This tape was found in her garbage. Why?

'Maybe she bought a DVD,' suggested Clara when he'd asked them for their theories. 'We've been slowly switching our collection over to DVD. All Peter's favorite movies eventually go screwy because he watches the good parts over and over.'

'Hello, everyone,' Gabri's cheerful voice called from the kitchen. 'I heard about the movie night. Am I too late?'

'The film just finished,' said Peter. 'Sorry, old son.'

'Couldn't get away earlier. Had to minister to the sick.'

'How is Inspector Beauvoir?' Gamache asked, walking into the kitchen.

'Still asleep. He has the flu,' Gabri explained to the rest. 'Am I feverish? Hope I didn't get it.' He offered his forehead to Peter, who ignored him.

'Well, even if you've picked it up we're not at risk,' Ruth commented. 'The chances of it jumping from Gabri to a human are pretty small.'

'Bitch.'

'Slut.'

'So who's looking after him?' Gamache asked, wondering if he should head for the door.

'That Agent Nichol showed up and booked herself in.

Even paid for it herself using little rolled up bills. Anyway, she said she'd look after him.'

Gamache hoped Beauvoir was unconscious.

Beauvoir was having a nightmare. Through his fever he dreamed he was in bed with Agent Nichol. He felt nauseous again.

'Here.' A woman's voice, quite pleasant, came to him.

Somehow the wastepaper basket had levitated and was right under his mouth. He heaved into it, though there was nothing much left in his stomach to bring up.

Falling back into the damp sheets he had the oddest sensation that a cool cloth had been laid on his forehead and his face and mouth had been wiped clean.

Jean Guy Beauvoir fell back into a fitful sleep.

'I brought dessert.' Gabri pointed to a cardboard box on the counter. 'Chocolate fudge cake.'

'Do you know, I think I'm beginning to like you,' said Ruth.

'What a difference a gay makes.' He smiled and started unwrapping it.

'I'll make coffee,' said Myrna.

Gamache cleared the plates and ran warm water in the sink to do the washing up. As he scrubbed the dishes and handed them to Clara to dry, he looked out the frosted window at the lights of Three Pines and thought about the film. *The Lion in Winter*. He went over the characters, the plot, some of the devastating repartee between Eleanor and Henry. It was a film about power and love warped and twisted and squandered.

But why was it so important to CC? And was it important to the case?

'Coffee'll take a couple of minutes yet,' said Clara, hanging the damp towel on the back of a chair. The room was already filled with the dark smells of fresh brewing coffee and rich chocolate.

'Could you show me your studio?' Gamache asked Clara, hoping to get far enough away from the cake to overcome the temptation to put his finger in it. 'I realize I've never seen your art.'

The two drifted across the kitchen toward the door to Clara's studio, wide open. Next to hers, Peter's studio was closed.

'In case the muse should try to escape,' explained Clara, and Gamache nodded sagely. Now he walked to the center of Clara's large, crowded studio and stood still.

The studio had tarpaulins spread everywhere and the comforting smell of oils and acrylics and canvas. An old, worn armchair stood in one corner, with stacks of art magazines creating a table on which stood a dirty coffee mug. He turned leisurely, stopping to stare at one wall that held three images.

He moved closer to them.

'That's Kaye Thompson,' he said.

'Well done.' Clara came up beside him. 'And that's Mother.' She indicated the next work. 'I sold Émilie to Dr Harris a while ago but look over here.' She pointed to the end wall where a huge canvas stood. 'All three.'

Gamache stood in front of an image of three elderly women, arms entwined, cradling each other. It was an amazingly complex work, with layers of photographs and paintings and even some writing. Em, the woman in the middle, was leaning back precipitously, laughing with abandon, and the other two were supporting her and also laughing. It ached of intimacy, of a private moment caught in women's lives. It captured their friendship and their dependence on each other. It sang of love and a caring that went beyond pleasant lunches and the remembrance of birthdays. Gamache felt as though he was looking into each of their souls, and the combination of the three was almost too much to bear.

'I call it *The Three Graces*,' said Clara.

'Perfect,' Gamache whispered.

'Mother is Faith, Em is Hope and Kaye is Charity. I was tired of seeing the Graces always depicted as beautiful young things. I think wisdom comes with age and life and pain. And knowing what matters.'

'Is it finished? It looks as though there's space for another.'

'That's very perceptive of you. It is finished, but in each of my works I try to leave a little space, a kind of crack.'

'Why?'

'Can you make out the writing on the wall behind them?' She nodded toward her painting.

Gamache leaned in and put on his reading glasses.

> *'Ring the bells that still can ring,*
> *Forget your perfect offering,*
> *There's a crack in everything,*
> *That's how the light gets in.'*

He read it out loud. 'Beautiful. Madame Zardo?' he asked.

'No, Leonard Cohen. All my works have vessels of some sort. Containers. Sometimes it's in the negative space, sometimes it's more obvious. In *The Three Graces* it's more obvious.'

It wasn't obvious to Gamache. He stepped back from the work, then he saw what she meant. The vessel, like a vase, was formed by their bodies, and the space he'd noticed was the crack, to let the light in.

'I do it for Peter,' she said quietly. At first Gamache thought he might have misheard, but she continued as though speaking to herself. 'He's like a dog, like Lucy. He's very loyal. He puts everything he has into one thing. One interest, one hobby, one friend, one love. I'm his love and it scares the shit out of me.' She turned now to look into Gamache's thoughtful brown eyes. 'He's poured all his love into me. I'm his vessel. But suppose I crack? Suppose I break? Suppose I die? What would he do?'

'So all your art is exploring that theme?'

'Mostly it's about imperfection and impermanence. There's a crack in everything.'

'That's how the light gets in,' said Gamache. He thought of CC who'd written so much about light and enlightenment and illumination, and thought it came from perfection. But she couldn't hold a candle to this bright woman beside him.

'Peter doesn't get it. Probably never will.'

'Have you ever painted Ruth?'

'Why do you ask?'

'Well, frankly, if anyone's cracked . . .' He laughed and Clara joined him.

'No, and you know why? I'm afraid to. I think she could be my masterpiece, and I'm afraid to try.'

'In case you can't do it?'

'Got it in one. There's also something scary about Ruth. I'm not sure I want to look that deeply into her.'

'You will,' he said, and she believed him. Gamache looked at her silently, his deep brown eyes calm and peaceful. She knew then all the horrible things he'd seen with those eyes.

Murdered and mutilated women, children, husbands, wives. He saw violent death every day. She looked down at his hands, large and expressive, and knew then all the horrible things they'd had to do. Handle the bodies of people dead before their time. Fight for his own life and others. And perhaps the worst of all, those fingers had formed loose fists and knocked on the doors of loved ones. To break the news. To break their hearts.

Gamache walked over to the next wall and saw the most astonishing works of art. The vessels in this case were trees. Clara had painted them tall and gourd-shaped, voluptuous and ripe. And melting, as though their own internal heat was too much for them. They were luminous. Literally luminous. The colors were milken, like Venice at dawn, all warm and washed and venerable.

'They're marvelous, Clara. They radiate.' He turned to look at her in astonishment, as though meeting the woman for the first time. He'd known she was insightful, and courageous and compassionate. But he hadn't appreciated that she was this gifted. 'Has anyone seen these?'

'I gave my portfolio to CC just before Christmas. She's friends with Denis Fortin.'

'The gallery owner,' said Gamache.

'The best in Quebec, probably in Canada. He has connections to the Musée d'Art contemporain and the Museum of Modern Art in New York. If he likes your stuff you're launched.'

'That's exciting,' said Gamache.

'Not really. He hated it.' She turned away, not able to look any human in the eye as she admitted her failure. 'CC and Fortin happened to be at Ogilvy's when I was there for Ruth's book launch. We passed on the escalator. I was going up and they were going down. I heard CC say to him it was a shame he thought my work was amateurish and banal.'

'He said that?' Gamache was surprised.

'Well, he didn't, but CC did. She was repeating what he'd said and he didn't contradict her. Then we'd passed and before I knew it I was out the door. Thank God for the vagrant.'

'What vagrant?'

Should she tell him? But she already felt skinned and lashed and had no stomach for further exposure even to this man who listened as though she was the only one on earth. She couldn't admit she believed God was a bag lady.

Did she still believe it?

She paused a moment and considered. Yes, came the simple and clear answer. Yes, she still believed she'd met God on the cold, dark, blessed streets of Montreal at Christmas. Still, she'd embarrassed herself enough this night.

'Oh, nothing. I gave her a coffee and felt better about myself. Seems to work like that, doesn't it?'

To kind and compassionate people, thought Gamache, but not to everyone. He knew she was holding something back, but chose not to press. Besides, it couldn't possibly have anything to do with the case and Armand Gamache had no stomach to breach someone else's boundaries just because he could.

'Did CC know you were there when she spoke?'

Clara pretended to think back, but she knew the answer. Had known it from the moment she'd seen CC on the escalator.

'Yes, we made eye contact briefly. She knew.'

'That must have been devastating.'

'I actually thought my heart would stop. I really believed Fortin would like my work. It never occurred to me he wouldn't. It was my fault, living in a fantasy like that.'

'When someone stabs you it's not your fault that you feel pain.'

He looked at her face now and at her fists, balled up, knuckles white, her breathing heavy as though pumping herself up. He knew Clara Morrow to be kind and loving and tolerant. If CC de Poitiers could produce this reaction in Clara, what must she have done to others?

And he added Clara's name to the long list of suspects. What was she hiding deep down in the room she kept locked and hidden even from herself? What had peeped out at him from that silence a few moments ago?

'Dessert.' Gabri poked his head into the studio.

TWENTY-TWO

'Who do you think killed CC?' Myrna asked, licking her fork and taking a sip of rich dark coffee. The combination of freshly ground and brewed coffee and chocolate fudge cake made Myrna almost light-headed.

'I think I first have to figure out who she was,' admitted Gamache. 'I think the murderer is hiding in her past.' He told them then about CC and her fantasy world. Like a storyteller of old, Gamache spoke, his voice deep and calm. The friends formed a circle, their faces glowing amber in the light from the fireplace. They ate their cake and sipped their coffee, their eyes growing wider and wider as the depth of the mystery and deceit became clear.

'So she wasn't who she pretended to be,' said Clara when he'd finished. She hoped triumph wasn't evident in her voice. CC was nuts after all.

'But why choose them as parents?' Myrna jerked her head toward the TV.

'Don't know. Do you have any theories?'

Everyone thought.

'It's not unusual for children to believe they were adopted,' said Myrna. 'Even happy children go through that stage.'

'That's true,' said Clara. 'I remember believing my real mother was the Queen of England and she'd farmed me out to the colonies to be raised a commoner. Every time the doorbell rang I'd think it was her, come to get me.'

Clara still remembered the fantasy of Queen Elizabeth standing on the stoop of her modest home in the Notre Dame de Grace *quartier* of Montreal, the neighbors craning to get a load of the Queen in her crown and long purple robes. And handbag. Clara knew what the Queen kept in that handbag. A picture of her, and a plane ticket to bring her home.

'But', said Peter, 'you grew out of it.'

'True,' said Clara, lying just a little, 'though it was replaced by other fantasies.'

'Oh, please. Heterosexual fantasies have no place at the dinner table,' said Gabri.

But Clara's adult dream world had nothing to do with sex.

'And that's the trouble,' said Gamache. 'I agree as children we all created worlds of our own. Cowboys and Indians, space explorers, princes and princesses.'

'Shall I tell you mine?' Gabri offered.

'Please, dear Lord, let the house explode now,' said Ruth.

'I used to dream I was straight.'

The simple and devastating sentence sat in the middle of their circle.

'I used to dream I was popular,' said Ruth into the silence. 'And pretty.'

'I used to dream I was white,' said Myrna. 'And thin.'

Peter remained mute. He couldn't remember any fantasies

he'd had as a child. Coping with reality had taken up too much of his mind.

'And you?' Ruth asked Gamache.

'I used to dream I'd saved my parents,' he said, remembering the little boy looking out the living-room window, leaning over the back of the sofa, resting his cheek on the nubbly fabric. Sometimes, when the winter wind blew, he could still feel it rough against his cheek. Whenever his parents went out for dinner he'd wait, looking into the night for the headlights. And every night they came home. Except one.

'We all have our fantasies,' said Myrna. 'Was CC any different?'

'There is one difference,' said Gamache. 'Do you still want to be white and thin?'

Myrna laughed heartily. 'No way. Would never occur to me now.'

'Or straight?' he asked Gabri.

'Olivier would kill me.'

'Eventually, for better or worse, our childhood fantasies disappear or are replaced by others. But not CC. That's the difference. She seemed to believe them, even to the extent of choosing the name de Poitiers. We don't even know what her real name was.'

'I wonder who her parents were?' said Gabri. 'She was in her late forties, right? So they'd probably be in their seventies at least. Like you.' Gabri turned to Ruth, who waited a moment then spoke.

> 'Long dead and buried in another town,
> my mother hasn't finished with me yet.'

'From a poem?' Gamache asked when Ruth had finished. It sounded familiar.

'You think?' said Ruth with a snarl.

> '*When my death us do part*
> *Then shall forgiven and forgiving meet again,*
> *Or will it be, as always was, too late?*'

'Oh, thank God. I thought we'd be without your poetry for one night,' said Gabri. 'Please, continue. I don't feel quite suicidal enough.'

'Your poetry is remarkable,' said Gamache. Ruth looked more stricken by his kind words than Gabri's insults.

'Fuck off.' She shoved Gamache aside and made for the door.

'The Shit's hit the Fan,' said Gabri.

Gamache remembered where he'd heard the poem. He'd read it in the car on his way down to start the case. He carefully retrieved *The Lion in Winter* from the video machine.

'Thank you,' he said to Clara and Peter. 'I have to get back to Inspector Beauvoir. Do you have one of your portfolios?' he asked Clara. 'I'd like to take it.'

'Sure.' She led him into her studio and over to her crowded desk. Turning the lamp on she riffled the stacks of papers. He watched her until his eyes wandered, drawn to something shining on the bookcase behind her desk. He stood still for a moment, almost afraid that if he moved the object would flitter away. Silently, slowly, he edged forward, creeping up on it. As he moved he put his hand into his pocket and withdrew a handkerchief. Reaching out, his hand steady and true, he delicately hugged the object in the handkerchief and picked it off its stand. Even through the cloth it felt almost warm.

'Isn't it beautiful?' said Clara, as he drew back and held the object under the lamp. 'Peter gave it to me for Christmas.'

In his palm Gamache held a glowing ball. A scene was painted on it. Three pine trees with snow heavy on the branches. Underneath was the word *Noël*, and below that, very lightly, was something else. A single capital letter.

L.

Gamache had found the Li Bien ball.

Peter Morrow looked as though he'd been cornered, and he had. When asked Clara had happily declared that the lovely ornament was the very first Christmas gift Peter had ever bought for her. Up until this year, she'd explained, they'd been too poor.

'Or too cheap,' said Ruth.

'Where did you get it?' Gamache asked, his voice polite, but with a firmness that demanded an answer.

'I forget,' Peter tried, but seeing the determination in Gamache's eye he changed his mind. 'I wanted to buy you something.' Peter turned to Clara, trying to explain.

'But?' Clara could see where this was going.

'Well, I was driving to Williamsburg to shop – '

'The Paris of the North,' explained Gabri to Myrna.

'Famous for its shops,' agreed Myrna.

' – when I passed the dump, and—'

'The dump?' Clara exclaimed. 'The dump?'

Now Lucy the dog started snaking between Clara's legs, upset by the frequency Clara had achieved.

'Careful, you'll shatter the ball,' said Ruth.

'The dump.' Clara's voice deepened and she lowered her head, her eyes glowering at Peter who wished, as Ruth had earlier, that maybe the house could just explode now.

'The Jacques Cousteau of dumpster diving has struck treasure again,' said Gabri.

'You found this,' Gamache held the Li Bien ball up, 'in the Williamsburg dump?'

Peter nodded. 'I was just looking, just for fun. It was a mild day so everything wasn't frozen together. I wasn't there long and that thing just caught my eye. You can see why. Even now just by lamplight it's glowing; you can imagine what it looked like in broad daylight. It was like a beacon. It was calling to me.' He looked at Clara to see if maybe that would work. 'I think I was meant to find it. Destiny.'

She remained unconvinced of the divinity of his gift.

'When was this?' Gamache asked.

'I don't remember.'

'Remember, Mr Morrow.' They all looked at Gamache now. The man seemed to have grown and now radiated an authority and insistence that silenced even Ruth. Peter thought a moment.

'It was a few days before Christmas. I know, it was the day after your book launch,' he said to Ruth. 'The twenty-third of December. Clara was home and could walk Lucy while I went Christmas shopping.'

'Christmas garbage sifting, don't you mean?' said Clara.

Peter sighed and said nothing.

'Where was it in the dumpster?' Gamache asked.

'Right on the edge, as though someone had reached up and placed it there, not just thrown it in.'

'Did you find anything else?'

Gamache watched Peter closely to see if he was lying. Peter shook his head. Gamache believed him.

'What is it? Why's it so important?' Myrna asked.

'It's called a Li Bien ball,' said Gamache, 'and it belonged to CC. She built her whole spiritual philosophy around it. In her book she described it, exactly like this, and said it was the only thing she had left from her mother. In fact, she said her mother painted it.'

'It has three pine trees on it,' continued Myrna.

'And an initial,' said Clara. 'L.'

'So that's why CC moved here,' said Gabri.

'Why?' said Peter, who'd been thinking of his own world of trouble ahead and not really concentrating on the conversation.

'Three pines?' said Gabri, walking over to the window and gesturing out. 'Three pines. Three Pines?'

'Three pines three times,' said Ruth. 'You're clicking your heels, Dorothy.'

'We're not in Kansas any more,' said Gabri. 'We're in?' he beseeched Peter.

'Three Pines,' said Peter, finally getting it. 'CC's mother was from here?'

'And her initial was L,' said Myrna.

Émilie Longpré lay in bed. It was early, not yet ten, but she was tired. She picked up her book and tried to read but it was heavy in her hands. She struggled to hold it, wanting to finish the story, wanting to know how it ended. She was afraid she'd run out of time before she ran out of book.

Now the hardcover lay heavy in her lap, feeling a little like David in her womb. She'd lain in this same bed, Gus beside her doing his crosswords and mumbling to himself. And her baby inside her.

And now she had only a book to keep her company. No, she roused herself. Not just a book. She had Bea and Kaye. They were with her too, and would be until the end.

Em saw the book, heavy with words, rise and fall on her stomach. She looked down at the bookmark. Halfway through. She was only halfway there. Émilie picked up the book again, this time holding it in both hands, and read some more, losing herself in the story. She hoped it would have a happy ending. That the woman would find love and happiness. Or maybe just herself. That would be enough.

The book closed again as Em's eyes closed.

Mother Bea could see the future and it didn't look good. It never had. Even in the best of times Mother had the gift of seeing the worst. It was a quality that hadn't served her well. Living in the wreckage of her future sure took the joy out of the present. The only comfort was that almost none of her fears had come true. The planes had never crashed, the elevators never plummeted, the bridges had remained solid spans. All right, her husband had left her, but that wasn't exactly a disaster. Some might even say it was a self-fulfilling prophecy. She'd forced him away. He'd always complained that there were too many in their relationship. Beatrice, him and God. One had to go.

It wasn't much of a choice.

Now Mother Bea lay in bed, snug in her soft and warm flannel sheets, the duvet heavy around her plump body. She'd chosen God over her husband, but the truth was she'd have chosen a good eiderdown over him too.

This was her favorite place in the whole wide world. In bed in her home, safe and sound. So why couldn't she sleep? Why couldn't she meditate any more? Why couldn't she even eat?

Kaye lay in bed issuing orders to the young and frightened infantry-men around her in the trench. Their flat, shallow helmets were askew and their faces dirty with muck and shit and the first flush of whiskers. The first and last, she knew, but chose not to tell them. Instead she gave them a rousing speech and assured them she'd be the first out of the trench when the time came, then led them in a heartfelt chorus of 'Rule Britannia'.

They'd all die soon, she knew. And Kaye curled herself into the tightest ball, ashamed of the cowardice she'd carried all her life like a child in the womb, so much in contrast to her father's obvious courage.

'I'm sorry,' said Peter, for the hundredth time.

'It's not that you got it from the dump, but that you lied about it,' Clara lied. It was that he'd gotten the goddamned thing from the dump. Once again, he'd given her garbage for Christmas. It hadn't mattered when they couldn't afford anything else. She'd make him something, because she was good with her hands, and he'd dumpster dive, because he wasn't, then they'd both pretend to like their gifts.

But this was different. They could afford it now, and still he'd chosen to shop at the dump.

'I'm sorry,' he said, knowing it wasn't enough but not knowing what was.

'Forget it,' she said.

He was smart enough to know that wouldn't be very smart.

Gamache sat beside Beauvoir. He'd made up another hot water bottle, though the fever had broken. Gamache could only find one hot water bottle and wondered what had happened to the other. Now he sat, sometimes watching Jean Guy and sometimes reading the heavy book in his lap.

He'd read Isaiah just to be sure then turned to the Psalms. He'd called their parish priest when he'd gotten back to the B&B and Father Néron had given him the reference.

'It was good to see you Christmas Eve, Armand,' Father Néron had said. Gamache waited for it. 'And meet your granddaughter. She looks like Reine-Marie, lucky child.' Gamache waited. 'It's so good to see a family together. Too bad you'll be in Hell and won't be able to spend eternity with them.' Ta da.

'Fortunately, *mon père*, they'll be in Hell too.'

Père Néron had laughed. 'Suppose I'm right and you're endangering your mortal soul by not coming to church every week?' he asked.

'Then I'll miss your cheerful company for eternity, Marcel.'

'What can I do for you?'

Gamache had told him.

'Not Isaiah. That's Psalm 46. Not sure which verse. One of my favorites, actually, but not very popular with the bosses.'

'Why not?'

'Well, think about it, Armand. If all anyone had to do to get close to God was be still they wouldn't need me.'

'Suppose the passage is right?' Gamache asked.

'Then you and I will meet for eternity after all. I hope it is.'

Now Gamache read the psalm, looking at Beauvoir every now and then over his half-moon glasses. Why had Mother lied and told him it was from Isaiah? She must have known the truth. And even more compelling, why had she misquoted the passage and written on the wall *Be Calm, and know that I am God?*

'Am I that sick?'

Gamache looked up and saw Beauvoir staring at him, clear-eyed and smiling.

'Your body isn't, young man. It's your soul I lament.'

'There's truth there, monsignor.' Beauvoir struggled to his elbow. 'You wouldn't believe my wicked dreams. I even dreamt Agent Nichol was with me.' He lowered his voice for the confession.

'Imagine that,' said Gamache. 'You're feeling better.' He took his cool hand off Beauvoir's cool head.

'Much. What time is it?'

'Midnight.'

'Go to sleep, sir. I'm fine.'

'Fucked up, Insecure, Neurotic and Egotistical?'

'Hope that's not from my next performance evaluation.'

'No. That's a bit of poetry.'

If that's poetry, thought Beauvoir, wearily subsiding once again into the welcoming bed, I can get to like it.

'Why're you reading the Bible?' he mumbled, half asleep already.

'It's about the writing on the wall at Mother's meditation center. Psalm 46, verse 10. It should read, *Be still, and know that I am God.*'

Beauvoir drifted away, comforted by the voice and the thought.

TWENTY-THREE

⌒

The bedside clock glowed 5:51. It was still dark and would be for a while. Gamache lay in bed, feeling the fresh freezing air from the slightly open window on his face, and the bed sheets warm around him.

It was time to get up.

He showered and dressed quickly in the cool room with its dark wood furniture, white walls and fluffy feather bedding. The room was elegant and way too inviting. Gamache tiptoed down the dark stairs of the B&B. He'd put his warmest clothing on and got into his huge parka. He'd shoved his tuque and mitts into the sleeve of his parka when he'd come in the night before, and now, thrusting his right arm into the armhole, he hit the blockage. At a practiced shove the pompom of the tuque crowned the cuff followed by his mitts, like a tiny birth.

Once outside he started walking, his feet munching on the snow. It was a brittle crisp morning but without a breath of wind and Gamache thought the forecast might actually be accurate. It was going to be a cold one, even by Quebec standards. Leaning forward slightly, head down, his mittened hands clasped behind his back, Gamache walked and thought about this baffling case with its embarrassment of suspects and clues.

Puddles of anti-freeze, niacin, *The Lion in Winter*, booster cables, Psalm 46:10 and a long lost mother. And that was only what he'd uncovered so far. CC was two days dead and what he really needed was an epiphany.

Round the Commons the case took him in the dark, though in winter the night was never pitch black. The snow covering the ground had its own glow. Past the homes of sleeping villagers he trudged, smoke from the chimneys rising vertically, past the darkened shops, though a hint of a light in the basement of Sarah's Boulangerie promised fresh croissants.

Round and round he went in the astonishing quietude and comfort of the hushed village, his feet crunching on the hardened snow and his breathing loud in his ears.

Was CC's mother asleep in one of these houses? Was it an easy sleep she enjoyed, or did her conscience startle her awake, like a home invader intent on violence?

Who was CC's mother?

Had CC found her?

Did Mom want to be found?

Was CC motivated by need for family or was there some other, darker, purpose?

And what about the Li Bien ball? Who'd thrown it away? And why not simply toss it into the frozen dumpster, smashing it into unrecognizable pieces?

Fortunately Armand Gamache loved puzzles. Just then a dark figure shot off the village green, racing toward him.

'*Henri! Viens ici,*' a voice commanded. For a dog with such big ears Henri didn't seem to hear. Gamache stepped aside and Henri skidded past with great glee.

'*Désolée*,' said Émilie Longpré, puffing as she approached. 'Henri, you have no manners.'

'It's a privilege to be chosen as Henri's playmate.'

They both knew Henri also chose his own frozen poop as a playmate, so the bar wasn't set so high. Still, Em gave a slight incline of her head, acknowledging his courtesy. Émilie Longpré was a dying breed of Québecoise. Les Grandes Dames, not because they pushed and insisted and bullied, but because of their immense dignity and kindness.

'We're not used to meeting anyone on our morning walk,' explained Émilie.

'What time is it?'

'Just past seven.'

'May I join you?'

He fell in beside her, the three of them making their slow progress round the Commons, Gamache tossing snowballs to an ecstatic Henri as one by one lights appeared in village windows. In the distance Olivier waved as he crossed from the B&B to the bistro. A moment later soft light came through the window.

'How well did you know CC?' Gamache asked, watching Henri skid lazily around on the frozen pond after a snowball.

'Not well. I only met her a few times.'

In the dark Gamache couldn't make out Em's expression. He felt handicapped but focused intently on her tone.

'She came to visit me.'

'Why?'

'I invited her. Then I met her a week or so later at Mother's meditation center.' Émilie's voice held a touch of humor. She could still see it. Mother's face the color of her caftan, which that day was crimson. CC, thin and righteous, standing in the middle of the meditation room, critiquing Mother's entire way of life.

'Of course, it's understandable,' CC condescended to Mother. 'It's been years since you've renewed your spiritual path and things get stale,' she said, mixing her metaphors and picking up a bright purple meditation pillow with two fingers, as evidence of Mother's woefully fossilized philoso-phy. And decorating scheme. 'I mean, since when has the color purple been divine?'

Mother's hands flew to the top of her head, her mouth open and silent. But CC didn't see any of this. She'd tilted her head to the ceiling, palms up, and hummed like a large tuning fork.

'No, there's no spirit here. Your ego and emotions have squeezed it out. How can the divine live among all these loud colors? There's too much you and not enough Higher Power. Still, you're doing your best and you're quite a pioneer, bringing meditation to the Townships thirty years ago—'

'Forty,' said Mother, finding her voice, though it was a squeak.

'Whatever. It didn't matter what you offered, since no one knew any better.'

'I beg your pardon?'

'I came here hoping to find someone with some karma to share.' CC had sighed and looked around, shaking her disil-lusioned, enlightened, bleached head. 'Well, my path is clear. I've been given a rare gift and I intend to share it. I'll be opening my home as a meditation center, teaching what I learned from my guru in India. Since my company and book are called Be Calm, that's what I'll be calling my meditation center. I'm afraid you'll have to change the name of your little place. In fact, I'm feeling it might be time for you to close altogether.'

Em feared for CC's life. Mother probably had just enough strength to throttle CC, and she looked as though she meant to.

'I sense your anger,' said CC, displaying an immediate grasp of the obvious. 'Very toxic.'

'Mother didn't take her seriously, of course,' said Em after she'd described the scene to Gamache.

'But CC planned to use the name of her center. That could have been a disaster for Mother.'

'True, but I don't think Mother believed it.'

'The center's called Be Calm. That phrase seems to keep coming up. Wasn't it the name of your curling team?'

'Where'd you hear that?' Em laughed. 'That must have been fifty, sixty years ago. Ancient history.'

'But interesting history, madame.'

'I'm glad you think so. It was a joke. We didn't take ourselves seriously, and didn't much care whether we won.'

It was the same story he'd heard before but he wished he could see her expression.

Henri limped over, lifting first one paw then the other.

'Oh, poor Henri. We've stayed out too long.'

'Should I carry him?' asked Gamache, feeling badly because he hadn't remembered that the biting snow could burn a dog's paw. Now he remembered last winter struggling to carry old Sonny the three blocks home when his feet couldn't take the cold any more. It had broken both their hearts. And he remembered hugging Sonny to him a few months later when the vet came to put him to sleep. And he remembered saying soothing things into the stinky old ears and looking into the weepy brown eyes as they closed, with one final soft thump of the ragged, beloved, tail. And as he felt the final beat of Sonny's heart Gamache had had the impression it wasn't that his old heart had stopped but that Sonny had finally given it all away.

'We're almost there,' said Em, her voice now thick, her lips and cheeks beginning to freeze in the cold.

'May I offer you breakfast? I'd like to continue this conversation. Perhaps the bistro?'

Émilie Longpré hesitated just an instant, then agreed. They dropped off Henri then made their way through the dawn to Olivier's Bistro.

'*Joyeux Noël*,' the handsome young waiter said to Gamache, showing them to the table by the freshly lit fireplace. 'It's good to see you again.'

Gamache held the chair for Em and looked after the young man going to the cappuccino machine to make their bowls of *café au lait*.

'Philippe Croft,' said Em, following his gaze. 'Nice young man.'

Gamache smiled delightedly. Young Croft. The last time he'd met Philippe, during an earlier case, he'd been less than likable.

It was just eight o'clock and they had the place to themselves.

'This is a rare treat, Chief Inspector,' said Em, surveying the menu.

Her hair was standing on end from the static caused when

she'd removed her tuque. But then so was his. They both looked as though they'd had a small fright. Now they sipped their coffees, feeling the warmth spread through their bodies. Their faces were rosy and their cheeks beginning to thaw. The smell of fresh brewed coffee mingled with the wood smoke from the young fire, and the world seemed cozy and right.

'Do you still want your curling lesson this morning?' Em asked. Gamache hadn't forgotten their date and was looking forward to it.

'If it isn't too cold.'

'This morning should be perfect. Look at the sky.' She nodded out the window. There was a delicate glow in the sky as the sun considered rising. 'Clear and cold. By this afternoon it'll be a killer.'

'May I suggest the eggs and sausages?' Philippe was at their elbow, his order pad ready. 'The sausages are from Monsieur Pagé's farm.'

'They're wonderful,' confided Em.

'Madame?' Gamache invited her to order first.

'I'd love the sausages, *mon beau Philippe*, but I'm afraid at my age they're a bit much. Does Monsieur Pagé still provide your back bacon?'

'*Mais oui*, home cured, Madame Longpré. The best in Quebec.'

'*Merveilleux*. Such luxury.' She leaned across the table to Gamache, genuinely enjoying herself. 'I'll take a poached egg, *s'il vous plaît*, on a piece of Sarah's baguette and some of your perfect bacon.'

'And a croissant?' Philippe looked at her playfully. They could smell the croissants baking in the shop next door, the connecting door open and eloquent.

'Perhaps just one.'

'Monsieur?'

Gamache ordered and within minutes he had a plate of sausages and French toast. A jug of local maple syrup was at his elbow and a basket of croissants steamed between them, accompanied by jars of homemade jams. The two ate and talked and sipped their coffees in front of the lively and warm fire.

'So what did you think of CC?' he asked.

'She struck me as a very lonely woman. I felt sorry for her.'

'Others have described her as selfish, petty, hurtful and frankly a little stupid. Not someone you'd choose to be with.'

'They're right, of course. She was desperately unhappy and took it out on others. People do, don't they? They can't stand it when others are happy.'

'Yet you invited her to your home.'

This was the question he'd wanted to ask since she'd mentioned it on their walk. But he'd needed to be able to watch her face.

'I've been desperately unhappy in my life.' Her voice was quiet. 'Have you, Chief Inspector?'

It wasn't a response he could have predicted. He nodded.

'I thought so. I think people who have had that experience and survived have a responsibility to help others. We can't let someone drown where we were saved.'

Now the room was very still and Gamache realized he was holding his breath.

'I understand, madame, and I agree,' he said finally. Gently he asked, 'Could you tell me about your sadness?'

She met his eyes. Then she reached into her cardigan

pocket and pulled out a ball of white Kleenex, and something else. On the table between them she placed a small black and white photograph, cracked and dusty from the tissues. She caressed it clean with one practiced finger.

'This is Gus, my husband, and my son David.'

A tall man had his arm across the shoulder of a lanky young man, a boy really. He looked to be a teenager, with long shaggy hair and a coat with wide lapels. His tie was also wide, as was the car behind them.

'This was just before Christmas 1976. David was a violinist. Well, actually, he only played one piece.' She laughed. 'Extraordinary, really. He heard it when he was a child, little more than a baby. Gus and I had it on the hi-fi and David suddenly stopped what he was doing and went right over to the console. He made us play it over and over. As soon as he had the words he asked for a violin. We thought he was kidding, of course. But he wasn't. One day I heard him practicing in the basement. It was shaky, and squeaky, but sure enough, it was the same piece.'

Gamache could feel the blood run from his hands and feet and into his heart, which gave a squeeze.

'David had taught himself the piece. He was six. His teacher eventually quit since David refused to practice or play anything else. Just the one piece. Willful child. Gus's side of the family.' She smiled.

'What was it?'

'Tchaikovsky's violin concerto in D Major.'

Gamache couldn't bring it to mind.

'David was a normal teenager. He played goalie on his hockey team, dated one of the Chartrand girls for most of high school, wanted to go to the Université de Montréal to

252

study forestry. He was a lovely boy, but not an extraordinary one, except in that one feature.'

She closed her eyes and after a moment one hand turned upward, exposing her slim wrist, blue with veins. The hand moved fluidly back and forth. The ghost notes filled the space between them and surrounded the table and eventually the entire bistro seemed filled with music Gamache couldn't hear but could imagine. And knew Em heard perfectly clearly.

'Lucky boy, to have found such a passion,' he said quietly.

'That's exactly it. If I hadn't ever met the divine I'd have known it in his face as he played. He was blessed, and so were we. Still, I don't think he planned to take it any further, but then something happened. He came home just before his Christmas exams with a notice. Every year the Lycée held a competition. All the musicians had to play the same piece, chosen by the committee. That year,' she nodded to the photo, 'it was Tchaikovsky's violin concerto in D Major. David was beside himself. It was to be held the fifteenth of December in Gaspé. Gus decided to drive him there. They could have taken the train or flown, but Gus wanted some time alone with David. You know what it's like, perhaps, with teenagers? David was seventeen and a typical boy. Not very talkative about his feelings. Gus wanted to let him know, in his own way, that his father loved him and would do anything in the world for him. This picture was taken just before they left.'

Em gazed down and her finger crept along the wooden table toward it, but stopped just short.

'David came in second in the competition. He called, so excited.' She could hear him still, breathless, as though unable to contain his happiness. 'They were thinking of staying to hear some other contestants but I'd been watching the weather and there was a storm coming in, so I convinced them to leave right away. You can guess the rest. It was a beautiful day, like today. Clear and cold. But it proved to be too cold, too bright. Black ice, they said. And the sun right in Gus's face. Too much light.'

TWENTY-FOUR

'So who's CC's mother?' Beauvoir asked. They'd been in the morning meeting in the Incident Room for half an hour and he was feeling like his old self again.

With one significant difference.

His old self had despised Agent Yvette Nichol, but this morning he found himself quite liking her and not quite remembering what had been the problem. They'd had breakfast together at the B&B and ended up laughing hysterically at her description of trying to warm up his hot water bottle. In the microwave.

'Sure you find it funny,' said Gabri, plopping two Eggs Benedicts in front of them. 'You didn't come home to find what looked like the cat exploded in the micro. Never liked the cat. Loved the hot water bottle.'

Now they all sat round the conference table listening to reports. The Li Bien ball had been produced and dusted for prints. They found three sets which had been transmitted to the lab in Montreal.

Nichol had reported her findings. She'd gone into Montreal to interview the school about Crie.

'I wanted to get more than just a report card. Seems she's considered a smart girl, but not very bright, if you follow. Plodding, methodical. I get the impression Crie was a bit of a blight for Miss Edward's School for Girls. The vice principal called her Brie once then corrected herself. Crie's best subject is science, though she was beginning to show some interest in the theatre. She'd hidden away for the past few years doing the technical stuff, but this year she was actually in the play. Bit of a disaster apparently. Stage fright. Had to be led off the stage. The other kids weren't very kind. Neither were the parents, apparently.'

'And the teachers?' Gamache asked.

Nichol shook her head. 'But there was something interesting. The tuition cheque bounced a few times. So I looked into their finances. Seems CC and her husband were living way beyond their means. In fact, they were a couple of months away from complete disaster.'

'Was CC insured?' Beauvoir asked.

'For two hundred thousand dollars. Richard Lyon comes from a modest background. Gained a degree in engineering from Waterloo but never achieved professional status. Went to work at his current job eighteen years ago. He's a kind of low-level manager. Organizes schedules. An under-achiever. He makes forty-two thousand a year, clears thirty. She hasn't seen a profit in the six years she's had her company. Does small interior design jobs here and there, but seems to have spent most of the last year writing the book and coming up with her own line of household items. Here.' Nichol tossed a catalogue onto the table. 'That's the prototype for the catalogue she was planning to put out, the one the photographer was working on, I guess.'

Beauvoir grabbed it. Li Bien soaps, Serenity coffee mugs, Be Calm bathrobes.

'CC had lined up a meeting for next week with Direct Mail Inc.,' Nichol continued. 'It's the biggest marketer of catalogue items in the United States. She was planning to sell them on her line. If she had, it would have been huge.'

'What do they say?' Isabelle Lacoste asked.

'I have a call in to them,' said Nichol, a smile she hoped said *thank you for asking* on her face.

'Any word from the lab on those pictures he took at the curling?' Beauvoir asked Lacoste.

'I've sent an agent to get the negatives developed. Should hear soon.'

'Good,' said Gamache, then told them about niacin, *The Lion in Winter*, and Psalm 46:10.

'So who's CC's mother?' Beauvoir asked the key question.

'There're a few women in Three Pines who're the right age,' said Lacoste. 'Émilie Longpré, Kaye Thompson, and Ruth Zardo.'

'But only one of them has the initial L,' said Agent Lemieux, speaking for the first time. He was watching Agent Nichol closely. He wasn't sure why, but he didn't like her, didn't like her sudden appearance and certainly didn't like this newfound camaraderie with Inspector Beauvoir.

'I'll check them out,' said Lacoste, and the meeting broke up.

Gamache reached for the wooden box on his desk, turning it over automatically to stare at the letters stuck to the bottom.

'What's that?' Beauvoir pulled up a chair beside the chief.

'A piece of evidence from another case,' said Gamache, handing it to Beauvoir. As he took it Gamache suddenly had the impression Beauvoir would be able to see something he hadn't. He'd look at the letters on the outside and inside and put it all together. Gamache watched the Inspector handle the box.

'One of your Christmas cases?'

Gamache nodded, not wanting to break Beauvoir's concentration.

'Collected letters? What a nutcase.' He handed the box back to Gamache.

Well, so much for intuition.

As he left Gamache bent down and spoke to Lacoste. 'Add Beatrice Mayer to your list.'

The curling stone thundered down the rough ice and hit the rock at the far end with a huge bang that moments later bounced off the hills surrounding Lac Brume. It was a bitterly cold morning, the coldest of the winter so far and the mercury still falling. By midday their flesh would freeze in seconds. The sun, teasing them with light but no warmth, hit the snow and magnified, blinding anyone not wearing dark glasses.

Billy Williams had cleared the curling surface on Lac Brume for them, and now he, Beauvoir, Lemieux and Gamache watched tiny Émilie Longpré straighten up, her breath coming out in jagged puffs.

Not long, thought Gamache. We'll have to get her in soon before she freezes. Before we all do.

'Your turn,' she said to Beauvoir, who'd been watching

her with polite attention. Curling was not to be taken seriously. As Beauvoir crouched and stared at the other end of the ice, twenty-five feet away, he could see where this was going. He'd astonish them with his natural ability. Soon he'd be fighting off pleas to join the Canadian Olympic curling team. He'd turn them down, of course, too embarrassed to be associated with such a ridiculous pastime. Though maybe, when he could no longer do any real sports, he'd consider joining the Olympic curling team.

Clara slipped into the claw-foot tub. She was still pissed off at Peter for dumpster diving, but was beginning to feel better. She slid down into the hot scented water, her toes playing with lumps of herbal bath, a Christmas gift from Peter's mother. She knew she should call to thank her, but that could wait. His mother insisted on calling her Clare and up until this year had given her cooking gifts. Books, pans, an apron once. Clara hated cooking and suspected Peter's mother knew it.

Clara swished her hands back and forth and let her mind wander to her favorite fantasy. The director of the Museum of Modern Art in New York knocking on her door. His car would have stalled out in the bitterly cold temperatures, and he'd need help.

Clara could see it all. He'd come into the house and she'd make him a cup of tea, but when she turned to give it to him he'd have disappeared. Into her studio. She'd find him there, staring.

No. Weeping.

He'd be weeping at the beauty, the pain, the brilliance of her art.

'Who did these?' he'd ask, not bothering to wipe the tears away.

She'd say nothing, just let him realize the great artist was before him, humble and beautiful. He'd declare her the greatest artist of her generation, or any other. The most gifted, astonishing, brilliant artist that ever lived, anywhere, any time.

Because she was nothing if not fair, she'd show him Peter's studio, and the chief curator of MOMA would be polite. But there'd be no doubt. She was the real talent in the family.

Clara hummed.

'Now kneel down, Inspector. You grab the handle of the rock as though you're going to shake hands.' She was bending over him. 'Now, you bring the rock back with your right arm and your left leg also swings back, then you bring both forward at the same time and slide down the ice, the rock leading the way. Don't shove it, mind. Just release.'

Beauvoir looked down the curling rink to her stone at the far end. It suddenly seemed very far away.

Gamache watched Beauvoir take a deep breath and bring his right hand back, the rock threatening to overbalance him already. Beauvoir remembered the silly broom and leaned over on it, feeling his boots begin to slip. This couldn't be right.

The rock thumped onto the ice and he gave a great heave, knowing he'd somehow lost the momentum he was meant to build up. His right arm shot out, still clinging to the stone, and his left leg scrambled for purchase. He could feel himself falling.

Beauvoir fell flat on the ice, arms and legs splayed, the stone still in his grip.

'Whale oil beef hooked,' said Billy Williams, laughing.

Clara was thinking about the movie the night before. It'd been a while since she'd watched a video. Almost all their movies were on DVD, mostly because Peter's favorite videos were ruined. He'd kept pausing them at his favorite spots to watch over and over and the tape had stretched. Gone wonky.

Clara sat up in the bath, bits of fragrant herbs clinging to her body. Could that be it?

'Honey, Mom's on the phone from Montreal, calling to thank us for our gift.' Peter walked in holding the phone. Clara waved him off, but it was too late. Wiping her hands she glared at Peter.

'Hello, Mrs Morrow. Well you're welcome, and Merry Christmas to you too. My job at the pharmacy? It's going very well, thank you.' She looked daggers at Peter. Clara hadn't worked at the pharmacy in fifteen years. 'And thank you for your gift. Very thoughtful. I'm using it now. Yes, *bon appétit*.' Clara hung up and handed the phone to Peter. 'Seems she gave me a pack of dried soup. Vegetable.'

Looking down at her toes, Clara noticed a pea bobbing on the surface, next to a bright orange rehydrated carrot.

'Did I win?' Beauvoir brushed himself off and stared at the curling stone at his feet.

'Depends what game you're playing.' Em smiled. 'You've definitely mastered the stationary stone game. *Félicitations*.'

'*Merci, madame*.' The terrible cold of the day was kind to the Inspector. It hid any blush he might have produced. As he looked at the rock sitting forlornly at his feet a grudging, and secret, respect for curlers was born in Beauvoir.

Gamache took out the photos his people had taken of the crime scene. Five curling stones were imbedded in the snow where Mother had 'cleared the house'.

An idea started to form in Gamache's mind.

TWENTY-FIVE

'I'm sorry, Chief Inspector Gamache isn't in, Mrs Morrow,' said Agent Lacoste, dragging her eyes from her screen to look at the woman in front of her.

'When do you expect him?'

'I'm not sure.' She looked at the clock. Almost noon. 'I would imagine he'll be back soon. Is it important?'

Clara hesitated. She didn't really know, but something told her it was.

'No. It'll wait.' She turned to go and caught sight of Yvette Nichol working on another computer. There was no love lost between the two women, though Clara was still baffled by the hostility this young agent had shown when they'd first met a year ago. Now Agent Nichol looked up from her desk, caught Clara's eye, and immediately looked back down.

Well, it's better than the evil eye I used to get, thought Clara.

The Sûreté officers were alone on the ice now. Émilie Longpré had gone to have lunch with Kaye in Williamsburg and Billy Williams had mumbled something about either going to practice for the World Cup of skiing or cutting wood for blast-off. It seemed to Gamache that Billy made perfect sense to everyone but him. Gamache couldn't understand a word the man said.

Gamache walked to the stands, sitting there for a long, cold moment staring at the ice, then at the spot where CC had sat, and died. Then he walked round the stands and over to where Billy Williams had parked his truck.

.'The murderer stood here,' said Gamache firmly, planting himself on the snow. 'He watched the curling, and waited. Just as CC got up to grab the chair in front, he attached the booster cables.'

'The lab's confirmed what we already knew,' said Lemieux. 'Mr Williams's cables were the ones used. They were found in his truck all blackened. But he says he attached them from his generator to the heating lamp, so how did someone take them from the lamp to the chair in the middle of the curling without being seen?'

'They didn't have to,' said Gamache. 'The murderer must have detached the heating lamp before anyone showed up, and clipped the cables onto the chair.' He strode from the phantom truck to the phantom lamp and further onto the ice, to the imaginary chairs. 'While everyone was at the community breakfast he took the cables from the lamp and clamped them onto the leg of the lawn chair, then took the other end off the generator.'

'But wouldn't people have noticed that the lamp wasn't working?' Lemieux asked.

'They did. At least two people talked about how cold it was, including Kaye Thompson. That was what made me believe that lamp was never on.'

'I still don't understand why no one saw anything,' said Beauvoir.

'Well, for one thing, any sound he made, his boots on the snow for instance, would be masked by the generator. And Mr Williams's truck was behind the stands. Not exactly hidden by them, but anyone in the stands would have to work to see it. The only people who could have seen anything were Kaye and CC. But there's more. At first I thought we were dealing with a very lucky person but now I think it wasn't luck but careful planning. The murderer chose his moment precisely. He waited until all eyes were guaranteed to be on the curling.'

Agent Lemieux tried to see it all. The curlers, the spectators, the two women in their lawn chairs. The electrified chair sitting just ahead of them.

'Something special happened in the match,' said Gamache, walking now toward the ice, then turning round to look at the two perplexed officers. 'Mother Bea cleared the house. It was a tradition. How many times have we heard that in the last two days? Some people come just to see that. And why? We found out today. In a sport that thrives on subtlety and finesse, that's the most passionate of plays. Almost violent. Imagine the sound of Mother's stone as she hurtles it down the ice with all the force she can muster. Imagine that stone hitting another stone at the far end, then that stone hitting another and another. An entire chain reaction. Within moments curling stones would be smashing off each other, going in all directions and causing a monstrous noise. Very exciting.'

'Riveting,' said Beauvoir.

'And noisy,' said Lemieux, and he had the satisfaction of

seeing Chief Inspector Armand Gamache turn to him, a huge triumphant smile on his face, his eyes lively with delight.

'Got it. That's it. What a perfect moment for murder. Who was going to tear their eyes from the spectacle? And who would hear the screams of a woman being electrocuted? It was perfectly timed.'

'But how did he know CC would even grab the chair, never mind at that very moment?' Beauvoir asked.

'Good question,' admitted Gamache, walking briskly toward the relative warmth of their car. The day was growing dangerously cold and it was getting hard to talk. 'And why didn't Kaye Thompson see anything? And how did the murderer unhook the cable and toss it back into Billy's truck again without being seen?'

The men got into the car and sat while it warmed up. Agent Lemieux's toes were numb and he scrunched them up and down in his boots trying to get the blood going. Beauvoir looked out the frosted window.

'Well, the curlers are off the list. They couldn't have done it. And if Myrna Landers sticks to her story and says Richard Lyon was beside her the whole time that lets him out, though I still think he did it.'

'What do you think, agent?' Gamache asked Lemieux.

'I think this doesn't make sense. The murderer had to feed her niacin at the community breakfast, spill anti-freeze behind the chair, make sure she was wearing boots with metal soles or nails, hook up booster cables and wait for the perfect moment, all without being seen. Then clean up after himself? It's just way too complicated. Why not just shoot her?'

'I wonder,' said Gamache.

*

The photographs from the lab arrived after lunch and the team huddled round anxiously as Gamache opened the envelopes. It was eerie to see the face of someone about to die. Gamache always expected to see in their eyes some foreboding, some premonition, but he'd looked at thousands of pictures just like these and never seen it.

Still, it was eerie. This was as close as they'd ever come to meeting the victim, and Gamache realized that the only photo he'd seen up 'til now was on the cover of her book and that was more a caricature. Now here she was, minutes before her time ran out. It was a shame she didn't seem to be enjoying herself. Instead she sat lemon-faced and defensive at the community breakfast. All around her people were animated, talking to neighbors, heads thrown back in laughter, but CC de Poitiers sat rigid. Beside her Richard stared down at his plate.

Was he planning murder? Were the sausages the curlers and the pancakes the chairs? Was the bacon the booster cable? And CC? What would she have been on his plate? The knife?

More pictures. Mother Bea and Myrna behind CC. CC posing with a group of suddenly glum villagers, as though CC was a cloud that had moved across their sky.

Then they were at the curling. CC in her chair, trying too hard to look like Audrey Hepburn on holiday in the Alps. But now something interesting appeared. CC's face was flushed. True, the sudden redness could be from the cold, but beside her Kaye was a delicate pink, not the purple CC'd become.

'Look.' Lacoste pointed to a picture. 'You can just see the blue of the anti-freeze by the chair.'

'Her mittens are off,' said Lemieux, pointing to another.

They were getting close. Gamache opened the next envelope. All eyes were fixed, all bodies leaning forward across the table as though trying to see the pictures a millisecond sooner. Gamache spread them across the table in a move that spoke of poker nights.

CC was on the ground. Ruth was gesturing. Olivier was bending over the body and Gabri was looking behind him, his eyes sharp and focused.

The next series of pictures showed the heroic and frantic efforts to save this woman no one liked. Clara walking away with Crie, trying to keep the girl from the grisly scene. Gabri beside Richard, holding his arm. Peter and Billy Williams running with CC toward the truck. The last one showed Billy's truck disappearing round a bend.

The pictures were eloquent, though abbreviated.

'Some are missing,' said Gamache, stern-faced. As he headed to the door, Beauvoir and Lemieux in tow, Agent Lacoste ran after him.

'Mrs Morrow's been trying to get you. And I've done a background search on the women who might have been CC's mother. Kaye Thompson's too old. Émilie Longpré had a child, but he died in an accident. Still, she could have had another. Given her up for adoption. But the most interesting thing I found is Beatrice Mayer. Beatrice Louise Mayer.'

With that information newly arrived in his head Gamache walked determinedly to the car, Beauvoir hurrying to catch up, in a reversal of roles Beauvoir found disconcerting.

Saul Petrov sipped coffee and sat in the easy chair by the window in his living room. Two days ago he'd have described the chair, in fact the entire chalet, as tacky. The fabric was dull and threadbare, the carpets worn, the décor dated. A collection of spoons from various Canadian destinations hung on the wall next to a washed-out photo of Niagara Falls.

But when he'd awoken today and wandered relaxed down the scuffed stairs, he'd thought he quite liked the house. And as the sun rose and the fireplace had been lit and the coffee perked Saul realized he really liked the place.

And now he sat in the sun as it streamed through the window and looked at the stunning view of the perfect, unblemished field in front of his rented chalet, the forest beyond and beyond that the mountains, all gray and craggy.

He'd never felt such peace.

Beside him on the table sat a Banff coaster and a roll of undeveloped film.

'Hello, Clara.' Gamache spoke loudly into his cell phone. It was so tiny it felt like something found in a Christmas cracker. 'It's Gamache. I'm on a cell and it's coming in and out. You were looking for me?'

'I . . . video . . . Peter.'

'Pardon?'

'The video last night.' Suddenly her voice was crystal clear and Gamache realized they'd crested a hill. But they'd be heading into a valley soon and through a forest and he was sure to lose the signal then. He hoped she got to the point fast.

'Peter has DVDs now,' she was saying. Faster, faster, he said to himself, but knew enough not to say out loud. Inevitably, telling someone to do anything faster slowed the whole thing down. The car was just heading down the long slope into the valley. 'Because his videos are all stretched out of shape. He stops them at his favorite spots and that stretches the tape.' Faster, faster, thought Gamache, seeing the valley approaching. 'Do you think CC did too?' Clara asked, her voice already fading.

'We're pretty certain she didn't throw it away because it was stretched out of shape.' He wasn't following her and now he could hear the static begin.

'. . . know that. Not too bad . . . need one.'

Then the line went dead.

Saul saw the car winding up his snowy drive. He picked up the film and held it in his palm as though, by osmosis, it might tell him what to do. As CC always had.

And then he had his answer. He was finally free. He felt light, buoyant for the first time in months. Years. He even felt bright, as though perhaps he could hold his own in a conversation, as though overnight he'd been buffed up, his shine restored.

He was no longer dull.

He smiled gently and gratefully and closed his eyes, feeling the sun warm and red through his lids. He could start again here, in this place with so much light. He could buy this charming, cozy chalet and maybe take pictures of the beauty he saw all around. Maybe he could track down the artist whose portfolio CC had savaged and tell him what had happened. And say he was sorry for his part, and maybe the artist would become his friend.

The men were getting out of the car. Sûreté officers, Saul knew. He looked at the roll in his palm, walked over to the fireplace, and threw it in.

TWENTY-SIX

—

'S it down, please.' Saul took their heavy coats and stuffed them into the closet, closing the door quickly before they tumbled out. He'd decided this was Day One, the beginning of a new life, and any new life should begin without regret. Saul Petrov had decided to tell everything. Well, almost everything.

Gamache looked around the room, and sniffed. There was a smell of burning, and not of the wood in the fireplace. This was more pungent, less natural. He felt his nerves sharpen and everything seemed to slow down. Was there a fire? An electrical fire perhaps? These old chalets were often slapped together by some backwoods pioneer who knew a great deal about the cycles of nature and almost nothing about wiring. Gamache's eyes narrowed as he scanned the walls, the outlets, the lamps for wisps of smoke, as his ears searched out a telltale crackling as the electricity leaped and arced and his nose struggled to identify the strange acrid smell.

Beside him Lemieux was suddenly aware of the chief's

heightened attention. He stared at Gamache, trying to figure out what the problem was.

'What's that smell, Monsieur Petrov?' Gamache asked.

'I don't smell anything,' he said.

'I do,' said Beauvoir. 'Smells like plastic or something like that.'

Now Lemieux could smell it too.

'Oh, that,' said Petrov with a laugh. 'I tossed some old film into the fire. Outdated stuff. I guess I should have just put it in the garbage. Wasn't thinking.' He smiled disarmingly. Gamache walked over to the fireplace and sure enough there was a sizzling blob of black and yellow. An old roll of film. Or maybe not so old. Either way, it was destroyed.

'You're right,' said Gamache. Petrov was used to people, especially CC, looking right through him, but this was a new experience. He had the impression Gamache was looking into him. 'You weren't thinking. That may not have been a wise thing to do.'

Petrov's new life was barely half an hour old and already he was feeling regret. Still, this quiet man looked as though he might understand. Petrov showed them to chairs then sat down himself. He was feeling almost giddy with anticipation. He could hardly wait to confess and get on with life. Start again. He almost felt tearful and was deeply grateful to this homicide inspector for hearing his confession. Saul Petrov had been raised a staunch Catholic and like most of his generation had rejected the church, the priests and all the trappings of religion. But, now, in this modest, even silly room where in place of stained glass there were plastic placemats stapled to the wall, he felt like falling to his knees.

Oh, for a fresh start.

'There's something I need to tell you.'

Gamache didn't say a word. Petrov looked into his kindly, thoughtful eyes and suddenly no one else existed.

'CC and I were having an affair. Had been for about a year. I'm not sure, but I think her husband knows about it. We weren't very discreet, I'm afraid.'

'When were you last together?' Beauvoir asked.

'The morning of the day she died.' It took a force of will to drag his eyes from Gamache over to the tense man in the other chair. 'She came over and we had sex. It was only a physical relationship, nothing more. She didn't care for me and I didn't care for her.'

There it was. A mean little thing. He exhaled, feeling lighter already.

'Did she tell you why she bought a place here?' Beauvoir asked.

'In Three Pines? No. I wondered that myself. She had a reason for everything, though, and most of the time it was money.'

'You think money motivated her?'

'It always did. Even our affair. I'm not stupid enough to think she slept with me for the great sex. It was to get a photographer cheap. Payment in kind.'

He was surprised how ashamed he felt. Even as he spoke it seemed unbelievable. Had he really given CC a break on his bill in exchange for sex?

'I could be wrong, but I had the impression CC bought a place here because there was something in it for her, and I don't mean peace and quiet. From what I could tell the only thing CC de Poitiers loved was money. And prestige.'

'Describe your movements on the day she died,' said Beauvoir.

'I got up about seven and lit the fire, then put on coffee and waited. I knew she'd come and sure enough around eight she arrived. We didn't talk much. I asked how her Christmas was and she shrugged. I feel badly for her daughter. Can't imagine having a mother like that. Anyway, she left about an hour later. We made arrangements to meet at the community breakfast.'

'When did she decide to go?'

'Sorry?'

'Well, did she decide to go to the breakfast and curling at the last minute, or was it something she'd planned to do for a while?'

'Oh, it was planned. I told her about it, but she already knew. They'd gone the year before, just after she bought the house here. She told me to get shots of her surrounded by common folk, her words not mine. So I went off to the breakfast and shot a couple of rolls, then we went to the curling. Cold as hell. My camera eventually froze up. Had to put it under my coat, under my armpit, to thaw it out. I was moving around, trying to get different angles. CC wasn't very photogenic, so it was important to get the right lighting and angles and preferably some other point of interest in the shot. That old lady sitting beside her was great. Face full of character and the way she looked at CC, fantastic.' Petrov threw himself back in the chair and laughed at the memory of Kaye glaring as though CC was something her dog had thrown up. 'And she kept at CC to sit still, sit still. CC didn't listen to many people. Anyone, actually, in my experience, but this old lady she listened to. I would too.

Scary as hell. And sure enough CC sat still. Kinda. Made my job easier, anyway.'

'Why was Kaye Thompson telling CC to sit still?' Chief Inspector Gamache asked.

'CC was a nervous sort. Always jumping up to straighten an ashtray or picture or a lamp. Nothing was ever right. I guess it finally got on the old girl's nerves. She looked as though she was about to kill her.'

Gamache knew it was just a figure of speech, and Petrov clearly didn't even realize what he'd said.

'We got your developed film from the lab this morning,' said Beauvoir, walking to the table and setting them out. Petrov followed as did the others. There on the table was a series of stills. CC's final moments, and beyond.

'Notice anything curious?' Beauvoir asked.

After a minute or so Petrov straightened up and shook his head. 'It looks like what I remember.'

'Nothing missing? Like, oh, the entire series of pictures from here to here? From CC alive to CC dead. The entire murder is missing.' Beauvoir's voice rose. Unlike Gamache, who could sit and chat with suspects all day hoping they'd eventually open up, Beauvoir knew the only way to handle a suspect was to show them who was boss.

'That's where the camera froze, I guess,' said Petrov, scanning the images, trying not to let the fear out, trying not to sink into the petulance and self-pity so much a part of his life with CC.

'That's convenient,' said Beauvoir, taking a deep breath. 'Or maybe I just inhaled the frame that shows the murder? What do you think? Did you burn the film that shows CC being murdered?'

'Why would I? I mean, if I have film of CC being murdered, wouldn't that prove I didn't do it?'

That stopped Beauvoir cold.

'I gave you all the rolls I shot that day. I promise.'

Beauvoir's eyes were narrow as he watched this little man cower. He's done something wrong, I know it, thought Beauvoir. But he couldn't figure out how to nail him.

The officers left, Beauvoir stomping to the car and Lemieux trailing behind, not wanting to become the target for Beauvoir's unexercised frustration. Gamache stood on the stoop squinting into the sun, feeling his nostrils contract in the bitter cold.

'It's lovely here. You're a lucky man,' and Gamache pulled off a glove and offered his hand. Saul Petrov took it, feeling the warmth of human contact. He'd been with CC so long he'd almost forgotten that most humans generate heat. 'Don't be a foolish man, Mr Petrov.'

'I've told you the truth, Chief Inspector.'

'I hope so, sir.' Gamache smiled and walked quickly to the car, his face already beginning to freeze. Petrov went into the warm living room and watched the car disappear round a bend, then he looked again on the bright new world, and wondered just how foolish he'd been. He rummaged through some drawers and found a pen and an unused Christmas card. He wrote a short message then headed into St-Rémy to find the mailbox.

'Stop the car,' said Gamache. Beauvoir applied the brakes then looked at the chief. Gamache sat in the passenger's seat staring out the window, his lips moving slightly and his eyes narrow. After a minute he closed his eyes and smiled, shaking his head.

'I need to speak to Kaye Thompson. Drop me off in Williamsburg, then get back to Three Pines and take *The Lion in Winter* over to Clara Morrow. Ask her to show you what she meant. She'll understand.'

Beauvoir turned the car toward Williamsburg.

Gamache had just figured out what Clara was saying in their garbled conversation, and if she was right, it could explain a great deal.

'Fuck the Pope?'

Gamache never thought he'd hear himself say that, even as a question. Especially as a question.

'That's what they said.' Kaye looked at him, her blue eyes sharp, but now veiled by something else. Exhaustion. Beside her on the sofa Émilie Longpré sat forward and listened, watching her friend closely.

'Why?' Kaye asked him.

It was, of course, the one question he asked all the time and now someone was asking him. He had the impression there was something he didn't understand going on, some subtext that was escaping him.

He thought for a moment, looking out the picture window of her modest room in the seniors' home. She had a splendid view across Lac Brume. The sun was setting and long mountain shadows cut the lake so that part was in blinding light and part in darkness, like yin and yang. Slowly the scene faded and he saw the boys in the trench, their young eyes filled with terror. They were being told to do the inconceivable, and, inconceivably, they were about to do it.

'I wonder whether they knew that words could kill,' said

Gamache, slowly, thinking out loud, seeing the defenseless, indefensibly young men preparing for death.

What did it take to do that? Could he? It was one thing to rush without thought into a dangerous situation, it was quite another to wait, and wait, and wait, knowing what was coming. And do it anyway. For no purpose. To no end.

'That's ridiculous. Yelling "Fuck the Pope" wouldn't kill a single German. What do you use for ammunition? When a murderer shoots at you what do you do? Run after him yelling *"Tabernacle!"*, *"Sacré!"*, *"Chalice!"*? I hope I'm never in a life and death situation with you. *Merde.*'

Gamache laughed. Clearly his insightful comment had failed to impress. And she was probably right. He couldn't begin to understand why the young men had yelled that at the Somme.

'I have pictures here I'd like you both to see.' He spread Saul's photographs on a table.

'Who's that?' asked Kaye.

'That's you, *ma belle*,' said Émilie.

'Are you kidding? I look like a potato in a laundry hamper.'

'You seem to be speaking to CC in a few of the pictures,' said Gamache. 'What were you saying?'

'Probably telling her to keep still. She kept wiggling. Very annoying.'

'And she listened to you? Why?'

'Everyone listens to Kaye,' said Em with a smile. 'Like her father, she's a natural leader.'

Gamache thought that wasn't totally true. He thought that of the three friends Émilie Longpré was the real leader, though the quietest.

'Our Kaye here ran Thompson Mills up on Mont Echo

for decades, all by herself. Trained and organized a bunch of mountain men, and they adored her. It was the most successful logging operation around.'

'If I could get some brute into a lye bath once a week I could get CC to stop fidgeting,' said Kaye. 'Never could stand the nervous sort.'

'We now believe de Poitiers wasn't her real name,' said Gamache, watching their reactions. But both women continued to stare at the photographs. 'We think her mother came from Three Pines and that's why CC came here. To find her mother.'

'Poor child,' said Em, still not looking up. Gamache wondered whether she was deliberately avoiding eye contact. 'Did she?'

'Find her mother?' said Gamache. 'I don't know. But we know her mother's name started with an L. Do you know of anyone?'

'Well, there is one,' said Émilie. 'A woman named Longpré.'

Kaye sputtered with laughter. 'Come on, Chief Inspector. You can't suspect Em here? Do you think she could abandon a child? Em could no more do that than she could win a curling match. Absolutely incapable.'

'Thank you, dear.'

'Anyone else?' he asked. There was a pause and both women eventually shook their heads. Gamache knew then they were hiding something. They had to have been. They'd both lived in Three Pines when CC's mother was there and back in the fifties in a small Quebec village a pregnant girl would have been noticed.

'Can I offer you a lift home?' Em asked after a long, uncomfortable silence.

Gamache bent to pick up the photographs and his eye caught something. Kaye looking particularly cross at CC, and CC staring ahead at the empty chair as though desperate to get to it. He knew then how the murderer had done it.

TWENTY-SEVEN

C lara and Peter Morrow turned their television and VCR on and Beauvoir shoved the tape into the slot.

He wasn't looking forward to this. Two hours of some old English movie where all they probably did was talk, talk, talk. No explosions. No sex. He thought he'd rather have the flu than sit through *The Lion in Winter*. Beside him on the sofa Agent Lemieux was all excited.

Kids.

Émilie Longpré dropped Gamache at the old Hadley house as he requested.

'Would you like me to wait?'

'No, madame, *mais vous êtes très gentille*. The walk back will do me good.'

'It's a cold night, Chief Inspector, and getting colder.' She pointed to her dashboard. The time and temperature were displayed. Minus fifteen celsius already and the sun had just set. It was four thirty.

'I've never liked this house,' she said, looking at the turrets and blank windows. Ahead the village of Three Pines beckoned, the lights glowing and warm with a promise of company and an aperitif by a glad fire. With a wrench Gamache opened the car door, which screamed in protest, its hinges frozen and crying. He watched as Émilie's car disappeared over the small hill into the village, then he turned back to the house. A light could be seen in the living room and a hall light went on after he'd rung the bell.

'Come in, come in.' Richard Lyon practically yanked him through the door then slammed it shut. 'Terrible night. Come in, Chief Inspector.'

Oh, for God's sake, don't sound so hearty. Can't you just once sound normal? Try to be like someone you admire. President Roosevelt, maybe. Or Captain Jean Luc Picard.

'What can I do for you?' Lyon liked the sound of his voice now. Calm and measured and in control. Just don't fuck up.

'I need to ask you some questions, but first, how's your daughter?'

'Crie?'

Why was it, Gamache wondered, that every time he asked about Crie, Lyon seemed perplexed, almost surprised to discover he had a daughter, or that anyone cared.

'She's doing all right, I suppose. Ate something for lunch. I put the heat up so she's not so cold.'

'Is she speaking?'

'No, but then she never did much.'

Gamache felt like shaking this lethargic man who seemed to live in a world of cotton batting, insulated and muffled. Without being invited Gamache walked into the living room and sat down opposite Crie. The girl's clothes had changed.

Now she wore white shorts that strangled her legs, and a pink halter top. Her hair was in pigtails, and her face blank.

'Crie, it's Chief Inspector Gamache. How are you?'

No reply.

'It's cold in here. Do you mind if I give you my sweater?' He removed his cardigan and draped it over her bare shoulders, then turned to Lyon.

'When I leave I suggest you put a blanket round her and light the fireplace.'

'But it doesn't throw much heat,' said Lyon. Don't sound petulant. Sound strong, sound like the man of the house. Sound decisive. 'Besides, there's no wood.'

'There's wood in the basement. I'll help you bring it up, and you're probably right about the heat, but the fire is cheerful and bright. Those things are important as well. Now, I have some questions for you.' Gamache walked out of the living room and into the hall. He didn't want to spend much time there. He wanted to meet Myrna in her bookstore before it closed.

'What was your wife's real name?'

'De Poitiers.'

'Her real name.'

Lyon looked completely at sea. 'Not de Poitiers? What're you saying?'

'She made that up. You didn't know?'

Lyon shook his head.

'What are your finances, Monsieur Lyon?'

He opened his mouth then clamped it shut before the lie could escape. There was no longer any need to lie, to pretend to be something and someone he wasn't. CC was the one who insisted and had made him go along. Pretend they were born to be in a house like this, the manor house, the one on the hill. Born to greatness. Born to riches.

'I signed over my pension to buy this house,' he admitted. 'We're in way over our heads.'

He was surprised how easy that was. CC had told him they could never admit the truth. If people knew what life was really like for them, they'd be ruined. But deceit and secrecy had brought them to ruin anyway. And now Richard Lyon told the truth and nothing bad happened.

'Not any more. Your wife was insured for hundreds of thousands of dollars.'

Something bad just happened, and now Lyon deeply regretted telling the truth. What would President Roosevelt do? Captain Picard? CC?

'I don't know what you're talking about.'

Lie.

'Your signature's on the policy. We have the documents.'

Something very bad indeed was happening.

'You're an engineer by training, and an inventor. You could easily hook up the booster cables that electrocuted your wife. You'd know that she'd need to be standing in water and have bare hands. You could have slipped her the niacin over break-fast. You knew her well enough to know she'd take the best seat under the heat lamp.' Now Gamache's voice, which had been so reasonable it somehow added to the nightmare, grew very quiet. He reached into the satchel and brought out a photograph. 'What's troubled me from the very start was how the murderer knew CC would grab the chair in front of her. It's not the sort of thing people do. Now I know. This is how.'

He showed Richard Lyon the picture. Richard saw his wife

in the minute or so before she died. Beside her Kaye was saying something, but CC's attention was riveted on the chair in front.

Richard Lyon blanched.

'You, sir, would know too.'

'I didn't do it.' His voice was tiny and reedy. Even the voices in his head had fled, leaving him alone now. All alone.

'He didn't do it,' said Myrna twenty minutes later.

'How d'you know?' Gamache asked, settling into the rocking chair. He stretched his long legs out in front of the woodstove, which was radiating heat. Myrna had stirred up a hot rum toddy for him and it sat on a stack of *New York Review of Books* on the blanket box between them. Gamache was thawing out.

'He sat beside me on the bleachers the whole time.'

'I remember you told me that, but is it possible he left for a few minutes without you noticing?'

'As you were walking here from the old Hadley house would you have noticed if your coat had fallen off, just for a few minutes?' She had a twinkle in her eye as she asked.

'Maybe.' He knew what she was getting at, and didn't want to hear it. Didn't want to hear that his perfect suspect, his only perfect suspect, couldn't have done it because Myrna here would have noticed the sudden absence of Lyon's body heat, if not his personality.

'Look, I don't have any love for the man,' she said. 'Someone over a period of years has screwed Crie up to the point where she's almost comatose. At first I thought she might be autistic, but after spending a few minutes with her

I don't think so. I think she's run away, inside her head. And I think Richard Lyon's to blame.'

'Tell me.' Gamache picked up his warm mug. He could smell the rum and the spices.

'Well, let me be careful here. In my opinion Crie's been emotionally and verbally abused all her life. I think CC was the abuser, but there are generally three parties to child abuse. The abused, the abuser and the bystander. One parent does it but the other knows it's happening and does nothing.'

'If CC emotionally abused her daughter, would she also have abused her husband?' Gamache remembered Lyon, frightened and lost.

'Almost without a doubt. Still, he's Crie's father and he needed to save her.'

'And didn't.'

Myrna nodded. 'Can you imagine what it was like living in that house?' Myrna's back was to the window and she couldn't see the old Hadley house, but she could feel it.

'Should we call Family Services? Would Crie be better somewhere else?'

'No, the worst is over, I think. What she needs is a loving parent and intense therapy. Has anyone spoken to her school?'

'They say she's bright, in fact her grades are very high, but she doesn't fit in.'

'And probably never will now. Too much damage done. We become our beliefs, and Crie believes something horrible about herself. Has heard it all her life, and now it haunts her, in her own mother's voice. It's the voice most of us hear in the quiet moments, whispering kindnesses or accusations. Our mother.'

'Or our father,' said Gamache, 'though in this case he said nothing. She said too much and he said not enough. Poor Crie. No wonder it led to murder.'

'We live in a world of guided missiles and misguided men,' said Myrna. 'Dr Martin Luther King, Junior.'

Gamache nodded, then remembered something else.

> *'Your beliefs become your thoughts*
> *Your thoughts become your words*
> *Your words become your actions*
> *Your actions become your destiny.*

Mahatma Gandhi,' he said. 'There's more, but I can't remember it all.'

'I didn't know the Mahatma was so chatty, but I agree with him. Very powerful. It starts with our beliefs, and our beliefs come from our parents, and if we have a sick parent we have sick beliefs and it infects everything we think and do.'

Gamache wondered who CC's mother was and what beliefs she'd filled her daughter with. He sipped his toddy, his chilled body finally warming up, and looked around.

The store felt like an old library in a country house. The walls were lined with warm wooden shelves, and they in turn were lined with books. Hooked rugs were scattered here and there and a Vermont Castings woodstove sat in the middle of the store with a sofa facing it and a rocking chair on either side. Gamache, who loved bookstores, thought this was just the most attractive one he'd ever met.

He'd arrived a few minutes before five, passing Ruth. The elderly poet again stopped halfway across the village green and plunked down on the icy bench. He looked out Myrna's window now and saw her there still, rigidly and frigidly outlined in the cheerful lights of the Christmas tree.

'Well, all children are sad,' quoted Gamache, 'but some get over it.'

Myrna followed his gaze.

'Beer walk,' she said.

'Beer walk,' repeated Robert Lemieux. He was in the Morrow home, having wandered away from the television set. Clara and Inspector Beauvoir were still there, eyes like satellite dishes, staring at the screen. The only sign of life Lemieux had seen in Beauvoir since *The Lion in Winter* had begun was the occasional gasp. Lemieux had tried to get into it, but found himself drifting off to sleep. He had visions of his head slipping onto Beauvoir's shoulder, mouth open, drooling. Best to get up and walk around.

Now he stared out the window and Peter Morrow joined him.

'What's she doing?' Lemieux pointed to the old woman sitting on the bench while the rest of the village huddled indoors or scurried through the night that felt as though the air itself would freeze solid.

'Oh, that's her beer walk.'

Lemieux shook his head. Pathetic old drunk.

When Myrna finished explaining Gamache walked to his coat, feeling inside each pocket until he came to what he was looking for. The copy of Ruth's book found on Elle's body.

He returned to his seat and opened it, reading at random.

'She's a remarkable poet,' said Myrna. 'Too bad she's such

a mess as a person. May I?' She reached out for the book and opened it at the beginning. 'Did Clara lend you this?'

'No. Why?'

'Well, it's inscribed to her.' Myrna showed him. 'You stink, love Ruth.'

'Clara's "You stink"?'

'Well, she did that day. Isn't that funny? She said she lost it. I guess she found it again, though you say you didn't get it from her?'

'No, it's part of an investigation.'

'A homicide investigation?'

'You said she lost it after the signing? Where?' Gamache was leaning forward now, his bright eyes focused on Myrna.

'At Ogilvy's. She'd bought the book at Ruth's launch, had it signed and then we had to leave.' Myrna could feel his energy and felt herself getting excited, though she didn't know why.

'Did you come straight back?'

'I got the car and picked her up outside. We didn't stop anywhere.'

'Did she go anywhere else before you picked her up?'

Myrna thought about it and shook her head. Gamache stood up. He had to get over to the Morrow place.

'Well, there was one thing she told me the next day. She bought some food for this old beggar outside. She—' Myrna stopped herself.

'Go on.' Gamache turned at the door.

'Nothing.'

Gamache just stared.

'I can't tell you. It's for Clara to say.'

'The beggar's dead. Murdered.' He held up Ruth's book and said softly, 'You need to tell me.'

TWENTY-EIGHT

~

Peter ushered Gamache into their home and took his coat. There was a definite smell of popcorn and the sounds of a Gothic choir in the background.

'They're just finishing the movie,' said Peter.

'It's over,' said Clara, popping into the kitchen to greet Gamache. 'Even better the second time, I think. And we found something.'

They walked through to the living room to find Jean Guy Beauvoir staring at the screen, wide-eyed, as the credits rolled.

'*Mon Dieu*, no wonder you English won on the Plains of Abraham,' he said. 'You're all nuts.'

'It does help, in war,' agreed Peter. 'But we're not all like Eleanor of Aquitaine or Henry.' He was tempted to point out that Eleanor and Henry were actually both French, but decided that would be rude.

'You think not?' Beauvoir asked. He'd seen enough of the Anglos in Quebec to make him wonder. It was their secrecy that always scared him. He couldn't figure out what they were thinking. And if he couldn't figure that out, he couldn't begin to know what they'd do. He felt exposed and endangered around the English. And he didn't like it. Frankly, he didn't like them, and this film had done nothing to change his mind.

Terrifying.

'Here.' Clara pressed the rewind and the tape whizzed. 'It's at about minute seventeen. The tape goes strange.'

Gamache had finally figured out Clara's garbled message. Video tapes stretch when someone stops them at the same spot often enough. And when they stretch, the picture goes wonky. Clara's message had been that if Peter stopped his videos at an important point and the tape stretched, then maybe CC had done the same thing.

'There is a spot where the tape goes strange,' said Lemieux. 'But we watched it over and over and nothing's happening there.'

'I think you'll find', Gamache turned to the young officer, 'that there's a reason for every frame of this film. And there's a reason CC stopped it there.'

Lemieux blushed. It was the same lesson all over again. There's a reason for everything. Gamache had spoken matter-of-factly, but they both knew this was the second time he'd had to tell Lemieux that.

'OK, here we go.' Clara sat down and hit the play button.

A barge was approaching the dreary shore. Katharine Hepburn, as an aging Eleanor, was wrapped in shawls, splendid and brittle. There was no dialogue, just a long, pastoral shot of the boat, the oarsmen and the queen arriving.

The barge was almost at the shore, and the tape went strange. Just for a moment. It squirmed.

'There.' Clara hit pause. 'Here, let me show you again.'

Twice more she rewound and hit play and twice more Eleanor arrived for her devastating Christmas with her family.

Clara paused the picture at the very moment it went squiggly. The prow of the barge almost filled the screen. No faces were visible. No actors at all. Just leafless, lifeless trees, a near dead landscape, gray water and the bow of the boat. Nothing. Lemieux might be right, thought Gamache.

He leaned back on the sofa and stared. Eventually the pause released itself and Clara had to rewind, play and pause again.

The minutes went by.

'What do you see?' he asked everyone in the room.

'The boat,' said Clara.

'Trees,' said Peter.

'Some water,' said Beauvoir, anxious to say something before everything was taken.

Lemieux could have kicked himself. There was nothing left to say. He caught Gamache looking at him with amusement, and something else. Approval. Better to say nothing than say something just for the sake of speaking. Lemieux smiled back and relaxed.

Gamache turned back to the screen. Boat, trees, water. Was it just a coincidence CC had stopped the movie here? Was he trying to read way too much into this? Had she stopped just to get a drink or go to the washroom? But the tape wouldn't stretch from just one pause; she'd have to have stopped it here many times to cause the damage.

He got up and stretched his legs.

'No need to keep staring. There's nothing there. You were right, and I was wrong. My apologies,' he said to Lemieux, who was so stunned he didn't know what to do.

'I'm sorry,' said Clara, walking with them back to the mudroom. 'I thought I was on to something.'

'And you might have been. You have an instinct for crime, madame.'

'You flatter me, monsieur.'

Had Peter been a dog his hackles would have risen. Try as he might he couldn't quite get over his jealousy of Gamache and his easy relationship with Clara. In the mudroom Gamache pulled a book from his coat and presented it gently to Clara. After speaking to Myrna he had an inkling of what he was about to do, and wished he didn't have to.

'How kind, but I already have Ruth's latest book.'

'But not this one,' he said almost in a whisper. Peter strained to hear the words, as did the others.

Clara opened the book and smiled broadly. 'You stink, love Ruth. You found it. The one I lost. Did I drop it on the road, or at the bistro?'

'No, you dropped it in Montreal.'

Clara looked at Gamache, puzzled. 'And you found it? But that's not possible.'

'It was found on the body of a dead woman.' He said the words slowly and carefully, giving her every chance to hear them and to understand. 'She was found outside Ogilvy's, just before Christmas.' Gamache was staring at Clara, examining her face, her reactions. Still she looked puzzled, amazed. Nothing more.

'She was a vagrant, a bag lady.'

And now he could see the light go on. Her eyes opened slightly wider and she brought her head up and away from him, as though repulsed by his words.

'No,' Clara whispered and went very white. She breathed

into the silence a couple of times. 'The old woman, the bum on the street?'

The silence stretched on, all eyes watching Clara as she struggled with this news. Clara felt herself falling, not to the floor, but way below it, into the abyss filled with crushed dreams.

I've always loved your art, Clara.

No. That means the vagrant wasn't God after all. Just a pathetic old woman. As delusional as Clara. They both thought her art was good. And they were wrong. CC and Fortin were right.

Your art is amateurish and banal. You're a failure. You have no voice, no vision, no worth. You've wasted your life.

The words ground into Clara, weighing her down and dragging her over the edge.

'Oh, my God,' was all she could think to say.

'Peter, could you make a cup of tea, please? Hot and sweet?' Gamache asked and Peter was both annoyed Gamache had thought of it and grateful for something to do.

'Go back to the Incident Room and see what progress Agent Lacoste has made,' Gamache whispered to Beauvoir quickly, then he turned back and led Clara into the living room, kicking himself once there because he hadn't given Beauvoir the video to take back. He hoped he wouldn't forget it.

'Tell me about it,' he said to Clara once he had her seated by the warm fire.

'I stepped right over her on my way into Ogilvy's. It was the night of Ruth's book launch. I felt badly about that, all my good fortune and all.' She left the sentence hanging, knowing Gamache would understand. Once again she saw the scene. Leaving the launch, buying the food, getting on the fateful escalator. Passing CC.

Your art is amateurish and banal.

Walking in a daze into the cold night and wanting to take off down the street, howling and crying and shoving all the revelers aside. But instead bending over the vagrant, the heap of stinking shit and despair, and meeting those rheumy eyes.

'I've always loved your art, Clara.'

'She said that?' Gamache asked.

Clara nodded.

'Did you know her?'

'Never saw her before.'

'But you must have,' said Agent Lemieux, speaking for the first time in an interrogation, the words jumping unbidden from his mouth. He clamped his mouth shut and looked at Gamache, waiting for the reprimand. Instead Gamache was looking at him with interest. Then he turned back.

Relieved, Lemieux listened, but wanted to squirm in his seat. He found this whole exchange deeply unsettling.

'How do you explain it?' Gamache asked, watching Clara closely.

'I can't.'

'Yes you can,' Gamache encouraged her, exploring, probing, asking her to let him in. 'Tell me.'

'I think she was God. Thought she was God.' Clara struggled to compose herself, clamping her throat against the tears.

Gamache sat quietly, waiting. He looked away, giving her the semblance of privacy. Staring at the television he saw in his mind's eye the frozen image of the barge. No. Not the barge, just the prow. With a design. A sea serpent. A snake. No. A bird.

An eagle.

A shrieking eagle.

And Gamache knew then why CC had stopped the tape just there. He had to get to the Incident Room before Lacoste left. The clock on the mantel said just after six. It might already be too late. Gesturing to Lemieux he whispered in the young man's ear. Lemieux left the room quickly and quietly. A moment later Gamache saw him hurrying along the front path and out the gate.

Gamache cursed himself for forgetting to give the video to Lemieux to put back in the evidence box. He had a sneaking suspicion he'd leave without it himself. Peter arrived with the tea and Clara roused herself.

'I need to ask you this again, Clara. Are you sure you'd never seen Elle before?'

'Elle? Was that her name?'

'That's what the police report called her. We don't know her real name.'

'I've thought about it a great deal since that night. Myrna also asked. I didn't know her. Believe me.'

Gamache did.

'How did she die?' asked Clara. 'Was it the cold?'

'She was murdered, shortly after she spoke to you.'

TWENTY-NINE

⌒

Armand Gamache actually remembered to take *The Lion in Winter* back to the Incident Room. He placed it on his desk and went over to Lacoste's computer where the others were huddled. He noticed Agent Nichol sitting at her own desk and waved her over.

'Lemieux told me what you wanted,' said Lacoste, glancing at him quickly. 'Look at this.' Her computer screen was split in two, with near identical images on either side. The head of an eagle, stylized and screaming.

'This one', Lacoste pointed to the one on the left, 'is the emblem of Eleanor of Aquitaine.'

'And that one?' Gamache pointed to the other half of the screen.

'That's CC's corporate logo. It's on the cover of her book, kind of. It's all smudged, a not very good reproduction, but that's what it is.'

'You were right,' said Beauvoir. 'CC stopped the video at minute seventeen to get a good look at the front of the boat.

She must have recognized it as Eleanor's emblem, and wanted to copy it.'

'Everything makes sense,' murmured Lemieux.

'How'd you make the connection?' Beauvoir asked.

'I had an unfair advantage,' admitted Gamache. 'Lyon showed me CC's book and pointed out the logo. It's unforgettable.' So this explained the ridiculous choice of a belligerent eagle as a logo, he thought. It was Eleanor's emblem.

'There's something I need to show you.' Gamache walked over to his satchel and removed the photographs taken by Saul Petrov. The team pulled their chairs up to the conference table while Gamache spread them out.

'I figured out why CC grabbed the chair in front of her,' he said, nodding to the series of pictures. 'It's all there.'

They stared and after a minute Gamache took pity on them. They were all tired and hungry and Agent Lacoste had a long drive back to Montreal.

'See here?' He pointed to one of the early shots of CC watching the curling. 'The chair looks fine, right?'

They nodded.

'Now look here.' He pointed to one of the last pictures of CC.

'My God, it's so obvious. How could I have missed it?' Beauvoir looked from the pictures to Gamache in astonishment. 'It's crooked.'

'So?' said Lacoste.

'Over and over again the people who knew her, or even met her casually, said the same thing. CC obsessively rearranged everything around her. A chair like this', Gamache pointed to the tilted chair, one corner sunk into the snow, 'was guaranteed to get a reaction. The only surprise is that it took her so long.'

'Except, as you pointed out,' said Nichol, 'the chair was just fine to begin with. Someone must have shoved it off kilter.'

Gamache nodded. Was that what was on the roll of film Petrov burned? Did it show a villager casually wandering by and leaning on the chair? Did the villager then go to the generator and wait for CC to get up? And when she did all he had to do was attach the booster cables, and bang. Murder.

It was brilliant and almost elegant.

But who did it? Richard Lyon was the perfect suspect. He knew his wife would reach for the chair that had gone askew.

'That photographer was hiding something,' said Beauvoir.

'I agree,' said Gamache. 'He burned a roll of film in his fireplace just before we arrived. I think it was of the murder.'

'Why would he destroy it, though?' asked Lemieux. 'As he said, if he had a picture of the murderer it would prove his own innocence.'

'What about if he planned to use it for blackmail?' Nichol asked.

'But why destroy it? You'd keep that film safe, wouldn't you?' said Lacoste and received a disconcertingly friendly smile.

Bitch, thought Nichol. She looked around and noticed Gamache watching her. Does he know? she wondered. He was standing there so smug and comfortable, surrounded by his team. And her on the outside, always on the outside. Well, that would change.

'Why destroy pictures of CC being murdered?' Gamache

asked himself, sitting down and staring at the photographs. 'Unless he's trying to protect the murderer.'

'Why would he do that? He doesn't know anyone round here, does he?' asked Lemieux.

'Look into Saul Petrov's background,' Gamache said to Nichol. 'Find out everything you can about him.' He rubbed a weary hand over his eyes.

Walking to his desk he picked up the video and took it to the evidence room. The small box of items from CC's garbage was on the floor. He took out the inventory sheet before placing *The Lion in Winter* back into its spot, then replaced the sheet, gazing at the familiar list. Cereal boxes, bits and pieces of food now tossed but inventoried, the video, a broken bracelet, a boot box and Christmas wrapping. It was a mundane list, except for the video. And the bracelet.

Gamache put on gloves and started rummaging through the box, like a mini-dumpster dive. After a minute the cardboard box was empty, save for a dirty little thing curled in the corner, like an unwanted puppy at the shelter. It was brown and filthy and broken. But what it wasn't was a bracelet. Gamache put on his half-moon glasses and picked up the object, dangling it at arm's length. He breathed in sharply then brought it closer to his face, peering at the small object hanging from the worn leather strap.

It wasn't a bracelet, it was a necklace. With a pendant. A small, tarnished, dirty head. The face of a shrieking eagle.

Gamache knew CC, fastidious, obsessive CC, had never worn this filthy thing. But he knew who had.

Slowly Armand Gamache rose, the images and thoughts tumbling one on top of another. He walked the necklace back to his desk then brought out two documents: the drawing by the police artist and an autopsy photograph of Elle.

When he'd first seen the autopsy photographs of Elle he'd seen a smudging on her chest. It was circular and regular and a different color from the rest of the filth on her body. It was a kind of tarnish that came off impure metal when it reacted to sweat. As soon as he'd seen the autopsy photo he'd known Elle had worn a necklace. A cheap necklace but it must have been precious to her.

But there was other evidence she'd worn a necklace. There was a small dark bruise at the base of her neck, probably made when the leather strap was broken. And the cuts in her hand. He'd sent Agent Lemieux over to the Old Brewery Mission to ask whether anyone remembered Elle wearing a necklace. They did, though none had gotten close enough to be able to say what it was. He'd searched for it in the box of evidence but had found nothing. He'd known then that if he found the necklace he'd find her killer.

Well, he'd found the necklace. In Three Pines, one hundred kilometers away from the frozen Montreal street where Elle was found, and the necklace was taken. How had it ended up here?

Armand Gamache closed his eyes and the events played there, in the movie house of his mind. He could see Elle's murderer struggling with her. The murderer had grabbed the necklace and broken the cord. Then Elle had grabbed it back, pressing it so violently into her palm as she was strangled that it cut into her hand, like a cookie cutter. Gamache had asked the Sûreté artist to connect the bloody dots and try to recreate what the necklace had looked like.

Now he looked at the drawing. The artist had made a

stylized circle, with a bite taken out, and a kind of neck. It hadn't made sense at the time, but now it did. The bite was the eagle's mouth, open and screaming. The rest was its head and neck.

So Elle had died grasping her necklace. Why had Elle valued it so much she'd died holding it? And why had the murderer taken the time to pry it from her hand?

And then what? Gamache leaned back in his chair and folded his hands over his stomach. Any sounds in the room, in the village, in Quebec, receded. He was in his own world now, with the murderer. Just the two of them. What had he done, and why?

He'd taken the pendant from Elle's dead hand and brought it back home. And he'd put it in the garbage. CC's garbage. Gamache could feel himself getting close. It was still murky, far from clear, but the headlights were shining bright now, cutting through the night. Before he got to who, Gamache needed to know why. Why hadn't the murderer just fled? Why take the time to pry this necklace from Elle's hand?

Because it was a screaming eagle. It was a tarnished, filthy, cheap version of what he'd seen on the screen earlier that evening. The emblem of Eleanor of Aquitaine, the logo for CC de Poitiers and the necklace of the beggar were the same.

The murderer had taken it because it proved something more terrible than who killed Elle. It proved that Elle and CC were connected. They shared more than a symbol.

Elle was CC's mother.

'Come on,' said Beauvoir, holding out his gloved hand for the necklace. 'Some dead vagrant was CC de Poitiers's mother?'

Gamache was on the phone, dialing. 'That's right.'

'I'm confused,' said Beauvoir and Lemieux was glad he said it. Nichol, at her computer, stole looks over to the three men talking. She watched as Lacoste got up and joined the men.

'*Oui, allô,*' said the Chief Inspector. 'Is Terry Moscher there? Yes, I'll hold.' He covered the mouthpiece with his hand. 'What are the chances the dead vagrant and CC both have the same emblem? A butterfly, maybe. A flower, I'd give you that. They're pretty common. But that?' He gestured to the pendant hanging from Beauvoir's fist. 'Who do you know who'd wear that for decoration?'

Beauvoir had to agree if he bought a necklace with an insane eagle on it for his wife she wouldn't thank him. It was more than a coincidence, but did it make them mother and daughter?

'Yes, hello, Monsieur Moscher? It's Chief Inspector Gamache. I'm well, thank you, but I have a question for you. You mentioned that Elle signed the register the few times she stayed at the Old Brewery Mission. Would you mind finding the entry again? Yes, I'll hold.' He turned back to his team. 'We'll send the necklace to the lab to be tested.'

'I'll take it back with me,' said Lacoste.

'Good. We should get the results in less than a day. It'll tell us about fingerprints, but there's also blood on it. Yes, I'm still here.' He turned back to the phone. 'I see. Yes. Could you fax me a copy of the page right away? And I'll send an agent over tonight to pick up the ledger. *Merci infiniment.*'

Gamache hung up, looking reflective.

'What? What'd he say?' Beauvoir asked.

'I've been a fool. When I asked him the other night to

check the register he confirmed that Elle had signed it. Or at least I thought that's what he said and meant.' The fax rang and started printing. They all watched as the paper took its excruciating time, inching out of the machine. Finally it was done and Beauvoir snatched up the paper, scanning the signatures.

TV Bob
Frenchie
Little Cindy
L

'L,' he said softly, handing the sheet to Gamache. 'L, not Elle.'

'Her name was L,' said Gamache, taking the paper back to his desk and picking up the Li Bien ball. He turned it over until the signature was visible. L. Exactly the same as the ledger.

Whoever had made this exquisite work of art years ago had recently signed into the Old Brewery Mission in Montreal to escape the killing cold. She'd become a vagrant, a homeless bag lady. And finally, a body with a closed file in homicide. But now Gamache felt he'd at least brought her home. To Three Pines. L was CC's mother. He was sure of it. But that meant something else. L was dead. CC was dead.

Someone was killing the women in that family.

THIRTY

~

Gamache and Beauvoir hurried into their coats and boots, Beauvoir remembering to press the remote start on his car keys, to at least give it a minute or so to warm up.

'Just a moment.' Gamache took off his tuque and returned to his desk, picking up his phone and dialing. 'This is Chief Inspector Armand Gamache of the Sûreté du Québec. Is this the duty officer?'

Beauvoir was almost out the door when he turned back and signaled to Nichol to join them. She leaped from her desk.

'No.' Gamache covered the mouthpiece of the phone and turned to Nichol. 'You stay here. Agent Lemieux, you come with us.'

Stunned, as though slapped, Nichol stood still and watched as Agent Lemieux hurried past, giving her a slight apologetic smile. She could have killed him.

Beauvoir looked at the chief for a moment, puzzled, then hurried into the cold. He thought he was prepared for the outside world, but he was wrong. The temperature had plummeted even further and now it burned his skin as he walked, then trotted and finally ran the few yards to his car. The vehicle was struggling to keep turning over, its fluids sluggish and near frozen. The windows were etched with frost and Beauvoir opened the groaning door and grabbed a couple of scrapers. Shavings of frost jumped from the blades as though he was a carpenter whittling a car. Lemieux joined him and the two men furiously scraped the windows. Tears obscured Beauvoir's vision as the bitter cold found every inch of exposed flesh.

'I called ahead. He's expecting us,' said Gamache, getting in and automatically buckling up even though they were going less than a kilometer. On any other night they'd walk. But not tonight.

Up ahead was their destination. Beauvoir had been so intent on getting the car going he hadn't thought about where they were headed. Now, as he applied the brakes, the reality hit. The old Hadley house. Last time he was here he'd been coughing up blood. This place seemed to crave blood, and fear. Lemieux jumped out of the car and was halfway down the walk before Beauvoir could even stir himself. He felt a heaviness on his arm and looked at Gamache beside him.

'It's all right.'

'I don't know what you mean,' snapped Beauvoir.

'Of course not,' said Gamache.

Finally the door opened and Lyon stepped back into the hall to let them in.

'I'd like to see Crie, please.' The Chief Inspector was cordial but firm.

'She's in the kitchen. We're just sitting down to eat.'

Lyon's eyes were blank, bewildered. It was as though,

Beauvoir thought, he'd been hollowed out. He wondered what echoed round in Lyon's head. He looked around. Last time he'd been there the electricity had been off and all he'd seen was what was visible by flashlight. It wasn't much. Now he was surprised to see it looked like a regular home. But then, that was the real horror of these places and these people. They looked normal. They sucked you in, then slowly the door swung shut and you were trapped. With a monster. Within a monster.

Stop thinking that, his mind commanded. This is just a normal house. This is just a normal house.

'She's just through here.'

The men followed Lyon into the kitchen. Beauvoir was surprised to find it smelled good, like home cooking.

'Ms Landers came over with some food,' Lyon explained.

Crie was sitting at the table, a plate cooling in front of her.

'She's not eating much these days.'

'Crie, it's Chief Inspector Gamache again.' Gamache sat in the chair next to her. He laid his large, expressive hand over her dimpled white one and left it there gently. 'I just wanted to make sure you're all right. Is there anything I can do?' He waited a long minute for the answer, which never came. 'I'd like to ask you a favor.' His voice was even and friendly. 'Could you eat some dinner? I know you don't have much of an appetite, but it's good for you, and we want to keep you healthy and beautiful.'

The room was silent. She stared straight ahead, her expression unchanging. Finally Gamache rose.

'Goodnight, Crie. We'll see you soon. If you need anything I'm staying just down the hill at the B&B.'

Gamache turned and nodded to his men and Lyon, then left the room, all of them following including Lyon, who found it strangely relaxing to be around this man who took charge.

'We believe we've found CC's mother,' he said to Lyon in the front hall.

'Who is she?'

'Well, we don't know her name, but we think she was from Three Pines. What we do know is that she was murdered just before Christmas.' Gamache watched closely and believed he saw a flicker of something race across Lyon's face but then was gone.

'Murdered? Both of them? CC and her mother? But what does that mean?'

'It means someone might try to kill your daughter,' said Gamache, his eyes hard on Lyon, full of meaning and warning. 'The local police are sending a car – '

'It's arrived sir,' said Lemieux, who'd noticed the head-lights.

' – so there'll be a guard here twenty-four hours a day. Nothing will happen to that girl. Do I make myself clear?'

Lyon nodded. Things were happening so fast. Too fast. He needed time to think.

Gamache gave a brisk nod and left the house.

Olivier threw another log on the open fire at the bistro and stirred it. Jean Guy Beauvoir and Chief Inspector Gamache were talking quietly at their table by the fire. The bistro was half full, and a small murmur of conversation filled the room. Olivier picked up their bottle of red wine and refilled their glasses.

'Here comes your dinner. *Bon appétit.*' He smiled and left.

A steak frites was placed in front of Beauvoir, sizzling from the charcoal fire, the French fries thin and seasoned, a small dish of mayonnaise waiting for them on the side. Beauvoir sipped his wine, swirling the dark liquid around lazily and looked into the fire. This was heaven. It'd been a long, cold day but it was finally over. Now he and Gamache could talk and chew over the case. It was Beauvoir's favorite part of the job. And if it came with a charcoal steak, fries, wine, and a lively fire, so much the better.

A rack of lamb, sending out an aroma of garlic and rosemary, sat in front of Gamache, tiny potatoes and green beans rounding out the plate. Between them on the table sat a basket of steaming rolls and a small dish of butter balls.

Across from him Gamache had moved his napkin so that the plate could be put down and now Beauvoir noticed the doodle Gamache had made. Upside down he read it.

B KLM. The L circled over and over again.

'L's box,' said Beauvoir, recognizing the letters. 'Must have been collecting those letters for years. Compulsive. Like her daughter. I wonder if those things run in families?'

'I wonder.' The warmth, the wine, the fire, the food were all seducing Gamache. He felt relaxed and pleased with the progress of the day, though worried about Crie. Still, he knew she'd be safe. He'd warned Lyon. They were watching. Armand Gamache was still convinced Richard Lyon was their man. Who else could it be? He ate his lamb, enjoying the subtle flavors. 'Why did the murderer stop to take the necklace out of L's hand, Jean Guy?'

'It must have been important. Maybe it implicates him, gives him away.'

'Maybe.' Gamache took a roll and ripped it in two, sending a flurry of flakes falling onto the wooden table. 'Why did he kill L? Why kill CC? Why kill them both? And why now? What happened that the murderer had to kill them both within days?'

'CC was about to sign a contract with that American company. Maybe it was to stop her doing that.'

'But why stop her? She'd be worth much more afterwards. Besides, I have a feeling that American contract was another of CC's delusions. We'll see. But even so, why kill her mother?'

'Was L from Three Pines, do you think?'

'I do, and we need to concentrate tomorrow on finding people who knew her. I have another one for you.' Their plates were just about empty now and Beauvoir was mopping up the juices from his steak with a roll. 'Why throw the video away? It was perfectly good, as we saw.'

A waitress took their plates and a cheese platter arrived.

'These are all from the monastery at Saint-Benoît-du-Lac,' said Olivier, waving a cheese knife over the platter. 'Their vocation is making cheese and Gregorian chants. All their cheeses are named after saints. Here's Saint-André, and this one's Saint-Albray.'

'And this one?' Beauvoir pointed to a large wedge on the wooden platter.

'That would be Saint-Blue Cheese,' said Olivier. 'And this is Saint-Cheddar. Damn. Another good theory blown.' He cut them off slices of each and left a basket of baguette and crackers.

'I know how he feels.' Gamache smiled, spreading Saint-André on a thin cracker. They ate in silence and Gamache looked at the younger man across the table. 'What's bothering you?'

Beauvoir peered over the rim of his glass then drained the last of his wine just as their cappuccinos arrived. 'Why'd you order Nichol to stay behind?'

'Are you upset that I countermanded you?'

'No,' Beauvoir said, but knew that was indeed part of it. 'I don't like my orders contradicted, especially in front of the team.'

'You're right, Jean Guy. I wouldn't normally do it.'

Beauvoir knew that to be the truth. In all the years they'd worked together it had only happened a handful of times, and then only in the most dire situations.

Was this a dire situation? Gamache was sitting forward now, his face suddenly weary. And Beauvoir could have kicked himself. Why hadn't he seen it before?

'You don't trust her, do you? You don't trust Nichol.'

'Do you?'

Beauvoir thought for a moment, then nodded his head. 'She's impressed me. As you know, I have no love for the woman. I thought she was a complete disaster on her last case, but this time? I think it's possible she's changed. But you don't?'

Gamache waved his hand slightly as though dismissing the suggestion. It wasn't very convincing.

'What is it?' Beauvoir leaned forward now. 'Tell me.'

But Gamache was silent. There was only one thing, in Beauvoir's experience, that could produce that kind of silence in his boss.

'My God. It's not the Arnot case? Tell me that isn't it.' He could feel his anger, and his dinner, rising. He felt this way whenever he thought of Pierre Arnot and what he'd done. To others, to the Sûreté. To Gamache. Surely, though, it was past. And it couldn't possibly have anything to do with Nichol. Could it?

'Tell me,' he demanded. 'Enough.' Now the younger man was almost shouting. He caught himself, looked around to see if anyone else had heard, and lowered his voice to an urgent growl. 'You can't keep this from me. You can't take this on yourself. You did the first time and Arnot almost killed you. What is it with Nichol and Arnot?'

'Leave it be, Jean Guy.' Gamache reached across the table and gently tapped Beauvoir's hand. 'There is no connection. I'm just wary of her, that's all. Nichol is certainly more agreeable than she was last time. Maybe I'm being too hard on her.'

Beauvoir studied him for a moment. 'Bullshit. You're humoring me now. What do you really think?'

'It's just a feeling.' Gamache smiled wryly, waiting for Beauvoir to roll his eyes.

'Your feelings aren't always delusional.'

'Just sometimes? It's not important, Jean Guy.'

Gamache sipped his cappuccino and wondered whether he was turning cynical at last, thinking people couldn't and didn't change. All the evidence was that Agent Yvette Nichol had shed her arrogance and that huge chip she lugged around. Since joining them the day before she'd proved she could take orders, could take guidance and criticism. She'd worked hard and proved herself a self-starter, and had done good work finding out about Crie. And she'd even booked herself into the B&B, and had paid for it herself.

This was indeed a new Nichol.

So why don't I trust her?

Gamache leaned back in his chair and signaled Olivier, then turned back to Beauvoir.

'I owe you an apology. I shouldn't have countermanded your orders, and certainly not in front of the team. May I offer you a cognac?'

Beauvoir recognized the bribe, but was willing to take it. Olivier delivered the amber drinks in their plump glasses and the two men discussed the case, talking about everything but thinking about only one thing. Agent Yvette Nichol.

THIRTY-ONE

T he alarm sounded at twenty past two in the morning. The siren blasted through the frozen air and into every house in the village, traveling through fieldstone and mortar, through thick pink insulation and clapboard, through sweet dreams and restless sleeps, and announced a nightmare.

Fire.

Gamache leaped out of bed. Through the wail he could hear footsteps and shouting and the phone ringing. Tugging on his dressing gown he looked down the corridor and saw the vague outline of someone else in the darkness.

Beauvoir.

Downstairs he heard a woman's voice, high and strained.

'What is it, what's happening?'

Gamache took the stairs rapidly, Beauvoir silent and following.

'I don't smell smoke,' said Gamache, striding up to Nichol who was standing in the door to her room wearing pink flannel pajamas. She was wild-eyed and hyper-alert. 'Come with me.' His voice was even and composed. Nichol could feel herself breathing again.

As they descended they heard Gabri and Olivier calling to each other.

'It's along the Old Stage Road. Ruth has the address,' Olivier shouted. 'I'm heading over.'

'Wait,' said Gamache. 'What's happening?'

Olivier stopped in his tracks as though seeing an apparition.

'*Bon Dieu.* I'd forgotten you were here. There's a fire. The siren's coming from the train station telling all the volunteer firefighters to get there. Ruth just called to tell me where the fire is. I'm the driver of the pump truck. She's going there directly with Gabri.'

Gabri jogged down the corridor from their mudroom in his insulated khaki and yellow firefighter's garb, reflecting strips round his arms, legs and chest, a black helmet under his arm.

'I'm off.' He kissed Olivier on the lips and squeezed his arm before running into the bitter cold.

'What can we do?' Beauvoir asked.

'Get into your warmest clothes and meet me at the old railway station.' Olivier didn't look back, disappearing into the night, his parka flapping as he ran. Lights were appearing at homes all round the village.

All three raced upstairs, reassembling in minutes near the front door. Running across the village green Beauvoir could barely breathe for the searing cold. With each breath his nostrils froze shut and the air was like an ice pick in his sinuses, shooting pain through his forehead and making his eyes tear and freeze. By the time they were halfway to the train station he could barely see. Of all nights for a fire, he thought, struggling to keep his eyes open and his breathing even. The cold was already inside him, as though he was naked, his sweaters and jeans and warm clothing useless against this barbarous chill. Beside him Nichol and Gamache were coughing, also trying to catch their breaths. It was like inhaling acid.

The siren stopped as they got partway across. Beauvoir didn't know what was worse, the shriek of the alarm or the shriek of the ground as though the earth itself was crying out in pain with every step they took. In the dark he could hear invisible villagers coughing and stumbling, rushing like doughboys toward God knew what Hell.

Three Pines was mobilized.

'Put those on.' Olivier pointed to firefighting clothes hanging neatly in open lockers. The three of them did as they were told and soon the place was full of other volunteers. The Morrows, Myrna, Monsieur Béliveau and a dozen or so more villagers all rapidly and without panic putting on their equipment.

'Em's started the phone chain, and the buses are warming up,' Clara reported to Olivier, who nodded his approval.

Glum-faced they stood at the wall staring at the huge map of the township.

'Here's the fire. Down the Old Stage Road toward St-Rémy. About four kilometers along there's a turnoff to the left. Seventeen rue Tryhorn. It's a kilometer up on your right. Let's go. You come with me.' He gestured to Gamache and the others and strode toward the pumper truck.

'That's Petrov's place. I'm sure of it,' said Beauvoir, swinging up into the truck beside Gamache while Nichol squeezed into the back seat.

'What?' said Olivier, heading the huge truck toward the Old Stage Road, the other vehicles following.

'My God, you're right.' Gamache turned to Olivier, shouting over the noise. 'There's someone in the house. His name's Saul Petrov. Could it be a false alarm?'

'Not this time. A neighbor called in the report. She saw flames.'

Gamache stared out the window watching the headlights slice into the night along the snow-covered road, the truck almost outpacing the light.

'Minus thirty,' said Olivier, as though to himself. 'God help us.'

There was silence in the cab then as they tore along, the vehicle skidding slightly on the ice and snow. Ahead they could see other vehicles turning.

What met them was even more horrible than Gamache imagined. He felt like a pilgrim in Hell. A pumper truck from Williamsburg had just arrived and was spraying water on the burning house. The water was freezing almost before it hit the flames and the spray was coating everything in a layer of ice. The volunteers looked like active angels coated in crystals as they directed their spray to the fire. Men and women of all ages worked together in well disciplined teams. Icicles hung from their helmets and clothing and the unscorched parts of the house looked like glass. It was like something out of a particularly macabre fairy tale, both spectacularly beautiful and horrible.

Gamache leaped out of the truck and made for Ruth Zardo, standing nearby in her fire chief's outfit, directing operations.

'We'll soon need another water source,' she said. 'There's

a pond here somewhere.' Peter and Clara turned to look for evidence of a frozen pond, but all they saw was darkness, and snow.

'How'll we find it?' Peter asked.

Ruth looked around and pointed. 'The neighbor'll tell you.'

Peter ran to the pumper truck and grabbed a power auger while Clara ran to a woman standing alone, her gloved hand to her mouth as though she was in danger of inhaling the horror she was witnessing. Within moments the Morrows and the woman were no more than a flashlight bobbing in the distance.

The burning house was illuminated by the headlights of cars swung into preordained positions for that very purpose. Gamache knew a leader when he saw one, and now he understood why the people of Three Pines had elevated Ruth to fire chief. Gamache suspected she was used to Hell so this held no terror. She was calm and decisive.

'There's someone in that house,' he shouted above the roar of the water and flames and rumbling vehicles.

'No, the owners are away in Florida. I asked the neighbor.'

'She's wrong,' Gamache shouted. 'We were here earlier today. It's rented to a man named Saul Petrov.'

Now he had Ruth's complete attention.

'We need to get him out.' She turned to look at the home. 'Gabri, call an ambulance.'

'Already have. It's on its way. Ruth, the house is almost gone.'

The implication was clear.

'We need to try.' Ruth looked around. 'We can't leave him in that.' She gestured to the house. Gabri was right. Half of it was engulfed, the flames hissing and roaring as though the firefighters were using holy water on a home possessed. Gamache didn't think ice and fire could live together, but now he saw it. An ice house burning.

The firefighters were losing.

'Where's Nichol?' Beauvoir shouted into Gamache's ear. The noise was almost deafening. Gamache swung round. She couldn't have wandered off. She couldn't be that stupid.

'I saw her go over there,' Monsieur Béliveau, the grocer, his face covered with ice from the spray, yelled.

'Find her,' said Gamache to Beauvoir, who took off in the direction Monsieur Béliveau pointed, his heart pounding. Don't be that stupid, please, dear Lord, don't be that stupid.

But she was.

Beauvoir ran, following the footsteps in the snow. Fuck her, his mind screamed. The prints went directly into the back door of the house. Fuck, fuck, fuck. He turned round twice, desperately hoping he'd see her outside. He shouted her name into the house, and heard nothing back.

Fuck, his mind shrieked.

'Where is she?' Gamache was at his elbow, calling into his ear. It was a little quieter round this side, but not much. Beauvoir pointed to the door and saw Gamache's face harden. Beauvoir thought he heard the chief whisper 'Reine-Marie', but decided it was a trick of the scene, the turmoil creating its own conversation.

'Stay here.' Gamache left, returning a minute later with Ruth.

'I see what you mean,' Ruth said. The elderly woman was limping badly and her words were muffled, her face frozen. Beauvoir's own face was numb and his hands were getting there. He looked at the firefighters, the baker, the grocer, the handyman, and wondered how they did it. They were covered in ice, and squinting into the spray and flames, their faces black from the smoke. Every minute or so they'd sweep their huge gloved hands in front of their faces to knock the icicles from their helmets.

'Gabri, get half a dozen hoses over here. Concentrate on this part of the house.' Ruth waved at the quarter of the structure that wasn't yet in flames.

Gabri understood immediately and took off, disappearing into the smoke or spray, Beauvoir could no longer tell them apart.

'Here,' she turned to Gamache, 'take this.' She handed him an axe.

Gamache took it gratefully and tried to smile but his face was frozen. His eyes were watering furiously from the smoke and extreme cold and every time he blinked he had to struggle to get his eyes open again. His breath came in rasps and he could no longer feel his feet. His clothing, damp from the sweat of the adrenalin rush, was now cold and clammy and clinging to his body.

'Damn her,' he said under his breath, and advanced on the house.

'What're you doing?' Beauvoir grabbed his arm.

'What do you think, Jean Guy?'

'But you can't.' Beauvoir thought his mind would explode. What was happening was inconceivable and moving at lightning speed. Too fast for him to keep up.

'I can't not,' said Gamache, staring at Beauvoir, and the frantic noise seemed to recede for a moment. Beauvoir dropped his grip on Gamache.

'Here.' He took the heavy axe from the chief's hand. 'You'll put someone's eye out with that. Come on.'

Beauvoir felt as though he'd just walked off a cliff. Still, like Gamache, he had no choice. He wasn't capable of seeing the chief walk into a burning building alone. Not alone.

Inside, the house was eerily quiet. Not silent, but it seemed like a cloistered monastery compared to the tumult outside. The electricity was off and both men turned on their flashlights. It was at least warm though the reason didn't bear thinking of. They were in the kitchen and Beauvoir knocked against something, sending a wooden box of cutlery clattering to the floor. So ingrained was his upbringing he actually considered stooping to clean it up.

'Nichol,' Gamache shouted.

Silence.

'Petrov,' he tried again. Silence, except for the dull roar that sounded like a hungry thing growling. Both men turned and looked behind them. The door into the next room was closed, but beneath it they could see a flickering light.

The fire was approaching.

'The stairs to the second floor are through there.' Beauvoir pointed to the door. Gamache didn't answer. He didn't need to. Outside they could hear Ruth issuing orders in her slurred, frozen voice.

'This way.' Gamache led Beauvoir away from the flames.

'Here, I found something.' Beauvoir yanked open a trap door in the kitchen floor and shone his light down. 'Nichol?'

Nothing.

He could see a ladder and handed his light to Gamache, hardly believing he was about to do this. But he knew one thing: the sooner this was over, the better. He swung his legs

321

into the hole, found the ladder and climbed down quickly. Gamache gave him his flashlight and shone his own down as well.

It was a root cellar. Cases of Molson beer, wine, boxes of potatoes and turnips and parsnips. It smelled of dirt and spiders and smoke. Beauvoir shone his light to the far end and saw a wave of smoke rolling its slow motion way toward him. It was almost mesmerizing. Almost.

'Nichol? Petrov?' he shouted, for form's sake, backing toward the ladder. He knew they weren't there.

'Quickly, Jean Guy.' Gamache's voice was urgent. Beauvoir poked his head out of the trap door, noticing the door to the next room was smoking. Soon, they both knew, it would burst into flames.

Gamache hauled him out of the hole.

The noise was mounting as the flames approached. Outside the shouts were growing ever more frantic.

'These old houses almost always have a second stairway up,' said Gamache, sending his flashlight beam around the kitchen. 'It'll be small and maybe boarded up.'

Beauvoir yanked open cupboards while Gamache pounded on the tongue-in-groove walls. Beauvoir had forgotten the home of his *grandmère* in Charlevoix, with its tiny secret staircase off the kitchen. He hadn't thought of it in years. Hadn't wanted to. Had buried it deep and covered it over, but here he was in a strange house, on fire, and now the memory decided to come back. Like that smoke in the basement it rolled inexorably toward him, slowly engulfing him, and suddenly he was back in that house, in that secret stairway. Hiding from his brother. Or so he thought until he'd grown bored and tried to leave. The door had been locked from the outside. He had no light and suddenly he had no air. The walls closed in, crushing him. The stairs moaned. The house, so comforting and familiar, had turned on him. His brother had said it was an accident when the hysterical child had been found and removed but Jean Guy had never believed it, and had never forgiven him.

Jean Guy Beauvoir had learned at the age of six that nowhere was safe and no one could be trusted.

'Here,' he shouted, staring into the half doorway. He'd taken it for a broom closet, but now his flashlight showed a set of steep, narrow steps leading up. Shining his light to the top he saw the trap door was closed. Please God, not locked.

'Let's go.' Gamache moved ahead of Beauvoir into the stairway. 'Come on.' He looked back, puzzled, as Beauvoir hesitated then entered the dark, narrow space.

The stairs were built for tiny people from a century ago, undernourished Québecois farmers, not the well-fed Sûreté officers of today, wearing outsized winter firefighting clothing. There was barely enough room to crawl. Gamache took off his helmet, and Beauvoir did the same, relieved to be free of the cumbersome piece of equipment. Gamache edged up the narrow steps, his coat scraping the walls. It was black up ahead and their flashing lights played on the closed trap door. Beauvoir's heart was pounding and his breathing fast and shallow. Was the smoke getting thicker? It was. He was sure he could feel flames at his back and turned to stare behind him, but saw only darkness. It wasn't much of a comfort. Please, let's just get out of here. Even if the entire second floor was in flames, that was better than being entombed in the stairway.

Gamache put his shoulder to the trap door and shoved.

Nothing happened.

He shoved again, harder. It didn't budge.

Beauvoir looked back down to where they'd been. Smoke was seeping under the door below. And the door above was locked.

'Here, let me through.' He tried to shove past Gamache, even though a piece of paper wouldn't get by. 'Use the axe,' he said, his voice rising. He could feel his skin tingling and his breathing coming in quick shallow gulps. His head felt light and he thought he might pass out.

'We need to get out of here,' he said, hitting the walls with his fist. The stairway had him by the throat and was choking him. He could hardly breathe now. Trapped.

'Jean Guy,' Gamache called. His cheek was on the ceiling, his body pressed against it. He couldn't go forward and he couldn't go back and he couldn't comfort Jean Guy, who was panicking.

'Harder, push harder,' Beauvoir shouted, his voice rising in hysteria. 'God, the smoke's coming in.'

Gamache could feel Beauvoir cramming his body against his in an effort to get further from the smoke and flames.

We're going to die here, Beauvoir knew. The walls were closing in, dark and narrow, binding and suffocating him.

'Jean Guy,' Gamache shouted. 'Stop it.'

'She's not worth it. For God's sake, let's go.' He was shouting and tugging at Gamache's arm, dragging him back down into the darkness. 'She's not worth it. We have to get out of here.'

'Stop it,' Gamache commanded. He turned as much as he could in the tight area, Beauvoir's flashlight hitting his face, blinding him. 'Listen to me. Are you listening?' he barked.

The frantic tugging eased. The stairwell was filling up with smoke now. Gamache knew there wasn't much time. He strained to look past the light and catch the face beyond.

'Who do you love, Jean Guy?'

Beauvoir thought he must be hallucinating. Dear God, was the chief about to quote poetry? He didn't want to die with Ruth Zardo's dreary words in his ears.

'What?'

'Think of someone you love.' The chief's voice was insistent and steady.

I love you. The thought came to Beauvoir without hesitation. Then he thought of his wife, his mother. But first was Armand Gamache.

'Imagine we're here to save them.' This wasn't a suggestion, it was an order.

Beauvoir imagined Gamache trapped in this burning house, injured, calling his name. Suddenly the narrow staircase wasn't so narrow, the darkness not as threatening.

Reine-Marie, thought Gamache, over and over, and had thought ever since he'd known he had to enter the burning building. Not after Agent Yvette Nichol. Not Saul Petrov. But Reine-Marie. The idea of saving her erased all thoughts of personal safety. No fear existed or could exist. All that mattered was finding her. Nichol became Reine-Marie and terror became courage.

He shoved and shoved against the door. He coughed now and could hear Beauvoir coughing as well.

'It moved,' he shouted to Beauvoir, and redoubled his efforts. Someone, he realized, must have put a piece of furniture on it. A refrigerator by the feel of it.

He stepped back for a split second and gathered himself.

He stared at the door and was silent. Then he closed his eyes. Opening them, he gave it a mighty heave. It moved enough to wedge the axe into the gap. Using it as leverage he forced the trap door up, the smoke pouring in and blinding him. He buried his face in his shoulder, trying to breathe through the clothing. He heard and felt the piece of furniture tumble to the ground and the door flew open.

'Nichol,' he bellowed, taking in a lungful of smoke then coughing it out again. He could barely see but the flashlight told him he was in a small bedroom. A chest of drawers was on its side beside the trap door. Beauvoir scrambled out after him, noticing that the smoke was heavier here than in the stairway. Time was almost up.

Beauvoir could hear the fire close now and feel its warmth. He'd gone from freezing cold to blistering hot in no time, something his *grandmère* said would be the death of him.

'Nichol! Petrov!' both men shouted.

They listened, then moved into the corridor and there it was. The wall of flames licking the ceiling then contracting as though drawing breath. Gamache moved quickly down the corridor away from it, crouching, and ducked into the next room, tripping over something as he stepped across the threshold.

'I'm here.' Nichol got to her knees and threw herself at Gamache. 'Thank you, thank you.' It felt as though she was trying to crawl into his skin. 'I am worth it. I really am. I'm sorry.' She clung to him as though drowning.

'Petrov? Listen to me. Where's Petrov?'

She shook her head.

'Right. Take this.' He handed her his light. 'Beauvoir, lead the way.'

Beauvoir turned and all three crouched and raced back down the corridor, toward the flames and smoke. Ducking into the small bedroom Beauvoir almost fell into the hole in the floor. It was hot. He shone his light down and could see a froth of smoke and flames beneath.

'We can't,' he shouted. The roaring was close now. Almost upon them. Gamache went to the window and broke it with his elbow.

'There,' he heard Ruth shout. 'Up there. Get the ladders.'

Within moments Billy Williams's face appeared at the window. Soon all three were staggering away from the building. Gamache turned to see the building swallowed up, bright orange embers, smoke and Saul Petrov shooting heavenward.

THIRTY-TWO

⌒

They woke up late the next morning to an enchanted day. The cold spell had broken and snow was falling heavily, lying thick upon the cars, the houses, the people as they languidly went about their lives. From his room Gamache could see Peter Morrow at the birdfeeder, pouring seed into it. As soon as he left black-capped chickadees and blue jays descended, followed quickly by hungry squirrels and chipmunks. Billy Williams was shoveling the rink, a rearguard action at best as the snow piled up behind him. Émilie Longpré was walking Henri. Slowly. Everyone seemed to be at half speed this day. Strange, thought Gamache as he showered and got into his corduroys, turtleneck and warm pullover, the village seemed more diminished by the death of the unknown photographer than by CC's.

It was ten in the morning. They'd gotten back to the B&B at six thirty. Gamache had run a long, hot bath and had lain in it, trying not to think. But one phrase kept coming back.

'I'm worth it, I really am,' Nichol had said, slobbering and weeping and grabbing at him. I'm worth it.

Gamache didn't know why, but it gave him pause.

Jean Guy Beauvoir had gone to bed after a quick shower, pumped. He felt as though he'd just run a triathlon and won. He wondered, briefly, whether curlers ever felt that way. He was physically at his limit. Cold, exhausted. But he was mentally buzzing.

They'd lost Petrov, but they'd gone into the burning building and saved Nichol.

Ruth Zardo had bathed then sat at her plastic kitchen table, sipping Scotch and writing poetry.

> *Now here's a good one:*
> *you're lying on your deathbed.*
> *You have one hour to live.*
> *Who is it, exactly, you have needed*
> *all these years to forgive?*

Yvette Nichol had gone straight to bed, filthy, stinking, exhausted, but feeling something else. She lay in bed, safe and warm.

Gamache had saved her. Literally. From a burning building. She was beyond buoyant, she was overjoyed. Finally, someone cared for her. And not just anyone, but the Chief Inspector.

Could this be hope?

The thought had warmed her and sent her off to sleep

wrapped in the promise of belonging, of finally taking a seat in the living room.

She'd told Gamache about Uncle Saul.

'Why did you go in there?' he'd asked when they were warming up in the school bus, elderly volunteers handing out sandwiches and hot drinks.

'To save him,' she'd said, feeling herself falling into his eyes, wanting to curl up in his arms. Not as a lover, but as a child. Safe and loved. He'd saved her. He'd fought his way through the fire, for her. And now he offered her something she'd longed for and looked for all her life. Belonging. He wouldn't have saved her if he didn't care for her. 'You'd said the photographer was in there and I wanted to save him.'

Gamache had sipped his coffee and continued to stare at her. He'd waited until no one else was around then lowered his voice. 'It's all right, Yvette. You can tell me.'

And she had. He'd listened closely, never interrupting, never laughing or even smiling. At times his eyes seemed full of sympathy. She told him things that had never left the walls of her immaculate home. She'd told him about stupid Uncle Saul in Czechoslovakia, who'd flunked out of the police and failed to save his family. Had he succeeded he'd have been able to warn them of the putsch, to protect them. But he couldn't, he didn't and he died. They all died. They died because they didn't belong.

'You went in there because his name was Saul?' Gamache had asked, not mocking, but wanting to be clear.

She'd nodded, not even feeling defensive or needing to explain or blame. He'd sat back in the seat, staring out the window at the still burning house, the efforts of the firefighters no longer to save it but to let it burn itself out.

'May I give you a piece of advice?'

Again she'd nodded, eager to hear what he might say.

'Let it go. You have your own life. Not Uncle Saul's, not your parents'.' His face had grown very serious then, his eyes searching. 'You can't live in the past and you certainly can't undo it. What happened to Uncle Saul has nothing to do with you. Memories can kill, Yvette. The past can reach right up and grab you and drag you to a place you shouldn't be. Like a burning building.'

He'd looked out again at the hungry, licking flames, then back at her. He'd leaned forward then until their heads were almost touching. It was the most intimate moment she'd known. In a soft voice he'd whispered, 'Bury your dead.'

Now she lay in bed, warm and safe. It's going to be all right, she said to herself, noticing the soft snow falling on the windowsill. She brought the duvet up to her chin and buried her nose in the bedding. It smelled of smoke.

And with the smell came a ragged phrase, shouted through the smoke. Cutting through and finding her curled on the floor, terrified and alone. She was going to die, she knew. Alone. And instead of the rescuers finding her, their words did.

She's not worth it.

She was going to burn to death, alone. Because she wasn't worth saving. The voice had belonged to Beauvoir. What didn't chase those words down that corridor, through the acrid smoke, was Gamache's voice saying, 'Yes she is.'

All she'd heard was the roar of the approaching fire, and her own heart howling.

Fucking Gamache would have left her to die. He wasn't looking for her, he wanted to find Petrov. Those were the first words out of his mouth when he'd found her. 'Where's Petrov?' Not 'Are you all right', not 'Thank God we found you'.

And he'd tricked her into telling him about Uncle Saul. Into betraying her father. Her family. Now he knew everything. Now he knew for sure she wasn't worth it.

God damn Gamache.

'It must have been arson,' said Beauvoir, shoveling scrambled eggs into his mouth. He was famished.

'Ruth doesn't think so,' said Gamache, spreading strawberry jam on his croissant and sipping his strong, hot coffee. They were in the dining room of the B&B, a warm, cozy room dominated by a huge fireplace and a window with a view of the forests and the mountains beyond, obscured now by the heavily falling snow.

Both men were whispering, their throats raw from the smoke and the shouting of the night before. Gabri looked like hell, and Olivier had closed the bistro and would only reopen for lunch.

'You're getting what you're getting this morning. No special orders,' Gabri had snapped when they'd shown up. Then he'd produced an exquisite breakfast of eggs and maple-cured back bacon, French toast and syrup. And steaming, buttery croissants. 'Fortunately for you, I cook when I'm stressed. What a night. Tragic.'

After he'd retreated to the kitchen Beauvoir turned back to Gamache.

'What d'you mean she thinks it wasn't arson? What else could it be? A main suspect, at the very least a witness in a murder case, dies in a fire and it isn't murder?'

'She says the neighbor saw flames shooting out the chimney.'

'So? Flames were shooting out everywhere. They were almost shooting out my ass.'

'The neighbor thinks it was an accident, a chimney fire. We'll see. The fire inspector'll be there now. We'll get a report by this afternoon. Sometimes a cigar is just a cigar, Jean Guy.'

'And when it bursts into flames, what is it then? No, sir. That was arson. Saul Petrov was murdered.'

The rest of the day was spent in slow motion, as everyone recovered from the fire and waited for the results of the fire marshal's investigation. Lemieux had found out that Saul Petrov's next of kin was a sister in Quebec City. An agent was despatched to break the news and gather more background.

After breakfast Beauvoir trudged through the knee-deep fluffy snow, kicking it ahead of him as he went house to house, interviewing villagers in the hope of finding someone who knew a woman with a name beginning with L who'd lived in the area forty-five years before. Lemieux searched the parish records.

It was a quiet, almost dream-like day, their lives muffled by exhaustion and the thick layer of gathering snow. Gamache sat at his desk. Behind him the volunteer firefighters cleaned the pumper truck and put their equipment in order. Occasionally he nodded off, his feet on his desk, his eyes closed and his hands folded over his stomach.

She's not worth it.

He startled awake. Beauvoir's voice, panicked, filled his head again, and again he smelt smoke. He dropped his feet to the floor, his heart racing. The volunteers were slowly going about their work on their side of the large room, but he was alone on his side. He wondered, briefly, what it would be like to join the volunteers, to retire to Three Pines and buy one of the old village homes. To put out his shingle. *A. Gamache, Détective privé.*

But then he noticed that he wasn't alone after all. Sitting quietly at a terminal was Agent Nichol. He thought for a moment, wondering whether he was about to do something very foolish. He got up and walked over to her.

'At the height of the fire, when we were trying to save you . . .' He sat down, forcing her to look at him. She was pale and radiated smoke as though it had seeped beneath her skin. Her clothes were ill fitting and slightly dirty, a grease stain on her lapel, dark smudges round her cuffs. Her hair was badly cut and falling into her eyes. He felt like giving her his credit card with instructions to buy nice clothes. He felt like passing his large, tired hand in front of her brow to sweep the dull hair from her angry eyes. He did neither, of course. 'Something was said. I suspect you heard it. One of us yelled, "She's not worth it."'

Now she looked at him straight on, her face full of bitterness.

Gamache stared back. 'I'm sorry,' he said. 'It's time for the truth, for both of us.'

He told her what he had in mind, his plan. And she listened. When he'd finished he asked her to keep it to herself. She agreed and thought two things. That he was probably smarter than she'd given him credit for, and that he was going down. After he was gone she brought out her cell phone and made a quick, discreet call.

'I decided to tell him about Uncle Saul,' she whispered. 'I

know, I know. It wasn't part of the plan. Yes sir. But I'm on the ground here and it was a decision I had to make at the last moment,' she lied. She couldn't possibly admit it had slipped out in a vulnerable moment. He'd think her weak. 'Yes, it was a risk, I agree. I was afraid he'd take it the wrong way, but I think it worked. It seemed to appeal to him.' At least that part was true. Then she told him everything Gamache had said to her.

By the end of the day more than eight inches of puffy snow had fallen. Not the kind that made good snowmen, but it made for great snow angels and Gamache could see kids flinging themselves into the fluffy whiteness, flapping their arms and legs.

The fire inspector had just left.

It would take a while, of course, but his initial finding was that the fire was caused by creosote.

'So someone set fire to creosote and killed Petrov,' said Beauvoir.

'Exactly,' confirmed the fire inspector. 'Petrov set fire to the creosote.'

'What?'

'When Petrov lit the fire that day he was killing himself, though he didn't know it. Creosote is a natural substance. It comes from wood that hasn't dried long enough. I suspect the chimney hadn't been cleaned in years and the wood was young, and . . .' The inspector raised his palms to the ceiling indicating the inevitable and not uncommon.

Saul Petrov had struck the match that had eventually killed him. It was an accident after all.

*

Gamache looked out the window at the fire inspector sweeping the snow from his pickup truck. The sun had gone down and in the light of the Christmas decorations he could see snow tossed into the air, like tiny storms, as villagers shoveled their walks and driveways. On the village green Ruth Zardo whacked at her bench to get the snow off then plopped down on it.

Must be five o'clock, thought Gamache, checking his watch, then picking up his phone he dialed Agent Lacoste. She was at the Sûreté lab waiting for the results on the necklace and the Li Bien ball.

'*Oui, allô?*'

'It's Gamache.'

'I'm in the car, almost there, chief. You won't believe what they found.'

Half an hour later the team had reassembled in the Incident Room.

'Look.' Lacoste handed the report to Gamache who put on his half-moon reading glasses. 'I decided to drive it down rather than tell you about it. Thought you'd need to see for yourself.'

His brows were drawn together in concentration, as though struggling through a document in a little known language.

'What?' snapped Beauvoir, reaching out to take the papers. But Gamache didn't hand them over. Instead he continued to stare at them, turning from one page to the next then back again. Finally he looked up at them over his glasses, his deep brown eyes puzzled and worried. Almost in a dream he handed the pages to Beauvoir, who snatched them up and started reading.

'But this is bullshit,' he said after a minute skimming the information. 'It doesn't make sense. Who was the technician?' He checked the signature at the bottom and grunted. 'Still, must have been an off day.'

'I thought so too,' said Lacoste, enjoying the looks on their faces. After all, she'd had the hour and a half drive down from Montreal to think about the results. 'I had him do them twice. That's why I'm late.'

The papers made their way round the room, arriving at Agent Nichol last.

Gamache took them back and placed them neatly in front of him. The room was silent while they all thought. The fire crackled in the woodstove and the coffee bubbled and perked, sending little puffs of aroma into the room. Lacoste got up and poured herself a cup.

'What do you think it means?' Gamache asked her.

'It means Crie is no longer in danger.'

'Go on.' Gamache leaned forward, his elbows on the table.

'It means we've found out who killed L, and that person's no threat to Crie,' said Lacoste, watching their faces as she spoke. Gamache, she could tell, was with her, though one step behind. Beauvoir was listening, struggling to keep up, and the other two were simply baffled.

'What're you talking about?' demanded Beauvoir impatiently. 'The genetic tests say clearly L was CC's mother. We got that from the blood samples taken at the autopsy.' He tapped the report in front of Gamache.

'That's not the interesting part,' said Gamache, separating one of the sheets and handing it to Beauvoir. 'This is.'

Beauvoir took the sheet and read it again. It was the tests done on the necklace. The blood on the screaming eagle pendant belonged to L, but they already knew that. He looked at the next paragraph. The one describing the blood on the leather strap.

Same blood type, of course. Blah, blah, blah. Then he stopped. Same blood type, but not the same blood. It wasn't L's blood on the leather. It was CC de Poitiers's. But what was CC's blood doing on the necklace?

He looked over at Gamache who was at his own desk now, grabbing a file and bringing it back to the conference table. He opened it and skimmed a few pages, then slowed down and read more carefully.

'There. Is that what you mean?' He handed CC's autopsy report over to Agent Lacoste, who read the part he indicated and nodded, smiling.

'Got it.'

Gamache leaned back in his chair and exhaled deeply.

'Crie isn't in any danger from the person who killed L because that person's already dead.'

'The photographer,' said Lemieux.

'No,' said Lacoste. 'CC de Poitiers. She killed her own mother. It's the only thing that makes sense. CC grabbed the necklace from her mother's neck and broke it. That bruised the back of L's neck, but it also cut into CC's hand. Her palm. See here in the autopsy report for CC? Her palms were scorched but the coroner mentions another wound, partly healed, underneath. CC killed her mother then took the necklace from her dead hand and threw it in the garbage here.'

'So who threw out the video and the Li Bien ball?' asked Beauvoir.

'CC as well. Three sets of fingerprints were on the Li Bien ball: Peter and Clara Morrow and CC's.'

'But they would be,' persisted Beauvoir. 'It belonged to her. No one else ever got to see it, never mind touch it.'

'But if someone else had stolen it then thrown it away,' reasoned Gamache, 'there'd be a fourth set of prints.'

'Why would CC throw out the Li Bien ball?' asked Lemieux.

'I'm only guessing,' said Lacoste, 'but I think it was guilt. Two things in her house reminded her of her mother. *The Lion in Winter* video and the Li Bien ball. I think they had nothing to do with evidence. I think she threw them out because she couldn't stand to see them.'

'But why put the video in the garbage and take the Li Bien ball all the way to the dump?'

'I don't know,' admitted Lacoste. 'It's possible they were done on different days. Maybe she tossed the video at the same time she threw away the necklace, but it took her a while to get round to the Li Bien ball.'

'It would have been more precious,' agreed Gamache. 'She'd have hesitated to destroy it. It'd become a symbol of her family, her philosophy, her fantasies. That's probably why she couldn't bring herself to just throw it away, but placed it gently in the dumpster.'

'CC killed her own mother,' repeated Beauvoir. 'Why?'

'Money,' said Lacoste, who'd had time to think about it. 'She was about to meet with American buyers, hoping to sell her philosophy to them. She'd market Li Bien and make a fortune.'

'But that was probably fantasy on her part,' said Lemieux.

'Maybe, but as long as she believed it that's all that mattered. Everything was riding on selling Li Bien to the Americans.'

'Then along comes a drunken bag lady as a mother,' nodded Gamache, 'putting the lie to her carefully constructed life. Something had to die, either her dream or her mother. It wasn't much of a choice.' He looked down at the box in his hands. He turned it over, yet again.

B KLM.

Why had L collected those letters? He opened the box and his index finger swam through the other capital letters. Ks, Ms, Cs, Ls and Bs.

Slowly he closed the box and placed it on his desk, staring into space. Then he got up and walked round the room. Round and round he went, with a measured, unhurried pace, his head down and his hands clasped behind his back.

After a few minutes he stopped.

He had his answer.

THIRTY-THREE

⌒

'Madame Longpré.' Gamache rose and bowed to the slight woman in front of him.

'Monsieur Gamache.' She nodded slightly and accepted the chair he held for her.

'What can I get you?'

'An espresso, *s'il vous plaît.*'

The two of them settled into the bistro, their table slightly to one side of the fireplace. It was ten o'clock the next morning and flurries were falling. It was one of those not uncommon but still extraordinary meteorological phenomenons that happened in Quebec in the winter: it was snowing and sunny at the same time. Gamache glanced out the window and marveled. Crystals and prisms, delicate and fragile, floated by and lay soft on Three Pines. Pink and blue and green sparkled from the trees and the clothing of villagers strolling through it.

Their coffees arrived.

'Have you recovered from the fire?' she asked. Em had been there, along with Mother and even Kaye. They'd spent the night serving sandwiches and hot drinks and providing blankets for the freezing volunteers. They'd all been exhausted and Gamache had decided to wait until this morning before speaking to Émilie.

'It was a horrible night,' he said. 'One of the worst I can remember.'

'Who was he?'

'A man named Saul Petrov.' Gamache waited to see if there was any reaction. There was only polite interest. 'A photographer. He was taking pictures of CC.'

'Why?'

'For her catalogue. She was planning to meet with an American company in hopes of interesting them in her project. She had aspirations of becoming a style guru, though her aspirations seemed to have gone beyond style.'

'A kind of "one-stop" shop,' suggested Em. 'She'd refurbish you inside and out.'

'CC de Poitiers dreamed big, that's certain,' agreed Gamache. 'You said you met CC a few times, but did you ever meet her family? Her husband and daughter?'

'Only from a distance, not to speak to. They were at the Boxing Day curling, of course.'

'And the Christmas Eve service at the church here, I understand.'

'C'est vrai.' Em smiled at the memory. 'She's deceptive, the daughter.'

'How so?' Gamache was surprised to hear this.

'Oh, not in a devious way. Not like her mother, though CC wasn't as deceptive as she would have liked to believe. Far too transparent. No, Crie was shy, withdrawn. Never looked you in the eye. But she had the most enchanting voice. Quite took our breath away.'

Émilie cast her mind back to the Christmas Eve service in the crowded chapel. She'd looked over at Crie and seen a girl transformed. Joy had made her lovely.

'She looked just like David when he played Tchaikovsky.'

And then that scene outside the church.

'What are you thinking about?' Gamache asked quietly, noticing a troubled look settling on Em's face.

'After the service we were standing outside. CC was on the other side of the church. It's a short cut to their home. We couldn't see her, but we could hear her. There was also the strangest sound.' Émilie pursed her lips, trying to recall it. 'It was like Henri on the wood floors when I don't clip his nails. A clicking, only louder.'

'I think I can solve that mystery for you,' said Gamache. 'I believe those were her boots. She'd bought a pair of baby sealskin mukluks as a Christmas present for herself. They had metal claws attached to the soles.'

Em looked surprised and disgusted.

'*Mon Dieu*, what must He think of us?'

'You said you could hear more than her boots?'

'She screamed at her daughter. Tore into her. It was awful.'

'What about?' asked Gamache.

'What Crie was wearing. True, it was unconventional. A pink sundress I believe, but CC's main complaint seemed to be Crie's voice, her singing. Her voice was divine. Not the way Gabri uses the word, but really divine. And CC mocked her, belittled her. No, it was more than that. She eviscerated her. It was horrible. I heard it all and did nothing. Said nothing.'

Gamache was silent.

'We should have helped her.' Émilie's voice was quiet,

calm. 'We all stood there on Christmas Eve and witnessed a murder, because that's what it was, Chief Inspector. I'm under no illusion about that. CC killed her daughter that night, and I helped.'

'You go too far, madame. Don't mistake dramatics for a conscience. I know you feel badly about what happened and I agree, something should have been done. But I also know what happened outside the church wasn't isolated. The tragedy of Crie's life is that's all she's known. It became like the snow outside.' They both looked out the window. 'The insults piling up until Crie disappeared under them.'

'I should have done something.'

They were both silent for a moment, Émilie looking outside and Gamache looking at her.

'Blizzard coming tomorrow, I hear,' said Em. 'There's a storm warning out.'

'How much's expected?' This was news to him.

'The weather channel said we might get thirty centimeters. Have you ever been caught in a snowstorm?' she asked.

'Once, driving to the Abitibi region. It was dark and the roads were empty. I got disoriented.' He saw again the swarm of snow in his headlights, the world narrowing to that brilliant funnel. 'I made a wrong turn and ended up in a cul de sac. The road kept narrowing. It was my own fault, of course.' He leaned forward and whispered, 'I was stubborn. Shh.' He looked around.

Émilie smiled. 'It'll be our little secret. Besides, I'm sure no one would believe it. What happened?'

'The track got narrower and narrower.' He demonstrated with his hands, guiding them to a point until he looked like a man at prayer. 'It was nearly impossible to make out the road any more. By then it was really a path, and then,' he turned his hands over, palm up, 'nothing. All that was left was forest and snow. The drifts were up to the car doors. I couldn't go forward and couldn't go back.'

'What did you do?'

He hesitated, not sure which answer to give. All the answers that sprang to mind were true, but there were levels to the truth. He knew what he was about to ask her and decided she was owed the same respect.

'I prayed.'

She looked at this large man, confident, used to command, and nodded. 'What did you pray?' She wasn't letting him off the hook.

'Just before this happened Inspector Beauvoir and I had been on a case in a small fishing village called Baie des Moutons, on the Lower North Shore.'

'The land God gave to Cain,' she said unexpectedly. Gamache was familiar with the quote, but he hadn't run across many others who were. In the 1600s when the explorer Jacques Cartier first set eyes on that desolate outcropping of rocks at the mouth of the St Lawrence River, he'd written in his diary, *This must be the land God gave to Cain.*

'Perhaps I'm attracted to the damned.' Gamache smiled. 'Maybe that's why I hunt killers, like Cain. The area's barren and desolate; practically nothing grows, but to me it's almost unbearably beautiful, if you know where to look. Out here it's easy. Beauty is all around. The rivers, the mountains, the villages, especially Three Pines. But in Mutton Bay it's not so obvious. You have to go looking for it. It's in the lichen on the rocks and the tiny purple flowers, almost invisible, you have to get on your knees to see. It's in the spring flowers of the bakeapples.'

'Did you find your murderer?'

'I did.'

But his inflection told her there was more. She waited, but when nothing more came she decided to ask.

'And what else did you find?'

'God,' he said simply. 'In a diner.'

'What was he eating?'

The question was so unexpected Gamache hesitated then laughed.

'Lemon meringue pie.'

'And how do you know He was God?'

The interview wasn't going as he'd imagined.

'I don't,' he admitted. 'He might have been just a fisherman. He was certainly dressed like one. But he looked across the room at me with such tenderness, such love, I was staggered.' He was tempted to break eye contact, to stare at the warm wooden surface where his hands now rested. But Armand Gamache didn't look down. He looked directly at her.

'What did God do?' Émilie asked, her voice hushed.

'He finished his pie then turned to the wall. He seemed to be rubbing it for a while, then he turned back to me with the most radiant smile I'd ever seen. I was filled with joy.'

'I imagine you're often filled with joy.'

'I'm a happy man, madame. I'm very lucky and I know it.'

'C'est ça.' She nodded. 'It's the knowing of it. I only became really happy after my family was killed. Horrible to say.'

'I believe I understand,' said Gamache.

'Their deaths changed me. At some point I was standing

346

in my living room unable to move forward or back. Frozen. That's why I asked about the snowstorm. That's what it had felt like, for months and months. As though I was lost in a whiteout. Everything was confused and howling. I couldn't go on. I was going to die. I didn't know how, but I knew I couldn't support the loss any longer. I'd staggered to a stop. Like you in that snowstorm. Lost, disoriented, at a dead end. Mine, of course, was figurative. My cul de sac was in my own living room. Lost in the most familiar, the most comforting of places.'

'What happened?'

'The doorbell rang. I remember trying to decide whether I should answer the door or kill myself. But it rang again and I don't know, maybe it was social training, but I roused myself enough to go. And there was God. He had some crumbs of lemon meringue pie on the corner of His mouth.'

Gamache's deep brown eyes widened.

'I'm kidding.' She reached out and held his wrist for a moment, smiling. Gamache laughed at himself. 'He was a road worker,' she continued. 'He wanted to use the phone. He carried a sign.'

She stopped, unable for a moment to go any further. Gamache waited. He hoped the sign didn't say *The End is Nigh*. The room faded. The only two people in the world were tiny, frail Émilie Longpré and Armand Gamache.

'It said *Ice Ahead*.'

They were silent for a moment.

'How did you know He was God?' Gamache asked.

'When does a bush that burns become a Burning Bush?' Em asked and Gamache nodded. 'My despair disappeared. The grief remained, of course, but I knew then that the world wasn't a dark and desperate place. I was so relieved. In that moment I found hope. This stranger with the sign had given it to me. It sounds ridiculous, I know, but suddenly the gloom was lifted.'

She paused a moment, remembering, a smile on her face.

'Annoyed the hell out of Mother, I'll tell you. She had to go all the way to India to find God and He was here all along. She went to Kashmir and I went to the door.'

'Both long journeys,' said Gamache. 'And Kaye?'

'Kaye? I don't think she's made that journey and I think it scares her. I think a lot of things scare Kaye.'

'Clara Morrow has painted you as the Three Graces.'

'Has she now? One day that woman will be discovered and the world will see what an astonishing artist she is. She sees things others don't. She sees the best in people.'

'She certainly sees how much the three of you love each other.'

Em nodded. 'I do love them. I love all this.' She looked around the cheerful room, the fires crackling in the grates, Olivier and Gabri talking to customers, price tags dangling from chairs and tables and chandeliers. When he'd been annoyed at Olivier one day Gabri had waited on tables with a price tag dangling from himself.

'My life's never been the same since that day I opened the door. I'm happy now. Content. Funny, isn't it? I had to go to Hell to find happiness.'

'People expect me to be cynical because of my job,' Gamache found himself saying, 'but they don't understand. It's exactly as you've said. I spend my days looking into the last room in the house, the one we keep barred and hidden even from ourselves. The one with all our monsters, fetid and rotting and waiting. My job is to find people who take lives. And to do that I have to find out why. And to do that I have to get into their heads and open that last door. But when I come out again,' he opened his arms in an expansive movement, 'the world is suddenly more beautiful, more alive, more lovely than ever. When you see the worst you appreciate the best.'

'That's it.' Émilie nodded. 'You like people.'

'I love people,' he admitted.

'What was your God doing to the wall in the diner?'

'He was writing.'

'God wrote on the wall of the diner?' Em was incredulous, though she didn't know why. Her God walked around with a prefabricated construction sign.

Gamache nodded and remembered watching the grizzled, beautiful fisherman at the screen door to the fly-filled diner that smelled of the sea. He'd looked back at Gamache and smiled. Not the radiant, full frontal beam of a few minutes earlier, but a warm and comforting smile, as though to say He understood and that everything would be all right.

Gamache had gotten up and slid into the booth and read the writing on the wall. He'd pulled out his notebook, stuffed with facts about death, about murder and sorrow, and he'd written down the four simple lines.

He knew then what he had to do. Not because he was a brave man or a good man, but because he had no choice. He had to return to Montreal, to Sûreté headquarters, and he had to sort out the Arnot case. He'd known for months he had to do it, and yet he'd run from it and hidden behind work. Behind dead bodies and the solemn, noble need to find killers, as though he was the only one on the force who could.

The writing on the wall hadn't told him what to do. He knew that. It'd given him the courage to do it.

'But how do you know you did the right thing?' Em asked, and Gamache realized he'd said all that out loud.

The blue eyes were steady and calm. But something had shifted. The conversation seemed to have another purpose. There was an intensity about her that hadn't been there before.

'I don't know. Even now I'm not absolutely sure. Lots of people are convinced I was wrong. You know that. I'm sure you read about it in the papers.'

Émilie nodded. 'You prevented Superintendent Arnot and his two colleagues from killing more people.'

'I stopped them from killing themselves,' said Gamache. He remembered that meeting clearly. He'd been part of the inner circle of the Sûreté then. Pierre Arnot was a senior and respected officer in the force, though not by Gamache. He'd known Arnot since his days as a rookie and the two had never gotten along. Gamache suspected Arnot thought him weak, while he thought Arnot a bully.

When it was obvious what Arnot and two of his top men had done, when even his friends couldn't deny it any longer, Arnot had had one request. That they not be arrested. Not yet. Arnot had a hunting cabin in the Abitibi region, north of Montreal. They'd go there and not return. It was decided it was best, for Arnot, for the co-defendants, for the families.

Everyone agreed.

Except Gamache.

'Why did you stop them?' Émilie asked.

'There had been enough death. It was time for justice. An old-fashioned notion.' He looked up and smiled into her face. After a moment's silence he continued. 'I believe it was right, but I still struggle sometimes. I'm like a Victorian preacher. I have doubts.'

'Really?'

Gamache looked into the fire again and thought long and hard. 'I'd do it again. It was the right thing to do, at least for me.'

He looked back at her and paused.

'Who was L, madame?'

'Elle?'

Gamache reached into his satchel and brought out the wooden box, turning it over to reveal the letters taped to the bottom. He pointed to the L. 'L, Madame Longpré.'

Her eyes, while still holding his, seemed to drift and focus on a spot in the distance.

Ice ahead. They were almost there now.

THIRTY-FOUR

⁓

'She was our friend,' said Émilie, holding Gamache's eyes. 'We called her El, but she signed her name with just the letter L.' Em felt calm for the first time in days. 'She lived next door to me.' Em pointed to a small Québecois house with a steep metal roof and tiny dormers. 'Her family sold it years ago and moved away. After El disappeared.'

'What happened?'

'She was younger than the rest of us. Very sweet, very kind. Some children like that get picked on. Other kids know they won't fight back. But not El. She was one of those children who seemed to bring out the best in others. She was bright, in every way. A shining child. When she walked into a room the lights went on and the sun rose.'

Em could still see her, a child so lovely no one was even jealous of her. Perhaps, too, they all sensed that someone that kind and good couldn't last long. There was something precious about El.

'Her name was Eleanor, wasn't it?' Gamache asked, though he was certain of the answer.

'Eleanor Allaire.'

Gamache sighed and closed his eyes. There. He'd done it.

'El, short for Eleanor,' he whispered.

Émilie nodded. 'May I?' Her tiny hands reached across the table and took the box, holding it in open palms as though inviting it to fly away. 'I haven't seen this in years. Mother gave it to her when El left the ashram in India. They went there together, you know.'

'She was the L in B KLM, wasn't she?'

Em nodded.

'Mother Bea is B, Kaye is K and you're M. Bea, Kaye, El and Em.'

'You're very clever, Chief Inspector. We would have been friends anyway, but the coincidence of our names all sounding like letters of the alphabet appealed to us. Especially since we all adored reading. It also seemed romantic, a kind of secret code.'

'Is that where Be Calm came from?'

'You figured that out as well? How?'

'There were too many references to Be Calm in this case. Then I visited Mother's meditation center.'

'Be Calm.'

'Yes, but it was the writing on the wall that gave it away.'

'That seems to happen to you a lot. Must be helpful in your trade to have the answers written on the wall.'

'It's recognizing them that's the trick. It was a misquote and that didn't seem in character. Mother might give the impression of being not of this world, but I suspect she's very much here. She'd never have put *Be calm, and know that I am God* on her wall unless she meant to.'

'Be still, and know that I am God,' quoted Em correctly.

'That was El's problem. She couldn't be still. Kaye was the one who noticed that we could put our letters together and make a word, sort of. B KLM. Be calm. Close enough to make sense to us, and far enough away to make it a secret. Our secret. But you figured it out, Chief Inspector.'

'Took me far too long.'

'Is there a time limit on these things?'

Gamache laughed. 'No, I suppose not, but sometimes my own blindness takes my breath away. I'd been staring at these letters for days, knowing they were significant to El. I even had the example of Ruth's poetry book. *I'm FINE*. The capital letters all stand for some other word.'

'*Mais non*. What?'

'Fucked up, Insecure, Neurotic and Egotistical,' he said, slightly embarrassed about using a swear word in front of such a dignified woman, but she didn't seem to mind. In fact, she was laughing.

'*J'adore Ruth*. Just when I think she's loathsome she does something like that. *Parfait*.'

'I kept staring at the letters on the box and assumed the space between the B and the KLM wasn't significant. But it was. It held the answer. It lay in what wasn't there. In the tiny space between letters.'

'Like those wild flowers in the land God gave to Cain,' said Em. 'You have to look hard to see it.'

'I didn't think it was a deliberate space. I thought that was where the C went,' Gamache admitted.

'The C?'

'Open the box.'

Em did and stared for a very long time. She reached into

the box and brought out a tiny letter. Balancing it on her finger she showed it to Gamache. A C.

'She put her daughter into the box too,' said Em. 'This is what love looks like.'

'What happened?'

Em cast her mind back again, to the days when the world was new. 'El was a pilgrim soul. While the rest of us settled down, El grew more restless. She seemed frail, fragile. Sensitive. We kept pleading with her to be calm.'

'You even called your curling team Be Calm,' said Gamache. 'That was another clue. You only ever spoke of three members of the original team, but a curling team has four. Someone was missing. When I saw Clara Morrow's picture of the three of you as the Graces there seemed to be someone missing. There was a hole in the composition.'

'But Clara never met El,' said Émilie. 'Never even heard of her as far as I know.'

'That's true, but as you said, Clara sees things others don't. She created the work with the three of you forming a sort of vase, a vessel she called it. Only there's a piece missing, a crack. Where El would be.

> *Ring the bells that still can ring,*
> *Forget your perfect offering,*
> *There's a crack in everything,*
> *That's how the light gets in.'*

'What an extraordinary poem. Ruth Zardo?'

'Leonard Cohen. Clara used it in her piece. She wrote it on the wall behind the three of you, like graffiti.'

'There's a crack in everything, that's how the light gets in,' said Émilie.

'What happened to El?' He remembered the autopsy photographs. A filthy, emaciated, pathetic old drunk on the slab. A world away from the shining young woman Em had described.

'She wanted to go to India. She thought maybe there her mind would still and she'd find peace. The rest of us drew straws and it was decided Mother would go with her. It's ironic that El didn't much like India but Mother found the answers to questions she didn't even know she had.'

'Mother,' said Gamache. 'Beatrice Mayer. Very clever as well. I asked Clara why everyone calls Bea Mother and she suggested I figure it out for myself.'

'And you did.'

'Took me a long while. It wasn't until I was watching *The Lion in Winter* that I got it.'

'How so?'

'It was made by MGM. Metro, Goldwyn, Mayer. Mayer. It's pronounced the same way as *mère*. French for mother. Beatrice Mayer became Mother Bea. I knew then I was in the company of people who loved not only books, but words. Spoken, written, the power of words.'

'When Kaye asked why her father and the other boys would have screamed "Fuck the Pope" as they ran to their deaths you said maybe it was because they knew that words could kill. Kaye dismissed it, but I think you were right. I know words can kill. I saw it on Christmas Eve. You might consider it melodramatic, Chief Inspector, but I saw CC murder her daughter with words.'

'What happened to El?' he asked again.

*

Beauvoir brought the car to a halt and sat for a moment. The heater was on and the car seats had warmed. On the stereo Beau Dommage was singing 'La complainte du phoque en Alaska'. He'd necked to that at school dances. It was always the last song and always brought the girls to tears.

He didn't want to leave. Not just because the car was so comfortable, filled with warm and sticky memories, but because of what awaited him. The meditation center sat bathed in sharp morning sun.

'Bonjour, Inspecteur.' Mother smiled, opening the door before he knocked. But the smile didn't extend to her eyes. It barely left her lips, which were tight and white. He could sense her tension and felt himself relax. He had the advantage now and knew it.

'May I come in?' He was damned if he was going to ask, 'Mother, may I?' He was also damned if he was going to ask why everyone called her Mother, though he was dying to know.

'I was under the impression this wasn't your favorite place,' she said, regaining some ground on him. Beauvoir didn't know what it was with this woman. She was squat and unattractive. She wobbled instead of walked and her hair stuck out in all directions. And she wore sheets, or perhaps curtains, or maybe they were slipcovers. By all standards she was ludicrous. And yet there was something about her.

'I came down with the flu when I was last here. I'm sorry if I behaved badly.' Although it caught in his throat to apologize Gamache had pointed out that it actually gave him an advantage. And he'd noticed, over the years, that it was true. People felt a certain superiority if they thought they had something on you. But as soon as you apologized they had nothing. Pissed them off.

Now Beauvoir felt equal to Madame Mayer.

'Namaste,' she said, putting her hands together in prayer and bowing.

Damn her. He felt off balance again. He knew he was meant to ask, but didn't. Taking his boots off he strode through to the large meditation room with its soothing aqua walls and warm green-carpeted floor.

'I have some questions for you.' He turned to watch Madame Mayer waddle toward him. 'What did you think of CC de Poitiers?'

'I've already told the Chief Inspector about that. In fact, you were here, though I suppose you might have been too ill to listen.'

She was exhausted. Her compassion was spent. She didn't care any more. She knew she couldn't keep this up much longer, and now she yearned for the end. She no longer woke in the middle of the night and worried. Now she simply didn't go to sleep.

Mother was dead tired.

'CC was delusional. Her entire philosophy was crap. She'd taken a bunch of teachings and mashed them together and come up with this poisonous idea that people shouldn't show emotions. That's ridiculous. We are emotion. That's what makes us who we are. Her idea that truly evolved people feel no emotions is ridiculous. Yes, we want to be in balance, but that doesn't mean not feeling or showing things. It means the opposite. It means,' now Mother was getting worked up, too exhausted to contain herself any longer, 'it means feeling things fully, passionately. It means embracing life. And then letting go.

'She thought she was so great, coming here and lording

it over us. Li Bien this, Be Calm that. All her tasteful white clothes and furnishings and bedding linens and stupid aura pillows and calming baby blankets and God knows what other crap. She was sick. Her emotions were denied and stunted and twisted and made into something grotesque. She claimed to be so balanced, so grounded. Well, she was so grounded it killed her. Karma.'

Beauvoir wondered whether karma was an Indian word for irony.

Mother radiated anger. It was how he liked his suspects. Out of control, liable to say and do anything.

'And yet you and CC both called your places Be Calm. Doesn't calm mean placid? Showing nothing?'

'There's a difference between flat and calm.'

'I think you're just playing word games. Like you did with that.' He pointed to the wall where the quote was stenciled. Then he walked over to it.

'Be calm, and know that I am God. You told Chief Inspector Gamache it came from Isaiah, but doesn't it actually come from Psalms?'

He loved this part of the job. He could see her deflate in front of him, surprised she didn't make a little squealing sound. Slowly he brought out his notebook.

'Psalm 46 verse 10. Be still, and know that I am God. You lied and you intentionally put a misquote on your wall. Why? What does Be Calm really mean?'

They were both still then. Beauvoir could hear her breathing.

Then something happened. He saw what he'd just done. He'd broken an elderly woman. Something shifted and he saw before him a beaten old lady, with wild hair and a plump sagging body. Her face was very white and wrinkled and soft and her hands were veined and bony and trembling.

Her head was bowed.

He'd done this. He'd done it on purpose and he'd done it gleefully.

'Eleanor and Mother stayed at the commune for six months,' Em told Gamache, her hands suddenly restless, playing with the handle of her espresso cup. 'Mother was getting deeper and deeper into it but El started to get agitated again. Eventually she left, came back to Canada, but not back home. We lost track of her for a while.'

'When did you realize she was unstable?' Gamache asked.

'We'd always known that. Her mind would race. She couldn't concentrate on any one thing, but hopped about from project to project, brilliant at them all. But, to be fair, if she found something she liked she'd become possessed by it. She'd bring all her talents, all her energies, to bear. And when she did that she was formidable.'

'Like Li Bien?' Gamache brought a cardboard box from his satchel.

'What else have you got in there?' Em leaned around the table to look at his leather satchel. 'The Montreal Canadians?'

'Hope not. They're playing tonight.' Em stared at his huge, careful hands as they peeled back the wrap, slowly revealing the object below. It stood on the table next to the wooden box, and for a golden moment Émilie Longpré was in her young body, staring at the Li Bien ball for the first time. It was luminous and somehow unreal, its beauty imprisoned beneath the layer of invisible glass. It was both lovely and horrible.

It was Eleanor Allaire.

Young Émilie Longpré had known then that they'd lose her. Had known then their luminous friend couldn't survive in the real world. And now the Li Bien ball had returned to Three Pines, but without its creator.

'May I hold it?'

Gamache placed it in her hands as he had the box and again she held it, but this time in hands closed tightly round it, as though hugging and protecting something precious.

He reached into his satchel for the last time and withdrew a long leather cord, stained with dirt and oils and blood. And dangling from it was an eagle's head.

'I need the whole truth, madame.'

Beauvoir was sitting next to Mother now, listening intently as he had when as a child his own mother had read stories of adventure and tragedy.

'When CC first came here,' Mother explained, 'she showed an almost unnatural interest in us.'

Beauvoir knew instinctively that by 'us' she meant Émilie, Kaye and herself.

'She'd drop in and seem to interrogate us. It wasn't a normal sort of social call even for someone as maladroit as CC.'

'When did you realize she was El's daughter?'

Mother hesitated. Beauvoir had the impression it wasn't to think up a lie, but rather to cast her mind back.

'It was a cascade. What put it beyond doubt for me was the reference to Ramen Das in her book.' Mother nodded to the small altar by the wall with its sticks of stinky incense sitting in holders on a brightly colored and mirrored piece of cloth. Stuck to the wall above it was a poster, and below that a framed photograph. Beauvoir got up and looked at them. The poster showed an emaciated Indian man in a diaper standing by a stone wall gripping a long cane and smiling. He looked like Ben Kingsley in *Gandhi*, but then all elderly Indians did to Beauvoir. It was the same poster he'd disappeared into during his last visit. In the smaller photograph the same man was sitting with two young western women, slim and also smiling, and wearing billowy nightgowns. Or maybe they were curtains. Or sofa covers. Astonished, he turned to Mother. Wild-haired, pear-shaped, exhausted Mother.

'That's you?' He pointed to one of the women. Mother joined him and smiled at his amazement and inability to conceal it. She wasn't insulted. It often amazed her too.

'And that's El.' She pointed to the other woman. While both the guru and Mother were smiling, the other woman seemed to radiate. Beauvoir could barely take his eyes off her. Then he thought of the autopsy pictures Gamache had shown him. True, Mother had changed, but in ways recognizable and natural, if not attractive. The other woman had disappeared. The glow gone, the radiance dimmed and dulled and finally extinguished beneath layers of filth and despair.

'Not many people know about Ramen Das. There was more, of course.' Mother plopped into a seat. 'CC called her philosophy Li Bien. I'd lived for over seventy years and only ever heard that phrase from one other person. El. CC called her business and her book Be Calm. And she used a logo only we knew about.'

'The eagle?'

'The symbol of Eleanor of Aquitaine.'

362

'Explain that to me, Mother.' Beauvoir couldn't believe he'd just called her Mother, but he had, and it felt natural. He hoped he wouldn't be suckling soon.

'We studied British and French history in school,' said Mother. 'Canada apparently had no history. Anyway, when we got to the section on Eleanor of Aquitaine El became obsessed. She decided she was Eleanor of Aquitaine. Don't look so smug, Inspector. You can't tell me you didn't run around playing cowboys and Indians or pretending to be Superman or Batman.'

Beauvoir snorted. He'd done nothing of the sort. That'd be crazy. He'd been Jean-Claude Killy, the world's greatest Olympic skier. He'd even told his mother she had to call him Jean-Claude. She'd refused. Still, he'd skied astonishing races in his bedroom, winning Olympic gold, often outrunning catastrophic avalanches, saving nuns and grateful millionaires along the way.

'El was searching even then, knowing something wasn't right, as though she didn't belong in her own skin. She found comfort in thinking she was Eleanor of Aquitaine, and Em even made her a necklace with Eleanor's heraldic symbol. The eagle. A particularly aggressive eagle.'

'So you put it all together and when CC moved here you realized she was El's daughter.'

'That's right. We knew she'd had a child. El had disappeared for a few years, then we suddenly got a card from Toronto. She'd gotten into a relationship with some guy who quickly disappeared, but not before getting El pregnant. She wasn't married and at the time, in the late fifties, that was a scandal. I'd known when she left India that she wasn't well emotionally. Her mind was brilliant and delicate and unbalanced. Poor CC, being raised in a home like that. No wonder the idea of balance was so important to her.' Mother looked at Beauvoir, stunned. It had just occurred to her. 'I felt no sympathy for CC, no compassion. At first, when we realized she was our beloved El's daughter we tried to invite her into our lives. I can't say we ever warmed to her. She was unlikable in the extreme. El was like sunshine, bright and loving and kind. But she gave birth to darkness. CC didn't live in her mother's shadow, she was her mother's shadow.'

'This was found in El's hand.' Gamache tried to say it gently, but knew there was no hiding the horror of it. 'El's mind might have been unbalanced, but her heart was steady. She knew what was important. Through all the years on the street she held on to these two things.' He touched the box and nodded to the necklace. 'The three of you. She surrounded herself with her friends.'

'We tried to follow her but she was in and out of hospitals and then finally put onto the streets. We couldn't imagine our El living on the streets. We tried to get her into shelters but she always left. We had to learn to respect her wishes.'

'When was CC taken from her?' Gamache asked.

'I don't know exactly. I think she was about ten when El was put into hospital.'

They were silent for a moment, each imagining the little girl taken from the only home she knew. Filthy, unhealthy place, but home nevertheless.

'When did you see El again?'

'Mother and Kaye and I often take the bus into Montreal and a couple of years ago we saw El at the station. It was a shock, seeing her like that, but we eventually got used to it.'

'And you showed her some of Clara's art?'

'Clara? Why would we do that?' Em was obviously confused. 'We never had long with her, just a few minutes, so we'd give her clothes and blankets and food and some money. But we never showed her Clara's art. Why would we?'

'Did you ever show her a picture of Clara?'

'No.' Again Em seemed baffled by the question.

Why indeed, thought Gamache.

I've always loved your art, Clara, El had said when Clara was down and distressed.

I've always loved your art.

Gamache felt the warmth of the fire on his face. He wondered whether El had ever had a cod quota or worked construction.

'How did you know El had been killed?' There was no cushioning that question.

Em had clearly been bracing for it and hardly reacted at all.

'We went back to Montreal on December twenty-third to give her a Christmas gift.'

'Why go back? Why not give her the present after Ruth's book launch?'

'El was a creature of habit. Anything outside her routine upset her. A few years ago we tried to give her a gift early and she didn't react well, so we learned. It had to be the twenty-third. You look puzzled.'

And he did. He couldn't believe a woman living on the streets followed a Day Timer. How'd she even know what day it was?

'Henri knows dinner time and when it's time for his

promenade,' said Em after Gamache had told her what was bothering him. 'I don't want to compare El to my puppy, but in the end she was like that. Almost all instinct. El lived on the streets; she was crazy, covered in her own excrement, obsessive and drunk. But she was still the purest soul I've ever met. We looked for her outside Ogilvy's, then the bus station. We eventually called the police. That's when we found out she'd been killed.'

Em broke eye contact, her self-possession slipping. But still Gamache knew she'd have to endure one more question.

'When did you know it was her daughter who killed her?'

Émilie's eyes widened. '*Sacré*,' she whispered.

THIRTY-FIVE

'No,' Beauvoir screamed at the television. 'Stop him. Defense, defense.'

'Watch it, watch it.' Beside him Robert Lemieux was twisting on the sofa, trying to check the New York Ranger who was racing down the ice at the New Forum.

'He shoots!' the announcer screamed. Beauvoir and Lemieux leaned forward, all but clasping hands, watching the tiny black dot on the screen shoot off the Ranger stick. Gabri was gripping his easy chair and Olivier's hand was stopped halfway to the cheese plate.

'He scores!' the announcer shrieked.

'Thomas. Fucking Thomas.' Lemieux turned to Beauvoir. 'They're paying him what? Sixteen zillion a year and he can't stop that.' He gestured to the screen.

'They're only paying him about five million,' said Gabri, his enormous fingers delicately spreading a piece of baguette with Saint-Albray cheese and dabbing a bit of jam on top. 'More wine?'

'Please.' Beauvoir held out his glass. It was the first hockey game he'd watched without chips and beer. He quite liked the cheese and wine change-up. And he was realizing he quite liked Agent Lemieux. Up until this moment he'd seen him as a piece of mobile furniture, like a chair on wheels. There for a purpose, but not to be friendly with. But now they were sharing this humiliating defeat at the hands of the crappy New York Rangers, and Lemieux was proving himself a staunch and knowledgable ally. Granted, so were Gabri and Olivier.

The *Hockey Night in Canada* theme was playing and Beauvoir got up to stretch his legs and walk around the living room of the B&B. In another chair Chief Inspector Gamache was making a call.

'Thomas let in another,' said Beauvoir.

'I saw. He's coming too far out of the net,' said Gamache.

'That's his style. He intimidates the other team, forces them to shoot.'

'And is it working?'

'Not tonight,' Beauvoir agreed. He picked up the chief's empty glass and wandered away. Fucking Thomas. I could do better. And while the commercials were on Jean Guy Beauvoir imagined himself in net for the Canadians. But Beauvoir wasn't a goalie. He was a forward. He liked the limelight, the puck play, the panting, the skating and the shooting. Hearing an opponent grunt as he was forced into the boards. And maybe giving him an extra elbow.

No, he knew himself enough to know he'd never make a goalie.

That was Gamache. The one they all depended on to make the save.

He took the filled wine glass back and put it on the table by the phone, Gamache smiling his thanks.

'*Bonjour?*' Gamache heard the familiar voice and his heart contracted.

'*Oui, bonjour*, is this Madame Gamache, the librarian? I hear you have a book overdue.'

'I have a husband overdue, and he is a little bookish,' she said, laughing. 'Hello, Armand. How are things going?'

'Eleanor Allaire.'

There was a pause.

'Thank you, Armand. Eleanor Allaire.' Reine-Marie said the name as though part of the novena. 'Beautiful name.'

'And a beautiful woman, I've been told.'

He told her everything then. About Eleanor, about her friends, about India and the daughter. About being the crack in the vessel, and finding herself on the streets. About CC, taken from her home, raised by God knows who, searching for her mother and even going to Three Pines.

'Why did she think her mother would be there?' Reine-Marie asked.

'Because that was the image her mother had painted on the Christmas decoration. The Li Bien ball. The only thing CC had from El. She was either told or must have guessed that the three pine trees on the ball meant the village where her mother was born and raised. This afternoon we spoke to old-timers and they remember the Allaires. Just the one daughter, Eleanor. They left almost fifty years ago.'

'So CC bought a home in Three Pines to search for her mother? I wonder why she did it now? Why not years ago?'

'I don't think we'll ever know for sure,' said Gamache, sipping his wine. In the background he could hear the *Hockey Night in Canada* theme. Reine-Marie was watching the game as well this Saturday night. 'Thomas isn't having a good night.'

'He should stay closer to the net,' she said. 'The Rangers have his number.'

'Do you have a theory why CC would suddenly decide to search for her mother now?'

'You said CC had approached an American company about a catalogue?'

'What're you thinking?'

'I was wondering whether maybe CC waited until she felt she was a success.'

Gamache thought about it, watching the players on the television pass the puck up the ice, lose it, skate furiously backwards as the other team charged. Beauvoir and Lemieux fell back into the sofa, groaning.

'The American contract.' He nodded. 'And the book. We think that's why El moved from the bus station to Ogilvy's. CC had posters put up advertising her book. One was at the bus station. El must have seen it and realized CC de Poitiers was her daughter, so she went to Ogilvy's to find her.'

'And CC went to Three Pines to find her mother,' said Reine-Marie. It was heartbreaking to think of the two wounded women searching for each other.

An image sprang to Gamache's mind of frail little El, old and cold, shuffling the long blocks, giving up her prized place on the subway grate in hopes of finding her daughter.

'Shoot, shoot,' the guys in the living room were shouting.

'He shoots, he scores!' the announcer yelled to wild applause from the New Forum and near hysteria from Beauvoir, Lemieux, Gabri and Olivier, who were hugging and dancing around the room.

'Kowalski,' Beauvoir called to Gamache. 'Finally. It's three to one now.'

'What did CC do in the village?' Reine-Marie asked. She'd turned the television off in their sitting room to concentrate on the conversation.

'Well, she thought one of the elderly women was her mother so she seems to have interviewed them all.'

'And then she found her mother at Ogilvy's,' said Reine-Marie.

'El must have recognized CC. I think she must have approached and CC paid no attention, thinking it was just another bum on the street. But El would have been insistent. Following her, maybe even using her name. But even then CC might have put it down to the vagrant's knowing her name from the book. Finally I think El became desperate and opened her front to reveal the necklace. That would have stopped CC dead. She'd have remembered the necklace from her childhood. It was made by Émilie Longpré. There was no other like it.'

'And CC would have known then the woman was her mother,' said Reine-Marie, softly, imagining the scene and trying to imagine how she'd feel. Yearning to find her mother. Longing not only for her mother but her mother's approval. Longing to be scooped up in those old arms.

And then to be confronted by El. A stinking, drunken, pathetic bag lady. Her mother.

And what had CC done?

She'd lost her mind. Reine-Marie guessed what had happened. CC had grabbed the necklace and yanked it off her mother's neck. Then she'd grabbed the long scarf and she'd pulled and pulled, tighter and tighter.

She'd murdered her mother. To hide the truth, as she'd done all her life. Of course that's how it must have been.

What else could have happened? CC might have done it to save the American contract, thinking she'd lose it if they knew the creator of Li Bien and Be Calm had an alcoholic vagrant for a mother. Or she might have done it thinking she'd be ridiculed by the buying public.

But it was more likely she never even thought of those things. She acted instinctively, as had her mother. And CC's instincts were always to get rid of anything unpleasant. To erase and disappear them. As she had her soft and indolent husband and her immense and silent daughter.

And El was a huge, stinking unpleasantness.

Eleanor Allaire died at the hands of her only child.

And then the child had died. Reine-Marie sighed, saddened by the images.

'If CC killed her mother,' she asked, 'then who killed CC?'

Gamache paused. Then he told her.

Upstairs in the B&B Yvette Nichol lay on her bed listening to the *Hockey Night in Canada* music and the occasional outbursts from the living room. She longed to join them. To discuss Thomas's new contract and whether the coach should be blamed for the horrible season, and whether Toronto had known Pagé was injured when they'd traded him to the Canadians.

She'd felt something for Beauvoir, that night when she'd nursed him, and the next morning when they'd breakfasted together. Not a crush, really. Just a sort of comfort. A relief, as though a weight she never even knew she was carrying had been lifted.

And then the fire, and her stupidity in going into the building. Another reason to hate stupid Uncle Saul. It was his fault, of course. Everything bad that happened to the family could be traced back to him. He was the rot in the family tree.

She's not worth it. The words had scalded and burned. She hadn't known how bad the injury was at first. You never do. You go sort of numb. But with the passage of time it had become clear. She was gravely wounded.

Gamache had spoken to her, and that had been interesting. Had actually helped. If only to make it clear what she had to do. She picked up her cell phone and dialed. A man's voice answered, the hockey game playing in the background.

'I have a question for you,' Gamache said, his change of tone alerting Reine-Marie. 'Did I do the right thing with Arnot?'

Reine-Marie's heart broke, hearing Armand ask that. Only she knew the price he'd paid. He'd put on a brave and firm public face. Not Jean Guy, not Michel Brébeuf, not even their best friends had known the agony he'd gone through. But she knew.

'Why are you asking now?'

'It's this case. It's become about more than murder. Somehow it's about belief.'

'Every murder you've been on is about belief. What the murderer believes, what you believe.'

It was true. We are what we believe. And the only case where he'd seriously been in danger of betraying what he believed had been Arnot.

'Maybe I should have let them die.'

There it was. Had he been driven by his ego in the Arnot case? His pride? His certainty that he was right and everyone else was wrong?

Gamache remembered the hushed and hurried meeting at Sûreté headquarters. The decision to let the men commit suicide, for the good of the force. He remembered raising his objections and being voted down. And then he'd left. He still felt a pang of shame as he remembered what happened next. He'd taken a case in Mutton Bay, as far from headquarters as he could get. Where he could clear his head. But he'd known all along what he had to do.

And the fisherman had put it beyond doubt.

Gamache had jumped on a plane and headed back to Montreal. It was the weekend Arnot had chosen to go to the Abitibi. Gamache had made the long drive up. And as he got closer the weather had closed in. The first storm of the winter had descended, rapidly and brutally. And Gamache had become lost and stuck.

But he'd prayed and pushed and finally the tires had gripped and the car had headed back the way it had come. Back to the main road. The right road. He'd found the cabin and arrived just in time.

As Gamache entered Arnot had hesitated then jumped for his gun. And in that instant, as Arnot lunged, Gamache had known the truth of it. Arnot would see the others dead then he'd disappear.

Gamache had leaped across the room and grabbed the gun first. And suddenly it was over. The three men were taken back to Montreal to face trial. A trial that no one wanted, except Armand Gamache.

The trial had been a very public affair, rending the Sûreté and the entire community. And many blamed Gamache. He'd done the unthinkable. He'd taken the matter public.

Gamache had known this would happen, and that was why

he'd hesitated. To lose the respect of your peers is a terrible thing. To become a pariah was hard.

> *And, when he thinks, good easy man, full surely*
> *His greatness is a-ripening, nips his root,*
> *And then he falls, as I do.*

'And when he falls, he falls like Lucifer,' said Gamache in a whisper.

'Never to hope again.' Reine-Marie finished the quote. 'Are you that great, Armand, that your fall is legend?'

He gave a short laugh. 'I'm just feeling sorry for myself. I miss you.'

'And I miss you, dear heart. And yes, Armand, you did the right thing. But I understand your doubts. They're what make you a great man, not your certainties.'

'Fucking Thomas. Did you see that?' Beauvoir was standing in front of the television, his hands on either side of his head, looking round. 'Trade him!' he shouted at the screen.

'Now, who'd you rather be tonight?' Reine-Marie asked. 'Armand Gamache or Carl Thomas?'

Gamache laughed. It wasn't often he let his doubts wash over him, but they had that night.

'The Arnot case isn't over, is it?' said Reine-Marie.

Agent Nichol came down the staircase and caught his eye, smiling. She nodded then joined the group, who were too preoccupied to notice.

'*Non, ce n'est pas fini.*'

THIRTY-SIX

—

One by one the lights went out in the homes of Three Pines, and eventually the huge Christmas tree went out as well, and then the village was in darkness. Gamache got out of his chair. He'd turned the lights out in the living room after everyone had gone to bed, and had sat there quietly, enjoying the peace, enjoying watching the village put its head to the pillow. He quietly put on his coat and boots and went outside, his feet munching the snow. Émilie Longpré had said Environment Canada had issued a storm warning for the next day, but it was hard to believe. He walked to the middle of the road.

All was silent. All was bright. He tilted his head to stare at the stars. The entire sky was brilliant with them. He thought perhaps this was his favorite part of the day. Standing under a winter's sky, the stars looking as though God had stopped a storm and the millions of flakes were suspended in the air. Bright and cheerful.

He didn't feel like walking, had no need to pace. He had his answers. He'd just come out to be with himself in the middle of Three Pines, in the middle of the night. So at peace.

They woke up next morning to a storm. From his bed Gamache could see it. Or, more precisely, he could see nothing. Snow had plastered itself against his window and even created a small drift on the wood floor where flakes had rushed through the open window and landed in the room. The room was freezing and dark. And silent. Totally silent. He noticed his alarm clock was off. He tried a light.

Nothing.

The power had been knocked out. Climbing out of bed he closed his window, put on his dressing gown and slippers and opened his door. He could hear some hushed voices down below. On the main floor he met a magical sight. Gabri and Olivier had lit oil lamps and hurricane candles. The room was made up of pools of amber light. It was exquisite, a world lit only by fire. The fireplace was on and threw flickering light and heat. He moved closer to it. The furnace must have been off for hours and the house had chilled.

'*Bonjour, monsieur l'inspecteur,*' came Olivier's cheerful voice. 'The heat's back on, thanks to our emergency generator, but it'll take an hour or so for the house to warm up.'

Just then the place gave a shudder. '*Mon Dieu,*' said Olivier. 'It's really kicking up outside. News last night said we could get fifty centimeters, almost two feet.'

'What time is it?' Gamache asked, trying to get his watch close to an oil lamp.

'Ten to six.'

Gamache woke the others and they breakfasted as the

original inhabitants of this old stagecoach inn might have. By firelight. On toasted English muffins, jam and *café au lait*.

'Gabri plugged the oven and the espresso machine into the generator,' explained Olivier. 'No lights, but we have the necessities.'

The electricity was back on but flickering by the time they fought their way across to the Incident Room. The snow slashed out of the sky, hitting them sideways. Leaning into it and bowing their heads they tried not to lose their way in the short slog across the familiar village. The snow drove into them, finding its way up their sleeves and down their collars, into their ears and into every cranny of their clothing as though searching for skin. And finding it.

At the Incident Room they unwound their scarves, shook packed snow from their sodden tuques and kicked their boots against the building to get the worst of the snow off.

Lacoste was stuck in Montreal with the storm and would spend the day at headquarters. Beauvoir spent the morning on the phone and finally found a pharmacist in Cowansville who had recorded selling niacin in the last few weeks. He decided to head over there, even though the snow made the roads almost impassable.

'Nothing to it,' he said, exhilarated to be at the end of the case and heading into a storm. The hero, the hunter, challenging the odds, meeting adversity, fighting the worst snowstorm anyone had ever seen anywhere. He was astonishing.

He dashed out, only to find the new snow up to his knees. He waded through to his car and spent the next half hour shoveling it out. Still, it was fluffy and light and brought back memories of prayed-for storm days off school.

The storm didn't keep the villagers inside and a few were doing their errands on snowshoes and cross-country skis, barely visible through the gusts. Beauvoir's was the only car on the road.

'Sir.' Lemieux came up to him an hour later. 'I found this under the door.'

He held an envelope, long and thick and damp from melted snow.

'Did you see who brought it?' Gamache looked from Lemieux to Nichol. She shrugged and went back to her computer.

'No sir. In this storm someone could be right at the building and we wouldn't know.'

'Someone was,' said Gamache. On it was written in precise, exquisite script, 'Chief Inspector Armand Gamache, Sûreté du Québec'. He tore it open, dread rising in him. Scanning the two pages rapidly he shot to his feet and strode across the room, throwing his coat on and not even bothering to do it up before plunging into the brutal day.

'May I help?' Lemieux called after him.

'Get your coat on. Agent Nichol, come here. Get your coat on and help clear my car.'

She glared at him, no longer bothering to hide how she felt, but did as she was told. Working hard the three of them had his Volvo dug out within minutes, though the snow just kept piling up.

'Good enough.' He yanked open the door and threw the scraper and shovel in. Lemieux and Nichol raced to the other side of the car, trying to be the first to get into the passenger's seat.

'Stay here,' Gamache called before shutting the door and

379

heading out. The tires spun, trying to get a grip. Suddenly the car lurched forward. Looking in the rearview mirror Gamache saw Lemieux still hunched over where he'd given the back of the car a push. Nichol was lounging behind him, her hands at rest on her hips.

Gamache's heart was pounding but he forced himself not to step on the gas. So much snow had fallen it was getting difficult to distinguish the road from the off-road. At the top of du Moulin he hesitated. The windshield wipers were working furiously, barely keeping up. Snow was piling high and he knew if he stopped too long he'd be stuck. But which way?

He leaped out of the car and stood on the road looking one way then the other. Which way? To St-Rémy? To Williamsburg? Which way?

He forced himself to settle down, to be calm. To be still. He heard the howl of the wind and felt the cold snow plaster against him. Nothing came. There was no wall for writing, no voice whispered through the wind. But there was a voice in his head. The brittle, bitter, clear voice of Ruth Zardo.

> *When my death us do part*
> *Then shall forgiven and forgiving meet again,*
> *Or will it be, as always was, too late?*

Jumping back in the car he headed as fast as he dared for Williamsburg, to where forgiven and forgiving would meet again. But would he be too late?

How long had that letter sat there?

After what seemed an eternity the Legion came into view. Driving beyond it he turned right. And there was the car.

He didn't know whether to be relieved or appalled. He pulled in behind and leaped out.

Standing on the brow of the small hill he looked out onto Lac Brume, snow hitting his face full on and near blinding him. In the distance, between gusts, he could just make out three figures struggling on the ice.

'Namaste, namaste,' Mother repeated, over and over until her lips dried and cracked and bled and she couldn't speak any more. The word was stuck inside and there she repeated it. But it kept sliding off the terror in her heart and could find no purchase. Mother fell silent with just her terror and disbelief to keep her company.

Kaye struggled in the middle, her legs barely working any more, propped up between her friends, as she realized she'd been all her life. Why had it taken until now to understand that? And now, in the end, for it was the end, she was totally dependent upon them. They held her up, sustained her, and would guide her into the next life.

She knew then the answer to her riddle. Why her father and his friends had cried 'Fuck the Pope' as they went to their deaths.

There was no answer. They were his words, his life, his path and his death.

This was hers. She'd spent her entire life trying to solve something that had nothing to do with her. She'd never understand and she didn't have to. All she had to understand was her own life and death.

'I love you,' she croaked, but the words were stolen by the wind and scattered far from old ears.

Em held up Kaye as the three stumbled further onto the

lake. Mother had stopped shivering or trembling and even her crying had stopped until there was just the howling of the storm.

They were near the end now. Em could no longer feel her feet or hands. The only consolation was that she wouldn't have to endure the pins and needles agony of feeling them thaw. The wind blew and through its keening she could hear something else. Across the lake there came the strains of a single violin.

Em opened her eyes, but all she could see was white.

Ice here.

Armand Gamache stood on the bank. The barbarian wind raced out of the mountains, across the lake, past the three women, past the buried curling rink and the spot where CC had died, gathering strength and pain and terror and finally hitting him in the face. He gasped for breath and clutched Em's letter, the white paper invisible against the white snow behind and in front and all around him. He was enveloped in white, as were they.

He took a step forward, yearning to race onto the lake after them. Every part of who he was demanded he save them, but he stopped, sobbing with the effort. In her letter Émilie had begged him to let them die, like the fabled Inuit elders who walked onto an ice flow and drifted to their deaths.

They'd murdered CC, of course. He'd known that since the day before. He suspected he might have known it for much longer. All along he'd known it was impossible no one saw the murder. Kaye could not have been sitting beside CC and not seen her killer.

And then there was the murder itself. It was far too

complicated. The niacin, the melted snow, the tilted chair, the jumper cable. And finally the electrocution perfectly timed for when Mother cleared the house, and all eyes and ears were on her.

And then to clear up the cable afterwards.

No one person could have done it without being seen

The bitter niacin was in the tea Mother served at the Boxing Day breakfast. Em had spread the anti-freeze when she'd delivered the chairs to the site. She'd sat in the chair herself, to keep CC away from it.

Kaye was pivotal. Gamache had assumed whoever had electrocuted CC had attached the cables to the chair first, then hovered around Billy's truck waiting for the right moment to attach them to the generator. But Em's letter said otherwise. They'd attached the cables to Billy's generator and then Kaye had waited for a signal from Em that Mother was about to clear the house. When it came, she'd gone to the empty chair, leaned on one corner to knock it off kilter, and attached the cables. From that moment on it had electricity coursing through it.

By then the niacin was working and CC had removed her gloves.

Mother was winding up to 'clear the house'. All eyes were on her.

The rock was thrown, moving like thunder down the ice, the stands cheering, everyone on their feet, and CC got up. She went forward, stepped in the puddle, put her bare hands on the back of the metal chair and that was it.

They'd taken risks, of course. Kaye had to detach the cord and throw it clear, a bright orange cord lying where no cord should be. But they'd gambled that everyone would be so focused on CC they could gather it up again. Em did so, and threw it in the back of Billy's truck. She'd almost gotten caught when Billy ran toward her to start the truck and clear the back for CC. She'd covered up by saying she'd had the same idea and was going to clean a spot in his pickup for CC and the resuscitation team.

The only thing Gamache had been missing was a motive. But Em and Mother had provided that.

Crie.

They had to save El's granddaughter from the monster who was her mother. They'd heard Crie sing, and they'd heard CC crush and humiliate her. And they'd seen the girl themselves.

Crie was clearly dying, suffocating beneath layers of fat and fear and silence. She'd withdrawn into her own world so far she could barely get out any more. CC was murdering her daughter.

Now he watched as the middle dot, the smallest of them, sank to the ground. The others stumbled and tried to pull her up. To go on a little longer. Gamache felt his knees quaking and he longed to collapse onto the snow, to bury his horror in his hands. To look away as the Three Graces died.

Instead he stood erect, the snow insinuating itself down his collar and up his sleeves, plastering against his face and into his unblinking eyes. He forced himself to watch as first one then the other sank to her knees. He stayed with them, a prayer on his cracked lips, repeated over and over.

But another thought insinuated itself.

Gamache looked down at the letter crushed in his hand, then back at the black sprawls on the snow. He was frozen for a moment, stunned.

'No,' he screamed and started forward. 'No,' he shouted and spun round, looking at his car behind him half buried already in the snow. As were the women. He ran toward the car, frantic to reach it.

It was too late, he knew, but still he had to try.

THIRTY-SEVEN

G amache turned the car and gunned it toward
Williamsburg, making straight for a *cantine* on rue
Principale.

'I need help,' he said at the door of the restaurant. All
eyes turned to him, a large stranger covered in snow and
making demands. 'I'm Chief Inspector Gamache of the
Sûreté. Three women are trapped on Lac Brume. We need
snowmobiles to get them.'

After a moment's pause a man rose from the crowd and
said, 'Em are ducks.' It was Billy Williams.

'I'm with you.' Another man stood up. Soon the place was
emptying and within minutes Gamache found himself
clinging to Billy as the fleet of snowmobiles screeched along
rue Principale and out onto Lac Brume.

The storm was howling and Gamache strained to see, to
guide Billy to the fallen women. He prayed they hadn't been
buried by the snow.

'They're around here somewhere,' Gamache cried into the
side of Billy's Canadian's tuque.

Billy slowed down. Around them other snowmobilers were following their lead, careful not to run the women over. Billy stood and gracefully moved his machine through the deep snow, looking for a lump, a bump, a body.

'High mechanics boat,' Billy yelled, pointing to a spot invisible to Gamache. They were in a whiteout now. Williamsburg had gone, the shore had gone, the other snowmobilers had disappeared into the storm. Billy turned his machine and made straight for a spot that looked like any other spot on the lake to Gamache. But as they approached some contours appeared.

The women had fallen, holding each other, and now they were indeed covered in snow. But Billy Williams had found them. He tossed off his gloves and while Gamache staggered through the deep snow to the women Billy put his fingers to his mouth and whistled. The sound cut through the howl of the storm. While Gamache fell to his knees and dug to get at Em and Mother and Kaye Billy whistled and by the time Gamache had uncovered the women, hands were reaching for them. The men hurried the three women back to their snowmobiles and within moments all were racing back to shore.

Gamache clung on to Billy. Everything was white. The snow was driving into them, making it near impossible to breathe never mind see. How Billy knew where the shore was was anyone's guess. Gamache had the impression they were heading further out onto the lake, away from the shore. He opened his mouth to shout at Billy, but closed it again.

He was disoriented, he knew. And he knew that he needed to trust Billy. He hugged the man and waited for the machine to hit the shore and climb the slight rise onto rue Principale.

But that didn't happen. Five minutes went by, then ten, and Gamache knew then that they were in the middle of Lac Brume. Lost. In a storm.

'Where are we?' he screamed into the tuque.

'Chairs might red glass,' shouted Billy, and kept going flat out.

Three minutes later, though it seemed an eternity, the snowmobile thumped into a small hill and Billy turned left. Suddenly they were in among pine trees. The shore, they'd made the shore, thought Gamache with amazement. He looked behind and saw the line of other skidoos following in their tracks.

Billy gunned his machine along a path and onto a street, not yet cleared of snow, though empty of vehicle traffic. Gamache looked for his car, knowing he had a long drive ahead of him to Cowansville hospital. But Billy had taken them another way.

Damn the man, thought Gamache. He's gotten us lost on the lake and now God only knows where we are.

'Loudspeaker,' shouted Billy, and gestured ahead.

There was a huge blue lighted sign. H. Hospital.

Billy Williams had taken them through the storm, across the lake and straight to the hospital.

'How did you know?' Beauvoir asked Gamache as the two men looked down at Kaye Thompson. She was hooked up to machines and IVs and bundled in a silver heating blanket. She looked like a baked potato. Like her father before her, she'd faced certain death and beaten the odds.

Gamache took from his pocket a balled up and sodden piece of paper. Handing it to Beauvoir, Gamache turned back to stare at Kaye and wonder what the last few days must have been like for her. Knowing what they almost certainly would do.

Beauvoir sat down and gently pried apart the paper until it again resembled a letter. It was written in a clear, old-fashioned hand, in beautiful French, by Émilie. It explained it all. How Crie had reminded Émilie of her son, David. So gifted, so joyous when creating music. When they'd heard CC attack Crie after the Christmas Eve service they knew they had no choice. They had to kill CC to save Crie.

'That explains a lot,' said Beauvoir, finishing the letter. 'The complexity of the crime, why Kaye claimed not to have seen anything. It all makes sense. It needed all three of them. The niacin was in Mother's tea, Émilie controlled when Mother would make all that noise at the curling, drawing everyone's attention away from CC. Kaye leaned on the chair, making it crooked. They knew CC would have to straighten it.' Beauvoir pointed to the letter on his lap. 'Madame Longpré begs you to let them kill themselves, and you were going to.'

He had no gift for subtlety, but he tried to make it sound less harsh than it was.

Gamache moved out of the emergency room and into the busy hallway. Doctors and nurses were rushing up and down, the emergency room clogged with car accident victims, skiers with broken bones, people suffering hypothermia and frost-bite from the storm. The two men found a couple of chairs and sat down.

'You're right, I was going to let them die.' He could barely believe he was saying that. 'I knew yesterday that they were the only ones who could have killed CC. Em's letter only confirmed what I'd guessed. But as I watched them struggle onto the lake I thought of Inuit elders and how they'd get on an ice flow and drift to their deaths, to save the community in a time of starvation. They'd give up their lives so that others would live. Then there were CC's boots.'

'The mukluks. Inuit boots. You're not saying there's an Inuk involved somehow?' Beauvoir wondered who that might be.

'No.' Gamache gave him a small smile.

'Good. So there were only three of them. I was afraid the whole village was involved.'

A young doctor hurried down the corridor toward them, wiping his hands.

'Chief Inspector Gamache? I've just come from Madame Mayer. It looks as though she'll live. Looks soft, but she's tough as nails. She has frostbite, of course, and moderate exposure. Interestingly enough, the snow might have saved them. It created a blanket when it fell and that helped insulate them. But the other woman? Émilie Longpré?' Gamache closed his eyes for the briefest of moments. 'I'm afraid she's already gone.'

Gamache had known. When he'd lifted her up she'd been impossibly light. He'd felt he had to hold on to her otherwise she'd float out of his arms. As he held her he'd poured all his prayers into her. But the vessel was cracked too deeply.

Émilie Longpré was curled in Gus's arms now, warm and safe and happy, listening to David play Tchaikovsky's violin concerto in D Major. Em was home.

'Madame Mayer's awake if you'd like to talk to her.'

'Very much.' Gamache started down the hall, following the doctor.

'Just one more thing,' said the doctor as they approached the door. 'Madame Mayer keeps repeating something over and over and I wonder if you can help us.'

'Namaste,' said Beauvoir. 'It means, the God in me greets the God in you.' Gamache turned to him, surprised. 'I looked it up.'

'No, I know namaste,' said the doctor, opening the door.

Gamache turned to Beauvoir. 'The Inuit boots. Émilie Longpré didn't mention them in her letter. She didn't know about them until I told her, and even then she didn't see the significance.' Gamache disappeared into Beatrice Mayer's room.

Beauvoir stood on the threshold of the room, alone. What was the chief saying?

And then it hit him. Like the Inuit, the Three Graces had tried to kill themselves to save someone else. To save the real murderer.

They hadn't killed CC. Someone else had.

From inside the room he heard Beatrice Mayer's voice.

'Fuck the Pope!'

Beauvoir brought the car up to the house, yet again. It skidded as he applied the brakes, as though it too didn't really want to stop there.

The old Hadley house was in near darkness, the path to the front door unshoveled and without footprints. No one had been in or out of the place all day.

'Should I call for backup?'

'No. I don't think he'll be surprised to see us. He might even be relieved.'

'I still don't understand why CC married him,' mumbled Beauvoir, looking at the closed door.

'His name,' said Gamache. 'Nichol gave me that answer.'

'How'd she figure it out?'

'Well, she didn't really, but she told me that she went into the fire to save Saul Petrov because of his name. Saul. She had an Uncle Saul and there's a collective guilt in her family about those who died in Czechoslovakia. Including Uncle Saul. It worked on a primal level. It wasn't rational.'

'Nothing she does makes sense.'

Gamache stopped, halfway up the path, and turned to Beauvoir. 'Everything makes sense. Don't underestimate her, Jean Guy.' He held the younger man's gaze a moment longer than necessary then continued his story. 'This whole case has been about belief and the power of the word. CC de Poitiers married the only man she could. She married another royal. Eleanor of Aquitaine's favorite son was Richard Coeur de Lion. Richard the Lionhearted. Richard Lyon.'

'She was attracted to the name, not the man?'

'Happens all the time. If you like someone named Roger, suddenly you feel kindly toward all Rogers.'

Beauvoir snorted. He couldn't remember ever feeling kindly, period.

'And the opposite is true,' Gamache continued. 'You hate a Georges, chances are you won't like any Georges at first. I know I do that. Not proud of it, but it happens. One of my best friends is Superintendent Brébeuf. Every time I meet a Michel I think of him, and immediately like the person.'

'You immediately like everyone. It doesn't count. Give me a bad example.'

'Okay. Suzanne. A Suzanne in junior school was mean to me.'

'Oh, she was mean to you?' Beauvoir's face was writhing in laugh lines.

'Very mean.'

'What did she do? Knife you?'

'She called me names. For four years. She followed me down the halls, through the arches of the years, down the labyrinthine ways of my own mind.'

'That last was a quote, wasn't it?' Beauvoir accused him.

'Afraid so. "The Hound of Heaven". And maybe she was. She taught me that words wound and sometimes they kill. And sometimes they heal.'

They were at the door and ringing the bell and it opened.

'Monsieur Lyon,' said Beauvoir, stepping across the threshold. 'We need a word.'

Gamache knelt beside Crie. A purple bathing suit was strangling her arms and legs.

'Who'll look after her?' Lyon asked. 'Will she be all right without me?'

Beauvoir almost demanded why he should suddenly care. Look what life with him had brought her to. Surely this could only be an improvement. But seeing Lyon's face, resigned, afraid, defeated, Beauvoir held his tongue.

'Don't worry,' said Gamache, straightening up slowly. 'She'll be looked after.'

'I should have stopped CC earlier. Never let it come to this. From the time Crie was born CC had it in for her. I tried a few times to speak to CC.' Lyon looked at Gamache, pleading for understanding. 'But I couldn't.'

All three men looked down at Crie sitting on the side of her bed surrounded by candy and wrappers, as though a chocolate storm had hit. She's the end of the line, thought Gamache, the final repository of all the fears and fantasies of her mother and grandmother. This was what they'd created. Like Frankenstein's monster. A patchwork of their own horrors.

Chief Inspector Gamache took her hand and held it, staring into those blank eyes.

'Crie, why did you kill your mother?'

Crie felt the hot sun tanning her face and her long, lithe body as she lay on the beach. Her boyfriend reached out and took her hands in his and held them as he looked with such kindness into her eyes. His young body gleamed and glistened as though enlightened and he drew her to him, kissing her gently and holding her.

'I love you, Crie,' he whispered. 'You're everything anyone could want. I don't think you know how beautiful you are, and talented, and brilliant. You're the most wonderful girl in the world. Would you sing for me?'

And Crie did. She raised her voice and the young man in her arms sighed and smiled with delight.

'I'll never leave you, Crie. And I'll never let anyone hurt you again.'

And she believed him.

THIRTY-EIGHT

⁓

The door opened even before Gamache and Reine-Marie knocked.

'We've been waiting for you,' said Peter.

'It's a lie,' shouted Ruth from inside the cozy cottage. 'We started drinking and eating without you.'

'Actually, she never stopped,' whispered Peter.

'I heard that,' shouted Ruth. 'Just because it's the truth doesn't make it less insulting.'

'*Bonne année*,' said Clara, kissing the Gamaches on both cheeks and taking their coats. This was her first time meeting Reine-Marie and she was exactly as Clara had imagined. Smiling and warm, kind and elegant in her tailored and comfortable skirt and shirt with camelhair sweater and silk scarf. Gamache wore a tweed jacket and tie and flannels. Beautifully cut and worn with easy elegance.

'Happy New Year.' Reine-Marie smiled. She was introduced to Olivier and Gabri, Myrna and Ruth.

'How're Mother and Kaye?' Peter asked, leading them into the living room.

'Recovering,' said Gamache. 'Still very weak, and feeling adrift without Em.'

'It's unbelievable,' said Olivier, perching on the arm of Gabri's chair. The fire crackled and a tray of drinks was on the piano. The Christmas tree made the always inviting room even cheerier.

'The oysters are on the piano, away from Lucy,' Clara explained. 'Only a Morrow would have a dog who loves oysters.'

'We saw the barrel as we came in,' Reine-Marie admitted, remembering the wooden keg full of oysters sitting in the snow near the Morrows' front door. She hadn't seen one of those in years, since her own childhood in the countryside. Barrels of oysters on New Year's Day. A Québecois tradition.

After getting plates of oysters on the half shell, thin slices of pumpernickel lightly buttered and wedges of lemon, the two joined the others in front of the hearth.

'How's Crie?' Clara asked, settling in beside Peter.

'She's in a psychiatric unit. Won't stand trial for a while, if ever,' said Gamache.

'How did you know she'd killed her mother?' asked Myrna.

'I thought it was the three women,' Gamache admitted, sipping his wine. 'They completely fooled me. But then I remembered those baby sealskin boots.'

'Wicked,' said Ruth with a slurp.

'In her letter Émilie described the niacin, the anti-freeze, the booster cables. But she left out one crucial thing.' Gamache had their undivided attention. 'Had they done all the things they describe in that letter, CC would still be alive. In her letter Émilie didn't mention the boots. But CC had to have been wearing the Inuit mukluks with the metal claws.

They were the key to this whole murder. I told Émilie about them yesterday and she was sickened. More than that, she was surprised. She'd heard CC clicking down the path after the Christmas Eve service, but she couldn't see her. She had no idea what had caused the sound.'

'None of us did,' said Clara. 'It sounded like a monster, with claws.' As she listened to Gamache a familiar Christmas carol moved through her mind. Sorr'wing, sighing, bleeding, dying, sealed in the stone-cold tomb. Ironically, Clara realized, it was from 'We Three Kings'.

'I realized the women couldn't have killed CC. But they knew who had,' Gamache said, his listeners, even Lucy, silent and staring. 'Mother told us everything. Kaye would only give us her name, rank and serial number, which was actually her phone number. Couldn't get a straight answer out of her.'

Gabri turned to Reine-Marie. 'I don't give him straight answers either.'

'Nor should you, *mon beau Gabri*,' said Reine-Marie.

'According to Mother, Kaye saw it all, and what she didn't see they figured out later. For instance, they didn't see Crie slip niacin into her mother's tea. But they did see her spill windshield washer fluid behind the chair. And Émilie saw her hanging around Billy Williams's truck. None of these things meant anything at first but when Kaye saw Crie deliberately put the chair off balance, and hook up booster cables to it, her curiosity was piqued, though she didn't expect murder. CC was concentrating on what was happening on the ice, of course, but when she grabbed the chair and was electrocuted Kaye knew at once what had happened. After all, she'd worked all her life in a logging camp. She knew about generators and boosters. Before going to help CC Kaye unhooked the cables and tossed them aside. In all the excitement they were stepped on and buried under the snow. While you were all working on CC Kaye started gathering up the cable. Em saw her and asked what she was doing. Kaye didn't have time to tell her everything; all she said was she had to get the booster cable back into Billy's truck. Émilie didn't need more of an explanation.'

'So they knew Crie had killed her mother,' said Myrna. 'But did they know that CC had killed her own mother?'

'No. Not until I told Em the other day. No, the death of CC had nothing to do with her killing her own mother. Not in a literal way anyway. Mother would probably say it was karma.'

'So would I,' said Clara.

'Crie killed her mother out of self-defense. She was finally so hurt she couldn't take it any more. It happens with children sometimes. They either kill themselves, or they kill their abuser. Émilie described Crie as deceptive, though not in an underhanded way. She meant Crie appeared flat, without a spark or talent. But she wasn't.'

'We heard her sing on Christmas Eve,' said Olivier. 'It was sublime.'

They all nodded.

'She's also a straight A student. Quite brilliant, especially in sciences. In fact, for the past few years she'd been in charge of lighting for the school plays.'

'Losers always are,' said Ruth. 'I was too.'

'This year her class studied, among other things, vitamins and minerals. The B complex. Niacin. She got ninety-four per cent on the Christmas exam. Crie was well equipped to know how to kill her mother.'

'I wonder whether the notion of an electric chair appealed to her,' said Myrna.

'Might have. We may never know. She's in a near catatonic state.'

'So you knew it wasn't the Three Graces, but how did you figure out it was Crie?' asked Peter.

'CC's boots. Only two people knew about them. Richard and Crie. I wanted to believe Richard had done it. He made the perfect suspect, after all.'

'Why do you say that?' Myrna sounded slightly offended and the others looked at her with curiosity. 'He dropped by the shop today with this.' She reached into her tote and pulled out what looked like a simple light glove. 'It's fantastic. Here, hand me that.' She waved to an open hardcover on the hassock. She slipped the glove on and held the book. 'Look. It's easy to hold. He's done something with the glove, reinforced it somehow. When you're wearing it, suddenly hardcovers feel even lighter than paperbacks.'

'Here, let me try,' said Clara. Sure enough the book sat snugly in her gloved hand, without strain. 'It's great.'

'He heard we didn't like hardcovers so he's been working on this.' Myrna handed it to Reine-Marie, who thought perhaps Richard Lyon had finally created something useful, and maybe even lucrative.

'He has a crush on you,' Gabri sang. Myrna didn't correct him.

'But you kept insisting Lyon hadn't left your side the whole time.' Gamache turned to Myrna.

'That's right.'

'And I believed you. So if not Richard Lyon it had to have been his daughter.'

'Crie took a hell of a chance,' said Peter.

'I agree,' said Gamache. 'But she had an advantage. She didn't care. She had nowhere to go and nothing to lose. She had no plan outside of killing her mother.'

'Five o'clock. Time to go.' Ruth stood up and turned to Reine-Marie. 'You're the first reason I've seen to believe your husband isn't a complete moron.'

'*Merci, madame.*' Reine-Marie inclined her head in a gesture reminiscent of Émilie. '*Et bonne année.*'

'I doubt it.' Ruth limped out of the room.

Richard Lyon sat in his workroom in the basement, tinkering with his Hardcover Hand, as he'd come to call it. Beside him on the workbench sat a Christmas card, received that morning in the mail. It was from Saul Petrov, apologizing for the affair with CC. He'd gone on to say that he'd had a roll of film of CC in compromising positions that he'd chosen to burn that morning. He'd kept the film with thoughts of blackmailing her one day, if she struck it rich, and had even considered holding on to it to do the same to Lyon. But he'd recently discovered a conscience he'd thought had gone for ever, and now he wanted to tell Lyon that he was sorry. Petrov ended the letter by saying he hoped one day they might be, if not friends, at least friendly, since they would almost certainly be neighbors.

It surprised Lyon how much the letter meant, and he thought perhaps he and Petrov might have been friends.

Gamache and Reine-Marie ran into Agent Robert Lemieux as they walked to their car outside the bistro.

'I plan to see Superintendent Brébeuf', said Gamache,

shaking the young man's hand and introducing Reine-Marie, 'and ask him to assign you to homicide.'

Lemieux's face opened in astonishment. 'Oh, my God, sir. Thank you, thank you. I won't let you down.'

'I know you won't.'

Lemieux helped him clear off his car while Reine-Marie used the washroom in the bistro.

'Poor Madame Zardo.' Lemieux pointed his snow scraper at Ruth, sitting on her bench on the village green.

'Why do you say that?'

'Well, she's a drunk. One of the villagers said that's her beer walk.'

'Do you know what a beer walk is?'

Lemieux started to say yes then wondered. Maybe he'd gotten it wrong. Jumped to a conclusion. Instead he shook his head.

'Neither did I.' Gamache smiled. 'Myrna Landers explained it to me. Ruth Zardo had a dog named Daisy. I met Daisy. The two were inseparable. Two stinky old ladies limping and growling through life. This past autumn Daisy grew weak and disoriented and finally the end was near. Ruth took her old friend on one last afternoon walk. It was five o'clock and they went into the woods where they'd gone each day. She took along a gun and when Daisy wasn't looking, she shot her.'

'But that's awful.'

'It's called a beer walk because most farmers before they put their family pets down take a twelve pack with them, get just drunk enough, and do the deed. Ruth was sober. It was an act of love and mercy and formidable courage. Later Olivier and Gabri helped her bury Daisy under the bench here. And every day at five Ruth visits Daisy. Like Greyfriars Bobby.'

Lemieux didn't understand the reference, but he understood he'd been wrong.

'You must be careful,' said Gamache. 'I'm counting on you.'

'I'm sorry sir. I'll do better.'

At Sûreté headquarters the phone rang and the Superintendent picked it up quickly. It was the call he'd been waiting for. After listening for a few moments, he spoke.

'You've done well.'

'I don't feel good about this, sir.'

'And you think I do? It makes me sick. But it has to be done.'

And it was true. The Superintendent was heartsick about the position he found himself in. But he was the only person who could bring Gamache down.

'Yes, sir. I understand.'

'Good,' said Michel Brébeuf. 'We're clear. I have another call. Keep me informed.' He hung up on Agent Robert Lemieux and took the next call.

'*Bonjour*, Superintendent.' Gamache's deep warm voice came down the line.

'*Bonne année, Armand*,' said Brébeuf. 'What can I do for you, *mon ami*?'

'We have a problem. I need to talk to you about Agent Nichol.'

At home again Yvette Nichol unpacked her suitcase, putting the dirty clothing into her drawers. Her father stood at the doorway, getting up his courage to speak. To start the New Year with the truth about fictional Uncle Saul.

'Yvette.'

'What is it?' She turned round, a dull gray sweater bunched into a ball in her hands. Her voice was petulant, a tone he'd heard her use with others with some satisfaction, but never with himself. Now he noticed the smell of smoke. It seemed to get stronger as he approached her, as though his daughter had been scorched.

'I'm proud of you,' he said. She'd told him about the fire, of course. But hearing her on the phone describing it from Three Pines had seemed unreal. Now, actually smelling the smoke, imagining her that close to the flames, he felt overcome with terror. Had he really come that close to losing her? For a lie? A fictitious Uncle Saul?

'I don't want to talk about it any more. I told you everything already.' She turned her back to him. For the first time. In one fluid, vicious, calculated move she changed his life for ever. She turned away from him.

Gutted, barely able to speak, Ari Nikolev tried to find the courage to tell his daughter she'd almost lost her life because of a lie he'd told. And retold. All her life.

She'd hate him, of course. Nikolev, staring at his daughter's back, had a vision of his life stretching forward for years, bleak and cold. All the warmth and laughter and love turned to ice and buried beneath years of lies and regret. Was the truth worth it?

'I want—'

'What do you want?' She turned back to him now, willing him to ask her again. To get her to open up. To get her to tell him again and again about the devastating fire until it became a part of the family lore, its jagged edges worn and softened by repetition.

Please, please, please, she silently begged him. Please ask me again.

'I want to give you this.' He reached into his pocket and dropped into her free hand a single butterscotch candy, its cellophane crackling as it landed, like the very beginning of a fire. As he walked down the gloomy corridor the smoke clung to him, in the way his daughter once did.

'Who were you speaking to?' Reine-Marie asked, getting into the car.

'Michel Brébeuf.' Gamache put the car into gear. The plan begins, he thought. As they drove out of Three Pines they passed a motorist who waved.

'Was that Denis Fortin?' asked Gamache, who knew the art dealer slightly.

'I didn't see, but that reminds me,' said Reine-Marie. 'I met a friend of yours in the bistro. He said it was good to see you again.'

'Really? Who?'

'Billy Williams.'

'And you understood what he said?' asked Gamache in amazement.

'Every word. He asked me to give you this.' She held up the small paper bag on her lap, protecting it from their latest family member. Henri sat in the back seat, listening alertly to their conversation and wagging his tail. Reine-Marie opened the bag to show Gamache a slice of lemon meringue pie. Gamache felt goose bumps on his arms.

'Look, there's a napkin in here with something written on

it,' said Reine-Marie, diving into the bag and pulling it out. 'Isn't that funny?'

Gamache pulled the car to the side of the road near the top of du Moulin.

'Let me guess,' he said, feeling his heart thudding in his chest.

> *'Where there is love, there is courage*
> *Where there is courage, there is peace*
> *Where there is peace, there is God.*
> *And when you have God, you have everything.'*

'How did you know?' Reine-Marie asked, her eyes wide with astonishment, her hands delicately holding the napkin.

In the rearview mirror Armand Gamache could see Three Pines. He got out of the car and stared down at the village, each home glowing with warm and beckoning light, promising protection against a world sometimes too cold. He closed his eyes and felt his racing heart calm.

'Are you all right?' Reine-Marie's mittened hand slipped into his.

'I'm more than all right.' He smiled. 'I have everything.'

ACKNOWLEDGEMENTS

—

As ever, and always, the first person to thank is Michael, my amazing, lovely, brilliant and patient husband.

Thank you to Gary Matthews and James Clark for fielding urgent questions about electricity. To Lili de Grandpré for making sure the French is correct, especially the swear words, which I, of course, never normally use, but apparently she does. Thank you to Marc Brault for lending me his fine name. To Dr Robert Seymour and Dr Janet Wilson for thinking about the medical issues and coming up with the answers I needed.

There's a fair amount of curling in *Dead Cold*, a sport I happen to love. I played it a bit in Thunder Bay and Montreal and respect the focus and poise the players have, never mind their ability to make amazing shots under pressure. It's a thrilling sport, despite what Inspector Beauvoir might think. I visited the Sutton Curling Club and spoke to Wayne Clarkson, Ralph Davidson and Bob Douglas, who explained strategy to me. Thank you for your time and patience.

I met Anne Perry at a mystery conference in Canada before

my first book, *Still Life*, had been published. She agreed to read it and became the first established writer to endorse the book, a massive event for any debut novelist. Anne Perry is lovely, both inside and out, and I'm deeply grateful to her for giving me the time of day, never mind the endorsement. I'm extremely grateful to all the other writers who also endorsed the book. This is no small task, having to read the whole thing on top of the million other calls on their time. But Margaret Yorke, Reginald Hill, Ann Granger, Peter Lovesey, Deborah Crombie and Julia Spencer-Fleming all gave me that time. And I will do it for others, if asked.

Many thanks to the wonderful Kim McArthur and her team.

And finally, thank you to Teresa Chris, my agent, for her wisdom and robust humour, and to Sherise Hobbs of Headline and Ben Sevier of St Martin's Press for making this book better and for doing it with such kindness and thoughtfulness.

I'm one lucky woman, and I know it.

If you enjoyed *A Fatal Grace*,
read on for the beginning
of the next Gamache case,
The Cruellest Month!

ONE

Kneeling in the fragrant moist grass of the village green Clara Morrow carefully hid the Easter egg and thought about raising the dead, which she planned to do right after supper. Wiping a strand of hair from her face, she smeared bits of grass, mud and some other brown stuff that might not be mud into her tangled hair. All around, villagers wandered with their baskets of brightly colored eggs, looking for the perfect hiding places. Ruth Zardo sat on the bench in the middle of the green tossing the eggs at random, though occasionally she'd haul off and peg someone in the back of the head or on the bottom. She had disconcertingly good aim for someone so old and so nuts, thought Clara.

'You going tonight?' Clara asked, trying to distract the old poet from taking aim at Monsieur Béliveau.

'Are you kidding? Live people are bad enough; why would I want to bring one back from the dead?'

With that Ruth whacked Monsieur Béliveau in the back of his head. Fortunately the village grocer was wearing a cloth cap. It was also fortunate he had great affection for the white-haired ramrod on the bench. Ruth chose her victims well. They were almost always people who cared for her.

Normally being pelted by a chocolate Easter egg wouldn't be a big deal, but these weren't chocolate. They'd made that mistake only once.

A few years earlier, when the village of Three Pines first decided to have an egg hunt on Easter Sunday, there'd been great excitement. The villagers met at Olivier's Bistro and over drinks and Brie they divvied up bags of chocolate eggs to be hidden the next day. 'Ooohs' and 'Aaaaahs' tinged with envy filled the air. Would that they were children again. But their pleasure would surely come from seeing the faces of the village children. Besides, the kids might not find them all, especially those hidden behind Olivier's bar.

'They're gorgeous.' Gabri picked up a tiny marzipan goose, delicately sculpted, then bit its head off.

'Gabri.' His partner Olivier yanked what was left of the goose from Gabri's massive hand. 'They're for the kids.'

'You just want it for yourself.' Gabri turned to Myrna and muttered so that everyone could hear, 'Great idea. Gay men offering chocolates to children. Let's alert the Moral Majority.'

Blond and bashful, Olivier blushed furiously.

Myrna smiled. She looked like a massive Easter egg herself, black and oval and wrapped in a brilliant purple and red caftan.

Most of the tiny village was at the bistro, crowded around the long bar of polished wood, though some had flopped down in the comfortable old armchairs scattered about. All for sale. Olivier's was also an antique shop. Discreet tags dangled from everything, including Gabri when he felt under-appreciated and under-applauded.

It was early April and fires crackled cheerily in the open grates, throwing warm light on the wide-plank pine floors, stained amber by time and sunlight. Waiters moved effort-lessly through the beamed room, offering drinks and soft, runny Brie from Monsieur Pagé's farm. The bistro was at the heart of the old Quebec village, sitting as it did on the edge of the green. On either side of it and attached by connecting doors were the rest of the shops, hugging the village in an aged brick embrace. Monsieur Béliveau's general store, Sarah's Boulangerie, then the bistro and finally, just off that, Myrna's Livres, Neufs et Usagés. Three craggy pine trees had stood at the far end of the green for as long as anyone remembered, like wise men who'd found what they were looking for. Outward from the village, dirt roads radi-ated and meandered into the mountains and forests.

But Three Pines itself was a village forgotten. Time eddied and swirled and sometimes bumped into it, but never stayed long and never left much of an impression. For hundreds of years the village had nestled in the palm of the rugged Canadian mountains, protected and hidden and rarely found except by accident. Sometimes, a weary traveler crested the hill and looking down saw, like Shangri-La, the welcoming circle of old homes. Some were weathered fieldstone built by settlers clearing the land of deeply rooted trees and back-breaking stones. Others were red brick and built by United Empire Loyalists desperate for sanctuary. And some had the swooping metal roofs of the Québécois home with their intimate gables and broad verandas. And at the far end was Olivier's Bistro, offering *café au lait* and fresh-baked croissants, conversation and company and kindness. Once found, Three Pines was never forgotten. But it was only ever found by people lost.

Myrna looked over at her friend Clara Morrow, who was sticking out her tongue. Myrna stuck hers out too. Clara rolled her eyes. Myrna rolled hers, taking a seat beside Clara on the soft sofa facing the fireplace.

'You weren't smoking garden mulch again while I was in Montreal, were you?'

'Not this time,' Clara laughed. 'You have something on your nose.'

Myrna felt around, found something and examined it. 'Mmm, it's either chocolate, or skin. Only one way to find out.'

She popped it in her mouth.

'God.' Clara winced. 'And you wonder why you're single.'

'I don't wonder.' Myrna smiled. 'I don't need a man to complete me.'

'Oh really? What about Raoul?'

'Ah, Raoul,' said Myrna dreamily. 'He was a sweet.'

'He was a gummy bear,' agreed Clara.

'He completed me,' said Myrna. 'And then some.' She patted her middle, large and generous, like the woman herself.

'Look at this.' A razor voice cut through conversation.

Ruth Zardo stood in the center of the bistro holding aloft a chocolate rabbit as though it were a grenade. It was made of rich dark chocolate, its long ears perky and alert, its face so real Clara half expected it to twitch its delicate candy whiskers. In its paws it held a basket woven from white and milk chocolate, and in that basket sat a dozen candy eggs, beautifully decorated. It was lovely and Clara prayed Ruth wasn't about to toss it at someone.

'It's a bunny rabbit,' snarled the elderly poet.

'I eat them too,' said Gabri to Myrna. 'It's a habit. A rabbit habit.'

Myrna laughed and immediately wished she hadn't. Ruth turned her glare on her.

'Ruth.' Clara stood up and approached cautiously, holding her husband Peter's Scotch as enticement. 'Let the bunny go.'

It was a sentence she'd never said before.

'It's a rabbit,' Ruth repeated as though to slow children. 'So what's it doing with these?'

She pointed to the eggs.

'Since when do rabbits have eggs?' Ruth persisted, looking at the bewildered villagers. 'Never thought of that, eh? Where did it get them? Presumably from chocolate chickens. The bunny must have stolen the eggs from candy chickens who're searching for their babies. Frantic.'

The funny thing was, as the old poet spoke Clara could actually imagine chocolate chickens running around desperate to find their eggs. Eggs stolen by the Easter bunny.

With that Ruth dropped the chocolate bunny to the floor, shattering it.

'Oh, God,' said Gabri, running to pick it up. 'That was for Olivier.'

'Really?' said Olivier, forgetting he himself had bought it.

'This is a strange holiday,' said Ruth ominously. 'I've never liked it.'

'And now it's mutual,' said Gabri, holding the fractured rabbit as though an adored and wounded child. He's so tender, thought Clara not for the first time. Gabri was so big, so overwhelming, it was easy to forget how sensitive he was. Until moments like these when he gently held a dying chocolate bunny.

'How do we celebrate Easter?' the old poet demanded, yanking Peter's Scotch from Clara and downing it. 'We hunt eggs and eat hot cross buns.'

'*Mais*, we go to St Thomas's too,' said Monsieur Béliveau.

'More people go to Sarah's Boulangerie than ever show up at church,' snapped Ruth. 'They buy pastry with an instrument of torture on it. I know you think I'm crazy, but maybe I'm the only sane one here.'

And on that disconcerting note she limped to the door, then turned back.

'Don't put those chocolate eggs out for the children. Something bad will happen.'

And like Jeremiah, the weeping prophet, she was right. Something bad did happen.

Next morning the eggs had vanished. All that could be found were wrappers. At first the villagers suspected older children, or perhaps even Ruth, had sabotaged the event.

'Look at this,' said Peter, holding up the shredded remains of a chocolate bunny box. 'Teeth marks. And claws.'

'So it was Ruth,' said Gabri, taking the box and examining it.

'See here.' Clara raced after a candy wrapper blowing across the village green. 'Look, it's all ripped apart as well.'

After spending the morning hunting Easter egg wrappers and cleaning up the mess, most villagers trudged back to Olivier's to warm themselves by the fire.

'Now, really,' said Ruth to Clara and Peter over lunch at the bistro. 'Couldn't you see that coming?'

'I admit it seems obvious,' Peter laughed, cutting into his golden *croque-monsieur*, the melted Camembert barely holding the maple-smoked ham and flaky croissant together. Around him anxious parents buzzed, trying to bribe crying children.

'Every wild animal within miles must have been in the village last night,' said Ruth, slowly swirling the ice cubes in her Scotch. 'Eating Easter eggs. Foxes, raccoons, squirrels.'

'Bears,' said Myrna, joining their table. 'Jesus, that's pretty scary. All those starving bears, rising from their dens, ravenous after hibernating all winter.'

'Imagine their surprise to find chocolate eggs and bunnies,' said Clara, between mouthfuls of creamy seafood chowder with chunks of salmon and scallops and shrimp. She took a crusty baguette and twisted off a piece, spreading it with Olivier's special sweet butter. 'The bears must have wondered what miracle had happened while they slept.'

'Not everything that rises up is a miracle,' said Ruth, lifting her eyes from the amber liquid, her lunch, and looking out the mullioned windows. 'Not everything that comes back to life is meant to. This is a strange time of year. Rain one day, snow the next. Nothing's certain. It's unpredictable.'

'Every season's unpredictable,' said Peter. 'Hurricanes in fall, snowstorms in winter.'

'But you've just proved my point,' said Ruth. 'You can name the threat. We all know what to expect in other seasons. But not spring. The worst flooding happens in spring. Forest fires, killing frosts, snowstorms and mud slides. Nature's in turmoil. Anything can happen.'

'The most achingly beautiful days happen in spring too,' said Clara.

'True, the miracle of rebirth. I hear whole religions are

based on the concept. But some things are better off buried.'
The old poet got up and downed her Scotch. 'It's not over
yet. The bears will be back.'

'I would be too,' said Myrna, 'if I'd suddenly found a village
made of chocolate.'

Clara smiled, but her eyes were on Ruth, who for once
didn't radiate anger or annoyance. Instead Clara caught something far more disconcerting.

Fear.